SORCEROUS

A RISE OF THE CHARIOTEER NOVEL
BOOK ONE

SUSAN LASPE

Jerry,

Remember —
Not all curses are as dreadful
as they seem!

~ Susan Laspe

Copyright © 2021 by Susan Laspe

All rights reserved.

No part of this book may be reproduced in any form or by any electronic or mechanical means, including information storage and retrieval systems, without written permission from the author, except for the use of brief quotations in a book review.

Printed in the United States of America

First Printing, 2021

ISBN 978-1-7377188-1-9

Cover Art by: Susan Laspe

Cover Layout by: Susan Laspe, Kelsey Gietl

Year of the Frog Publishing, LLC

6209 Mid Rivers Mall Dr. Ste 202

St. Charles, MO 63304

http://susanlaspe.com

❊ Created with Vellum

For my Family

"Men are so quick to blame the gods: they say that we devise their misery. But they themselves—in their depravity—design grief greater than the griefs that fate assigns."

— HOMER, *THE ODYSSEY*

PART I
ORACLE

"Of all creatures that breathe and move upon the earth, nothing is bred that is weaker than man."
— Homer, *The Odyssey*

PROLOGUE

Holy Saturday, April 18, AD 1356
Chaddesden, Derbyshire, England

A new season. A new start. An end to tragedy.

That was what Brynwen hoped as she helped her aunt and uncle unpack their wares at the Chaddesden village market. Saturday market days were always busy, but today was special. Spring weather had arrived at last, and the entire village turned out. Even with the winter's incidents, everyone looked forward to the Easter season with great anticipation.

Beside her, Aunt Joan busied herself with arranging her homemade preserves in jars on the narrow table.

Snippets of gossip carried to Brynwen as she removed the bundle from the wooden crate proffered by her Uncle Walter. With nimble fingers, she unwrapped the brown-spotted eggs nested within and set them with care in the large display basket.

"T'ain't right," said the aged woman with a crooked back. She glared a rheumy eye at the miller's lad at the next table. "It's never cost over four."

The lad with reddening cheeks answered in a quiet tone, and Brynwen didn't catch his response. *Must've raised their prices again,* she thought with a sigh.

"...Kytte and the cow...not found..." came another voice drifting to her from a couple of tables away. "Looked everywhere all this morn'."

The hair on the back of Brynwen's neck stood on end. *Oh, no! Is Kytte missing too?* Brynwen didn't know her well, but the girl had a free spirit. However, after everything that had happened, one could never be so sure. Brynwen leaned toward the speaker to catch more of the conversation, praying she had misheard.

A shadow fell over her, causing her to jump and almost topple the egg basket. "Brynwen!" said her friend Catelin. The thin girl's brown eyes creased with worry as she jammed her empty basket down on the table. Before Brynwen could catch her breath, Catelin continued in a rush. "Costin's disappeared, and his wife is frantic."

"Not Costin!" Brynwen said, a lump forming in her throat. Brynwen had helped with the birth of his first son only the week before. Last she had seen Costin and his wife, joy had filled their home with the recent addition to their little family. And now this. "When did it happen?"

"Just two nigh' ago," Catelin replied. "Went to tend to the sheep and never came back."

Brynwen's shoulders sagged, her hands moving over the eggs of their own accord. It was just like the others. She leaned forward and lowered her voice to a whisper. "Have you heard anything about Kytte?"

Catelin shook her head. "Only bits and pieces of gossip around town, but nothin' definite. She and the cow went missing before her family awoke for the morning milking."

"I hope she is all right."

"Aye, me too," Catelin said. "My mum nearly didn't let me come to the market today. All day and night, she worries and cries, rarely leaving the house. It's becoming a right nuisance." For the first time, Brynwen noticed the worry lines etching their way into her young friend's face.

This isn't right, she thought. *Why is this happening to us?*

A new determination grew in Brynwen's chest. She had to keep positive, if only for her friends' and family's sakes. She squeezed Catelin's hand. "We must remain strong, Catelin. All we can do now is pray the new lieutenant and his knights will figure out what's happening and put an end to it once and for all."

"And if they don't?"

She shrugged. "Then I suppose we'll all need to keep our chickens and cows inside, as I hear livestock are next to go."

CHAPTER 1

Holy Saturday, April 18, AD 1356
Chaddesden, Derbyshire, England

Lieutenant Padric de Clifton's chestnut roan horse gave a hopeful whinny as the red doors of the barracks stables came into view.

"I promised you extra oats this morning, Firminus. And extra oats you shall have, after our harried morning. Then we must be off again."

Knights, squires, pages, and workers, each in their designated livery, bustled about on their own errands. Most nodded a greeting as Padric rode by.

A half mile away, the bells of St Mary's church tolled the hour. Out of habit, Padric listened as the twelve bells plus one rang. Noon. He wondered if he could expend a few extra minutes to change out of his grime-smattered uniform. The captain wanted answers, and Padric had nothing as of yet to share with him. After their hard riding of the morning, Padric's once red and black uniform now resembled a brown and gray rag. Even the butcher's pigs were cleaner than himself.

"Padric!" came a shout from behind. "Sir Padric, there you are. May I have a word with you?"

Padric slowed the horse to a halt and waited for the caller to catch up. Firminus puffed his annoyance at the delay.

The man stopped short of Firminus, hands hitching up his tunic to reveal white, skinny ankles. He bent over with hands on his knees to catch his breath. Dark curls accented with gray bounced with the effort, and his rumpled white tunic and scarlet cloak hung in disarray. His tall, wiry body heaved deep lungfuls of air. The man was no sportsman, his studious nature overtook any need for exercise or nourishment. Padric wondered if he had run all the way from Derby.

"Signore Fiori," Padric said, stifling a chuckle at the older man's expense. "Why the hurry? Have your pupils run out on you again?"

Gregorio Fiori waved an arm in annoyance, his Roman nose flaring. "Tat was entirrrely yourrr fault-a, encourrraging dem to become soldiois like-a you." His Italian accent was more pronounced when he was flustered.

Padric did laugh this time. "It was a misunderstanding, I assure you. I merely explained to them that if they studied hard, they had the potential to enlist and excel. My only error lay in not ensuring they listened to the initial part. And I told you less mathematics will get you better supporters." Throughout his years of study, Padric could never help teasing him.

Gregorio let out a snort and stood at his full height. He shook his finger at Padric, his careful English returning. "Latin and Greek are just as important. How can my greatest pupil be my worst supporter?" He chuckled and shook his head. But then he peered around, and his expression became solemn. "In all honesty, there is a matter of which I would discuss with you." Pulling a gold chain out of his shirt, Gregorio twirled the attached silver and blue pendant with agitation. The strength of the thin gold always amazed Padric, as the heaviness of the pendant would break the links of an ordinary chain.

Padric wanted to decline but could not ignore the pleading of his old tutor. "Of course. We can speak whilst I feed Firminus." He slid from the chestnut horse to walk next to his old tutor. The horse would have taken off on its own toward the stable if Padric had not kept a tight grip on the reins.

"Patience, Firminus," Padric laughed. "I vow a couple extra minutes will not cause you to perish from hunger. I saw the stablehand give you an extra helping of hay just last night."

Pfft.

"I think Firminus does not agree with you, young Padric," Gregorio said with a grin. "Your stablehand coddles him."

"I heartily concur, Signore."

The old tutor looked around, stuffing the pendant back under his worn tunic. "I would prefer to discuss the matter at my apartment. There is something you must see."

Padric rubbed a hand on the nape of his neck, his fingers brushing the dirty blond curls hanging over his uniform collar. He needed a haircut, but there never seemed to be time.

"I see. Forgive me, Signore, can I call on you later, after this afternoon's business is settled? We have another missing girl to find." *And her cow.* The Captain of Derby had set the assignment of finding Kytte on Padric's shoulders, and would allow no loitering.

"*Sì, sì,* I understand. Come to my apartment as soon as you can. Today," he emphasized, "as I must leave town on urgent family business on the morrow."

"All the way to Italy? Nothing dire, I hope."

"Not so far as that, there are some still in England. I shall await your arrival?"

"I shall come directly."

Padric caught a passing page and entreated him to bring a bit of food from the kitchens. The wide-eyed youth departed with haste.

Entering the large stable, Padric scooped up a handful of oats for his hungry horse, who gobbled them up greedily. However, before he could get his fill of the grain, Padric gathered the reins and nudged Firminus around. The horse glanced with longing toward the food bin before complying to his master's urging. On his way out, the page handed Padric a small bundle of cheese and bread, which he promptly placed in his saddlebag.

Padric sighed. "Back to business, Firminus."

Off at a gallop, Padric streaked past the neat hedges and flowering gardens of Baron Godfrey Wilmot's two-story, red stone manor. Past the gardeners bending over their work.

The hedgerows ended soon after that and a copse of trees took up the landscaping. Padric thought he saw a stag with the most intricate set of antlers he had ever seen staring at him through the neat trees. A red mark covered its heart.

How peculiar.

Firminus gave a short whinny, causing Padric to turn his gaze forward. Two knights marched just ahead. He pulled the horse to a stop.

The stag was gone when he glanced back to the trees. Had he imagined it?

"Sir? Are you all right?" came a voice nearby.

Startled, Padric spun around in the saddle.

"Oh," he said. "'Tis only you, Sir Leowyn. Sir Aeron," he said, acknowledging the two men in red and black uniform shirts.

They were two of the knights in his unit. Leowyn, one of his newer recruits with a mop of white-blond hair and a genuine smile always on his lips. He raised an eyebrow.

Padric grinned. "Forgive me, Sir Leowyn, you startled me, is all."

Aeron Drefan held his shoulders casually, regarding the lieutenant with mild amusement. In stark contrast to Leowyn, Aeron stood with an easy grin, brown eyes, impeccable uniform, and jet black hair. Of all of the men in his unit—or in all of Derbyshire for that matter—he was the most well put-together knight of minor rank. The majority of his earnings appeared to go toward his clothing and appearance. Women's and maids' eyes followed him whenever he marched by. No two men could be different, yet they got along well enough. That was why Padric had partnered them together.

"Did you see something, sir?" asked Aeron.

"It was the strangest thing. I thought I saw the most peculiar creature, a stag with great antlers. One moment it was there, and the next it was gone."

Aeron raised an eyebrow. "A stag, eh? It's a bit early for stags to be roaming about, isn't it?"

"I suppose it is," Padric replied.

"Maybe it was feeling peckish," Leowyn suggested.

"On your way to the guard post?" Padric asked, changing the subject.

"Aye," Aeron replied. "I suppose we should head on, Leo." He shared a look with Leowyn and they turned to go.

"I will join you as far as the guard post," Padric said, flicking Firminus's reins and matching their pace.

The north side of the Nottingham Road boasted a small red stone guard station. Sitting atop a bald spot on the grassy hill, a pair of knights in red and black uniforms stood guard. It gave a fair view of the surrounding countryside, including the baron's manor and the villagers' homes. Leowyn and Aeron were to switch shifts with George and Will. Beyond that lay the tall hedgerow and iron archway that marked the end of Wilmot property, then to miles of farmland.

They walked in companionable silence until they reached the red stone structure. After a few words, Padric bid the group farewell as he continued on the road toward the archway.

The bleating of sheep and sharp bark of a dog came from just ahead, and a couple of sheep popped into view around the tall hedges and archway lining Chaddesden's border.

Padric made it to the archway when a blanket of black clouds enveloped the entire sky in a matter of moments.

The bleating of the sheep intensified.

Padric gaped at the sudden change in weather. Never had he seen anything like it. A small voice in the back of his mind set off an alarm.

Then everything went black.

CHAPTER 2

*P*adric blinked.

Firminus reared up on his hind legs, nearly toppling Padric over his back. The knight held on for dear life, calling his horse to calm down, and tugging on the reins.

When at last Firminus settled to a mere tremor of agitation, Padric tumbled from the saddle. He shot to his feet and with both hands grabbed the horse's head. At first, Firminus resisted, but then yielded to his master and looked him in the eye.

"Hush boy, hush." Padric said it as much for Firminus as for himself. His own heart crashed against his ribcage. "'Tis over now. I think."

At last, Firminus stilled. As his their pulses settled down, Padric realized daylight had resumed. Whatever had happened was over.

What had *just happened?*

Stomach twisting, Padric took in his surroundings again. He was still on the Nottingham Road, but where?

To his left, he spotted a healthy farm with a little brown cottage set upon a small hillock about twenty yards away. To the right of the road was another farm, its cottage behind a row of trees.

There was not a knight or guard post to be seen. No archway or neat hedgerows.

He gathered they were about two miles east of Chaddesden. *Two miles?*

Padric tried to recall everything from the last few minutes, but it was all such a muddle. One moment he was near four other knights, the next, out here in the middle of farmland by himself.

"Firminus?" he said. "Do you know how we arrived here?"

The horse shook its dark main.

A sick feeling formed at the pit of Padric's stomach. There was no way he could have gone two miles without realizing it...was there? Or was this an *occurrence* he had heard so much about of late, finding oneself in a different location than the moment before?

Kytte! Padric had almost forgotten about the missing maid.

Still in somewhat of a daze, Padric prepared to get back in the saddle when he heard a shout from behind.

Two men argued in the open, one clearly dominating the confrontation. A smattering of sheep loitered around the farmland, munching on sprigs of crops. At the heels of the shepherd's feet sat a mangy sheep dog.

He recognized the farmer and shepherd in question.

As well as the sheep and dog—had Padric not seen sheep over near the Wilmot estate only a couple minutes ago?

"That cannot be good," Padric said. He sighed and tugged Firminus's reins toward the dispute. He would have to deal with this first.

The farmer Dunstan had a reputation for his short temper. If the burly farmer was in a foul mood, the poor shepherd Arold, opposite him, would receive more than just an earful of idle threats. One unsuspecting peddler who had ridden over Dunstan's carrots had found himself with a broken leg, his tunic bundled up and thrown in with the pigs. Even though he spent some time in the stocks for his behavior, Dunstan always managed to get himself into trouble again sooner or later. Neighbors gave the farmer unflattering nicknames for a reason: the Brawler, the Bully, the Beater.

Arold cringed as Dunstan shook his fist in the air when Padric approached. The farmer's seven children and wife, with infant at her hip, stood at a distance to witness the spectacle.

"You will get those sheep off of my property this instant, or I'll—"

"Master Dunstan," Padric said, halting to within an arm's reach of both men. He crossed his arms. "May I be of some assistance?"

"You can get this poor excuse of a shepherd off my premises. They are eating up all my cabbages."

"'T'were an accident, I tell you," Arold said, his whole body shaking, bracing himself for a beating.

The farmer took a menacing step forward.

Padric said, "Hold, Master Dunstan. Pray, tell me what happened."

Dunstan fumed. "Arold deliberately led his sheep into my fields and told them to chow down. He's sore after the last time I drove him off my property."

"That's not how it happened!" Arold protested. "We—"

"You lie!" Dunstan raised his fist higher.

Padric dove between the two, shoving his hands up at the enraged farmer.

"Master Dunstan! Please restrain your anger a moment longer. We have yet to hear Arold's side."

"But—"

The knight slit his eyes and drew his mouth into a thin line.

That shut the farmer up.

"Now, Master Arold," Padric said, turning to the old shepherd. "Please tell us what happened in your own words."

"Well, sir," the timid shepherd said, eyes darting to and away from the farmer, "I was leading the sheep to the far end of the potter's field—they have good grazing there, they have—seeing as no one wants to go over there—when it got all cloudy and dark and I couldn't see nuthin'. The sheep started runnin' this way an' that. I was following their bleating and barking, nicking my shins on the stones in the field." He leaned down to rub his gnarled leggings. "And then suddenly the sun was shining and we was here. And the sheep was so nervous they got to nibbling the first things they saw." He waved his hand at the partially eaten vegetables. Arold once again placed both hands on his staff as protection against the red-faced Dunstan.

The blood drained from Padric's face.

"And where were you when it became dark?" asked Padric, his throat tight. He refrained from telling them he had the same experience. It bothered him how often he had to ask this question of late. Now, however, he could honestly say he believed them.

"We was just crossing the main road, a little ways from the baron's nice grass."

It was them!

It was all Padric could do to keep his calm. *Right. Steady on, it will do no good to panic in front of these people.*

The potter's field was a couple of miles to the north of Baron Wilmot's park, but Arold, like Padric and Firminus, had somehow managed to redirect himself to Dunstan's farm, about two miles away from Chaddesden.

"So, you have no idea how you arrived here?" Padric asked.

"No sir, I was just following the sheep."

Padric held in his grimace. Any hope he had that the farmer could shed light on what happened was shattered.

"And the sheep went amok the moment it became dark," Padric confirmed. "No wolves or foxes to scare them?"

"Aye, black as night, it was! But no other creatures were about that I saw."

Dunstan thrust a fist in front of Arold's staff. "Liar! There's not a rain cloud in the sky. It's barely half day."

"It's the honest truth." Arold looked at Padric imploringly. "I b-beg pardon, Master Dunstan."

Dunstan growled and eyed first Arold, then the knight. "Well, what're you going to do about it?"

"It is all right, Arold," Padric said, placing a hand on the shepherd's shoulder. "But mayhap call your sheep so they stop eating the crops?"

"Oh, aye, sir." Arold bowed over and over again. "Aye." He placed two fingers to his lips and blew a sharp three-note whistle. The dog's ears perked up and he replied with a deep bark. Yapping all the while, it ran circles around the white sheep, shoving them away from the plants and onto the road. Arold followed in quick succession, Dunstan keeping sharp watch till the destructive creatures were out of sight back toward the Potter's field.

Minutes later, as he mounted his horse again, Padric reflected that it was a miracle, really, that the farmer refrained from taking out his rage on the shepherd and his flock. Dunstan was all bluster today.

Arold was not the first to relate this tale. Since December, a rather abnormal number of occurrences, similar in nature, happened to the villagers and farmers in and around Derbyshire. At first no one thought anything of it. Another tall tale to fill the cold nights at the ale house. However, after the tenth similar report came to the captain of Derby within a fortnight of the first occurrence, doubt spread.

Now, as he rode back to the barracks, a sense of foreboding added to the knots in Padric's gut. When one of these occurrences—such as he and Arold experienced—happened, something much worse took place at the same time.

Which meant something else might have happened near the guard post when Padric and the sheep were relocated down the road.

To go after Kytte, or his knights?

Padric faced Firminus to return to Chaddesden, if only to verify his knights were still at their posts. He prayed they were there.

And no, he told himself, he was not abandoning Kytte, only making a slight circuitous route.

CHAPTER 3

The Nottingham Road led to the village of Chaddesden, located two-and-a-half miles east of the city of Derby. Covering one hundred eight acres, Wilmot Manor was the largest home in Chaddesden. Much of the land around it was farmland. The knights' barracks resided between the manor and village square.

Since the onset of the year, the need for extra knights had taken precedence to protect the people who lived in and around Derbyshire. It even gave squires extra duties to help cover the need. Padric and the knights in his unit were even more important, given their grave additional objective by the High Sheriff of Nottingham and Derby.

Pushing the horse to full speed past the last two farms, Padric could just see the manor towering over the trees in the distance. Moments afterward, the red guard post came into view with the two guards in attendance.

Padric began to breathe easier.

Until he got closer.

Two guards stood in stolid stances, alert with straight shoulders and polished spears in their right hands. One with dark hair, the other boasting bright red. No blond-haired knight in sight. A flutter of tension gripped Padric's chest.

Where was Aaron's partner Leowyn? George was not in sight, either. The latter knight held the previous shift with Will.

Please let me be wrong about the occurrence.

Padric halted directly in front of the be-freckled guard, attempting to keep his facial features and voice completely calm.

"Will," Padric said, "what are you doing here? Did your shift not end a while ago, along with George?"

The guard's cheeks flushed scarlet, highlighting the freckles on his nose, which only appeared when he was nervous or heavy with drink. "Lieutenant." He nodded slightly. "I'm here, sir, because Leowyn didn't make it to his post. Sir."

"Is he ill?" *Please be ill.*

The guard scrunched his features. "Nay, sir. Well, I'm not sure, sir. T'was more like 'e just vanished, sir."

Padric felt he would cry. "What do you mean 'vanished'?"

A drop of sweat flicked off Will's chin. "I—'e just—well…"

"Aeron?" Padric asked, turning to the other guard.

"Lieutenant." The ebony-haired Aeron Drefan continued to stare straight ahead and waited expectantly for his superior to speak.

"What has happened to Leowyn?"

"To be truthful," Aeron said, "I know not, sir. He was with me, but then he…he wasn't."

Padric swallowed down the pang of worry pulling at his insides. His tongue was heavy as he said, "Explain."

"He—we—parted from you, then marched to our post. When I turned the corner to my post, the sky grew black and when it lightened again, he was gone." He licked his lips. "Did…uh…did you see the clouds, sir?"

"I did, unfortunately."

The young man's nostrils flared. "I looked back, but he was nowhere to be seen. In fact…when I looked behind me, I was no longer at the guard post, but just outside the manor's boundaries. I blinked and I was over *there.*" He pointed toward the edge of the manor's grounds near where Padric had entered but moments ago.

Will cleared his throat. "It happened just as he says, sir. He rounded the corner, then next thing I knew, I found meself standing by that shrub, George beside me. Aeron stood over there, alone. Leowyn was gone."

Feeling defeated, Padric could have beat himself for not being able to stop whatever fate befell Leowyn. The knight was near four others, and yet no one could do a thing about it.

"I assume you searched for him," Padric said. It seemed almost shallow to be so thorough, but nevertheless the captain of Derby would wish a full report. Yet another missing persons report to add to the ever-growing pile of unsolved cases.

Cases he and his knights were supposed to solve.

"We did, sir, upon my honor, high and low," Aeron replied. "All around this area and behind the trees and shrubs. There's not a sign of him about anywhere. We thought mayhap he was sick and ran back to his cot. We sent George back to look for him while Will stayed here."

"I suppose George found no sign of him, either."

Both guards shook their heads.

He took a mental breath before relaying his unexpected encounter with Dunstan, Arold, and the sheep.

Afterward, he changed the subject. "Did either of you see a young girl named Kytte and her cow this morning? Or anything else strange?"

Both knights shrugged. Will replied, "Now that you mention it, I do recall hearing sheep and a shepherd approaching near the edge of the property just before...er..." He nodded about the strange event. "I s'ppose it could have been Arold, but I didn't see 'im cross the road. No maid or cow, though. Why?"

"They have been missing since early this morning and no one has heard anything about them."

Alarm glinted in Aaron's eyes. "Sir, you don't suppose she and Leowyn had an occurrence?"

"I do not suppose," Padric said aloud, his throat tightening.

I know.

CHAPTER 4

Not twenty yards from the guard post, Firminus stumbled and huffed.

Padric pulled the reins. "What is it, Firminus?" he asked, leading the horse to the side of the road. He dismounted and patted the horse's neck affectionately. The horse answered with another puff from his long nose.

They had only gone as far as the wall to the baron's gardens, not a hundred paces from where he had left Aeron and Will at the guard post.

After a short examination, he discovered a small rock wedged tightly between his shoe and hoof to be the cause of Firminus's discomfort. A pang of guilt tightened Padric's chest. He wondered how long the poor creature had been dealing with the rock. What with the day's events, there had been little time to show his horse proper care. Yet that was no excuse.

"You deserve an extra apple for dinner, my friend," he said, straightening up. He stretched a hand to his saddle bag for a tool to dislodge the rock.

A strange sensation overcame him, as though a sudden dark cloud overhead blocked the sun.

The swish of fabric followed by urgent fingers gripped his arm like a vice. Tight enough to leave a red welt. Digging his heels into the ground, Padric caught a glance at a shorter figure in a rumpled brown cloak, the hood drawn low to conceal his face. The soft, worn cloth displayed a number of carefully sewn patches of differing colors and patterns.

Padric struggled to yank his arm back. "See here," he demanded. "Let go at once!" *He is quite strong for someone so small.* Padric reached for the dagger at his side—

"Stop it!" hissed the stranger. A *woman's* voice. With untold strength, she dragged him toward a copse of trees. "I am here to help you, you dolt!"

Dumbfounded, Padric allowed the woman to lead him away. Still holding onto his arm with one hand, she guided him through a small opening in the shrubs outside the boundary to the Wilmots' estate. Firminus followed behind without complaint.

Padric wondered if the gardeners saw him being led away. If that were so, they would have certainly made noise about it.

"Here," she said. They halted in a secluded stand of trees, well hidden in shadow from the midday sun. She dropped his arm abruptly.

"Who are you?" he asked. She removed the hood, and his blood ran cold.

In the partial light, her face appeared young, the shadows and dark hair hiding half her features. Her eyes shone a deep purple and seemed to read his very soul. Yet as she spoke, her voice sounded young, but—almost...timeless. He had a distinct impression that she had been around much longer than her appearance revealed.

Ridiculous. He shook his head slightly to dispel the thought.

"Who are you?" he asked again, his wary nature returning, still unsure how he had allowed this woman to drag him away from the road.

"It matters not who I am. I have come to offer you aid in your journey, young Padric de Clifton of Chaddesden."

"What journey? How—how do you know my name?"

"It does not matter," she repeated, eyes narrowed, jaw set. "But you must mark my words."

"What words? What are you talking about?"

"Listen carefully, young warrior. Everything will depend upon it." Without warning, she stretched to full height, face to the sun. Purple irises altered to ebony.

Her eyes transfixed on him, dazzling, drawing him in. He could neither avert nor close his own. A sharp ache formed behind his eyes, and he let out a gasp of surprise as it intensified with each heartbeat.

The woman then breathed a verse in Latin, of all things. Ancient, but he could understand it well from church and his Latin instructor:

> *Ut heres aurigae quondam feres maledictum*
> *Auri repete obscurissimae amuletum*
> *Noctis ut deleas immemoratae vis telum*
> *Et liberes illos cuius petis priusquam*
> *sol suum consequitur verticem altissimum.*

> As the heir to the charioteer of old
> Thou wilt bear a curse of gold.
> Reclaim the amulet of darkest night
> To destroy the weapon of untold might,
> And rescue those of whom you seek
> Ere the sun attains its highest peak.

As the verse progressed, it was as though someone etched on his brain with a fiery quill. Each letter, each Latin word was emblazoned into his mind. His head seared with fire, and he fell to his knees, panting. The woman slumped against a tree, exhausted.

After an interminable amount of time, the pounding subsided to a more bearable throb. The initial shock over, Padric gaped at the woman, his heart hammering wildly in his chest. *What was that?* He stood and stumbled back a step, feeling his head, making sure it was still intact. It was.

When he blinked, the verse stared at him, new and raw, the Latin words she spoke moving across his vision as if reading words on a page.

All was a muddle as he stared at the woman.

"What...what have you done to me?"

She raised her head to look him straight in the eye. It was all he could do not to flinch.

"Mark me well, you must believe all I have said. I have seen it—the destruction." Her eyes grew wide again, a vision of horror trapped on her face, as though witnessing some terrible act occurring directly behind the unsuspecting lieutenant's shoulder. "There will be untold devastation. It will consume all of Britain and much of the continent. Everything—all you hold dear—will be wiped away. You must not let this happen." She lunged forward and grabbed hold of Padric's tunic. He jumped at the sudden attack and seized her wrists.

Again, her irises shifted color, and he gazed into the abyss, black as any moonless night. Around him, bright, swarming flames engulfed the ear-splitting cries of those being consumed by a towering inferno.

Tongues of fire encircled Padric and the woman, licking at their feet. The trees, her cloak, everything within sight. His lungs filled with burning smoke, choking off his breath.

CHAPTER 5

"We must flee!" he cried.

Involuntarily, Padric gasped and cast about for their means of escape. Heart hammering, he dropped the woman's hands to block his face from the flames and blinding smoke. The flames abruptly faded.

Once again, they were surrounded by the grove of trees, leaves bright with the first fruits of spring. Birds called to one another from above. Not a scar or bit of ash in sight.

"What sorcery is this? You are a witch."

Her black eyes swirled as she shook her head. "Not witchcraft. The truth. If you do not act."

The words vibrated in Padric's thoughts, amid the now-ever-present-Latin verse.

If not witchcraft, then...something else. Her vision reminded him of the Greek and Roman lessons he had learned from his tutor Gregorio Fiori. Lessons steeped in ancient mythology: tales of sorcery and gods and ancient monsters. Of prophecies and oracles. *Where did those thoughts come from?*

The connection clicked like lightning. The world and everything he knew came crashing down to splinter at his feet.

What did he really know about the world? About anything? If what she said was true, then these were not just stories made up by a blind poet thousands of years ago.

Was his hunger playing with his mind? He never ate his midday meal.

Calming his racing heart, he regarded the woman before him. Except for her purple irises and extraordinary power of ramming prophetic words into his very brain, she appeared otherwise normal. Clothed in a travel-worn, brown woolen cloak and homespun blouse and long skirts, this woman resembled nothing like how he imagined an oracle from the mythology texts to appear. She could be anyone from Chaddesden or Derby. She must have been a visitor, for she was someone he certainly would remember. How far had she traveled?

Padric licked his lips, considering his options. *I am a knight*, he reminded himself. *Act like one.* He needed more information about this woman and her prophecy. Though his limbs yet trembled, he forced his body to compose itself into one of thoughtful contemplation. He hoped.

He asked, "What demon sent you here?"

She smirked. "Come now, you can do better than that."

So much for that. "If no demon, then I do not suppose Momus and Thalia, the gods of jests, sent you to me." The stories of these two Roman gods were among Gregorio's favorites to repeat.

The woman raised her eyebrow.

"I was afraid not," Padric said, and folded his arms across his chest. He blinked again, and the bright prophetic text flashed through his vision. If she were a witch, he thought it better to play along. At least until he could ascertain if she spoke the truth or not. "You have traveled some distance to deliver your message, in an ancient language, no less. I admit, you have seized hold of my attention to the fullest. Pray listen, for I am no Hercules or Ulysses. I control no army, only a small regiment of soldiers. How am I to fulfill this prophecy and save the world?"

"If you know your history and lore, you would recognize that even the most common person can accomplish the most extraordinary things."

"And yet, why should your gods choose me?"

She shrugged. "It's not for me to say. I only deliver the prophecies."

"Surely there is more you can tell me."

"You have seen all I have seen. I am sure you are clever and can work it out."

Padric grimaced, the headache returning in force. The prophecy raced by when he blinked. "And it all rests on my shoulders, does it? I do not suppose the line, *'And rescue those of whom you seek,'* refers to the missing people from Derbyshire?" A war raged inside, urging Padric to leave and search for the girl with the cow—but also to stay and glean more information from the woman.

"See how quickly you are progressing?" she asked with a smirk.

Padric ignored the remark and guessed, "What is the Oracle of Delphi doing in England?"

The corner of the woman's mouth rose ever so slightly. "I am not the Oracle of Delphi."

"If not the Oracle or a witch, then who are you?"

The clop of horse hooves sounded from the road, causing Padric to spin around and draw his sword.

"Calm down, Sir Padric, 'tis only Hamon."

"Hamon?"

"Come," she said, passing the confused knight, a grin on her lips. "Meet my husband."

"Your husband?"

"You may stop repeating my every word now."

"I...yes, madam."

Grabbing Firminus's reins and gripping his sword handle, Padric stepped onto the road beside the woman. He espied a lone rider dressed in a light, rumpled cloak and simple travel clothes, on an old, dappled gray mare. The man was making his way toward the Wilmots' estate at a slow, weary gait. His brown hair fell in his haggard, unshaven face whenever he swiveled his head back and forth from the north to south sides of the road and back again.

"Hamon!" the woman cried.

The man halted his weary horse and spun in the saddle. His face lit up when he spotted her.

"Roana, there you are! I have looked everywhere for you." He slid off the horse, landing on the ground with a deep grunt. With quick steps, he rushed to the woman and gathered her in his arms. When he pulled away, he kept hold of her, his expression changing from relief to consternation. "Roana, you must come home at once. I have searched for you for days. What were you thinking, leaving without a word?"

He righted when he noticed Padric's uniform. Padric thought him to be about ten years his wife's senior. "I beg pardon sir, but my wife is having another one of her spells. It will pass when I get her home."

"He knows, Hamon," Roana said.

"Oh." Hamon's facial muscles relaxed.

"Aye," said Padric, "your wife is skilled with the power to instill fear into a man's heart." He wished to avoid an awkward conversation. "If all is well with you two, I must take my leave. I am afraid my duties in town cannot be delayed any longer."

Roana merely nodded. Her lips parted, but she bit her lip and remained silent.

Leaping onto the saddle, Padric motioned for his steed to depart in the opposite direction.

"Oh! One last warning," Roana said, chasing after Padric. "When you pass the inn tonight, turn left instead of right. A bit of silver will save your life."

"Why?" Padric asked, puzzled.

"You shall see."

PADRIC'S HANDS still shook as he steered Firminus away from the strange woman and her husband. Though as he gained distance from her, the more difficult it was to purge her from his thoughts. That, and the pounding headache from their encounter increased once more. The unusual Latin words she had spoken tumbled around and around—as though each word had branded itself in his brain. Whenever his thoughts wandered, the words blazed in front of his eyes. Roana's vision of the destruction of England and Europe was more often than not sure to follow. Fire and death, and millions of men, women, and children screaming as it engulfed them in flames. It frightened him and made his heart ache each time.

Taking deep breaths, he tried to order his thoughts once again.

"Firminus, did I dream the encounter? Do I dream even now?" No answer. "You saw her, yes? She was as real as the trees we passed by a moment ago, was she not?"

Firminus snorted his retort.

"I can scarcely believe what just happened. The destruction of half the world, Firminus. The end of *everything*. So many deaths, their faces contorted in agony and despair as they died by flame. And there was naught I could do but watch in horror, my feet pinned to the ground.

"More than anything, I wish to make sense of her proclamations for this...this hero's quest. A curse of gold, an amulet, and a weapon used to destroy everything. And the sun. What do all these things have to do with one another? I fear my knowledge of ancient prophecies has gone stale in the last two years. In my studies, the Oracle's prophecies were always riddles.

"Roana spoke in ancient Latin, which is not a'tall common here, in this age—even to most priests. Signore Gregorio can correct me, but the Romans of over one and two thousand years ago spoke in this same way. Yet if Roana is neither a witch nor the Oracle of Delphi, who am I thinking of? She looked nothing over the age of twenty-two, yet when speaking the prophecy, her very being gave the impression of a timeless entity."

The horse shook his dark mane.

"Your input is noted. The next mystery: *Who* is this charioteer? Myself—I am no one of import. My father is a knight, as was his father, and his before him. No charioteers in our family, for as many generations as I know.

"And the phrase '*and rescue those of whom you seek*'...Roana confirmed it refers to the unexplained disappearances. But by whom and for what purpose?"

The horse nodded, then shook his head.

Padric was at a loss. How he wished Roana would have imparted that information. But like the prophecies of old, they were never very clear. More than anything, he wished he had more proof to go off of instead of the remarkable word of a stranger. What if she were lying, or crazed? Then maybe he was crazed, too…

Nevertheless, as vague as it was, what Roana said gave him more information than he had before. It could explain the strange disappearances. He and his knights had a duty to protect the people of Chaddesden. They were tasked by the captain of Derby to find these people. Now Padric had a lead, but how could he share this idea with any of them? Who would believe him? One friend came to mind. Even so, Padric could end up in the stocks, at best. Ridiculed and stripped of his station, at worst.

He squeezed his eyes closed, his vision spinning as a child's peg top toy. "On a normal basis, I enjoy a good riddle. But mythology is Signore Gregorio's area of expertise. If only he had been there to witness the event."

Firminus bucked his head as Padric jumped in his seat.

"That is it, Firminus! If anyone is to know how to interpret Roana's poem, 'twill be him. The old tutor is, after all, the greatest authority of Roman literature and mythology in Derbyshire. If anyone were to give merit to her prophecy, it would be him. He is expecting me this afternoon, and we may be able to aid one another. Come, Firminus, we must make all haste to see him."

Snort.

Padric set his lips into a thin line, his excitement cut short. "After we see about Kytte, that is."

By this time, the constant barrage of blazing text whenever he blinked intensified his growing headache. Padric was so distracted that he missed Firminus' nipping at one of Wilmot manor's neatly trimmed hedgerows. The gardener would have Padric's head if any maltreatment happened to any part of his beautiful landscaping. Tugging the reigns, he managed to prevent Firminus from causing grave havoc on the bright green hedge. A gnawed small hole in the branch was the only discernible blemish. Nothing too conspicuous, Padric hoped with a sigh and drew a hand over his face in mortification.

If he could survive the day.

PADRIC WANTED to make a few more inquiries before reporting the disappearance of Leowyn and Kytte to the captain. A task he had to do much too often for his liking in the last few months. Captain Garrick de Clifton was a thorough man and demanded all the facts. Something Padric and his knights were not always able to provide, further adding to his irritation this day.

At times, Padric half regretted his promotion to lieutenant. His eighteen years on this earth never seemed to provide enough experience to deal with every problem that emerged. Hard pressed as he was, he had limited time for training and problem-solving—let alone sleeping and eating.

When he returned to the barracks in late afternoon, frustrated and exhausted, Padric scribbled a quick note and handed it to one of the young pages who loitered around the barracks seeking errands for extra coin. Padric had not forgotten about the old tutor's request, but Leowyn's disappearance took precedence.

After watering Firminus, he mounted the horse yet again and headed to the outskirts of Derbyshire to finish the day's duties. All the while bearing the nagging feeling that something much worse would befall Chaddesden before long.

AN HOUR LATER, Padric found Ranulf Rawlins, his sergeant, at the Brown Bear Inn, sipping the last dregs of his golden ale. He inclined his glass at Padric, directing him to a second mug of ale waiting for him on the worn oak table. Padric accepted it with a grim face. It hit the spot after a long day. A bowl of bread and cheese sat in a bowl next to Rawlins' elbow, and he helped himself to a bite. Rawlins had also ordered two bowls of steaming meat stew with carrots and leeks. It smelled divine, and he downed it in no time.

Taking in Padric's rumpled appearance, Rawlins raised his dark eyebrows, but said nothing. "We have found the farm maiden and her cow, safe, *sir*," he said. Rawlins had always emphasized the word sir ever since Padric's promotion nearly two months before. Coming from anyone else, it would be grounds for insubordination, but Padric knew Rawlins too well for that. They had been friends since childhood, causing mischief around the barracks while their fathers were on duty around Derby. When they were old enough, they trained as pages and then squires together. Earlier this year, Padric had urged Rawlins to apply for the lieutenant position, but the knight merely scoffed. He enjoyed soldiering too much, and being a sergeant was more than enough responsibility.

Padric had not realized how tense his shoulders were until that moment. "At last, we have some welcome news. Where were they found?"

Rawlins resumed the story: "She and her new beau, a field worker named Philip, were found in the forest."

"Mmm. And the cow?"

"She claims it was their chaperone." Rawlins snorted.

Padric grinned. "I suspect her parents were neither happy nor surprised when they learned the news."

"You should hear George tell it."

"Thank you, nay," Padric said with a half-hearted laugh. "At least that is one problem solved. I cannot express how relieved I am she is safe. Yet still we find nothing on Leowyn." His stomach churned.

"Nay, none of our knights found anything a'tall. Just like all the others."

"And yet..." Padric had been too distracted all day to see it. But now, clearing his mind to the issue at hand, a new fact nagged at him as he recalled his earlier conversation with Aeron and Will. "Yet...something different occurred this morning."

"How so?"

With hesitation, Padric fidgeted with the mug and considered the idea he wished to convey. "How many people have gone missing in Derbyshire since December?"

"We've been over this before."

"Humor me."

"I'd say nigh on ninety or so, with Chadd having the highest numbers."

Padric nodded. "And what do these people have in common?"

"They were alone; a few in small groups. Always laborers or military, both men and women. All between the ages of fifteen and thirty-five. None from the nobility—yet, anyway. A general disorientation occurs to anyone nearby at the time of a disappearance."

New mothers, a betrothed young man who was to be married in a couple of hours, farmers in mid-chore. Not particularly uncommon, but the occurrences were too close together to be coincidental.

Padric nodded. "And none took any belongings other than what was on their person. And Leowyn?"

Rawlins blinked. "Leowyn is a knight. What's that got to do with this inquiry?"

"He is a knight, yes—who disappeared in the presence of three other knights. Aeron was directly in front of Leowyn as he stepped around the corner of the guard post before blinking and finding himself further down the road. The other two knights came to their senses a few yards from their last known positions. But Leowyn was gone. I was near Arold the shepherd by the archway at the time, only for us to find ourselves and his sheep two miles away at Dunstan's farm a couple minutes later."

Rawlins took a generous pull of ale while he considered. "Could be something there. There've never been witnesses a'fore. If someone took Leowyn, why not take the whole lot as well? I don't suppose Aeron and the others'd be lying." He shook his head. "After all this time, why does Leowyn's disappearance differ from all the others? Why *now*?"

Why indeed?

Padric released a deep sigh. Despite Roana's prophetic utterance, *"and rescue those of whom you seek,"* he was loath to believe it was magic or anything related to the supernatural. The thought of a vision from the Lord to Roana came to mind. If the Lord spoke to her, he must act. On the other side of the coin, if Roana worked for the devil, she could be trying to trick Padric into losing his very soul. But he still had no proof her prophecy had any meaning one way or the other.

"That is what we must find out," Padric said. "If someone took them, they could be desperate, or getting careless, or...who knows? But why Leowyn, of all people? He is no different than the other knights. Why him in particular, and right in front of the others?"

Sparing a glance out the window, Padric clapped his friend on the shoulder. "Come, Rawlins, 'tis growing dark, and there is naught left we can do this day but return to the barracks. First, I must speak with my old tutor." He had not forgotten the old tutor's request to meet, and Padric managed to devise a way to lead into Roana's prophecy without making himself sound crazy in front of Gregorio.

Rawlins shrugged, standing up. "I'll come with you, and we can confer more along the way."

Sweat broke out on Padric's neck. "Ah, well, there is no need. You know how Gregorio can go on and on with his stories. I would not wish to keep you out all night."

"Come on," Rawlins replied, clapping Padric's shoulder with a thump. "I haven't seen the old codger in ages, me'self."

"Fine, then," said Padric, the ale in the pit of his stomach souring. "After you."

The boarding house where Gregorio Fiori had lived for the past six years was an ancient two-story building in the oldest quarter of Chaddesden. On the verge of being run down, the blue-painted facade was peeling off the red brick, something fierce. Padric always cringed as he climbed the creaky staircase, convinced the steps would splinter and disintegrate beneath him. "So, I can hear when guests arrive," Gregorio had said the first time his pupils Padric and John Wilmot had ventured to the older man's rooms.

But Gregorio did not open the door immediately when they ascended the stairs. Nor when Padric knocked. The splintering crack under the pale gray door was dark. Either Gregorio was asleep or out.

In no time, Rawlins retrieved the spare key from the housekeeper, and they jostled the door open.

The scene inside was not what Padric had expected to see.

"We are too late," he lamented.

Moving into the room, Rawlins lit the short, lone candle on the little oaken writing desk. The room was in disarray with sheets on the floor, a mostly empty clothing trunk, desk drawers pulled out, bookshelves half empty, and a few tomes scattered about on the floor. Gregorio had needed a cart to haul all of his books when Baron Wilmot hired the Italian to tutor his children and the son of his good friend Garrick de Clifton. Padric still remembered the first time he saw Gregorio Fiori. The tutor refused to greet the baron until he had finished reading a chapter in one of his books. Padric liked him immediately and giddily watched with John as the baron's face turned beet-red in frustration. But despite his quirks, Wilmot worked with the man. The only other tutor who would have been available had perished in the plague. In the seven years since the Italian had been in Chaddesden, he had acquired an even larger collection of texts, adding a third shelf to his room.

"I had hoped he would wait," Padric said, running a hand through his curls and studying the forsaken items on the floor.

Rawlins shrugged. "Why'd he leave?"

"He said only that there was a family emergency." Padric put a hand to his aching temple. "Drat, I should have made him more of a priority."

"What else could you do, with Leowyn missing...what's this?" Rawlins asked, picking up a hard bound book from the ground.

Padric peered over Rawlins' shoulder. Like the majority of the printed works that came to Chaddesden with Gregorio, this one was well-worn, its once-red leather turned to deepest umber. The title was in Latin: *Homen Odyssea Craece.*

"*Homer's The Odyssey.*"

Again, Roana's face filled his vision, her dark eyes glittering.

> *As the heir to the charioteer of old*
> *Thou wilt bear a curse of gold.*
> *Reclaim the amulet of darkest night—*

With the utmost effort, he cut off the rest of the verse before it consumed him. The ache in his temple worsened and he had to blink back tears. Once again, the prophecy crept up on him out of the blue, followed by screams, flames, and death. Utter destruction. Every time, it was all he could do to refrain from allowing its repetition to consume him. The letters and visions stung every time, a constant reminder of what he had to prevent at all costs. If he could believe it.

Rawlins eyed Padric and opened his mouth.

"That is one of Gregorio's favorite texts," Padric said quickly, forcing himself to remain composed.

"Really?" Rawlins asked, abruptly flipping through the pages. He had only learned to read enough to understand the reward advertisements posted by the captain. "Why would he leave it behind?"

"Wait," Padric said, as a page fell from between the bindings and fluttered to the floorboards. A separate piece of paper, folded into thirds. He snatched it up. Composed in the neat, cursive figures of his tutor, the letter was addressed: *To my best pupil.*

The letter was short, but to the point.

I apologize for my abrupt departure, but a grave concern has taken me away immediately. I am deeply aggrieved that we could not speak one last time. I would ask of you, if I may, to keep my precious books safe until my return.

Your Friend,
    Gregorio

Padric wondered why Gregorio had to rush his departure by a day. He did not even tell his landlady. Curious, what was the family emergency that he could not wait a few more hours to leave/ Also, Gregorio had left the *The Odyssey* for him. But if that was the case, then why was it discarded with everything else on the ground? Padric read the letter again. The tutor's request to *keep my precious books safe* must have some meaning, but what?

Perhaps, he thought, the book had not been discarded after all.

CHAPTER 6

Minutes later, Padric and Rawlins exited the boardinghouse, each with an armful of Gregorio's texts.

They were passing the door to The Portly Pig tavern when a glint of silver on the ground caught Padric's eye. Shifting the heavy tomes in his arms, he bent down to pick it up.

Something swished past his ear. Without thinking, he dove behind a small wooden hand cart, dropping the books in his haste. Rolling to his knees, his heart pounded, and he drew the dagger at his waist. Rawlins dropped his armload and pitched in the other direction behind a hay bale. Breathing heavily, Padric peeked his head around the cart and cast a glance into the darkening area. Except for loud talking and laughter emanating from inside the tavern, there was no one around.

Despite this, there, by the doorframe of the inn, he found a dagger lodged in the wood.

Padric ran shaky fingers through his hair, darting his eyes all around the area. Who was there? From where did they throw it? The only hidden place was the alley.

Rawlins looked at Padric, but remained silent when his lieutenant motioned at the knight. Without a sound, the sergeant nodded and shifted behind the hay bale and slunk toward the alley from the far side.

Dagger in hand, Padric crawled around the hand cart, keeping to the shadows.

Rawlins arrived at the alley first and sprinted into the shadows, deadly sharp knives clutched in both hands. Padric moved to follow the knight when Rawlin's dark face appeared next to him as though out of the ether.

"There's no one here," Rawlins said.

Padric nearly jumped out of his boots. "Rawlins, I told you never to do that!"

"Sorry—habit."

Rawlins had the annoying tendency to appear as if out of nowhere, a trait perfect for a knight, though he had never taught its mastery to anyone else, even his best friend. Padric half wondered if Rawlins was even aware he did it.

They checked the area again for anyone lurking, but there was no one.

Still wary, Padric strode over to the inn and pried the weapon from the wood to examine the blade. It was too dark to make out any great details, but he detected nothing of note, no etchings to reveal the owner or maker. Just a plain, tarnished metal hilt.

"What was that all about?" Rawlins said with a scowl. He plucked the dagger from Padric's grasp. Twirling it in his fingers, he asked casually, "Is someone after you?"

"Why do you think they are after me? They missed, either way."

"Did they?" he asked and pointed at Padric's ear with the blade.

Padric touched his now stinging and sticky ear. His hand came away with a trickle of blood.

Rawlins continued, "I take it by your face you don't know who did this?"

Padric's mind raced as he shook his head.

"Mayhap we should tell—"

"Nay! I am not getting my father involved in this."

The sergeant shrugged. "Suit yourself. But mayhap the assailant won't miss next time."

*Next time...*Did they miss by accident or on purpose? It could be some sort of sordid warning. But about what, exactly?

Padric scanned the ground for the shiny metal piece he had seen earlier. Finding it, he picked up the broken half of a silver pendant and ran his fingers along its smooth circular surface. Flipping it over, he was surprised at finding the familiar silver and blue of Gregorio's pendant. *How did it get broken in half?* He held it up to the remainder of the light. An inscription in another language—old, possibly ancient Latin—

His chest tightened.

A bit of silver will save your life.

Black eyes, more ebony than the deepest pitch, darker than a moonless night, rose in his vision. The verse came flooding back to him, searing his eyelids. Curse. Amulet. Weapon. Destruction. Gasping for breath, he staggered to the wall of the inn.

Rawlins gaped. "What the—"

The inn door slammed open, and a pair of grungy men stumbled out. They stared at Padric for several moments. Then one laughed heartily and the other reciprocated and they tottered off, a familiar off-key song in their throats.

"'Tis true," Padric whispered, more to himself than to Rawlins. "It has begun."

He turned his head to find Rawlins' sharp gaze on him. "Padric. What's going on?"

At that moment, Padric had a great urge to tell Rawlins everything—Roana, the prophecies, all of it. He blinked, his stoic friend staring at him with expectation. He opened his mouth to utter it, but what came out instead was, "'Tis nothing. Nothing that I can tell you at this juncture that will make any sense. To be honest, it has been a long day, and I tire from traveling from post to post in a fruitless search all day."

Then, picking himself off the wall, Padric put himself together, hefted his tutor's books, and stalked toward the barracks with a confidence he no longer felt, not answering any of Rawlins's questions. To add to his worries of the day, he now had a would-be assassin to worry about as well. He gripped Gregorio's precious belongings tightly to stop his hands from shaking.

A bit of silver will save your life.

His chest threatened to burst. *There is nothing for it,* he resolved. *I must take up this challenge set by Roana and whatever forces drew her to me. I will stop this weapon and rescue the kidnapped people.*

Somehow.

"Don't you think it strange," said Rawlins, at last giving up on Padric's silence, "that all this is happening right before we are to take the baron's daughter to Wolverhampton in less than a fortnight?"

That was another thing to add to his worries. Baron Wilmot wanted Padric to escort his daughter, Lady Miriel, to Wolverhampton personally. As her friend, Padric would have insisted on taking her anyway, especially in these times. Nevertheless, he had hoped to dissuade her from going, but she remained adamant. Miriel's trip would take a week at most, and if Roana's prophecy were real, that would give him less time to fulfill it.

"It could be a coincidence," Padric replied without conviction.

Rawlins didn't look one bit convinced. "Even so, if Leowyn isn't found, who'll replace him on our journey?"

"I have not had a moment to spare the thought, but Aeron or Serill come to mind. Mayhap Leowyn will still be found," he said, though he knew it was not to be. Leowyn was gone.

"There is always tomorrow," Rawlins said, his voice lacking confidence.

Padric nodded with uncertainty. Yet he could not shake the guilt for his failure. "It still sits ill with me of our missing squire Mainard. It has been a whole month since his disappearance. Rawlins," he said, his stomach clenching, "are we making a difference? How do we protect citizens when we cannot even protect our own? The force in Derby is stretched thin enough without our own knights and squires missing." Eight Derby knights and squires had disappeared since the beginning of the year. "We do not even know what enemy we face. We have no clues to follow—none that make sense, at the least." *Like a prophecy.*

Rawlins shrugged. "There's been no ransom, no reason—the missing farmers and laborers have no money or enough property to warrant the demand of money."

"Nor do the knights and soldiers who are missing," said Padric. "The captain surmises they could be captured and sold to traders of slaves bound for the Middle East and Africa."

"Aye, if that's so, why Derbyshire? Chaddesden is at the height of the missing numbers, but why not kidnap people from the coasts? We're nowhere near the seas. And where are the tracks?"

Padric bit his lip. "Again, we have no clues to follow. And we have circled back to our original quandary."

As his friend strode beside him toward the barracks, another urge to tell Rawlins of his encounter with Roana the prophetess pulled at him. Would he aid in the quest? A quick glance at Rawlins' stoic face quashed his desire. How could he even begin to tell the tale?

During their short journey, those deep black eyes constantly filled Padric's vision, along with their warning of death and destruction. Annihilation of the world. When his eyes were closed, he could still see every word of the verse Roana had proclaimed. Each time he blinked, the words emblazoned in golden-red letters behind his eyelids as though etched there only moments ago.

For the umpteenth time, Padric wondered how he was to rescue all the missing people of Derbyshire, let alone the whole world. Would this amulet of darkest night aid him in finding the weapon, or destroying it? Or, heaven forbid, all of the above?

Again, he studied Gregorio's silver pendant. It had saved him from a grievous, if not deadly, wound. In coming to find his tutor, he had found the answer he needed. Roana spoke true, and he had a duty to do.

He could picture the excitement in the old man's face when Padric described his most unexpected encounter. In all likelihood, Gregorio would beg Padric to describe every detail, every word. All hope of understanding the muddle that was his day had vanished with the sudden departure of the old tutor. Why did he depart so early, and in such a rush, leaving so much behind?

Even after two years since ending his tutelage with Gregorio and becoming a knight, the rich stories remained with Padric. And now they would haunt his very dreams.

What foul nightmare had he walked himself into?

THE CREATURE of Shadow fanned the blazing fire, the flames licking the cave's ceiling with yellow and red-orange tongues. Its master liked high flames, it reminded itself. High flames meant a bigger vision to see through. It did not matter that the cave was cramped as it was, with barely enough room for the creature and the fire. The master wished to see all. To make itself known to all, even if only to the Shadow and the insects of the little cave.

"Report," came a booming voice from the fire. The master's blurred face burst forth from the fire and blasted unwelcome heat into the Shadow's face. If it had eyebrows, they would have been singed. But the Shadow had never known eyebrows, or any hair—not for as long as it could remember. It could not even remember if at one time it had a name. And it had a very long memory...

"Report," the voice said again, the expression distorted by the angry flames.

The creature winced at the force of the words. Wrung its dark, bony hands together. "The knight is ready, Master. The precautions have been dealt with and he has already laid down the first stone for our cause."

"And our quarry?"

"The plan has been set into motion, and the quarry has been sent down another path. He will not suspect a thing. But..."

"What?"

Now the Shadow wished it had kept its mouth shut. "There is another force at work, trying to undermine our efforts."

"How can this be? We have planned everything accordingly."

"The Oracle has returned. We will deal with it." There was one more thing that was worrisome to the Shadow, but it would have to think more about it and its implications before mentioning anything to the master. Dig deep down into its memory. But it would come. In due time, it would come.

"You had better."

Then a whirlwind engulfed the fire, distorting the face even more. When the wind dissipated, the face was gone, and with it, the flames.

CHAPTER 7

Easter Monday, April 20, AD 1356
Two days later

Brynwen Masson leaned over the plot of betony, plucking out a few weeds that had crept up around the purple petals. She sighed. The herb garden had been neglected for only three days while she assisted Rosa the midwife, and already the weeds were rejoicing in their days of freedom. Yesterday's rain hadn't helped keep them in check, either.

They mocked her.

"Oh, but you shall not be smug for long, my friendly weeds. For you shall shortly be sent out to pasture!" If she expected the little invaders to be offended, they did not show it, standing firmly planted, tall as ever.

After removing what seemed like hundreds of plants, Brynwen sat back on her heels. Wiping a few loose wisps of auburn hair out of her eyes with her forearm, she peered out over the land. The early morning light shone so prettily over the green grass in the distance and the newly planted fields. She may never have traveled far enough away to have a true comparison, but to Brynwen this was the most beautiful place in the country. Even though she saw it every day, she still marveled that this sight was hers to behold. Not everyone was as lucky as her and her family in their plots of land.

Beyond her family's small cottage, she espied her two brothers and grandfather tending the fields. Her brother Samuel, aged nineteen and her senior by three years, held the plow in the fallow fields, followed by their grandfather Eduard.

"Heads up!" In the next field, her twin brother, Talfryn, threw a stick for his dog Finn into the air. Finn caught it mid-jump.

Brynwen smiled. Talfryn should have been plucking weeds and checking on the newly sprouted plants, but found himself distracted more times than not.

Their two white goats, Hay and Stack, also followed Talfryn—whether because they liked him or because he worked in the fresh, succulent food patch was uncertain. The goats and chickens tended to trail after him, picking up the loose crumbs that tumbled from his pockets. Even without food, animals tended to follow him everywhere.

Today Talfryn was having a hard time keeping the goats from eating all of the plants directly after he had so painstakingly cleared their weeds. Finn barked at them as if to say, "Don't eat vegetables, they taste horrible!" But the goats didn't seem to care, as long as they had their tasty meal. Talfryn shooed them off, only to saunter back and continue chewing on the crops when he had his back turned. It was no use putting them in the goat pen, as they broke out within minutes. Every time.

Brynwen chuckled and continued her work. Soon she would have to start making the mid-day meal as well as a paste for the midwife Rosa to approve before she went to visit a new patient in the family way.

The chamomile was being particularly arduous when two people, a man and a woman, made their way toward the farm cottage. The older woman was Joan, the wife of her Uncle Walter. She was crying, gripping a ratty handkerchief to her face. The young man holding Joan's other arm, trying to keep her steady as she cried, was Jasper, the youngest son from her first marriage. He looked just like his mother, dark hair and all.

Brynwen stood up as the two approached, brushing dirt and plant debris from her skirt before hastening toward the pair.

"What is it, Aunt Joan? What has happened?" She held out her arms, causing Joan to fling herself anxiously from Jasper into her niece's embrace. She rarely saw her aunt so flustered. Something was very wrong.

"Oh," Joan moaned. After another couple of moments of sobbing, she managed to stammer out, "It—it's Leowyn!"

Brynwen raised a worried eyebrow at Jasper. "What is wrong with Leo?"

Jasper was also clearly upset about his older brother, though he seemed to be able to keep himself together. He nibbled his lower lip. "We found out from Lieutenant de Clifton he'd gone missing when we went into town yesterday for Easter Mass." He ran a hand through his short brown hair. "The knights couldn't find him anywhere in Derbyshire. Even all his things are still on his bunk. Pa is beside himself, and we've all been out looking for Leo night and day. We've searched everywhere."

"Oh no, not Leo," Brynwen said, her chest tightening. He was like another brother to her. Why was she only hearing about this now?

Other than the rumor that a knight had gone missing from Chaddesden, Brynwen had no idea it had been her cousin. Brynwen had been chatting after Mass with some friends, commenting on the fair weather and the new, handsome Lieutenant Padric de Clifton, when her aunt and cousin approached said lieutenant in the churchyard. Watching the lieutenant's sunny countenance quickly fade when he saw them, Brynwen became unsettled. He directly led Aunt Joan and Jasper away to speak to them in private. Unfortunately, she was in the midst of something and forgot following up with her aunt until now.

As a knight, sometimes Leowyn was on duty during Mass, but the church had been so full that day, she had little concern about not seeing him.

Joan lifted her face from Brynwen's shoulder, bloodshot eyes peering straight into her own. Her blouse was drenched with her aunt's tears.

"My Leowyn is a good lad," Joan said defiantly. "He would never desert his post. Something's happened to him, I know it." Now she sniffed, blowing her nose into her handkerchief.

When Joan finished dabbing her nose, Brynwen hooked her aunt's arm through her own. "Here, Aunt, let me make you some nice chamomile tea. That should help soothe you a little." She wasn't sure what else she could do. Would talking to the lieutenant do any good? From what she heard about him, he was doing everything he could to find the missing villagers. Surely he would look for Leowyn, too.

Her aunt followed like a docile child, the occasional whimper escaping her lips. Jasper followed inside quietly.

She sat Joan down on a chair by the small table and then went back outside to pick some fresh chamomile flowers for the tea.

Talfryn rushed over and halted in front of her. Her other brother Samuel and their grandfather Eduard were not far behind him. The older man hobbled as fast as he could with his gnarled wooden cane.

"What's going on?" Talfryn asked with concern. "What's Aunt Joan upset about?"

Brynwen gave them the short version. She needed to get back to her aunt before the woman broke down and melted onto the floor.

Three pairs of eyes widened with shock.

"Not again," Samuel said.

"I can't believe it," Talfryn said. "I just saw him a few days ago."

Their grandfather's face paled as he leaned heavily on his cane. "Dear Lord, when will it end?"

"Can I help in any way?" Talfryn asked. "I can join the search. Or tend their animals, if need be."

"Count me in," Samuel said.

The men all moved for the door.

"Wait." Brynwen stepped into their path. "Aunt Joan is very upset right now. I don't know how much she is able to talk."

Eduard nodded his understanding. "Aye, this is women's work, lads. Brynwen, will you let her know we're here if she needs us?"

"Thank you, Grandfather, I will."

With that, the men nodded and turned toward the fields, giving Brynwen room to go about her task.

Once back inside, she reserved some water from the fire for the tea which was thankfully still hot from breakfast.

Her cousin Jasper stood awkwardly by his mother, who was now finally sitting quietly, staring at nothing and furiously wringing her hands. "Can I help with anything?" he asked.

Surprised at his willingness to help in the kitchen, Brynwen recovered quickly. "Yes, could you please pour some water from the pot into the mugs over there?"

He smiled, apparently happy to be doing *something* other than watching helplessly as his mother cried her heart out. If Brynwen ever asked her brothers to help her with anything remotely related to the cooking or cleaning, they would conveniently find pressing matters needing their attention elsewhere—such as finding firewood, even if the wood basket was full to the brim.

Brynwen watched Jasper thoughtfully for a moment as he picked up the mugs. Then she pivoted toward the little cupboard with her herb supplies and took what she needed to the table near the window where she started crushing the chamomile petals with her mortar and pestle.

Next to the table sat a small bowl of beads where she had painstakingly made a beaded bracelet for her cousin Alice. She presented it to her on her wedding day almost nine months before. Alice and Brynwen were more like sisters—she was the first person Alice told about her pregnancy shortly after the wedding, insisting Brynwen be the midwife. She had been in the midst of creating another set of bracelets for Alice and the baby when she learned of her disappearance in December. Not a trace could be found. Just like Leowyn.

Jack, Alice's husband, was under suspicion for a while, even though he was a good man and they had been childhood sweethearts. He loved Alice dearly and would never have harmed her for anything. Their kin had been farming in the same area for several generations, so Jack was well-known to them. Brynwen knew he wasn't to blame for Alice's disappearance or death, but it was killing her, not knowing what really happened.

Now that she was a midwife in training, Brynwen couldn't help but wonder if Alice was still alive, and if the child within her womb was safe. Was she scared? Or was she lying face down in a ditch somewhere? She fancied her cousin could have run away with a daring bandit, like Robin Hood. Alice constantly teased that she would indeed run away with the rogue if Jack didn't propose to her soon after they were of age.

And the other people missing from the area—what had happened to them?

Brynwen sighed inwardly as she poured the crushed chamomile into a small pouch to place into the steaming mugs that Jasper had obligingly poured. She placed just a hint of honey—a true treat now that Talfryn began beekeeping the previous summer—and handed one cup to Aunt Joan, the other to Jasper. The older woman's sobs quieted substantially after a couple of sips, the soothing tea working its magic at calming her frazzled nerves. Even though the day was warm, Brynwen placed a blanket over her aunt's shoulders.

When Joan finished the tea, Jasper returned the cup to Brynwen. As she took it from him, his hand brushed against hers and she stiffened, a flush filling her cheeks.

Trying to hide her blush, she ducked her head to soap up the cup in the wash basin.

"Why is this happening to us?" Brynwen asked.

Jasper peered out the window absently, maybe hoping to catch a sight of his brother Leowyn walking down the road. "I can't say. It's like we're bein' punished for something. Leowyn doesn't deserve this."

"Aye." She set aside the cup and attacked her mortar and pestle with a damp rag. "Becoming a knight was always his dream. I remember him trying to persuade Talfryn and Samuel to enlist with him years ago. Talfryn offered to join if he could bring his dog and goats. When Leowyn said he didn't think that was possible, Talfryn vowed to create his own army of animals. He even started carving helmets for them."

"Which the goats promptly ate." Jasper chuckled warmly at the memory.

Brynwen cracked a smile at the reverie. *It's good to see him smile after all of this*, she thought.

Joan coughedI meant and sniffled. Jasper's brows furrowed, and he was at her side in a moment.

A little while later, on their way out the door and back to their ceaseless search for Leowyn, Brynwen reassured them that her family was willing to help out in any way they could. "Let us know what you need. Anything. Maybe Uncle Walter's found something by now."

Joan cupped Brynwen's face with wrinkled, calloused hands. "My dear child. You're too young to have to deal with life's tragedies. Sixteen years is so young."

Brynwen patted her aunt's hand gently. *And yet some of my friends are already married.* "Perhaps, but no one has to bear it alone."

In hushed tones, Jasper thanked Brynwen for her help with his mother.

With tired eyes, Brynwen watched the two sad figures make their way back down the road toward their home. She knew it was hopeless, but she prayed Leowyn would return home soon. Though he might get into terrible trouble with his lieutenant and the baron, and get the whipping of his life from his stepfather, at least he would be home. And safe.

In quiet Derbyshire, where nothing ever happened and more than half the population this side of Chaddesden were kin, people were disappearing without any explanation over the last few months. Two were relations of hers as well as many other family acquaintances.

She could not fathom what was happening to quiet Chaddesden, but Brynwen had a sinking feeling it was far from over...

CHAPTER 8

April 29, 1356
Chaddesden

Talfryn was lost. Not lost in the sense of location, but in that he didn't know how to convince the guards to allow him to speak with Captain Garrick de Clifton.

The two guards in their matching crimson and black uniforms stood resolutely, their spears gleaming as though they had never been put to use.

He gulped inwardly. Well, he *hoped* those spears had never been used...

They completely ignored his dog, Finn, sniffing and licking their boots.

The young farmer had a right terrible time getting to the city garrison. It was market day, and it seemed the whole region was in the city to buy and sell wares. He'd left his sister, Brynwen, and Rosa the midwife to fend for themselves with the vendors. Finn wandered off twice. It wasn't too long until Talfryn found himself shuffled in and out of the crowd and almost passed the knights' headquarters completely.

This is why I like to stay home on market day.

Talfryn had prepared to make a great case to the guards. But the young farmer found himself stuttering his request when faced with the knights' determinedly blank stares. Afterward, he wondered if they were even listening to him at all. Were they told to merely "stand as statues," which could be taken to mean "listen like statues" as well?

He was about to restate himself when the men abruptly came to attention. They continued to stare forward, but no longer with blank expressions. The guard on the left's eyes darted to the side and then back just as quick. Talfryn inclined his head and almost went to attention with them. A young man with curly, dirty blond hair not much older than himself stood before them. His crimson and black garb—well-tailored tunic, trousers, and comfortable leather boots—were suitable for fighting and standing for long periods of time. An officer's badge was pinned to his shoulder. However, Talfryn couldn't remember which ranking it meant. Surely this wasn't the captain? The officer was much too young to be in charge of the whole garrison of Derby. Talfryn's cousin Leowyn knew everything about the military—a resource Talfryn would have utilized right now if he could.

The officer looked Talfryn over with an experienced soldier's eye, perhaps trying to size him up, but gave no indication as to his final assumption.

"May I help you?" the officer asked.

Talfryn avoided shuffling his feet. "I am looking for the captain. These fine gentlemen wouldn't let me in to see him."

"And with good reason. The captain is usually out at this time, training with the corps. He should be back presently."

With some relief, Talfryn said, "Ah, so you aren't the captain?"

The other man bristled, a sly smile raising his lip. "Oh no, only recently was I promoted to lieutenant. I have quite a ways to go before any promotion for captainship would be available to me."

"I see."

"I am Sir Padric de Clifton." He then glanced down at Finn. "And who is this fine creature sniffing up Smith's boots?" He leaned over and scratched behind the dog's ears. "Did he step into something funny, boy?" Finn's tongue curled in and then licked Padric's hand. "Quite the dog you have here."

"I'm Talfryn Masson, and Finn here is quite the guard dog. Makes friends with all the rabbits. Grandfather threatens to throw him out if he doesn't change his ways very soon."

Sir Padric laughed at that, the mirth reaching his eyes.

Talfryn decided right then he liked this lieutenant. He was beginning to see why Leowyn liked him so much.

They didn't wait long before the captain himself came walking up to them, his shoulders square and brow dotted with sweat.

Sir Padric straightened his stance. "Captain." He saluted.

Shoulders back, hair trimmed close to the scalp, and with a hint of gray just around the ears, the bearing of Sir Garrick de Clifton bespoke a man of great strength and agility. Blue eyes revealed cunning and yet comprised an air of compassion hidden around the edges. Over his leather jerkin, he sported armor chest plates that had a few dents, evidence of quite a bit of time in battle.

The captain eyed Talfryn but spoke first to his subordinate.

"Lieutenant, where have you been? We were supposed to train this morning. I ended up sparring with Simmons, and you know how he does not give me as much of a challenge as you do." Turning to Talfryn, he lowered his voice conspiratorially. "No one wants to beat on the captain."

"Precisely," Sir Padric joined in, raising an eyebrow. "Because the last one who did so, ended up doing stable duty for a week."

"He also cheated and broke my favorite lance." The older man gave an indignant look. "It was a gift from the baron, you know."

"The baron gives you a lance every year."

"Yes, but this one had a nice sharp look to it."

Sir Padric shook his head and rolled his eyes. And then he outright laughed.

Talfryn couldn't help but wonder that if they weren't related, any other knight might have been throttled and sent to the stocks or dreaded stable duty for that outburst of laughter.

"I am the only one who spars regularly with the captain," Sir Padric explained, "and gives him a good challenge because I am his son."

Talfryn smiled genially and nodded. He could see the resemblance in their faces and statures.

Finally, opening the door to his quarters, the captain bade the young men to enter. It was a sparse room with a long oak desk and two matching chairs placed evenly across from it, a wooden bench spanning the length of the wall by the door, and a bookshelf overflowing with thick tomes and ledgers.

"Who is your companion, Sir Padric? A new recruit?" the captain asked, intrigued. "I am Sir Garrick de Clifton. Please take a seat, young man."

"This is Talfryn Masson, sir," Sir Padric explained, sitting in the farthest chair. "He came to speak with you."

"Yes, sir," Talfryn quickly interjected. The bench squeaked as he sat down on the end nearest the door. "I wanted to speak with you, sir, about my cousin Leowyn. He was stationed in Chaddesden and hasn't been seen or heard of in more than a week. His mother—my aunt Joan—and my grandfather wanted me to ask if you had any news." He unknotted his fingers from his stained brown tunic. It was the cleanest tunic he owned. "My aunt and uncle have heard next to nothing about their son. You see, Leowyn's longed to be a knight in this city his whole life. His dream was to help keep citizens safe. As a child, he'd spend hours with the retired soldier Barney who wandered around the farms, hearing his war stories and practicing the drills. He would never desert."

Because of circumstances left by the plague and the never-ending war with France, there became a shortage of knights in the countryside. For the past seven years, men like Leowyn who would otherwise be laborers, had the chance to prove themselves worthy of knighthood. Talfryn's cousin would not let his dream slip away like a frog from a lily pad for anything in the world.

The captain crossed his arms over his chest, and his face quickly fell with lines of worry. He stared at the young farmer for a few heartbeats.

"Unfortunately, he has not returned. No one has seen him or will come forward if they have." He moved around his desk and plopped down in the vacant chair. He looked to his son.

Talfryn glanced at Sir Padric. The lieutenant's posture had gone rigid, and his face flinched in pain—or guilt. Talfryn wondered at it.

"Leowyn is in my employ, actually. He was stationed at Chaddesden estate on the morning of Holy Saturday, but by early afternoon he was gone. We have led exhaustive searches everywhere. Some mark it as happening alongside an *occurrence*."

Garrick shot the lieutenant a look—one that the lieutenant promptly ignored.

What does that mean?

Talfryn shot to his feet. "An occurrence?" That would explain things. He'd wondered such, but it was another matter entirely to hear it from someone with authority. "So something *has* happened to him?" *Like the others.*

The captain seemed to age ten years at that. "We are likewise convinced something has happened to Sir Leowyn. However, we merely have to keep all avenues open as options as protocol."

Sir Padric's shoulders slumped slightly, his eyes betraying a haunted look. Talfryn got the feeling the knight wished to be anywhere but in this room.

"I understand, sir," Talfryn said.

"Talfryn," Sir Padric said, "if any information about Leowyn turns up, we will send you word. Where do you live?"

"Thank you, I really cannot tell you how much my family and I appreciate it. I live about three miles northwest of here, near the forest boundary. I had best be finding my way back to the market. My sister will have wondered if I fell down a well."

With that, Talfryn gave his goodbyes to the two knights and closed the door behind him.

CHAPTER 9

May Day, 1356

Chaddesden, Derbyshire, England

Captain Garrick de Clifton drilled his son one more time.

"Of course, Captain," replied Padric, "we will keep directly to Icknield Street. No detours."

It was midmorning on the first day of May. The carriage and wagons were nearly ready to begin their journey. The hot sun sweltered at his back, and the sweat trickled in uncomfortable streams down his neck.

The Lady Miriel Wilmot had insisted on starting out after a small May crowning ceremony at Saint Mary's church at dawn. However, the servants had so many parcels, trunks, and food items to load into the wagon, it took extra time to place them just so and tie everything down properly. It appeared the lady was taking enough presents for the whole court, not just for her new nephew. Padric's mother, Tabitha, and sister, Chelsea, were in the midst of handing a final present wrapped in brown paper and a bright blue ribbon to the servants to place on the wagon.

"Perfect," Garrick replied. He smiled. "You know I have every confidence in your abilities, son, but we must take all precaution during these troubling times."

"Of course, sir. I understand." He blinked, the prophecy winking in and out of his vision, and the urgency of completing it before the solstice heavy on his mind. There had been no opportunity for him to work toward accomplishing the prophecy. Let alone finding out any information about Roana—where she came from and the credibility of her prophecies. The captain kept him too busy, and the one time he had asked for a few days off had ended in a curt dismissal. Regardless, he had one last chance to try.

In a low voice, Padric said, "I still warrant this trip is ill-timed. Mayhap we should wait until things are more...settled. Our knights' numbers are low enough as is."

"I dare say you know the Wilmots are a stubborn people. Short of setting them under house-arrest, I cannot ban the baron from doing anything he sets his mind to. Besides, the Sheriff of Nottingham has given a clearance of travel as no other...incidents...have occurred since Easter."

Since Leowyn's disappearance, you mean. Is that supposed to give me comfort?

"Sir, I seek permission to scout our route first to make sure 'tis safe."

"Permission denied. The hour already grows late. You will all stay together, and that is an order."

Discussion over.

Padric bristled at this treatment from his own father, but once the captain decided something, that was it. After telling the captain about his own occurrence and what happened, there was little Sir Garrick could do short of sending all the knights out to verify Leowyn's last known whereabouts. Again.

Now, two weeks after meeting Roana, Padric still saw the prophecy behind his eyelids whenever he closed his eyes. The first couple of days had been the most unnerving, then it lessened over time. Likewise, the vision of fire and flames remained vivid in his brain, ever the reminder of the mission he needed to fulfill.

A short time later, the wagon was overflowing and ready to go. The servants had secured everything so soundly that the only way anything could rattle loose was if the wagon were to fall off a cliff and hit the ground straight on. All that remained to be placed in the empty carriage was the lady herself.

Padric turned to his second in command. "Rawlins, are the men ready?"

"Yes, sir," came the reply. "All the men are a'saddle and waiting on your command, Lieutenant."

Padric could see the three knights ready, but wanted to keep good form. Especially for his first command. Sergeant Rawlins drew his bay roan away and barked the order to Serill and Byron to align their horses into formation. Strawberry-blond Serill was the younger brother of Padric's predecessor, replacing Leowyn in the company. Lastly, Byron, with an unruly head of brown hair, long nose, and laid-back demeanor had served in Derby for the past seven years. He and Serill had taken the first opportunity to enter the new lieutenant's command.

Baron Wilmot's servants, Anton and Fred, were in their places. Graying Anton whipped the reins of the wagon, conveying the lady's trunks, gifts, and food stuffs; and younger, bearded servant, Fred, alighted to the driver's seat of Miriel Wilmot's carriage.

"Good. Now we merely wait for Lady Miriel and Isemay."

The young knight nodded in agreement.

At last, the grand doors to the mansion were thrust open violently by a young maiden, her long golden curls bouncing at her shoulders. Lady Miriel had dressed in a beautiful, flowing pink traveling cloak that perfectly matched her traveling dress; but any fool could see the ugly frustration evident on her face and in the clenched fists at her side. An older version of Miriel, an elegant woman in a rich red dress and white wimple, followed quickly down the stairs, the deep furrows of her golden eyebrows the only thing aging her still beautiful features. Only a pace behind her, Baron Godfrey Wilmot's visage portrayed a less worrisome pose, yet Padric knew the man enough to see fear hidden there. Last out the door was a younger woman with thick ginger hair, Miriel's handmaiden, Isemay.

The handmaiden's flaming red hair was the only wild aspect about her. Many would call her timid and cooperative, yet she could hold her own when given enough cause. Docile was not the term Padric would use, but she could remain calm and collected even under intense stress. She was what was needed to dampen Miriel's volatile energy.

"But, darling, are four knights enough?" her mother asked.

"I do not need more guards, Mama," Miriel huffed, halting midway down the stone steps to glare at her mother. "Four is plenty. And besides, they have swords and other weapons. It's not as if we are going to Mongolia."

Padric hid his smirk. Mongolia was the little joke of everyone in the Wilmot household. To them, Mongolia was the end of the world, where one could fall off the edge if they wandered too close to it. London was far enough away. Why go all the way to Mongolia?

"My love," the baron directed toward his wife, "she is in good hands. These men are well trained. The captain handpicked them himself."

That was more or less true, as Garrick had picked Padric, who in turn chose the men from his own unit.

As the family neared, Padric dismounted and stepped over to the carriage. Fred lifted the latch to the door and held it open.

Miriel's eyes rested on the lieutenant, then lightened with a smile. "Padric!" She still refused to call him Lieutenant in public. Old habits, he supposed. "Will you please tell Mama how safe the journey will be? She expects there to be bandits around every corner."

Padric acquiesced with a steady voice, although his brain screamed otherwise. "It is a straight enough journey, m'lady. The carriage will be well-protected within the company."

"And you will not deviate from the main road?"

"Nary a wagon wheel shall go astray, m'lady. Straight to Wolverhampton. We shall take as few stops as necessary to rest the horses and the company."

Garrick stepped forward. "Everything is settled along the way. They are expected at the Eagle Inn at Burton-Upon-Trent this evening."

Wilmot put a gentle hand on his wife's arm. "It is well, my love. You know Padric will keep our Miriel safe."

Isemay touched her other arm. "The lieutenant is very capable, m'lady."

The baroness's eyes darted to Padric, as though she just now noticed him standing only two paces away. "I know it," she said and attempted a wan smile. "I just worry so." She turned back to her daughter and stretched out a hand to straighten the broach on her cloak. "Please promise you will not be a nuisance to the servants and the knights."

"Mama," Miriel said, "We shall be fine." Abruptly, she pivoted to face Padric, batting Lady Wilmot's hands away. "We are ready." Then thinking better of it, she embraced her parents and again approached the lieutenant.

Miriel lifted her hand to Padric expectantly. He took it and helped her alight into the carriage, then did the same for Isemay and fastened the door behind them.

Once he bid farewell to his family, Padric remounted Firminus and saluted the baron.

"Please take good care of our daughter and Isemay," the baron implored, genuine trust in his eyes. Isemay was like another daughter to him and his wife. "God you speed."

The baroness did not speak; however, her piercing gaze from beneath her wimple left Padric shifting uncomfortably. Her silent plea did not go unnoticed.

"M'lord and lady, I will do my utmost to keep them safe." He could promise no more.

He turned his mount, and the party departed the village.

෴

KNOCKING on her aunt and uncle's cottage door, Brynwen waited anxiously for it to open. She wanted to visit her distraught aunt to give her some comfort and some medicines she needed frequently before heading to her three patients' homes.

The door opened wide by Jasper, his brown eyes weary. They brightened when he saw her. "Ah, Bryn, come in, come in. My mam'll be thrilled to see you."

Brynwen kept the smile plastered on her face as she entered, the atmosphere plummeting as she entered the threshold. As though someone had died.

"Aunt Joan? I've brought some ointment for your wrists and fresh chamomile tea."

Brynwen gasped as she beheld the room before her. The place was in disarray: unwashed dishes lay in the large wooden wash tub. The pot boiled over the edges and splashed into the fire, causing steam to rise. Clothes and linen lay in a thick pile in the far corner, forgotten.

Joan sat at the table and removed her shawl. "Ah, Brynwen, 'tis so good to see you, my dear." She looked up from the fire, not seeming to notice the turmoil occurring in the pot.

Without a word, Brynwen set down the basket on the table, scooped up her apron in her hands, and removed the large pot off the hook and placed it on the cooler stones of the hearth. A soup of carrots, celery, and barley. She sniffed the contents, scrunching her nose at its lack of seasoning.

"I was trying to watch the pot, but got distracted," Jasper said, a large wooden spoon in his hand. He shrugged his shoulders.

Brynwen plucked the spoon from his fingers. "Here, let me just add a bit of seasoning to it…" She opened the small cupboard and pulled out salt, pepper, sage, and thyme, and sprinkled each liberally into the pot. She sniffed again, the aroma meeting her with satisfaction. "There, try that." She dipped the spoon into the soup and handed it to her cousin.

His eyes popped out. "How do you do that? Can you cook for us every day?" He froze, then said, "I mean, until Mam's feeling better."

"I wish I could, but I will help where I can." Now she wished she'd brought a meal for them. She wondered if another local girl could help some days until Leowyn returned. If he returned.

Letting Jasper spoon the soup into a wooden bowl, Brynwen moved again to the table. She pushed aside three jars for other patients and removed a jar of ointment, a mixture of comfrey, sage, and hyssop, and a jug of freshly brewed chamomile tea from her basket.

"Can I help you with anything, dear?" Joan asked.

Eyeing her aunt carefully, Brynwen removed two mugs from the cupboard. "Nay, not at all, Aunt. I have an ointment and some tea for you. Have you heard," she said, wishing to fill the stifling silence in the cottage.

"Yes?" Joan asked, her head shooting up, eyes filling with hope.

"Oh." Brynwen quickly realized her mistake. She bit her lip. "'Tis nothing, really. A trifle."

Grabbing Brynwen's hands, Joan leaned toward her. "What is it? Is it about my Leowyn?"

"Nay, Aunt. It's only that Lady Miriel is going on a journey." Her friend Catelin had informed her of the trip earlier that morning. Catelin was eager to tell the news. Hardly anyone had traveled through Chaddesden in months because of the occurrences, so this was news indeed.

"Oh?" Joan leaned back, her eyes losing the spark of a moment ago. "I hadn't heard." Things must be serious if Joan wasn't among the first to know of the local gossip. It put a lump in

Brynwen's throat.

"Well, Catelin told me...what's wrong, Jasper?" she asked as her cousin's mouth drew into a thin line.

She followed his gaze out the window. On the road in front of her family's farmland, a small company of four knights in red and black uniforms escorted a carriage and servants in livery with a cart filled to the brim with belongings. They were headed toward the west, away from Chaddesden.

"Well," said Jasper in an even tone. "It looks like the knights are leaving right now. That's likely the lady's carriage, too."

Before Brynwen could respond, the front door slammed open and Aunt Joan exited the small cottage at a staggering run toward the group, calling out to them and waving her arms excitedly.

At a loss, Brynwen and Jasper shared a look. Then they tore out of the cottage after the older woman.

"Aunt Joan, please stop!" Brynwen cried.

But the older woman ignored her and continued after the knights. Brynwen and Jasper caught up then.

"Lieutenant de Clifton!" Aunt Joan cried again, dragging the younger folk after her. The party's overladen wagon groaned, and the wheels squeaked so greatly that the knights didn't seem to hear her until she was a mere twenty paces away. At last, a couple of the knights noticed them and yelled up to the front of the line. The two young knights in the front turned their heads toward the family, then the blond lieutenant on the left held up a hand and the company abruptly halted.

Jasper grabbed Joan's shawled arm. "Mam, leave them be—"

The woman showed unexpected strength as she tore her arm out of her son's grasp. Eyes only on one man, she sidled up to the knight in charge, Lieutenant Padric de Clifton. Brynwen had only seen him from afar in Chaddesden, but now that she viewed him up close, she could see why the village maidens swooned over him. Dirty blond curls framed his handsome face and angular jaw. He held himself well in the saddle yet did not appear to flaunt his authority by shouting as she had seen from some other Derby knights. Even so, afraid that the lieutenant would berate her aunt for stopping their progress in such an ungainly fashion, Brynwen moved in to help.

She peered up at the lieutenant in apology. "I beg your forgiveness for our inconvenient approach, sir. My aunt has experienced...a hardship of late."

Instead, his green eyes looked on Aunt Joan with familiarity and he smiled warmly. This took Brynwen by surprise. He regarded Brynwen, then Jasper, then returned to Brynwen. "Not at all, Miss." He shifted his gaze to Aunt Joan, his grin faltering. "Alas, madam, I am loath to report that we have yet to find any trace of Leowyn."

"Nay," Joan said with a wail. "There must be something! Some sign of him."

"Please, Aunt Joan," Jasper said, gently taking her by the other arm. "They're doing their best."

"But they are leaving, Jasper," she wailed. Tears flowed freely down her cheeks. "They have given up on my eldest boy! On all of us!"

Brynwen's heart broke. "Nay, Aunt. Nay. They will return." She looked up searchingly toward the lieutenant again.

The knight gave Aunt Joan a small, sad smile. "I give you my word, madam, my knights continue the search. Whilst my company and I have another mission which takes us away, I have left strict directives for the remaining knights to search high and low for your son. Rest assured, we are doing all we can."

At last Joan nodded, somewhat mollified. "Thank you, Lieutenant," she said, moving forward and pressing firmly on his hand. "Thank you and may God bless you for all you have done for my Leowyn."

Lieutenant de Clifton nodded. Then without further ado, the company once again set off down the road to Wolverhampton. It was then that Brynwen heard the high-pitched voice of a young lady chatting away inside the carriage, seemingly oblivious to the incident which had occurred directly outside her window.

CHAPTER 10

Despite Captain Garrick's confidence in their safety, tension emanated from the knights and servants like steam from a kettle of boiling water. Padric wondered if his own trepidation caused the men to tense, or if it was a collective effort. Who knew what lurked behind every tree? Every bush? Even the horses sensed their masters' unease. Everyone except for Miriel, who appeared unhampered by everyone else's lowered spirits.

Leowyn's disappearance in front of witnesses a couple of weeks ago had spread throughout the barracks like wildfire. Any of them could disappear next at any moment.

The faster they reached their destination, Padric thought, the better.

Padric and his knights followed the River Trent south for three quarters of the journey. Then they planned to veer off southwest toward Miriel's sister's estate outside Wolverhampton.

After two days on the road, Padric discovered Miriel to be an adept traveler. Though she had only left Derbyshire a few times in her life, she seemed to thoroughly enjoy traveling, and thrived when not around her mother. The men made no comment of her incessant one-sided chatter with Isemay. Only two times did she find fault with the road conditions, or the interminable jostling of the carriage, which Padric thought was quite reasonable for her.

Padric had little chance to speak to Rawlins about Roana's prophecy and vision of destruction without someone else being present. Mostly, he could not figure out the best way to speak of it. He thought that once they left Miriel safely with her sister in Wolverhampton, they could go in search of the amulet and missing people. Even though he still had no notion how to find either one.

Again, he wished for Gregorio's input. Before leaving Chaddesden, Padric had gone through the books his tutor had left behind but found only stories of ancient myths and histories. A little about amulets in general, but nothing caught hit attention as important.

The third morning, Padric awoke with a start. *Someone is here!* Heart pounding to nearly bursting, he snatched up his sword, unsheathing it as he launch to his feet. Dawn had not yet broken.

Spinning in a circle, he readied to pounce.

But no assailant came. No sound broke the silence except the snores of sleeping men lying under their blankets around the dying campfire. To the side, Miriel and Isemay's pale yellow tent glowed in the low light but was otherwise untouched. Rawlins stirred. His eyes met Padric's and he reached for his sword.

Serill crashed into the clearing, sword ready. "Sir?" he asked too loudly, eyes darting around the clearing for any signs of trouble. "What happened? I was patrolling the perimeter and through the trees saw you draw your sword."

Struggling to compose himself, Padric combed a hand through his curls, then bent over to lift his scabbard and replaced the weapon with a slight click.

"'Tis nothing," Padric said above a whisper, thankful his blush was hidden by the darkness. "I thought I heard something, but it must have been only a hare speeding by."

"Aye, sir," Serill said. Without haste he spun on his heel and returned to his post.

Though he was still tired, Padric knew he would get little sleep before it was time to rise, so he stayed up and stoked the fire.

"Get some sleep, Rawlins," he muttered across the fire to his friend.

"There is something out there, I can feel it," Rawlins said. He rose from his bedroll. "I'm going to make another perimeter check."

The remainder of the morning had Padric on edge. On occasion he would cast a glance about the road, then to the trees. But there was nothing at all of note. This same course occurred again and again throughout the day—the hairs on the back of his neck rising—a sporadic feeling of someone watching them—his hand clutching at his sword hilt. It was as though whatever it was came and retreated with quick succession, not daring to halt for more than a moment at a time.

For the afternoon meal, they settled in a clearing close to the river. Padric sent Rawlins, Byron, and Serill out to secure the location while the servants settled the young women on the picnic blankets on the soft grass beneath a shady beech tree.

Exiting the canopy of the trees, Rawlins shook his head, his expression dour. "Nothing out of the ordinary on my perimeter check. But something's just not right."

Neither Serill nor Byron saw anything either.

Padric ran a hand through his hair, then down the back of his neck. Even though Rawlins, his best tracker, could find nothing, Padric could not shake the constant feeling of dread. He half wondered if he should turn the carriage around to return to Chaddesden.

Nibbling a piece of crumbly journey cake, Padric shifted and put his back to a young oak. A light rustling sound from behind grabbed his attention and he stiffened as he listened. Pivoting slightly, he ducked into the trees, drawing his bow and nocking an arrow in one swift, silent movement. A shadow hovered on the tree nearest him.

Pulse racing and bow ready, he leaped around the tree, bow raised.

A stag, the largest male he had ever seen, stood before them. Its antlers swirled intricately around its majestic head. On its chest, a red mark in the shape of a diamond stood out in contrast to its white fur. It leaped away and Padric let loose the arrow, but it swished harmlessly past the stag's antlers, impaling a defenseless beech tree.

Padric cursed under his breath. *Where did it go?* He circled around for a few minutes, but found no trace of any animal besides the horses in the company. No broken branches, no foot or hoof prints. After a fruitless search, he returned to camp, trying to remember where he had seen that stag—or one just like it—before.

Why do I care so much about a stag?

Rawlins smirked. "No fresh meat for the midday meal, then?"

Padric responded in a lower tone, "Even if I had killed it, we would have no time to dress it or find space for excess meat." *Thanks to Miriel's packing,* he wished to add. Still, something was off about it. He supposed it could have been the source of his uneasiness this morning. But what creature of that size leaves no trail?

He was tiring of unexplained happenings cropping up around him. Even Rawlins had noticed the differences. Padric had shrugged off his friend's questioning so far. Yet, if he wanted Rawlins and his knights to aid him with the prophecy, the time had come. If Roana's prophecy was a ruse or witchcraft, he would deal with the consequences later.

"There is something I need to discuss with you."

Miriel cleared her throat loudly, interrupting the discussion. "Come, Padric. Isemay and I are in a heated debate. I think my nephew's name should be Charles. It is a good, strong name. However, Isemay thinks he should be named after his grandfather, Guy. I think it is overused and stuffy. And confusing."

"It is a grand name," Isemay stated quietly. "And you do not call your father by the same name."

With a huff, Miriel folded her arms together. "Mama put you up to it, didn't she? She loves that name."

The redhead rolled her eyes. "We shall find out tomorrow, Miriel. It will not be the end of the world if his name is Guy or Frederick or Barrington."

"See what I mean? So much to discuss. I also like the names Oliver and Oswin. Well, Padric? What think you?"

Padric blinked at them, unable to follow their topic of conversation. "Whatever you think is best," he said absently. Then, losing his nerve, he moved off to the other side of camp to gather everyone to continue the journey. He would have to catch Rawlins later.

"How rude," Miriel said under her breath, though still loud enough for the whole of the camp to hear.

CHAPTER 11

The afternoon sun was pleasant, rather than overbearing. From inside her carriage, Miriel's voice prattled on about the young men from Derbyshire, talking Isemay's ear off. Padric cast a glance at his knights and found various forms of amusement and displeasure on their faces at the maiden's mostly one-sided monologue.

The sky became overcast with thick black clouds, throwing the small company into utter darkness.

"A thunderstorm?" Byron asked.

Padric sensed his horse's unease with the sudden shift in the weather.

Not again!

He drew up short, causing the company to a sudden halt.

The experience with old shepherd Arold came to mind: the sky becoming overcast in but seconds before finding themselves miles away, somehow resulting in Leowyn's disappearance. *Who is next?*

Not a sound came from any birds or woodland creatures from the forest. All was still. Padric scanned the open land, drawing his eyes over the river, then turned his attention toward the trees. The stag with the grand antlers and red diamond on its chest had returned to observe the little group—to observe *him*. Padric's blood froze. It was the same creature, and had it followed them—why?

It stared at him a few moments more before withdrawing into the forest.

When he brought his gaze back to the road, about thirty feet in front of them stood a woman.

She had golden hair the color of fresh straw and piercing blue eyes that shone with a marveling cleverness. Upon her person she wore blue robes made of the finest material, arms bare all the way to her shoulders, where a sheer, light cape descended to the ground. Not at all in the latest English fashion. It reminded him of the artwork depicted in some of Gregorio's ancient Roman texts. Alabaster fingers encompassed a long wooden staff with a swirling piece of silver metal ensconcing a translucent orb.

She might have been the most beautiful person he had ever seen had it not been for the utter terror she struck in his heart. Where in the blazes did she come from?

Miriel's voice emanated from the carriage behind him. "Sir Padric, why have we stopped?"

Ignoring her query, Padric managed to gather his wits. He drew himself to his full height in the saddle, placed his hand on the hilt of the sword at his side, and mustered as much dignity as he could, despite his hammering heart.

"Madam," Padric said, keeping his voice neutral. "What is your business here?"

She smiled at his question and his heart flipped in his chest. Whatever spell she was casting was surely working. Not one man in the company made a sound.

"Padric," Miriel repeated, peeking her head out of the curtained window, "who is that woman and why does she halt our procession?"

"Dear sir," said the woman in question to Padric, "I have come to make a proposition. I have need of some specimens to add to my collection." had heard that accent before, but could not place it.

She stepped forward.

He had been raised to never lift a weapon to a woman. The vow of a knight, the promise of a gentleman. But something about this woman screamed danger—not just to him but to everyone present.

"Hold," he warned, drawing his sword. "I will not warn you again."

The other knights drew their weapons.

Padric very much doubted she meant anything so innocent as requesting a pass to collect rocks from the riverbed. The way she studied the guards—with the intensity of a jovial predator—made him quite afraid to ask what exactly it was that she sought.

Not shifting his gaze from the stranger, he recalled the area from memory for anything worth accumulating. To the right stood the forest, which remained unnervingly still. There were varying sizes of gray stones by the river. Their worth was minimal at best, should she wish to sit upon any and gaze at the rushing river. To his immediate right, Rawlins shifted in his saddle. He and the other men waited to see what their leader would do about her. Padric needed to make a decision and fast.

But before he could, the mysterious woman lifted her staff off the ground. An intense blue light blasted from the orb.

The blinding explosion caused his horse to rear back, nearly throwing Padric from the saddle. Blinking rapidly, he raised his sword—

His limbs froze in place.

"What is thi—"

The very breath squeezed out of his lungs—choking off his air supply.

CHAPTER 12

*A*fter a few heartbeats, Padric managed to draw a strangled breath. His lungs burned with the effort. His arms would not budge one bit—they were still as stone. His head, legs, and body could not twitch an ounce. *What is this?* Was it fear or indecision?

No, neither...

What in the world? It was as if his entire body were bound by a tightly wrapped blanket of iron.

Paralyzed. Not even to lift his smallest finger.

His chest tightened.

In fact, all the men and horses seemed unable to move. Even Rawlins, the most mobile of the bunch, sat motionless on the horse beside him. Sweat trickled down the sergeant's forehead as his lips were locked in a perpetual sneer.

The woman gave a honeyed chuckle as she appeared to float forward and halted in front of Padric to pat him on the knee with a delicate white hand. A shot of ice seared throughout his body, from the tips of his toes to his ears. "I will not forget about you, I promise," she said, and continued on her way, eyes sparkling in mirth.

Again, Padric struggled with the invisible bindings, but they refused to budge.

Is this sorcery?

The swishing of her skirts stopped at the door of the carriage. He heard the click of the handle. The creak of the door. The groan of her weight upon the step leading into the carriage.

Miriel and Isemay!

Desperately he fought to free himself. To use his sword. Or reach his bow. Throw himself off his horse. *Anything.*

They were in danger and there was nothing he could do. A gut-wrenching panic twisted his insides. Did she want Miriel for ransom? He could not protect them. Not like this.

But panicking would get him no closer to the maidens' aid. He had to think.

He slowed his mind and tried to breathe.

Who am I?

A military man, born and raised.

He could envision the captain—his father—yelling at his men to use strategy and logic. "Think of this as a normal training exercise."

Those words resonated with him over the years during his training. Now he cleared his mind and thought of the predicament he was in.

What is this barrier that is blocking me from my goal?

I am not asleep, ill, or dead.

What is holding me here?

A witch.

Yes, but...

Invisible, unbreakable bonds.

Sweat poured down his face. This was taking too long. How did one break invisible, magical fetters? Could the process be akin to real restraints? It was worth a try.

Taking a deep breath, he poured his mind into picturing iron-clad manacles holding his limbs down. He imagined metal joints connected together, where their key slots were located—and he could swear he could now actually *feel* them! Smothering down his astonishment, he propelled all his concentration into unlocking the manacle from his right forearm. Forming some iron in his mind, a key took shape, similar to the one at his family home. That done, he drove the key into the invisible manacle on his right arm. It was a slow, painful process. Sweat streamed down his face. After what seemed an eternity, the fingers of his hand wiggled of their own accord and the manacle faded from view.

He sat for a heartbeat or two in wonder. *How did I do that?* Nothing felt different, except a sort of tingling sensation emanating through his free arm.

Do not stop now! the knightly voice within him cried. *The others still need help.*

He paused to hear the sorceress speaking with Miriel and Isemay within the carriage.

Again, Padric shoved away all distractions to concentrate on unlocking the second manacle. The key jammed in the lock. No matter how he wiggled it, it remained firm.

Not now, I am so close!

I...need to...

...Move!

The lock clicked with a loud *thunk*. Light flashed before his eyes, then he found himself teetering off the side of his horse, and barely managed to grab the saddle pommel to stop himself from plunging to the ground.

Breathing heavily, he heaved himself back to a sitting position.

It took a moment to register that his body was once again his own. He looked at his hands, front and back, and flexed his fingers. He wiggled his toes. No physical damage done. He had no desire to go through that ever again.

Did I just perform magic?

A shiver ran up and down his spine. If Roana was not a witch, this blonde woman most certainly was. Yet she resembled no witch described in stories by the old village women. *What does that make me?*

No time for that now, Miriel, Isemay, and the others need aid. Who knew what the witch—or sorceress—was up to now.

How did one even fight a sorceress?

Padric devised to start with what he knew.

He slid off the petrified horse's back, landing softly on the ground, half surprised that his legs moved without any stiffness after his short bout with paralysis.

When he stood to his full height, he deftly brought forth his sword and at the same time scanned the features of his frozen men. Rawlins's face was set in a contemplative sneer, as though he were surmising how to quickly dispatch the wicked woman. His right hand gripped the handle of his sword. The other two knights, Byron and Serill, were caught with impassive expressions. Being the guards directly to either side of the lady's carriage, they would have waited until the assailant was almost upon them before confronting her.

Sneaking over to the closed carriage, Padric leaned in against the warm wood, trying to make himself as flush as possible against it and inched toward the open curtained window. At the moment only the sorceress was chatting.

Were Miriel and Isemay frozen as well? Would they be in a frozen torment of having to listen to this enchantress talk incessantly about her precious collection, whatever it was?

The burgundy curtain was drawn aside enough that he could see Miriel's face. Her eyes were wide and locked on the enchantress, though her lower lip slightly twitched with the effort to remain completely poised. He let out a relieved sigh that the maiden was not petrified, though he could not tell how Isemay fared.

Miriel smiled pleasantly at the intruder. It was a look she gave to her parents when she was attempting to get away with something. "Nay," she said, almost timidly. "I am afraid I cannot join you, as..." She hesitated, obviously trying to think of a diplomatic approach. "As much as I would adore visiting your home and meeting your family. My sister just bore her first child, and I have already promised her that I would arrive promptly to assist her."

The woman's lips twisted into a half smile. "But you have other siblings with children, do you not? Surely one more child in the family is the same as another?"

Miriel's eyes widened. "Oh, nay, m'lady. You see, this is my sister's first child, and I have not seen her in ages, and she is very homesick. Having a family member with her will be a great help. I have been looking forward to this visit for quite some time. I could not possibly detour now."

Silence filled the carriage. Padric's skin prickled, and he could feel a certain frost in the air.

"Mayhap..." Miriel bit her lip. "Mayhap I could join you afterward—on my return trip home?"

"But by then, my dear, it will be too late. The solstice is nigh on the horizon."

Padric's eyes burned. Flames and destruction bombarded his vision for a brief moment.

Ere the sun attains its highest peak.

So it is the solstice! Was it her weapon he had to stop?

In a flash his focus shifted back to the women. A gleam in her sapphire irises, the sorceress raised her staff in the cramped carriage. His only chance at freeing them was by surprise. Chest tightening, he knew what he had to do.

Shoving the curtain aside, he thrust his sword through the open window, halting less than an inch away from slicing the sorceress's throat. The maidens in the carriage gasped in surprise.

"I would not do that," he said.

He might have imagined her eyes popping in the briefest surprise. "Interesting." She smirked despite her unexpected situation. "I shall have to keep an eye on you."

Padric regarded her carefully and kept his voice even. "Miriel, Isemay, pray join me outside."

Silently and with shaky hands, Miriel unlatched the door on the second attempt, and, picking up her skirts, exited the carriage. Isemay hesitated only a moment, trying to give the sorceress as wide a berth as possible. She stumbled down the step and almost landed in a heap on the ground. Padric would have helped the young woman, but he dared not lose his advantage over the sorceress. Thankfully, Isemay recovered and scurried to Miriel on the other side of the still-frozen Byron.

"Quickly, m'ladies—to my horse."

With a swish of skirts, the maidens dashed to the front of the party. Noting their safe distance from the carriage, Padric edged the sword slightly closer to the blonde-haired woman's neck, almost grazing the alabaster skin. "Now release my men," he said, "and I shall not be forced to slice your throat in front of a lady." An impulse to cut her head off then and there overtook him. Yet something stayed his hand. Even if he killed her, would the spell be released?

He was gambling and it could go one of two ways: either she released them all or she killed him and possibly everyone else on the spot. If she had wanted any of them dead, she would have already done so.

The sorceress gazed at him in silence, causing his stomach to twist at the suspense of awaiting their fate.

At last, she grinned mischievously, and her piercing sapphire eyes bore into his own. A doubled-edged dagger of thrill and dread iced his heart and he braced himself to make a final strike if she so much as moved a hairsbreadth.

"I concede," she said.

Surprise and relief warred against each other, but Padric kept his guard up.

"I shall release them." She lifted the staff, the orb as high as it would go in the little carriage. "But we are far from finished here."

A bright blue light radiated from the staff. The clouds cleared away from the sun in all directions.

Padric heard a cough behind him, and Rawlins blurted out several loud exhortations. Byron and Serill shuffled off their horses to protect the maidens.

Before another spell could be cast, Padric shoved his hand through the window and ripped the staff from her thin, powerful fingers. The very touch of the grained wood sent a ripple of spasms coursing through the muscles in his arm, then his entire body, leaving everything tingling for several seconds afterward. It was the strangest sensation he had ever experienced. Part of him wanted to ask what the staff had done to him, but the other half did not want to give her the satisfaction of knowing its effect on him.

Pure shock registered on the enchantress's face. Padric could not discern its meaning, but remaining near her was not an option.

The sensation lessened to a constant hum.

Byron marched up to Padric's side. "Sir." He was a bit shaken from the ordeal. Could he hear everything that had happened? "What will we do with this woman?" The knight looked anywhere but directly at the sorceress.

"We should kill her now!" Rawlins shouted, sword drawn, appearing next to Padric. "If she escapes, she'll be nothing but trouble."

"And if we kill her, what kind of knights are we? She has surrendered herself to us and is now under our protection. We have an obligation to uphold—"

"We must protect our own."

"We do not kill defenseless women."

"She is as defenseless as a fox in a chicken coop," Rawlins retorted.

Rawlins had a point. Who knew what the woman could do without her staff? Yet, murder was against everything the knights stood for. Let the city judges decide her fate. The other options were no less ripe with folly: they could neither let her stay here, nor take her with them.

Padric lowered his voice. "Rawlins, unless you know something I do not, we have had no sorceress training. I am doing the best I can with what we have. And right now, we have her source of power—the staff."

Rawlins tried staring Padric down, but the lieutenant would have none of it. Finally, Rawlins backed down and, with a deep scowl, moved to where Miriel and Isemay stood by the horses. Padric hated fighting with his friend, but sometimes they butted heads on certain aspects of their duties.

"Byron, bind and gag her," Padric said. "See how she likes being tied down. We shall stop at Wychnor and leave her in their gaol until we have decided what to do with her upon our return. Lady Miriel and Maid Isemay shall accompany us on the horses."

Byron returned with a rope and bound the blue-clad woman hand and foot. He blushed when he had to raise her dress a couple inches to tie her ankles together. The sorceress remained calm and looked amused at the knight's discomfort.

Trussed like a pheasant, and despite the sword tip against her exposed throat, the sorceress lifted her chin high. "You could come with me, Lieutenant. We could have a grand destiny together. The world would be forever changed. What do you say to that?"

Padric's ears burned in anger. "Those are grand words coming from a defenseless woman. If you move so much as a muscle—"

"Oh, I shall stay put for the moment. But rest assured, this slight inconvenience will only slow me down for a while, Lieutenant. Soon you shall have the chance to meet my very good friends."

"I look forward to their acquaintance," said Padric calmly, but inside he raged. He hoped her promise to be a bluff, but the smug expression in her sapphire eyes gave him doubt he dare not let anyone see.

Perhaps I should have blindfolded her, too. .

Byron gave the rope on the prisoner's ankles one last tug to ensure its security, then exited the carriage to attend to his skittish horse. Padric finally removed the sword from the woman's throat and hastened away from the carriage with her staff.

"No one is to speak to this woman, or you shall join her in the gaol in Wychnor." He then gave curt orders to lighten the cart of half its load, expecting Miriel to raise protest. To his surprise, she made no comment.

When he reached Firminus, Miriel and Isemay were clutching each other's hands, shivering in silent fright. Padric's heart sunk at seeing them this way. He wished he could have spared them this horrible situation and all remained in Chaddesden. But their home was now too far away to return to. Their best chance was to get to the next village.

Miriel's eyes were on the verge of tears. "Padric, is…is she…?"

"She is detained, m'lady. But we should be off before her so called friends arrive, if there are any." He mounted his horse, then lifted Miriel up behind him. Rawlins did the same with Isemay.

Padric took stock behind him to ensure that the rest of the knights and servants were ready to depart—and fast.

They set off at a canter, slower than Padric would have liked, given the circumstances. They would be late in reaching their rendezvous point.

Miriel let out a little yelp as the horse surged forward and she nearly crushed Padric's stomach as she held on for dear life, knocking the wind from his lungs. After she caught her breath, Miriel queried, "Will her friends follow?"

Padric was silent for a moment. As much as he wanted to spare her, avoiding the truth would be much worse.

"I cannot say for certain. And if they do, I know not how good their tracking skills are, nor how strong her magic is without this"—he nodded toward the staff—"but we may have a few miles or so before they catch up." *If we are extremely lucky.*

"Can we go faster?"

"Not if we wish to preserve the horses' integrity." He would have loved to give the horses free rein—to get to Wychnor as soon as possible—but it would be too hard on the creatures. And the next livery that might have fresh horses was several miles up the road. They were running on borrowed time.

The lieutenant scanned the countryside for any kind of hiding place, while also peering behind them for any signs of being followed, and to ensure the sorceress remained secure in the carriage. Serill confirmed the sorceress's whereabouts. Alas, that was the only good news, as there was only a craggy riverbed with the rushing river to the left of the road and thick forest to the right. No carriage or wagon could move through that. It forced them to stay on the road for now.

Padric heard the flapping of wings and then several large, dark shadows flitted to and fro above the small band of runaways—large enough to block out the sun when passing directly overhead. At least a dozen eagles—the largest he had ever seen, each with the average wingspan of two men. Padric's companions shouted as they sighted the oversized birds.

Padric scowled. They had only gone perhaps two miles. With no hiding place in sight, they continued racing along the road.

And then the birds descended.

CHAPTER 13

Miriel screamed in Padric's ear.

Knights shouted.

The crisp clank of metal reverberated as swords were unsheathed. Rawlins swiped at an oncoming eagle.

Padric quickly brought forth his bow and nocked an arrow, aiming for the closest assailant. Why were these eagles so large?

Another deafening screech, and he turned his head to find long, sharp talons near his face. They were easily the size of his head, a deadly razor-sharp claw at the end of each orange-yellow digit.

He ducked just in time as the claws grazed the top of his hair. Behind him, Miriel shrunk herself enough to dodge the attack. She cowered into Padric's back, tightly gripping his shirt, whimpering.

Counting their number was impossible, as they moved so swiftly, dodging in and around each other. If their intent was to confuse, it worked.

Padric's chest tightened. It was hard enough to protect Miriel on the ground, let alone from avengers in the sky. There was no place secure where he could set her down, either.

"Hold on, Miriel. We will get through this." It was all the encouragement he could give.

In a moment, Padric secured the staff to the saddle pommel. Then drawing his bow, he loosed arrows in rapid succession at the attackers. Letting loose, one arrow struck the center of an eagle's wing. The creature wobbled in the air for a moment, then gave a cry as it lumbered down and knocked the servant Fred off the carriage.

Padric exhaled in frustration at the first casualty to go down. He hoped they could fend off these beasts quickly and circle back for him.

With no one to drive the carriage, the horses continued in a weaving pattern down the road. Which meant no one was watching the sorceress. Already, two of the assailants circled over it.

They could not let her escape.

"Rawlins!" Padric shouted. "The sorceress!"

The sergeant nodded and urged his horse toward the speeding carriage.

Padric quickly nocked another arrow. He saw a few of them fall, but there were always more to take their place. Their number never seemed to dwindle, no matter how many were struck down. How was that possible?

Rawlins yelled unkindly at the eagle nearest the carriage while Serill struck another's talon with his sword, eliciting a screech from the bird. It soared up into the air. Covered in blood, the blond knight moved to fight the next feathered creature, his brows drawn tight.

When they returned home, Padric decided, they would train in attacks from the sky. One never knew when a sorceress's friends would come to visit.

Another assailant alighted on the lieutenant's right, nipping at his face. Padric shot straight upward, the arrow sinking into the soft tissue of the creature's stomach.

"Get away, get *away*!" Miriel wailed. She flailed an arm above her head to fend off another winged beast coming from behind.

It was impossible to get a clear shot at the attacker. Its large wings constantly beat and pushed at him, with the air they generated, throwing off his aim and balance. It's razor-sharp feathers left deep, smarting scratches on his neck and the leather of his quiver.

"Impossible," he said in shock. *These cannot be eagles. Even their feathers draw blood.*

The bird's talons enveloped Miriel's arms and began lifting her up.

"Padric!" She let out a horrified scream.

No!

Dropping his bow on his back sling, he grabbed the hem of her dress as he raised the staff to strike at the eagle.

"Hold on, Miriel!"

His feet struggled to stay in the stirrups as he stretched upward and clipped its leg with the sorceress's staff.

The eagle squawked, its sharp feathers batting Padric heavily from behind. The staff flew out of his fingers and stars danced around his vision. Then the creature leaned over and nipped at his forearm with a bronze beak, leaving a gash along the top of his left wrist. Padric bit back a cry of pain. Despite the throbbing, he somehow kept his grip on the hem of Miriel's dress.

"You cannot have her!" What did the sorceress want with her?

Just when he thought he would lose her, the injured talon opened, and the still-screaming Miriel wrenched an arm free to reach down to Padric. He swung at the other leg, jabbing at the ankle. It released her, and she fell onto the horse behind Padric with a thump.

The bird shrieked and tore off into the sky. Once it was high enough, it let out another shriek, and as one, the others stopped attacking and followed it.

Did they give up?

He spared a glance toward the carriage, but it it was nowhere in sight. Where had it gone?

Miriel clutched onto Padric even as he clasped her arm. There was no time for relief, however, as the terrified horses tore down the road at breakneck speed.

The wind swept by Padric too fast to get his bearings. Try as he might, he could not sway his horse's direction. Any of his usual attempts to soothe the crazed creature did little good.

The view of the river emerged. They had veered so far off the road that they were now cornered at a part of the River Trent that curved back in on itself.

Padric yanked on the reins, trying to deviate the course while calling for Firminus to stop.

The horses finally came to a halt at the edge of the riverbank, Firminus nearly bucking Padric and Miriel over his shoulder and into the water several feet below. A short, steep, craggy cliff was all that separated them from the river. Padric's heart plunged to his boots. *Too close.*

Firminus shuffled nervously, kicking rocks down the cliff.

Everyone was shaken. Not one eye remained still but shot glances in all directions, waiting for another attack.

Miriel, still hugging Padric tightly, sobbed and squirmed. After a moment of trying to regain his composure and breath, he patted Miriel on the shoulder. "It is all clear now, Miriel. We are safe for the moment." *But how long will that be?*

He inspected the small remaining members of the party that had set out from Chaddesden. Both the servants Fred and Anton were missing along with the carriage and laden cart—which meant the sorceress was missing as well.

Another pang of dread crept up his neck. The eagles could dice the carriage apart in seconds. If they freed the sorceress, it was only a matter of time before she returned. His blood iced over at the thought. Not for the first time, he doubted their likelihood of getting to Wolverhampton in one piece. He knew they needed to move, but they were in no shape to go anywhere for the next few minutes.

"Miriel, why not get down and check on Isemay?" To outer appearances, the red-haired girl looked calm, but Padric knew her well enough to know on the inside the bird attack shook her up.

The baron's daughter stilled, but after a moment, nodded.

"There is a good lass," he said. With care, he let Miriel down to earth by the arm, then dismounted. He wished he could comfort her more, but they were not out of harm's way yet.

On shaky legs, Miriel wound her way around knights and horses to Isemay.

Padric surveyed his men, trying to ignore the aches from the scratches he had received from the eagle-like creatures. A large bloody cut ran down Byron's cheek. Serill's red shirt sleeve was tattered, blood oozing down his hand and dripping onto the ground. Holding his wounded arm, Serill breathed heavily then nodded at his lieutenant.

Rawlins scowled as he dismounted. "What do we do now?" he asked bluntly. Padric knew that look. More than his pride was hurt in failing at the chance to kill every bird that had attacked them. Rawlins helped Isemay set her feet on the grass, her eyes frozen in terror.

Somewhere along the way Padric had lost the staff. *To the non-eagles?* he wondered. They were no ordinary bird, but he could not place them. That was a worry for later. Right now, he had to worry about the sorceress regaining her magic staff. He ran a hand through his sweaty hair, his mind whirling toward a desperate stratagem.

"First," he said, "we must let the horses rest. Do *not* let down your guard. The sorceress and birds could return at any moment."

Rawlins slapped a hand on his sword hilt. "We need to keep moving."

Padric peered at the horses, their sides heaving. He shook his head. "The horses are finished. We will have to go by foot the rest of the way. There should be a livery a few miles up the road, where we can obtain fresh mounts. If the servants do not arrive in a few minutes, two of us will go back for them and the prisoner. Then we must move swiftly—"

A sudden shift in the weather halted his speech. Black clouds rumbled in the distance as the wind picked up, rippling his sweat-drenched tunic in front of him. Firminus snorted and nudged Padric's shoulder.

Then everything became still.

CHAPTER 14

Staff in hand, the sorceress angled her blonde head toward Padric, her grin stretching from ear to ear. "We meet again, my darlings. Did you greet my friends? Are they not charming?"

Then she laughed.

Padric was tiring of their meeting like this. For several heart-pounding moments, he thought about drawing his sword to strike her down, but he figured she was prepared for him this time.

"We did, but they were dispatched post-haste," Padric replied. "Left with their tail feathers between their legs. Not such loyal friends after all, were they?"

The enchantress did not even flinch.

Stepping in front of the trembling Miriel, he placed a cautious hand on the pommel of his sword. The other knights followed suit. "What do you want with the women?" he asked.

The sorceress's laughter ebbed. "You did not care for my friends?" A false pout distorted her luscious red lips. "A pity, for they—well, most of them—enjoyed meeting you. And now that I have your attention…" She raised her arms, lifting the staff off the ground.

Not again. He needed to stall for time.

"What do you want with them?" he repeated.

The woman lowered her arms, impatience marring her features for an instant. Then the humor returned to cover it.

"Oh, they are not the only ones I came for. All of you will do nicely."

Padric was stunned. "For what purpose? What have we done to vex you so, that you attack us? Have we unwittingly trespassed upon your territory?"

She stepped closer. "As I advised you before, I came to your little group to give a proposition and to further my collection. The proposition end is complete. And now I have come to fulfill the second portion of my quest."

The wind shifted.

Unbidden, Roana's verse slipped into Padric's thoughts...

And rescue those of whom you seek...

...and a light snapped in Padric's brain. *A collection.* The missing people from Chaddesden and Derby—were they all a part of this "collection"? She and her friends were collecting them. But to what end?

"But why us? You obviously have not taken everyone in our village. Why only a select few?"

"They have certain...traits that I desire. Would you begrudge a woman for seeking only the best qualities in those with whom she is to work?"

He could find no fault in that logic. It was what any good commander would want from his knights. Yet that still did not make it right. The villagers and farmers had little choice in the matter.

Then out of the corner of his eye, Rawlins appeared. While the sorceress and Padric talked, the sergeant had managed to skirt his way around the horses to within fifteen feet away, just out of her line of sight. He needed another few moments to get into position.

"Who are you?"

Another wicked smile spread across her face. "I am called Circe. Perhaps you have heard of me."

Circe? As in the mythical Roman goddess? That was impossible.

Rawlins closed in on this so-called "Circe." The lieutenant made a split decision—it would likely fail, and his men and father would be furious with him later. But if it did succeed...

"Take me instead. I will do whatever you wish, only spare these men and women. They have families. Would you tear them from their loved ones?"

He could not look at the knights standing by him. Protecting them was his duty.

A hint of emotion played in the sorceress's bright eyes. But just as quick, they returned to amused determination.

"How touching," she said caressingly. "And utterly pointless. Every one of you is needed. Every. One." A cold, wicked wind swept up his spine. "But I do admire your willing sacrifice, as futile as it may be, Sir Padric of Derby."

Once again, she lifted the staff into the air.

Raising his sword, Rawlins dashed at her.

A set of antlers darted out of the trees.

The orb atop the staff glowed with a blue ethereal incandescence. All present were mesmerized by the enrapturing spectacle. The woman began a sing-song chant in ancient Latin.

Though the chant was lilting, the meaning of the words chilled him to the bone.

O antiquitatis dei
Clamorem meum audite
Affigite ad hos viros
Oculis vestris acribus.

Tribuite super
Hos viros scintillam
Bestiarum ferre
Stigmatem natorum.

O gods of yore
Hear my cry
Afix these men

With thine keen eyes.

Upon these men
Bestow the spark
Of creatures born
To bear the mark.

The sweet melody engulfed him. It slowed his racing heart.

As she sang, Padric could feel his body tingling. The sensation grew stronger and stronger, changing from a dull ache to a fierce throbbing in his stomach. Pulling, as though his insides were trying to exit through his navel. He let out a gasp and cringed.

Sistere facite
Tempus: vini bib'te
Ut dorsum curvetis
Et spinam nudetis.

Crescite ungues et saetas
Et dentes et ad ungulas.
Terram pedibus pulsate
A qua veneratis ante.

Make time hold fast.
Drink of the wine
To bend the back
And bare the spine.

Grow fur and claws
And tooth and nail.
Paw at the earth
From which you hail.

His insides tore apart, rearranging themselves. Each breath more excruciating than the last.

Sharp as knives, the power she wielded cut his concentration. Doubling over, a hand on his abdomen, he managed to slit his eyes open enough to see the other knights writhing, faces blanched, calling out. Two of them fell off their horses.

Miriel stood as stone, horrified shock keeping her limbs locked as she stared at the spectacle. She was otherwise untouched by the knights' and horses' affliction. Firminus whinnied beside them, kicking out in terror. His hoof nearly struck Miriel, who was too stunned to notice.

Thrusting out a hand to hold Firminus, Padric nearly passed out as he tried to straighten his back. Then he was patting Firminus, but no coherent words would come forth. It was effort enough to soothe the horse.

Except that his foot stuck to Firminus's leg. Panicking, he tried tugging it free, but his foot remained firmly affixed to the animal. Then slowly, his knee, then hip sunk into the fur, and disappeared from sight. "Nay!" he shouted fruitlessly. Trying to get away, the horse squirmed and inched closer to the embankment, taking Padric with him.

Small hands wrapped around his arm. "Padric!" Miriel screamed, barely audible over the sorceress, wind, and screaming men.

"Let go." He shook her hands off. She lunged for him again, but if he was consumed into the horse's body, he did not want to drag her along with him.

Circe continued chanting. Her long blonde hair escaped the bun and flowed freely around her face and shoulders, lips never breaking the pattern of her aria. But Padric couldn't listen anymore. He was sure he would pass out at any moment as the searing pain worsened. A blinding white light filled his vision. Then every piece of his body exploded.

A cry could be heard from a distance. Then he realized it was his own.

A blind panic filled his entire being as Firminus reared and bucked, Padric still attached and near to stomping on Miriel in the process. The horse's violent desperation loosened some of the rocks at the edge of the riverbed.

Stones crunched.

Air swished. Then...he was *in* the air, wind and rocks biting his ankles.

※

SWALLOWING half the River Trent was vile. Pain shot through Padric's entire body, alerting him to his surroundings. He pushed down the growing panic of drowning and tried to kick his legs.

His body felt so heavy. As if being attached to a cartload of stones. He pushed up with his arms until they grew tired. Then his legs finally started working and he hauled his face above the water.

And breathed.

And spluttered acrid Trent water.

And fell back under the waves again in exhaustion.

As Padric began to sink for the second or third time, the current took him along, and he thought it might be worth allowing it to take him. After all he had endured this afternoon, a bit of rest was deserved, was it not?

As he witnessed the bubbles exiting his mouth and nose to rise toward the surface, something in the furthest recesses of his mind jabbed at him. It poked and prodded. Until it awoke him from his lethargy.

Miriel and Isemay.

Rawlins and the other knights.

Firminus.

A last determination came to kick his legs and arms.

He emerged, spluttering again, gasping for air.

As he struggled to keep afloat in the rushing, sloshing river, he managed to turn his head back and discern the last traces of his men on the riverbank as they writhed against the spell of the sorceress while she stood over them. At least, where the men *had been*...All he could espy were small woodland creatures in their stead.

Miriel called to him. Begged him to return.

Try as he might to swim toward shore, the current was too swift. Too thick. And he was so tired.

Just before he was thrust around a bend in the river, he glanced at the sorceress, her staff still raised in the air. Despite the distance, those sapphire eyes glared directly into his. Pierced his very soul. Through the coolness of the water, hot lightning poured from his head to the very tips of his toes.

Then she was gone.

When at last Padric wheeled his head around, he sucked in a breath.

The water churned incessantly, and before he knew it, he was caught in a rowdy collection of rapids, battering him with heedless abandon at all angles. Wicked waves spraying water into his face with stunning force, dunking his head into the water too many times to count. At odd intervals, he imagined hearing diabolical laughter. Each time he emerged from the depths gasping for breath, he thought it would be his last. His muscles were spent when the chaos dissipated a hairsbreadth.

Blinking water from his waterlogged eyes, Padric believed the waves had abated, and he was free. However, when his vision cleared, his heart sank. Not more than ten yards ahead, in an untidy row within the river, stood a rather intimidating collection of burly boulders. And the rapids were leading him headlong into the fray!

CHAPTER 15

A dull ache ground behind Padric's eyes, bringing him to wakefulness. Another in his side urged him to shift off of whatever was digging into his rib, but the action only made it worse. His entire body felt bruised and broken.

Perhaps the pain would subside after a moment...

Or perhaps not.

Padric winced and attempted to roll onto his back and stretch his legs out—perhaps that would help—but they felt numb. In fact, as he mentally checked his body, everything below the waist felt numb. His chest iced over.

Am I paralyzed?

For a few more ragged minutes, he attempted to regulate his breathing. *How can I be paralyzed? I was walking only moments ago—was I not?*

Was he? His mind was a blank. A snow-white parchment of memories.

He managed to pry one eye open.

Then the other.

The attempt to lift his head ended in immediate regret. In a sharp intake of breath, his stomach twisted, and he found himself coughing up what felt like at least half a horse trough of water.

Clamping his eyes shut, he felt a sensation in his right leg. Moments later, his left. And then his right, then his left...

He knew not how to describe the sensation. It was as though ten appendages protruded from his body all at once. Each appendage was restless and urged him to get up and run to loosen his aching joints.

Run!

Padric's eyes shot open. *Run.* He had been running. But to where? *From* where?

Sharp rocks from the riverbed pressed against a grassy knoll. In the far end of his vision, a dense thicket of oak trees lined up to where the road should be. A quick glance at the River Trent's direction indicated he was on the west side of the river.

He did not remember coming here. Was there not something he was doing?

As he slid an aching arm under his chest, he thought his torso and legs felt quite heavy. Just like when he was in the water.

The water.

Rapid, jarring memories flooded back to him.

The sorceress.

Chanting.

The knights.

Miriel and Isemay.

And...the river.

With more fervor, he undertook to get up, but something was off. He looked down at his legs but only saw Firminus's legs and shoulder. A shudder rent his chest as he thought his legs must be crushed beneath the horse. Is that why they felt numb? But—

Where was the horse's head?

"Firminus," he whispered, his throat sore after heaving.

No response.

"Firminus?"

Silence.

A boulder lodged itself in Padric's stomach. With a sick feeling, he spread his hand over the horse's shoulder. Rough chestnut horsehair met the smooth skin of his abdomen and the cloth of his red and black jerkin.

"What is this?" he said, bile rising in his esophagus.

> *Grow fur and claws*
> *And tooth and nail.*
> *Paw at the earth*
> *From which you hail.*

Balling his fist in front of his face, he found his hand to be real. Pale skin. His own. Then he made a second pass at where his skin and horsehair met at his abdomen.

This cannot be.

> *As the heir to the charioteer of old,*
> *Thou wilt bear a curse of gold.*

No!

He blacked out for a moment. When again he regained his senses, he resumed his musings.

What did she do to me? To Firminus?

If his stomach had anything left inside, he would have lost it.

He then recalled his men—Rawlins, Byron, and Serill—writhing on the shore. Changing...and as Padric was rushed away by the river, he saw their unrecognizable forms lashing out. He could still hear their screams. Miriel and Isemay's screams...

And she—the sorceress, Circe—had changed them all.

Into...animals? Then why am I a...am I something out of a story—a myth?

> *Thou wilt bear a curse...*

Cursed...with magic. *Real magic.* It knocked his breath away, as he tried to fathom this new and terrifying fact. It was neither rational nor sane. But it was real. And it went against every fiber of his being.

"Vile sorceress!"

A wail called up from inside of him. A deep-seeded sorrow, dragging him down, down, down, until he wished to bury his head in the sand. Or run at full speed until his heart burst.

After waiting a few agonizing heartbeats to calm down, Padric made three resolutions. First, he must stand up. Second, he must rescue his friends. Third, he would ensure the sorceress would never hurt anyone ever again.

The second and third items he was the most unsure of how to accomplish, but he determined he would figure them out.

"One thing at a time," his father had always said.

Two weeks ago, after Roana's prediction of Gregorio's medallion saving his life from a flying dagger to his face, Padric had begun to believe in the prophecy. But then nothing more had occurred—until today. Nevertheless, even with Roana's prophecy, nothing could have quite prepared him for this.

Did she know the sorceress would come this very day? He should have turned the caravan around and returned home at the first sign of trouble—at the first sighting of the stag. Before that even, his first feeling of trepidation. Oh, how foolish and headstrong was he to have allowed their party to continue into her trap!

Stop wasting time and get up! Nothing can be done whilst you wallow in self-pity. What was done is done.

With care, Padric moved his legs. It was a strange sensation moving four legs instead of two. He imagined it like being an infant on hands and knees and attempting to crawl for the first time.

Eventually, he made it to his knees and hauled himself up on wobbly hoofs; flailing his arms somehow prevented him from falling down on his face.

A centaur, he thought with a grimace. *I have been transformed into a centaur.*

It all fit. An oracle. A sorceress. Now a centaur. He *had* found himself inside a mythology story.

A stab of guilt wrenched his stomach. Was he the only one to escape? The chance his comrades remained near the bend in the river was slim.

He wondered if anyone else had escaped the sorceress and if she would search for them. If so, he needed to find them, and soon.

On the ground next to where he had lain, his bow was worse for the wear. The scarred wood appeared as battered as he felt after having been dashed from boulder to boulder on his way through the river rapids. But it was in one piece, for which he was grateful. Most of the arrows in the quiver, though waterlogged, were also intact.

Stooping to pick up his sad bow, his hoof caught on a rock, and he tripped a couple of steps. It would take time, he realized, to ever become as graceful as Firminus was. Their merging would take time. There was no time like the present to try it, he supposed. He wondered if the other knights merged with their horses as well.

As Firminus's stiff muscles—or were they his own muscles now?—took tentative steps over the rocky terrain, a tightness stopped him in his tracks.

His sword was still strapped in its scabbard around his waist, but the belt no longer fit right. The place where the horse's shoulders met his waist, where Firminus's neck should be, was larger than his hips, and the scabbard lay at an awkward angle, making the sword hilt practically stab him in the gut. In moments he removed the weapon and slung the belt over his shoulder, then under the opposite arm and buckled the two ends together. It was not quite military form, but his father might give him points for creativity until he could find something better. Despite everything, Padric chuckled at the thought.

"I have tarried here long enough," he said aloud to any woodland animals that would listen to a strange creature out of myth.

Padric made it to the copse of large oaks and found landmarks of his location. If his bearings were correct, the river washed him close to five miles away from his friends, close to Burton-Upon-Trent.

He headed south, keeping among the trees to avoid notice. Now and again, he spied travelers traipsing in each direction. *Curious*, he thought, *there was absolutely no one on the road when we crossed it earlier.*

Soon he found the spot of their first encounter with the sorceress. Little was discovered regarding the ordeal. No prints made by foot, no horseshoes, nor wagon wheels. It was absolutely bare. Except for the marks left by more recent travelers, there was no suggestion that Padric's group had ever traveled this way at all.

The bend in the river where he had last seen his men and the sorceress revealed the same scenario. Nothing. Only the crumbled rock from where he fell, which could have happened naturally.

With clarity he recalled the events: the sorceress singing in Ancient Latin, her staff glowing so brightly. Rawlins moving in to attack her. And then the...transformation. Miriel screaming, the river, the men changing into animals.

Of course, it was imperative that he inform his father immediately about what had happened. He was not looking forward to confessing his failure in taking care of Miriel and Isemay. Let alone his unit and two servants. He had sworn to protect these seven people with his life, and yet they were taken right out from under his guard.

In order to gain back his honor and friends—and his legs—he must rescue them, each and every person whom she had taken. His eyes roamed the area one last time, searching for the least trace of evidence of the last few hours, for naught.

Something else nagged at his mind. The sorceress called herself Circe. Was she really a goddess, or someone pretending to be her? Before the last few weeks, he would have said myths were mere stories. Now, though, he was beginning to believe in them.

Padric was drawn from his dizzying thoughts by the shadow of darkened clouds forming overhead.

A shiver ran up his spine. A storm was brewing, the air thickening and making his skin clammy to the touch. This was no longer a safe place to stand.

Then he spotted the stag. Stationary among the trees, there was no mistaking its antlers and the red diamond over its heart, as it stared at Padric, its head angled to the side.

Padric frowned. There was something very off about this stag. Instead of running in the opposite direction when it saw the group of humans, it stayed to watch, hidden in part by the trees.

Of course, Padric thought, this was not merely any curious stag following along for scraps of food. It had been watching them all day, if not longer, awaiting its mistress's arrival to wave her staff and scoop them up. In fact, he was positive he had seen it the same day he received Roana's prophecy.

Anger coursed through Padric's bones. His fingers itched with longing for a hunt.

"Do you think you can follow me without consequence?" he shouted. "Returning to the scene of your mistress's misdeeds was a grave error on your part. I know who you are."

The antlered animal was the reason the little company had been targeted. If Padric captured it, maybe it would lead him to the others. To *her*. If nothing else, he would bar it from communicating with her, to announce that Padric was alive and seeking her out.

Perhaps the stag recognized the gleam in the hunter's eye, because it briskly retreated into the trees as Padric drew his bow and nocked an arrow.

"Beware stag. I come."

Circe's spy was now the hunted.

CHAPTER 16

Dragging out the sword from its scabbard, Padric found a bit of grass and leaves to dry it off. Now he stood under a thick tree, drips of rain falling haphazardly through the canopy, some tickling his neck and head. The darkness and rain from the night before had driven him from his prize, but he now he was on the hunt again.

With his new set of legs, he knew his clumsy steps would only manage to warn the creature of his coming, as it had for the hares and other woodland animals of the forest realm. Despite that, being a centaur had its advantages. He could run faster, for one—when he was not tripping over vegetation due to inexperience. At first, he was afraid his hind legs would lag, but a sort of instinct took over to move them almost of their own accord. Things he never thought about when growing up around horses. He had more respect for Firminus and all four-legged creatures now.

He regarded the weapon in his hands. It had been his grandfather's. Almost without thinking, he brushed his thumb along one edge of his sword to the tip, its smoothness calming and focusing his mind. *Loyalty.* Then his thumb slid its way down the other side. *Justice.* The memory of its being bestowed upon him when he won his spurs and became a knight, blessed by a priest, and swore to always protect the poor and the weak, returned to him. Padric always wielded it with pride. That day over a year ago had been his greatest achievement. And now look where it had gotten him. It seemed he was not worthy to wield the blade after all.

Padric shook his head wearily.

He had thought he was ready to be a lieutenant. It was what he had worked toward for so long. But now...perhaps he was mistaken. The baron of Chaddesden had given Padric his commission and trusted him to guard his daughter with his life. But Padric had failed utterly. How could he ever show his face to them again? How would anyone ever trust him going forward? His father would be disgraced as well to have such a worthless son. And now he most likely lost the one lead he had. Brilliant.

Run, the voice in the back of his mind had said. It was the most cowardly thing to do, he acknowledged with a groan. But would that solve anything? No. His friends and all who were missing from Derbyshire would still be lost. And he was the only one who knew what happened to them.

...rescue those of whom you seek
Ere the sun attains its highest peak.

Padric inhaled a deep breath.

The solstice. He had until then to rescue everyone. A mere six weeks away. If he did not catch the stag, all hope of finding them would be lost. And with it, the world.

AFTER A CHILLY NIGHT, the rain at last took a much needed break, although the clouds remained thick with perspiration. They would release their burden again soon enough.

For the hundredth time, his mind wandered to the puzzle that lay before him. What was it about his encounter with this Circe that so struck him? Her blue robes, such as he had seen in drawings from his studies of the Odyssey and other texts, of the ancient Romans. This woman spoke in a foreign accent, and her chant was in an ancient form of Latin that only Gregorio had taught him. Identical in language and style to Roana's prophecy. And, he surmised, she did something quite specific: she changed men into animals. It was not every mythical sorceress who did that. But what did modern—*modern?*—sorceresses specialize in? If he encountered any more, he would be sure to ask them.

Like it or not, this woman matched the Circe of those stories.

If she were a sorceress from ancient Roman mythology—and that was a grand if—why suddenly appear now, and in England, of all places? And where there was one, he thought with despair, there could be more.

Why would a goddess, lost in time, find her way to England to pluck people from their homes?

On the other hand, she may be only a mortal woman wielding supernatural powers that had nothing to do with mythology. She could have borrowed or inherited the name. What would she gain by that, other than to strike fear into people's hearts? Padric shook his head. He would be hard-pressed to find even a handful of people in Chaddesden or even Derby who could give him a worthwhile discussion about ancient Roman mythology. No, that prospect seemed less likely.

A druid, perhaps? Then why not go by a druidic god's name?

Padric rubbed his sore eyes. How he wished Gregorio or Rawlins were here to talk to about it.

A sound carried to him, and he sidestepped behind a tree, bumping his hindquarters on another tree trunk. Even Firminus, who did little more than nod or shake his head would be preferable over Padric's own dark thoughts.

A cacophony burst to his right. Aiming his nocked bow at the sound, he was surprised by a jumble of large birds bursting from a bush to his right. *Eagles!* Pulse racing, he released an arrow at the flock. Missed.

But no, it was only a flock of pheasants, as startled by him just as he was of them.

He could not help but release a low strained chuckle. His nerves were wound so tight, he felt sure to burst. Those pheasants were nothing like the eagles which had attacked his party yesterday.

"Hold," he said aloud for the forest to hear. He halted. Padric closed his eyes, remembering. Yes, the eagles had veered off to the north when they turned from the terrified group of humans and horses. Of course, that did not necessarily mean the sorceress had taken his friends in the same direction—but it was a start.

No, no, that was wrong. They were not eagles at all, but resembled another creature he had studied briefly in his Roman and Greek lessons. The bronze beak and razor-sharp wings were from a flock of creatures the hero Hercules fought in his sixth labor: Stymphalian birds.

An incident came to mind of a day early in his studies with Signore Gregorio.

Padric, aged twelve, laboriously read the story aloud in Latin whilst Signore Gregorio paced around the room, commenting every so often at his pupil's lack of inflection. Out of the corner of his eye, Padric spied his friend John Wilmot doodling a passable rendition of a bird at the bottom of his parchment. Engrossed in his endeavors, the lad failed to notice the tutor's shadow hovering over him. When at last he felt the signore's eyes boring into his parchment, John tried to hide the offending drawing—too slow.

Swiping the paper out of his pupil's hand, the tutor studied the drawing. "This is not bad, but the wings are incorrect," he said, slapping the paper down onto the desk. Taking up the quill from John's petrified fingers, Gregorio dipped the quill and drew some rough strokes onto the drawing. "The wings of a Stymphalian bird looked more like this, and the beak...like...so." Holding up his work to the students, both stared unblinking at their tutor. Their old tutor would have flogged them both for such an mishap. Yet Gregorio was very different in his encouragement of imagination.

When Padric and John recovered and asked more about the Stymphalian bird, Gregorio mumbled that he read a plethora of books and then pointed at the tome for Padric to continue reading where he had left off in Hercules's sixth labor. John and Padric eyed each other at the avoidance, then shrugged their shoulders and read on with decidedly more interest.

Padric would have laughed at the memory had he not met the creatures in person. And how similar the John-Gregorio ink drawing was to the real thing left no room for argument.

Whatever their name, the birds' trail would be minimal at best. And there was so much land to the north, he would have little time to scour the whole of it. Not before she finished with her captives—whatever that might mean.

The prophecy had not forsaken him. He could sill see it whenever he closed his eyes:

> *As the heir to the charioteer of old*
> *Thou wilt bear a curse of gold.*
> *Reclaim the amulet of darkest night*
> *To destroy the weapon of untold might,*
> *And rescue those of whom you seek*
> *Ere the sun attains its highest peak.*

Padric inhaled deeply.

The solstice. He had until then to rescue them. A mere six weeks away.

As if in answer to a prayer, Padric spotted the stag winding its way through a field a few hundred yards ahead. A grin rose up his cheeks. The chase would resume after all.

※

THE MOONLESS NIGHT carried on as rain tore down in sheets, wind whipping in all directions in simultaneous bursts. Scarce could Padric see anything in front of him, but he knew the stag had come this way. He could smell it, sense it. Over the course of five days from when the sorceress appeared, it heightened many of his senses since becoming, for lack of a better term, a centaur. The rain gained momentum. He slowed to a trot in case of rabbit or mole holes in the waterlogged earth. The deluge continued this way, pelting him with harsh bursts until his entire body became one huge throbbing ache.

Lord, a little break in the rain would be most welcome about now. He sent up the soggy prayer and scanned the area around him. Sure that the dark mass looming ahead was the dense forest near Chaddesden, he figured the stag should have sped in that direction, at the least, to find some cover from the storm. And from him.

Lightning struck somewhere behind him. Too close, he thought, as the thunderclap sounded within a second. Raw energy from the blast attacked his senses, and he fought to keep his ground.

The horse lodging inside him panicked. *Danger! Get out of the open!* He strained to reign in the feelings that threatened to devour him. As he tried to swallow down the impending dread, his legs moved of their own volition, taking him closer to the trees with each long stride.

Finally, the rain and wind gave way enough for him to see the tree line come into focus. And there it was—the stag—standing at the edge of the trees, waiting for him. Baiting him to follow, as though playing a game. This was not the first time Padric sensed the stag toying with him. He had, after all, been chasing the animal for days. Garrick had taught his son to be a good game tracker, but this deer was an expert at backtracking and hiding its trail.

Padric was past frustrated with the beast. At another stage in his life, he might pursue the stag out of principle. But this wasted time he did not have. There were alternative means to locate Circe—he just had to find them. The only good news was that it led him toward home and getting reinforcements.

Thunder sounded in the heavens above him, sending the stag into the dense thicket. Picking up the pace, Padric reached the first tree without a hitch. Keeping to the path, the rain subdued to an annoying drizzle as he hurried along. But the thunder and lightning struck as bright and loud as before, each time creating more uncomfortable static in the air.

As if on cue, the stag emerged directly in front of him and hightailed it down the path. A shimmer of what appeared to be feathery wings sprouted from its back and a long feathery tail fanned down and swept the wet earth. Taken aback momentarily, the hunter snapped to attention and with deft fingers ripped an arrow from its quiver and brought forth the bow. "This is it!" he yelled into the rain and launched into a run.

Exiting the dense forest, Padric was gained momentum when a brilliant flash of light blinded him. The immediate return of an explosion of wood, leaves, and thunder followed. He skidded in the mud and blinked. As his eyesight returned to normal, he saw someone—a maiden with a dim lantern near the massive, burning tree trunk. She jumped as the very top of the tall oak sent sparks and branches into the air. Screaming, the maiden covered her head and scrambled under the tree, slipping on the slick ground.

A long, loud crack sounded at the base of the trunk, and the whole thing came tumbling down toward her.

Though sluggish in the thick mud, Padric put on speed. *Run!* He willed her. The thick branches were almost upon her as he neared, and he bellowed to her above the rain and thunder, "Look out!" as a large protruding branch swung down toward her back.

CHAPTER 17

Brynwen had sent Uwen back to his home when the large drops started spotting the ground. "I'll be fine. Home is just a little past the forest." The boy was not much younger than her, but he worried about his mother and his new baby sister. It was a difficult birth, and the child struggled to breathe for the first few minutes out of the womb. But Rosa did her magic by rubbing her favorite elixir all over the baby's chest and little neck, and then her breathing became easier. Exhausted, Rosa, the midwife, told Brynwen to go home before the heavy storm clouds opened up.

Uwen was uncertain about leaving Brynwen by herself, but she assured him she would be fine, and he turned around. Now she progressed through the forest, lantern in hand, unable to move faster as the darkness and sheets of rain impaired her vision. The path became exceedingly muddy, her shoes growing heavier each time she lifted her feet. The lightning and thunder chased her through the forest. The trees thinned to open ground, and she recognized the gigantic oak tree looming thirty feet away. After that, home was another quarter mile. She could do this.

Just a little further.

As she approached the great oak, a flash blinded her, the coinciding thunderclap knocking her onto her knees. Struggling to stand, the mud clung to her shoes, keeping her in place. A loud crack sounded at the tree base.

Maybe this wasn't such a great idea after all.

Stuck in the mud, Brynwen watched in horror as the bark at the base of the trunk splintered apart. Frantically, she tried to move her feet again, but no luck. Could she pull her feet out of the shoes?

The tree groaned under its own weight.

It's falling!

Then another sound like thunder stormed up behind her. Heart thumping in her chest, too late she heard the shout "Look out!" before a hand clamped onto her arm flung her into the air, landing with a thud on the ground, rolling over and over until she stopped in a puddle, dazed. Her lantern rolled a few more feet, then winked out.

But just before the tree crashed to the earth, she caught a glimpse of a man on horseback standing where she had just been. Then the oak slammed heavily to the ground, its fire sizzling out from the heavy rain.

"Oh!" she cried, scrambling to her feet on the slippery ground. Still dizzy from the impact with the earth, she stumbled to the fallen oak. She had to find out if the horseman was still alive.

The smoldering fire provided enough light to guide her to the tree. Her breath caught as she took in the damage. Could he survive that?

"Hello?" she cried out as she fought her way through foliage and stiff branches toward the trunk of the fallen oak. Branches and twigs tore at her clothes and flesh, but she continued on, ignoring the stinging scratches she received.

No answer came, but it would be almost impossible to hear over the loud rain.

She cringed as another flash of lightning struck in the distance behind her, closer to Chaddesden this time, followed by a hearty peal of thunder.

"Over here," said a male voice.

He was well hidden by the branches. She plunged into the oak's remains, twisting under small limbs and climbing over the larger ones, receiving scratches and long red gashes for her pains, and she called out again. This time came an answer, and pretty close, too. It seemed an eternity before she finally found him.

"I'm here," she said to her savior in the growing darkness as the last of the embers burned out. She extended her hands out to comfort him and feel the damage. "I am Brynwen Massen. What is your name?" Her teeth chattered from the cold, making it difficult to keep her voice from shaking. From what she could tell with her hands, a thick branch lay across his chest, and another rested against his waist, pinning him to the ground. Beyond that, she was barred by the oak's carnage. Her heart sank. "Are you..." she began, trying not to sound alarmed. "Are you in much pain? Where does it hurt?" She could not see his face but could sense his fear.

He took a shallow breath. "It is not...so very bad," he said, then grimaced. His voice was young and strong. She guessed he was about the same age as her older brother, Samuel. "Forget me," he continued. "Are you unharmed, Miss? I...feared I was too late." Genuine concern trilled his voice, and his calloused hand moved to cover hers, giving it a gentle squeeze. Propriety begged her to pull her hand away at such a forward act. But then she decided he must be in too much pain to think straight. She clutched his hand, willing to instill some of her essence and comfort into him, to take away his agony. Here he was, possibly broken under this tree, and *he* had the good grace to ask after her health. What if he never walked again...or died? Her heart broke a little more.

"Pray, what is your name?" she asked.

"I am Padric...de...Clifton."

Padric de Clifton, the lieutenant from Chaddesden? The combination of rain flowing into her eyes with the darkness of the night made it impossible to make out her savior's face. What was he doing out here, riding around in the storm? She had almost forgotten the horse he rode.

"Sir, your horse. Is it..." *Dead?*

Silence gripped the lieutenant, and she thought he might have passed out. But then he replied, "I cannot say, exactly."

She wondered what that meant but put it aside for later. "I have to get you out." Alas, it was impossible by herself. If only she had not sent Uwen home, he could have run for help.

He shook his head. "I...might be able to..." He tried to shift, but that only made it worse, and he let out a gasp. He shuddered and cried out in agony, then his whole body convulsed.

"Sir...*sir!*" But she was powerless against his seizure. The branches around him shook violently and dropped leaves everywhere. Then with a sigh he stilled.

"Sir de Clifton!" Brynwen cried.

Hands shaking, she brought a tentative hand to his mouth, his whiskers scratching the backs of her fingers. There were breaths. Steady. Alive. He had only fainted. But how long could he last?

"I will return with help," she said, though she knew he couldn't hear her. She hastened home as quick as the debris and mud and darkness would allow her, sending up a quick prayer to the Lord that her savior wouldn't die underneath the broken oak tree.

CHAPTER 18

The rain stopped by the time Brynwen dragged her two brothers and grandfather to the tree at predawn, the sun's rays barely peeking over the green tops of the forest and the fog.

Please be alive, please be alive, she prayed for the hundredth time since leaving the lieutenant.

Her lantern remained where it had fallen on the ground, caked with mud. All of the oil had spilled out leaving a glossy sheen on the wet ground.

As her eyes took in the scene before her, the breath caught in her throat.

Memories of the event ripped through her mind—her legs frozen in the mud, not doing her bidding to *run*. The caress of branches bearing down on her, grazing her back, her neck. The bone chilling fear of being crushed to death. Then the strong arm flinging her from danger.

Now in the daylight, the devastation of last night's storm truly hit home. The once great oak lay before them in a gnarled mess. Green leaf carnage littered the soggy ground within a couple of yards from it. The very tip of the tree was charred, and what was left of the leaves near the top were brown and curled in on themselves, as though trying to protect themselves from the flames left by the lightning.

If not for the knight coming along when he did, their positions would be reversed. He lay trapped under the tree in her stead, all because she wanted to get home. Neither of them should have survived that.

How could anyone survive that?

Her stomach churned just thinking about it.

"He is in there," she said, voice shaking. She found the place where she had broken twigs on her way to the wounded man.

"Sir de Clifton," she called, "I have returned with help." A shiver ran up her spine, imagining the poor man lying in pain or dying. Or even dead... *No, don't think that.* "Sir de Clifton?"

Her brothers, Talfryn and Samuel, climbed where Brynwen indicated while Eduard stayed behind. The brothers used their hatchets and saws to clear a path to the fallen knight. The slow, careful movements of her brothers' sawing and hacking at the branches grated at her already fraying nerves. *Move faster,* she urged inwardly. *A mother in the midst of labor could move faster than you lot!* Oh, why hadn't she brought a tool to help out?

She knew she should be more forgiving, as they were trying their hardest, but—

"Talfryn, be careful with that, you could cut him!"

Her twin brother let out a breath.

Again, she called to the lieutenant, but her calls remained unanswered.

He is dead, she mourned. *And it is my fault. I should have pulled him out right then. I should have run faster. I—*

"There's no one here," Samuel called, casting his eyes all around. Talfryn was equally perplexed.

"What?" Brynwen squeaked.

Samuel shrugged. "Only a saddle, a bed roll, and saddlebags. *Someone* was here, but not now. There are two depressions in the earth here, one heavier than the other, and some drops of blood."

Brynwen's chest tightened. "How can that be, Sam? He couldn't have gotten out—not in his condition."

Talfryn scratched his head. "You said he had a horse?"

"Yes, he rode it as he tossed me away from the tree."

"But did you see it?"

"Well...not clearly. It all happened so fast."

Her grandfather Eduard leaned forward on his cane. "Well, if he is as injured as you say, he can't have gotten very far. I say we split up and search for him." The boys nodded. "If anyone sees him, call out."

She tried to swallow the lump in her throat. Yes, maybe he did escape. But where would he go? Even so, the tightness in her chest lessened.

The group split up, Samuel and Eduard continuing down the road toward the forest while Talfryn searched more extensively in the tree and then headed south. Brynwen was to check the stream.

Turning down the path toward their home, she sent cautious glances at every little noise. A cricket singing. Scurrying squirrels in the grass. Birds chirping and swooping overhead and behind her in the forest. Yet she found no sign of the lieutenant. With ginger movements she picked her way toward the stream, which lay at the bottom of a grassy and rocky embankment. Maybe he had somehow managed to escape the tree and went for a drink of water.

Upon reaching the edge of the hill, Brynwen paused. The fog was denser down the hill closer to the stream. Glancing into the haze, she spied a figure on hands and knees at the edge of the water. Was it him? She took a deep breath and ventured down the hill.

Oblivious to her presence, and with halting and deliberate movements, the figure dunked his head into the clear rushing water. As she neared, she noticed a red and black shirt wadded into a careless heap on the grass, his shirtless upper half bloodied and dirty. Smooth, muscled back and arms, above a thin waist. The trousers he wore were made of no fabric she had ever seen. They were gray, almost like fur, making his legs appear contorted.

She was about to call to him when the fog lessened around him for an instant and made her halt abruptly. The trousers were not, in fact, trousers at all. They...were *real fur*. The strange gray legs curled under him, ending in dark hoofs, much like her family's goats, Hay and Stack.

Then his head bobbed and something on the top of his head glinted in the partial sunlight.

She blinked, cringed, convulsed, and wanted to be sick—all at the same time.

Was this even the same person—err—creature?

A sound from behind made her jump.

"Bryn, did you find something?" Talfryn said, stopping at her side.

She merely stared at the figure some distance away.

Talfryn squinted. "Hmm, do you think that's him? And what's with his legs?"

"I'm not entirely sure. Are those...goat legs?" Again, her stomach twisted. She was glad she had missed breakfast.

"Mayhap he merely likes kid skin."

"You are impossible," she said, and shoved his arm.

The glint of metal in the grass next to the creature caught her eye. A sword, and recently cleaned, too. Beside it lay a black scabbard, a bow, and a battered quiver half-full of arrows.

"Let's find out if it's your savior," said Talfryn.

"Are you insane? What if he is a demon?"

"Then why would he rescue you? Do you really believe that rubbish?"

She honestly didn't know how to answer.

He took that for a no. "Then let's go say hullo." He started off toward the man, pulling out the hatchet from his belt. "Just in case."

"If it is indeed him," she said. "Or it ate him. After you."

With a confidence she didn't at all possess, she followed her brother, weaponless except for her soggy satchel. With quiet steps, they made their way around the man-goat-thing, who was still oblivious to their presence—she hoped.

Heart racing, Brynwen stooped low and clutched his sword hilt, liberating the weapon from the grass. The sword was much lighter than expected. Leowyn had once said the weight of the weapon was supposed to be balanced in the hilt precisely for the wielder. This was a beautiful piece, made by a master craftsman, and engraved with a careful hand. She probably should have grabbed the dagger instead, but that would require getting closer to the demon.

Jaw set, Talfryn stood to the other side and waited.

The man-goat raised his head from the rushing stream, making Brynwen jump backward with a start. Water trickled down his hair and chin and then back into the stream. The dirty-blond hair on his head was already bouncing up in large round curls, failing to cover the little ivory horn protruding a couple of inches above his ear. A tiny twig was entangled in his hair.

She crinkled her nose in disgust at the sight of his horns. If this wasn't a demon, then what was?

The twins eyed each other, both motioning for the other one to make the first move. Then Brynwen put on her brave face. All her anxiety and fear were pushed into her arms as she pointed the sword at the young man's neck. Frantic thought swirled around her head: Should she finish him now? Cut off his head? Before he killed her and her family. Their friends. Maybe he was responsible for all the disappearances. She had never killed anyone before...

She bit her lip. *Am I crazy? Holding a sword at someone's throat?* Maybe she should have waited for Samuel and Grandfather before attacking this creature. Or bring other some knights with them.

Then the man's body tensed. With caution, his right hand reached out and patted the grass where the sword had been. Then, he turned his head with caution. Seeing the sword point only inches from his face, his eyes sparked, but otherwise betrayed no emotion.

Despite the nasty gash that marred the skin above his eyebrow and the whiskers on his chin—she recognized him immediately. It was veritably Lieutenant Padric de Clifton from Chaddesden.

And he was now a demon.

But why would he save her life? A fluttering arose in her stomach.

Perhaps she should say something before she and Talfryn killed him. Keeping her eyes on him and struggling to keep a scowl on her face, she opened her mouth, willing her voice to stay calm.

"Do not move," she said.

CHAPTER 19

*B*rynwen wished her hands would stop shaking.

The lieutenant's sharp gaze traveled up the sword, until it met Brynwen's hands, her arms, her chest, neck, then face. Surprise flitted across his mossy green eyes. Then his shoulders relaxed in relief and a smile crept up his lips. "I see you survived your journey home."

Not the reaction Brynwen was expecting. She became self-conscious about her haggard appearance as his eyes took in her mostly dried but mud-caked dress, arms, and face. With a scowl, she lurched the sword tip closer to his nose.

He reeled back, landing on his hip, his goat legs slipping out from under him. Keeping his face away from the sharp blade, he leaned back on his left arm and winced, raising a hand to his chest. Brynwen's healer's heart gasped at the sight of the deep purple bruises that spread down from his collarbone to his abdomen. Probably cracked ribs. Besides the ugly gash trailing blood down his cheek, bloody cuts and scrapes marred his entire body from his jaunt with the tree. She was surprised he was able to hold himself up at all. And he had risked his life for hers...

"Lieutenant?" Talfryn asked, all astonishment. He lowered his hatchet. "It is you, isn't it?"

Lieutenant Padric de Clifton spared a glance in the farmer's direction in surprise. "Yes. You are Leowyn's cousin. Talfryn, right?"

His guard let down, Talfryn's eyes revealed both recognition and confusion.

Surprised, Brynwen glared at her brother. "You *know* him?"

"Yes, Leowyn is in his unit in Chadd."

"Affirmative," Sir de Clifton said. "Your brother came to me to ask after Leowyn's whereabouts."

Brynwen's face flushed. She had forgotten Talfryn mentioned meeting the knight and captain when he went to in Derby.

Padric flashed another smile at Brynwen. "Thank you for returning my sword to me. Proper etiquette would be to offer it hilt first, though. But the blade is very sharp, I would not wish you to cut yourself."

The spell broken, Brynwen's mouth now seemed to work. "What *are* you?" She berated herself for the way her voice shook and jabbed the sword at him again.

He leaned back. "What? I am Padric de Clifton."

"Nay, you are not. Your face is the same. But your goat legs and horns are of a demon. A changeling—that is what you are." She was proud of herself for identifying him.

Stunned, Sir Padric raised an open palm to her. "Nay, you misunderstand. I only woke up this way this morning—"

"Do not try to dissuade me, you foul creature. You tried to seduce me to help you. And then you turned yourself into...into this, or a squirrel or snake, and were able to get yourself out all along. Probably turned into a chipmunk or a rat. You will get help, yes, but only to your death. You shall not take away any more innocent people from this land." She guessed at the last bit.

"Nay, Miss Bry—"

"Do not say my name, foul creature."

"Where is your horse?" Talfryn interjected.

Sir Padric's head flinched back slightly. "My horse?"

Talfryn continued. "Brynwen said she saw a rider with a horse fall under the tree."

The demon's nostrils flared, his face losing all color. He hesitated a moment, then said in a softer voice, "'Twas only me." The twins stared at him expectantly. "The horse was *me*," he clarified.

Brynwen huffed. "I distinctly saw you *and* a horse."

The lieutenant groaned and rubbed his face with his hand. "Last evening, I was both man *and* horse. But I assure you I am no demon or changeling. A week ago, I was a normal man. Human. *Mortal.* This was done to me by a…sorceress' curse." He paused, eyes glistening. "She turned me into a centaur, and then this morning a faun."

"A sorceress?" Brynwen asked. "Why would a sorceress change you?"

"'Tis the truth. As God is my witness—"

"God cannot help you should you prove to be the Devil's own. If all you say is true, then what happened?" As an afterthought, she added, "What have you done with Leowyn, Alice, and the other missing people from Chaddesden?"

"I—" His eyes darkened. "I know you do not believe me. But I have been searching for Leowyn and the others for weeks—months. What you see before you is the result of that failed search. But I now have a lead of their whereabouts, regardless. Or, I had one, until this morning."

A silent standstill occurred for several heartbeats. If that was true, then his saving her had cost him more than just a few cracked ribs. Her heart twisted. With new eyes she looked the young man over again. For the first time, she noticed he wore no clothing. Her cheeks heated and she squeezed the weapon tighter, trying to keep her eyes on the water behind him, just beyond his gorgeous face.

Noting her sudden discomfort, he looked down. Face flushing deepest scarlet, he shot his right hand out to grab the discarded shirt and threw it across his lap.

Of course, she'd grown up with two brothers, but still….

Talfryn snickered.

Looking more than helpless now, Lieutenant de Clifton exhaled. "Pray, put down my weapon. I know my appearance is alarming, but you have no reason to fear me, I assure you. By your leave, I must get to Derby. The captain must know what has happened, and I have been removed far too long as it is." He made a move to stand, but Brynwen kept the sword tip up.

Talfryn returned the hatchet to his belt. "And what, pray tell, has happened?"

Without hesitation, the lieutenant answered, "The sorceress attacked us on the road and my party was captured: the lady Miriel Wilmot, her companion Isemay, their servants, and some good men from my unit."

"Taken by the sorceress. Why?" Brynwen asked.

"I do not know," Sir Padric said, his neck cording with tension. "But I will find her and get them back."

A heaviness weighed down Brynwen's shoulders. She had heard Lady Miriel's group never made it to Wolverhampton. If a sorceress changed him into this creature, what did she do to the others? The sword became too heavy for her arms. She lowered the blade to the grass but did not drop the hilt as she studied the young knight before her. Could he be believed? She wanted to. Still, it was such an amazing story, she needed more information.

"How *did* you escape the tree?"

The lieutenant closed his eyes, head tilting back a tad, exhaustion washing over his features. "The sorceress must still be toying with me. When I awoke this morning, I found myself thus... changed...and I managed to squeeze out from under the branches. I am not sure how to explain it, but I could sense, or smell, the water, and thirst overtook me. Firminus helped, I think. It seemed to take the better part of an hour to crawl my way here, shortly before you arrived."

Before Brynwen could ask who this Firminus was, and his whereabouts, Sir Padric's head began to droop. Heart and head contending, Brynwen's healer instincts took over, and dropping the sword, knelt beside the wounded knight. Even if he turned out to be a demon, she could not stand to see him suffer. Even if her very soul was blackened for helping such a one.

Mossy green eyes lifted to hers, not pleading, but not relenting. "I must find the captain. 'Tis most urgent."

She shook her head. "You shan't make it to Derby today." His eyes dropped. "But mayhap we can deliver a letter for you?" At that, his expression brightened. Hope. And somehow, she found herself pulled toward wanting to help him.

The twins made to lift him, but he insisted on standing on his own. Blushing, Brynwen turned around to fix her filthy hair, then picked up his arrows and quiver while he shimmied with deliberate care into his ruined tunic. Not even the best seamstress in Derby could return the piece of cloth back to its former glory.

Talfryn helped his sister with the lieutenant's weapons. "He was taller a week ago," he whispered. Looking at him, she had also thought Sir Padric seemed taller in Chaddesden on Easter Sunday. But that was weeks ago.

Eduard and Samuel caught up to them a few minutes later, horrified by Sir Padric's appearance. It took Brynwen and Talfryn a few minutes to explain about the cursed knight's predicament before they finally calmed down.

Talfryn chatted as they walked back to the farm. Sir Padric de Clifton remained silent, concentrating on putting one shaky hoof in front of the other. The sight of the hoofs still unsettled Brynwen, but she imagined it was worse for the knight to whom they belonged. She and Talfryn walked to either side of the lieutenant, impressed that he made it to the cottage door before collapsing.

CHAPTER 20

The calming scent of chamomile roused Padric from his lethargy. As he slowly became more aware, the drumming of dull pain spread throughout his body. Everything was stiff. Someone was in the room with him, their clothes swishing around as they moved, scraping cooking utensils. He cracked an eye open. He lay on a straw cot in a small cottage.

The crackle of a fire and a whiff of something salty—soup or stew—made his stomach growl something fierce. How long had it been since he had eaten?

It took several moments to identify where he was. Then a vague memory of stumbling inside, Talfryn and his brother holding him upright, and collapsing on a cot, then nothing. Until now.

His eyes scanned the small cottage room. A light wooden workbench took up one whole side of the wall closest to the door. It was filled with many different types of plants in a number of forms and colors. A variety of dried and fresh leaves and petals lay arranged in neat piles by color and size. Above the bench hung several dried, withered plants clamped along a string, most of which he knew not the names to. At the center of the room stood a small table with four chairs. A cabinet and finely built shelf stood tall and proud on the next wall to the left. The straw cot he lay on resided at the corner of the room farthest from the door. Lastly, the overlarge hearth with a workable chimney—more extensive than in other local farm cottages—housed a good-sized fire.

He blinked, and the prophecy danced across his eyes, and all his recent memories returned. The stag he had chased for days was likely long gone by now, its tracks covered by the night's rain. Padric bit back a groan. Loathe as he was to leave his comfy cot, he could not stay. There were other places he needed to be.

His new furry legs were awkward and quickly entangled in the bedding as he tried to sit up. *These blasted goat legs!* he bemoaned. *What good is being a half-man and half-goat? The Roman gods must truly be laughing at me now, turning me into a faun for their sport.* The more he struggled with the blankets, the fiercer his annoyance and the ache in his body became. With effort, he refrained from letting out a groan as a searing pain shot up his side, throwing his eyes wide. Letting out an undignified grunt, he fell back down again, then gasped as unrelenting jagged daggers stabbed at his ribcage. His vision swam, dark spots everywhere.

"Oh, now you've done it," came an annoyed voice through the fog of pain.

Warm hands lifted him under the arms and settled him on the straw bed. The hands patted him down, replacing the poultices and ointment cloths which he had so unceremoniously knocked off in his foolish attempt to sit up.

He rubbed clumsy fingers over his forehead. "I...beg your forgiveness," he croaked through gritted teeth.

"As you should." Brynwen stepped back, placed her hands on her hips, and scowled. Then, seeing his evident pain, her eyes shifted to a spark of concern. "You really should not move so soon. Not for a couple of days, at least. You are lucky to have only two cracked ribs."

The maiden standing before him was much changed from earlier. Her long, damp auburn hair was braided and hanging down her front. She wore a cream-colored blouse with a dark blue skirt and brown patched work apron. Red scratches from the fallen oak tree marked her face, hands, and arms, but would fade in no time. He noticed how her hazel eyes sparkled as she glared down at him. Her now clean face resembled her brother Talfryn, though her features were daintier. Quite attractive, in fact. Even when she scowled.

The healer's hands reached toward him and smoothed the gray blanket back over the poultices and his chest without causing discomfort. Hands that were adept at comforting the sick. As she leaned over him, her long auburn braid dangled off her shoulder like a pendulum. The scent of honeysuckle and lavender rushed his senses. Padric breathed it in with welcome. It dismayed Padric to see the mixed emotions crossing from her eyes to her pursed lips.

He recalled her threatening him with his own sword, calling him a demon, and he could not help but grin at the memory. Part of him wanted to learn more about her. The other part advised to keep his distance, lest he scare her away again. He had warned himself that—and thus, as he found out so rudely this morning—he did not have complete control over his own body. *Circe* had captured that part of him, changing into whatever creature she wanted.

Padric tried to speak, rasping out a few words. His throat felt like sandpaper.

With a soft voice Brynwen said, "I will get you some tea with honey. That should help a little." Then she stepped toward the fireplace.

He nodded, instantly regretting the action, and closed his eyes for a few moments as Brynwen leaned over the stewpot.

Stories from his childhood of old bent women with dried herbs and small dead bats and crows strewn all over their homes was the first thing that came to mind. A witch's hovel? Surely not...

Still, the thought of a witch lingered in the back of his mind as Brynwen returned with a piping cup of tea. The flavorful tea filled his stomach and warmed him, the chamomile's fragrance calming his head and other aches.

By the time she had finished making a fresh poultice, which she explained was made with comfrey, hyssop, and a lavender ointment, he was nearly finished with the tea.

"I thank you, Miss Brynwen, for the hospitality. But I really must be on my way. My father must be made aware of the situation at once. I am much improved after your ministrations and the tea, I assure you." In fact, he did feel better, but not enough to walk the road to Derby. But she need not know that.

"Nay, you're still not fit to journey. You will need to stay at least a few days longer. And in your condition..." She eyed his hoofs under the blanket. "I would imagine you'd not wish to be made a spectacle."

His chest tightened. That confounded enchantress! She had made such a mess of things. How was he to fulfill a prophecy when he was flat on his back for a week or more? When his heart settled down somewhat, he said, "You must understand, I need to go."

"And you must understand that your body needs time to heal. You can't crack two ribs and be ready to run a foot race after only a day."

"Mayhap I can," he argued. "I am a quick healer." He was becoming irritable with this lass's attitude. Did she not know the world was at stake? Well, no, he supposed she did not. But a little thing like two cracked ribs could not stop him from his mission.

She crossed her arms. "Fine, then let me see you get up right now."

Padric glared at her, then made to get up. Except that his body refused to move, as though it perceived the pain it would be in if he did.

After a few more moments of internal battle with himself, he sighed. "Fine, I concede. You are the healer, and I dare say you know what is best. But I will be on my feet on the morrow or the day after."

Brynwen smiled. The first true smile since he had been captured under the tree. Was that only a few hours ago?

"That is better. I am the healer here, and I say you must stay in bed and rest."

Padric bowed his head slightly. "I concede to your wisdom in this matter, dear lady. Then might I have a bit of parchment, a writing implement, and a razor?"

The healer raised an eyebrow. Then realization sparked in her eyes, followed with a grin. "Ah. That can all be arranged. I will have one of my brothers deliver the missive directly to your father."

"My thanks," Padric said, eyes growing tired. "I am truly in your debt."

Brynwen said nothing as she grabbed the requested quill, ink, and a small roll of parchment from the cupboard and climbing the ladder for her brothers' razor. She returned quickly, and he detected the hint of a smile raise the corner of her lips.

A flutter trilled in his abdomen.

He lay back, a warm feeling creeping up his chest. He began to feel better.

Brynwen held out the razor to Padric, but then thinking better of it, pulled the implement back. Padric looked at her quizzically.

"Ah-ah. Do you know how to use this? You may cut yourself. Mayhap you need a bit of instruction before you slit your own throat?" A wry smile formed on her lips.

Padric feigned a look of hurt. "Lady, you do me to the quick. But mayhap I *might* need some instruction. Would you dare supervise such a perilous endeavor?"

"I accept the challenge." For a fleeting second Padric had second thoughts when she glanced overlong at the razor.

With set face, Brynwen set down the parchment and quill and set to work with the razor, and, to Padric's great relief, did not cut his face or throat. After a thorough job, he thanked her.

"Now, I best be off to midwife. One of our patients is due any day now."

"How long have you been an apprentice?"

"About a year now. Rosa the midwife has taught me a great deal and I still have so much more to learn. Really, I must be off. I will have Talfryn take the note into town for you."

A quick note it was, for his eyes grew heavy. When finished, he could swear he only blinked once and then Talfryn was there, holding the note in a grimy hand.

The farmer smiled down at Padric. "Feeling better, friend?"

"Tolerable, thank you."

"My sister is a good healer. One of the best." Talfryn rolled the message between his fingers. "I will deliver this straight off."

Padric rubbed a sore rib. "Be as discrete as you can. If you have time to wait for an answer, I would be grateful."

"Of course. Anything else, my liege?" A wry grin swept up his cheeks.

Padric replied with a grin of his own, "That will do, knave."

The farmer chortled and made a wide, clumsy bow. His arcing hand swatted a jar of ointment on the table. The bottle spun, dangled dangerously off the side of the table, but Talfryn righted it just in time. Padric tried not to laugh, lest his ribs burst.

"My thanks to you," he said. "And your sister. And that she did not impale me when she had the chance."

Talfryn grinned from ear to ear, eyes bright. "You know, I think you are growing on her."

Padric's heart picked up pace ever so slightly. "Why do you say that?"

"She hasn't made you eat nettles." Another laugh, then he was out the door.

CHAPTER 21

Padric remained in the bed, his soup bowl untouched while the little farming family sat around the table in the tiny cottage. Samuel ate with his betrothed's family that night. The smells wafting up from Padric's bowl were amazing, yet his stomach was too knotted to eat. He was heartsick. How was he to defeat the sorceress if he could not keep his own head? Like a madman, he had chased after the stag and had failed to capture it. It was as if it knew his every hunting move. And he still had no information regarding the sorceress's whereabouts.

"Lad, are you sure you will not sup this evening?" Eduard asked.

Padric sighed deeply, making his ribs ache with the effort. "I thank you kindly, sir, but I have no appetite."

Brynwen swung her head around, her braid twisting off her shoulder. "You really must eat. To keep up your strength. To do...whatever it is you need to do."

"What *is it* you need to do?" Talfryn asked.

Eduard leaned over and slapped his grandson's head. "That is not how we treat guests."

"Excuse me. I was just curious, is all."

"Leave it be, Talfryn," said Eduard.

Brynwen eyed her brother. "Tal, did you deliver the message to the captain?"

"Nay, actually." Talfryn wiped his mouth with a finger. "I didn't go to Derby."

"But—"

"Before you get all mad, the letter was addressed to Baron Wilmot's residence. To his son John."

"John? Why is this?" Eduard and Brynwen each looked to Talfryn and then to Padric.

Brynwen peered at Padric with a skeptical eye. "Why wasn't it sent to the captain of Derby? I thought you were desperate to see him?"

All eyes on him, Padric's cheeks flushed. He ran a hand through his hair, grazing a curved horn. He winced out of contempt of magic. "I changed my mind."

They remained silent.

Padric ruminated for a moment. "I started writing the letter to my father. But then, after a great deal of contemplation, I realized it to be a poor decision. As much as I know my father would want to help, it would be a disaster. He would send his whole battalion out to rescue the captives. The captain is a powerful man and an outstanding leader, and the men would follow him willingly. But despite his best efforts and intentions, she would either smite them all or else turn everyone into animals. Either way, they are doomed. He cannot know. I must go it alone."

Talfryn's jaw dropped.

"She," Brynwen said thoughtfully. Then with more force, "Who is *she*?" Setting her spoon in her bowl, she scooted her chair away from the table and moved to within a foot of the wounded knight. "Why won't you tell us what is going on? You show up practically at our doorstep in animal skin, and mention this sorceress's power, but give little detail. What are you afraid of, Sir Padric? That we will learn the truth from someone else? We know you are aware of what has become of our cousins and friends. How are we supposed to help you, to *trust you*, if you will not tell us the truth?"

Eduard glowered. "Brynwen, leave the poor lad alone. He needs rest and—"

"Nay, Miss Brynwen is right," Padric said, attempting to sit up straight, with difficulty. "I have imposed myself upon you. I did not wish to bother you with my plight, but in truth I find that I already have. You deserve to know what has befallen your family. It is by all means the most bizarre tale you shall ever hear."

Eduard grinned, his thin cheeks scrunching with the effort. "Son, the moment my grandchildren found you, the most bizarre tale we had ever heard died like last year's harvest."

Padric chuckled, then caught his breath as pain lanced up his ribs. "I suppose you are right. Then brace yourselves, for I am not much of a storyteller."

Haltingly at first, Padric began the tale. He started with the occurrence and Leowyn's disappearance, then the ill-fated journey with Miriel and his knights, the stag, the sorceress, and the Stymphalian birds. The only thing he refrained to mention was the Oracle and her prophecy about the amulet and the end of the world on the summer solstice. He felt that including them would only frighten and worry the farmers more.

"The sorceress is very beautiful and very powerful. You know about Roman mythology, yes?"

The three gave Padric a blank stare. *This is starting out well.*

"Pagan gods and goddesses, brave heroes and frightening monsters," he said.

Brynwen's eyes lit up. "Oh, yes! Some in Derby call Durand the bard the god of...of love. They called him something strange. Cooper? Coopie?"

"Ah, yes, Cupid," Padric replied. Not exactly the best example, but it would suffice for their purposes.

Talfryn rolled his eyes. "Mainly the drunk lasses say that."

"They do not!" Brynwen retorted.

"Marlon doesn't lie," Talfryn said.

"Marlon doesn't know everything. He is the town drunk."

"The point is," Padric inserted before things could escalate, "that thousands of years ago, people came up with stories, creating the gods and goddesses to explain how the world and everything in it came to be. They began to pray to these deities and the gods in turn sent heroes on quests to slay vicious monsters and save maidens and cities from destruction."

"These gods and goddesses—they were indeed powerful?" Brynwen asked.

"Quite so."

"Like our God in heaven?"

"Not quite. It is difficult to explain. But, you see, the situation I am in—we are all in—is a myth come to life. A sorceress calling herself Circe is behind this. In Roman mythology, Circe was a goddess and sorceress who seduced the hero Ulysses. In Homer's story *The Odyssey*, she changed Ulysses' men into animals. I have given it considerable thought over the last few days, and I am certain it is she. Like the goddess, this woman sang the sweetest, most alluring songs that fill you with longing. A sort of siren. I admit that I was drawn to her at first." He averted his eyes in admission.

"She had you enthralled, did she?" Talfryn said with a smirk.

"Yes." His eyes grew wide. "Nay—nay, not like that. The first time I saw her, my limbs froze in place. She had power over us all. Except Miriel and Isemay, who remained unfazed."

Brynwen furrowed her eyebrows. "You mean, they were unaffected, or what?"

"I am not entirely sure. But the sorceress asked them if they would like to help her out with something. They refused."

"And these maidens. Are either of them your sweethearts? Is that why you wish to get them back so desperately?"

"What?" Heat flushed Padric's cheeks. "Oh, nay. They are as sisters to me. My younger sister Emily is great friends with both of them. Emily was asked to travel with us, but Mother did not condone the idea of sending both of her children away in such troubling times."

"Your mother has sense," agreed Brynwen. "But tell me, you said the men in your unit were changed into animals. But not the maidens?"

Padric closed his eyes, recalling the event. "They did not change, as far as I could tell, as I was being swept away down the river." He furrowed his brow. "Nay, I do not think they changed a'tall."

"How extraordinary."

"If the knights were turned into animals, why were you only half-turned?" Talfryn wondered.

"That is what I have been delving to discover for myself. But I cannot dwell on that. I must find Circe and defeat her before the solstice."

"Why the solstice?"

Padric berated himself for the slip. He was so involved in the conversation, that one little concession from the prophecy stormed out of his mouth. Not only could he not forget the prophecy, he could not keep it secret to save his life.

"It...makes sense," he said. "In ancient times, the longest day of the year was a time of celebration and power for the druidic and Roman gods. The goddess Circe is up to something, and it has to do with the solstice. I am aware that the ancient peoples of this isle regarded specific places holy for their pagan gods. Stonehenge, or any henge, for that matter. Roman legions built shrines and temples to their gods and goddesses in their numerous fortresses and cities throughout their empire. The question, to my mind, becomes not in which location Circe resides, but which may have the greatest advantage during the solstice."

Eduard had been silent throughout the tale, and now Padric noticed the old man as he crossed himself, his face beet red. "All this talk of gods and goddesses. 'Tis blasphemy! We are Christians, not pagan-devil-worshipers! Are you not a Christian, young man?"

Padric was taken aback. During these times, that was a serious allegation. "Of course, sir. I proclaim to be no such believer in other deities. And yet, here we are. I concede, it does make one wonder about such things as the existence of other gods."

Eduard and Brynwen gasped in horror, but Padric held up a hand. "I only wish to say that, while I have only come into contact with one of these beings, I do not have sufficient information on all other deities. For the sake of argument, let us call them 'immortal beings.' I do not say we should worship them; I only surmise that these immortal beings might exist. *If* indeed the sorceress is Circe."

"What of demons?" Talfryn asked. "Could this Circe be a demon? Brynwen thought you were one earlier."

Brynwen glared at her brother, her cheeks coloring the deepest shade of crimson.

"I have heard that argument," Padric said, remembering all too well the incident of earlier at the stream. The way Talfryn held his hatchet, and the determined look in Brynwen's eyes as she held Padric's own sword to his throat. "In fact, my tutor has an entire tome on the subject. It mentions how strong the ancient deities were, with powers unlike what they imagined demons to possess. Greater, even. But my tutor did not take much stock in that theory."

"Then why did he have the book?" asked Brynwen.

"Because books are his life, and he could not bear the thought of anyone else owning it. He is rather stubborn in that regard."

Eduard considered Padric carefully, but then finally nodded. "I suppose that all makes sense. But I don't like it."

"There is not much of this to like," replied Padric.

"Tell me," Brynwen said at last, inching closer. "How do you plan on finding her lair?"

Padric sucked his teeth. "Ah, that is the question. After attacking us, the Stymphalian birds flew north. I can only assume they were headed toward her lair. But as to her exact location, I cannot say. There was one person who I think can help. My old tutor, Gregorio Fiori—*if* I can find him."

Talfryn's eyebrows raised. "The Italian? Didn't he kill someone?"

Padric rolled his eyes and sighed. Here it was again, the story no one would forget, or ever let Gregorio live down. "It was a misunderstanding. He was near a youth who drank too much and thought Signore Fiori poisoned him. But he is a good and honest man and would never do something so deplorable. The boy recovered, but the Italian's reputation never did.

"However," Padric continued, "Signore Fiori did extensive research on the Roman fortresses in England and might have intelligence which could aid in locating Circe." And for all he knew also lead him to the amulet.

"And then you plan on defeating Circe by yourself." Brynwen leaned forward, her face close to his.

"Of course. I cannot ask anyone else to go." *Fulfill the prophecy on my own.* Yet the words felt empty as they spilled from his mouth.

"I will come." Talfryn stood up quickly, nearly knocking the chair over onto its back.

Padric gaped at Talfryn incredulously. That was the last thing he had expected.

"No need to ask," Talfryn said. "I volunteer."

Brynwen gasped as though she had been slapped in the face. "Nay, Talfryn, you cannot go. Tell him, Grandfather." She spun to plead with Eduard.

Eduard got to his feet in alarm. "Talfryn, you foolish boy. Don't go around saying such things. People will believe you are serious."

Talfryn looked down at his grandfather with defiance. "But, Grandfather, 'tis no jest. I really do want to go." Under his grandfather's stern gaze, Talfryn appeared as a small boy being punished for taking two biscuits instead of one. "I *need* to go."

"Talfryn, it is not your responsibility," Padric said calmly. Talfryn might mean well, but he knew nothing of fighting. And this business with magic—it could be dangerous. He could not guarantee his safe return. "This is my fight. I must go alone."

Talfryn seemed to read Padric's thoughts. "I know I am no soldier. But I must go. My cousin Leowyn and I are close, and I can't leave him trapped in that sorceress's snare. It's my turn to be responsible now. He would do the same for me. And we have other family members and friends who were taken as well. I can't stand by as they suffer."

"Young man," Eduard said, "you cannot be serious. I beg you to reconsider."

Talfryn could only shake his head.

Brynwen said, "Talfryn, this is ridiculous. Forget it. You are not going with this man. He will lead you to ruin."

For the first time, her words stung, and Padric's resolve cracked. Was that what he was doing—slowly breaking their family apart?

"Bryn, if you think he will get me killed, then mayhap you should come with us, to guard me from harm," Talfryn joked. But the maiden scrunched her eyebrows, seeming to seriously consider her brother's suggestion.

Brynwen shook her head. "I have my patients, and Rosa needs me here. Besides, who will milk the cow? You know she is picky and prefers you handling her. *You cannot go.*"

"That's Grandfather's notion," Talfryn retorted. "You or Samuel can milk her just as well."

Eduard stood there, spluttering. "I cannot believe you are even considering this—this madness! We are farmers, Talfryn, not warriors. I forbid you to go."

Talfryn reached his full height and towered over the older man. "You would forbid a man to fight for his family and friends? What sort of a man do you want me to be? I finally have something to fight for, and you are against it."

"Because it is *dangerous.*"

"But isn't it worth the risk?"

With a sharp eye, Padric scrutinized the young farmer as a lieutenant would size up a new recruit. It was hard to admit, but Talfryn was a likely candidate for the city guard. He was young, strong, and full of drive. He could easily be trained with some fighting skills. Under normal circumstances, Padric would be the first to dissuade Talfryn from going. It was too personal. Yet, Padric could not with any sincerity say that his own reasons for going were entirely objective either. Talfryn did not ask for vengeance, only the deliverance of his loved ones.

"Do you promise to do everything that I ask and train as I see fit?" Padric asked.

Talfryn blinked, taken aback, then nodded agreeably.

A feeling crept up on Padric, and he could not say why, but he dared not peer at Brynwen. The sensation of her eyes boring little holes into the base of his skull was enough to give his arms gooseflesh.

"Then by all means, you may join me," Padric said. He managed an encouraging smile. "Assuming, of course, your grandfather gives permission."

The old man's shoulders slumped, another ten years seeming to age him in moments. He hesitated, then nodded in assent.

Padric turned his head to find Brynwen staring at him, as though wishing to throw a dozen daggers at his heart. Without a word, she stormed out the door, slamming it for good measure. Padric sat in shock.

"That's not good," Talfryn said. "But don't worry, she'll be back." Nevertheless, Padric could read the doubt spreading over Talfryn's face.

CHAPTER 22

*H*ours later, Brynwen paced the little cottage's lower room in the dark. Even with the moon shining brightly outside, its illumination through the window was blocked by the curtain, and the tiny lit candle on the table did little to brighten the room. She could barely see anything but shadows all around her. The wretched faun slept soundlessly in her grandfather's bed, while Grandfather snored in the corner on his makeshift cot.

The revelation of a sorceress stealing people from their homes had been improbable when Sir Padric first brought it up. Since her cousin Alice had gone missing, Brynwen held firm to the belief that the mother-to-be had not run away, but was taken without her consent. Now, Sir Padric made claims that Brynwen's belief was correct—but not in the way she had ever envisioned. She had pictured bandits or slave traders. This was completely out of her depth or understanding.

Brynwen knew nothing about magic, but understood the issue could not be cured with herbs and chamomile tea. If so, she would have made a poultice to rival St. Mary's church, or filled the county's widest ditches with her tea. How she wished it were that simple! But no, they were faced with a magical being who could steal people at her own whim. A *goddess*. The word left a sour taste in her mouth.

Sir Padric had lost his human legs at the price of magic. Brynwen had lost her cousins at the same price. Were Alice and Leowyn changed into animals the same as Sir Padric's other knights? There was no way of knowing, and that pierced Brynwen's heart more than anything. What was the sorceress doing to them right now? Were they in agony? Why did she take them? This half-man-half-beast lying in her grandfather's bed was the closest she had to answers, and yet he was nearly as clueless as she was.

After a few more rounds of pacing, she realized her hands needed to do something. She lugged a handful of carrots and celery from the cupboard and started chopping them for the morning's porridge. She needn't worry that the chopping would wake everyone in the house, as Eduard's snores could be heard to the edges of their property. The task was completed before she had even realized it. Still riled up, she found there was naught else to do but pace some more.

She stopped just short of Sir Padric's bed, another wave of frustration flowing from her bosom to her cheeks.

After Talfryn's insane proclamation to join Sir Padric's quest, and the knight's approval of said request, Brynwen stopped listening. Well, almost completely stopped listening. The blood in her body boiled. She could have murdered the young lieutenant right there. How dare he wish to take her brother away from her? She had already lost her mother and father to the plague. Now she might lose Talfryn to a different kind of plague. She could not bear to lose him. If possible, she would lock him in a stockade and throw away the key before letting anything like that happen to him.

But now...

Now she stared down at Sir Padric. Dark shadows veiled much of his handsome face. The shape of his fine nose. Eyes closed in sleep. The curls resting on his crown, and the point of a horn sticking out of those curls, discolored to bone white in the dark. His breathing was steady.

Even though their conversations since he came to stay with them had been unassuming at best, there was really nothing to point out that he was evil. What did she really even know about him?

She thought it odd how someone could seem so angelic as they rested. Yet again she wondered if Sir Padric had a dark heart, consciously leading her brother away to his doom. Could this faun in fact be a demon, as she had believed when first beholding him that morning at the stream? Had the sorceress turned him from a human with a soul to a demon with evil intent?

English hospitality dictated, "When interacting with strangers, you may be entertaining angels." Guests were to be treated with the utmost care and neighborliness, bending one's back to provide comfort and safety. They never mentioned how to protect one's family in case the stranger was discovered to be less than honest.

A tear traveled down her cheek.

"Mayhap I should show you how to use it first." His voice was soft, almost inaudible.

"What?"

"Before you cut my throat with that knife." Sir Padric's eyes opened to slits, the candlelight flashing in them, but he otherwise remained still.

Puzzled, Brynwen looked down at the young man. "What are you talking about?"

"If you are going to kill someone with a knife, you should have formal training. So you do not cut yourself in the process."

Oh! She had forgotten about the knife. A quick glance down to see the glint of candlelight reflecting off the blade confirmed it. Quickly regaining her composure, she set her shoulders back. "And why would I cut myself? I am a skilled healer and cook. I chop herbs and vegetables daily."

"So, you are a killer. I knew it," he said with a steady voice.

Brynwen was taken aback. She bristled on the defensive. "I haven't killed anyone."

"But those poor herbs and vegetables. Innocent of all crimes, and yet you pick them from their beds, hack them to tiny bits, crush them, and boil them to a frenzy. How is that not killing without remorse?"

The herbalist stared at Sir Padric in shock. Then her lip rose into a half smile, and she found herself giggling. "I suppose I am, aren't I? But if I am a killer, then you are a cannibal."

Sir Padric feigned horror. "How could you say that of me?"

"We ate a goat last night."

Sir Padric thought about it for a moment, then grinned, the candlelight glinting off his teeth. "I concede, then, to cannibalism. Much to my chagrin, I am a conspirator in your crimes, as I ate the evidence. We are both to blame in this sordid conspiracy."

He chuckled lightly. Again, she laughed with him, her heart lifting. Then remembering her grandfather, she glanced in his direction to ensure he remained asleep.

When Brynwen looked down again, she lifted the knife closer to her face. The smile dissolved. With her other hand, she slid her fingers along the smooth edge. Her heart ached, and she slid onto the chair beside Sir Padric's bed, all anger snuffed out like a candle. Yet her heart still ached.

"I don't think I could," she admonished.

"I know how you feel."

"How do you know?"

"Because I would not be able to bear it, were it the other way around. If my sister left home too young. Circe took my friends from me, without asking, and I was left behind." Padric's hand slid from atop the blanket and covered her hand holding the knife, sending a shock of lightning through her arm. His fingers, calloused from years of training with the weapons of knighthood, were warm. The action made her pulse race, and she quickly removed her hand from his.

"I am so sorry, Brynwen. I did not think how it would affect your family before I agreed to let Talfryn join me. But he is old enough to make his own decisions." His eyes eagerly searched hers for understanding. "Even your grandfather sees that."

"I know," she admitted. "I know I should let him go. And he can take care of himself. I...I am so scared. I've already lost so much. First my parents, and now my cousins and friends. I cannot lose him, too. Or be left behind. We have never been apart for more than a day."

They remained silent for a few minutes. Long enough that he might have fallen asleep. She caught herself almost nodding off.

"You will not lose him," he said. "You have my word." He squeezed her hand for reassurance. She squeezed back, finding that she wanted so much to believe him. To believe that his words were more than empty promises.

"You will bring him back to me?"

A flicker caught his eye, and he did not speak right away. She could feel the shift in his demeanor. Something was wrong, but she could not place what it was. At last, he answered.

"He will return home. I promise." A half-hearted smile raised his lips and lingered for only a moment.

What wasn't he telling her? She wanted to press him, but he closed his eyes.

After a few moments of silence, she rose and stretched.

The old ladder creaked as she climbed up to her pallet. At the last step, she worried her bottom lip and decided she did trust Padric—that he would take care of Talfryn.

But would he take care of himself?

CHAPTER 23

A reply letter from Sir John Wilmot arrived a week later. Brynwen handed it to Sir Padric.

The wounded knight read the letter eagerly. "I am to visit the mansion before dawn on the morrow, if I can manage it."

"Can you?" she asked. Her patient walked around the cottage, and a little outside, but his movements were slow. She wasn't sure if it was her poultices and ointments, or his determination to get better, or a combination of the two, that helped him heal faster. Whatever the case, it pleased her that his ribs were healing quicker than expected. However, it meant that he would take Talfryn away with him all the sooner.

"I can," he replied with set jaw.

Brynwen eyed him. "Fine, but Talfryn and I will be prepared to drag you back to the farm at the first sign of fatigue."

"Fine," he replied, taking the challenge.

On the morning of their visit to the mansion, Brynwen cast a wary glance around the late spring blooms and neat square hedgerows of the Wilmot mansion's courtyard garden. The sun had not yet peeked its nose over the horizon. Her eyes met her brother's. Never in their lives had they imagined they would ever be traipsing upon this bit of earth.

They had timed their arrival to avoid the guard shift change. Sir

Padric grumbled about having to sneak around men from his own unit, but there was naught to do about it. Garbed in the longest tunic the farming family owned, as well as a pair of Talfryn's trousers, which Brynwen had modified, Sir Padric took a wobbly step up the back stair. If no one looked directly at the bottom of his tunic, they might not notice the hoofs. She hoped.

Sir Padric wrapped his knuckles upon the door. He set his shoulders back, looking every bit the knight, sans uniform. However, there was no fooling Brynwen how labored his breathing or the ashen quality of his face. She had to give him credit, though—he never once slowed down or stopped for a break on the way to the mansion.

The door opened a crack, and Sir John Wilmot stuck his handsome head out, his dark hair swept back and tied with a small dark blue bow. Made of fine quality fabric, the young nobleman's tunic and leggings, Brynwen could not help but note, matched the bow in color. Sir John peered around the grounds and then opened the door wider and ushered the three inside, shutting the door quietly behind him.

"John," Sir Padric said with a wide grin and clapped his friend's arms amicably.

"Sir Padric, it is good to see you up and about," Sir John said with a mirror grin, "after the ordeal you referenced in your letter—though I am most surprised that you were able to make it a'tall. I feared you would send an emissary in your stead." He looked appreciatively at Brynwen, who was quick to avert her eyes and bow her head.

"I am much improved," Sir Padric stated, though his cheeks were quite pale.

"I am most anxious to learn about this secret mission of yours and about my sister." He looked anxiously at Sir Padric. "I only wish I could go with you. But I know you will apprise me later, yes?"

"Of course. That goes without saying. I regret that this is the only time we have to meet before you depart for London."

Brynwen raised an eyebrow. She had not asked what Sir Padric had said in his letter to Sir John, and he never divulged the information. She wondered at Sir John's complete trust in Sir Padric. The faun had said they knew each other since infancy, and would do anything for each other. They were almost brothers. If Brynwen were in Sir John's place, she would be demanding answers instead of waiting for all the information. But Sir John must have quite a bit of patience and trust in Sir Padric. Then again, she trusted Talfryn before nearly anyone else.

"As do I. Come along." Sir John turned and bade the others follow. They headed down a hallway with redwood walls and floors. Adorning the walls were framed paintings of landscapes and family portraits with so much detail, they appeared to be merely on the other side of a window than within paint and canvas. Up a sturdy staircase they climbed, every few steps bringing with it a new family portrait. Small children, individual portraits or in groups, as well as adults lavishly adorned in clothing of finest silks of all colors and fashions.

Turning around to comment to Talfryn, Brynwen discovered her brother was not behind her. He was still on the landing, studying the railing at the base with great concentration. He made to caress the strong wood with his hands, but never touched the grain, as though afraid to ruin it.

"Talfryn, come on," she said testily. Honestly, she did appreciate the craftsmanship that went into the building of this home, but her brother could get stuck on building materials all day. But after building the glorious hearth in their home as a birthday present to their mother less than a year before she died, Talfryn fell in love with anything made of stone. He had been an apprentice stone mason for a short time, showing great skill for the craft. However, after a couple of years, the older man sickened from an infection and died. A new stone mason took his place but brought his own apprentice and refused to take on a second one. Talfryn had been devastated to return to the life of a farmer.

Brynwen's eyes popped as she paused at the top of the stairs. The landing opened to an expansive hallway, doors leading off in both directions. Sir John took the left route and they found themselves in a bedroom. Whenever passing the mansion, Brynwen would always imagine that each room was at least two or three times larger than her own little cottage. But she was quite mistaken with this room. It was actually a little smaller than her home. The bed took up most of the space, with a chest of drawers made of cherry oak, with a large, round framed mirror, washbasin and ewer, a matching set of trunks, and a small writing desk by the window with an elegant wooden chair. Another door stood near the bed, closed.

"I have not been in your room for quite some time," Sir Padric remarked, looking around. "I see you never replaced the handle to that drawer." Hand on his ribs, he was hunched forward slightly. The long walk and flight of the stairs had been taxing on him. Again, Brynwen wondered if they should have waited another day or two before making this trip.

Sir John laughed. "You yanked it off."

"It was already loose."

"Whatever the reason, I think it looks more rustic now." He laughed heartily. "Of course, you are welcome to any of my clothing. I shan't require all of them where I am going."

"I thank you. When do you join the fleet?"

"Within the fortnight, I would imagine. My first orders should arrive any day now."

Sir Padric leaned close to Brynwen and whispered, "John has a weakness for the latest fashions. He is the most stylish man in all of Derbyshire."

"That is not an understatement, by any means." The baron's son smiled jovially. "My tailor bills alone could send Father to the poor house. I admit to the joy in making him squirm, just the minutest bit. Father hopes the military will do wonders in easing my collection to more modest tastes." He chuckled. "Come along. If you do not see anything of mine that suits you, Martin's wardrobe should retain some clothing, though he is a little smaller than you. And the tomes you requested," Sir John said, motioning toward a tower of seven thick, leather bound books. "The guards in your unit did not question my explanation when I came to get them from your belongings."

"Which was?"

"Research."

"Ah," Sir Padric said, not keeping back a grin. "They know never to stand between a scholar and their books. Thank you, John. I am confident I shall find what I need."

"I will leave you to it, then. You can find me down int he study should you need anything. I will retrieve you before the household returns."

"Be safe," Sir John said. "And God speed on your journey and Miriel's safety. You do promise to tell me what is going on?"

Sir Padric nodded. "When I can. I promise, I *will* bring her back."

"I trust you," his friend said.

The door closed, and Sir Padric had already settled himself on the edge of the bed.

"We should probably start with finding a tunic of some sort," Brynwen said. "Talfryn, take a look in the wardrobe. I'm going to check on Sir Padric's bandage."

Talfryn turned his nose up and made a deep bow, flinging one arm high into the air with great exaggeration. "Yes, m'lady."

Brynwen gave him a stern look, biting on her lip to stifle her laugh. "Oh, get on!"

Her brother stood up, smirked, and then opened the door to the wardrobe, giving a whistle as he entered. "These are most fancy."

Brynwen raised an eyebrow and turned back to her charge, who had already removed his large shirt. "Where does it hurt most?" she asked.

"Breathing is difficult at the moment. I think the bandage might be too tight."

"Or you have bruised your ribs again with too much exertion. I told you it was too soon to walk all this way." She sighed. "Since you were not moving about too much before this morning, I did not think to lessen the knotting." She proceeded to fix this and was indeed glad to see the poultices and salves being of benefit to his ailments. The bruises were lessening and turning a terrible shade of chartreuse—a sure sign of healing. It would take time for the cracks in his ribs to heal, but he was progressing nicely. And he enjoyed her chamomile tea, which helped him relax, and seemed to brighten his countenance every time he took a sip.

Talfryn emerged from the wardrobe holding a long piece of tartan material. Its greens, browns, and white stripes jumbled together in a ghastly fashion. His face beamed brightly.

"What is that?" Brynwen asked.

"It is tartan material," Talfryn returned.

Brynwen put a hand on her hip. "Yes, I know that. But what is it for?"

"Oh, well, I was thinking, what if we take it and wrap it around Sir Padric's middle…like this…" He bade Sir Padric stand and proceeded to wrap the cloth around the faun's waist.

Sir Padric frowned. "Like a skirt?"

"Yes! It would be perfect and would hide your legs."

"Ummm….no."

Talfryn became indignant. "Why not?"

"Would *you* wear it?"

"Well, I…not in public…"

"*That's* settled, then." Brynwen pointed at the wardrobe. "Go take that horrid thing back and find something *useful*." Sometimes she forgot they were the same age.

Downcast and allowing the tartan material to bunch on the floor, Talfryn shuffled away, dragging the plaid cloth after him. Brynwen almost felt sorry for him, but knew he would bounce back in a few minutes with another dreadful find.

When she looked again at Sir Padric, his head was down, body shaking, and clutching at his side. "Oh!" Brynwen's eyes grew wide. She gasped and reached toward him. The bandages were too tight!

Then he snorted. "'Not in public.'" A wide grin spread over his face, and he shook in mirth. He flinched at the pain, but the smile never faded.

Finding her fears unfounded, the knot in her stomach loosened. "Hold still," she demanded, a giggle forming in her throat, "else you'll burst your bindings." She finished redressing Sir Padric's bandages.

A terrible racket came from the back of the wardrobe, cutting their laughter short. She was about to go in after her brother to see what the commotion was, when he stepped out, his hands behind his back. Talfryn's eyes lit up, he opened his mouth…

"Ah—" Brynwen raised a quick finger. "Is it something useful?"

The wheels churned behind her brother's eyes. Then he hung his head. "Never mind." He sighed heavily, then spun around and trudged back through the door.

Sir Padric and Brynwen exchanged confused glances, a burst of laughter escaping both of their lips at the same instant.

Sir Padric said through tears, "Mayhap he requires assistance."

Brynwen conceded with a nod. Stepping over to a set of large cherry oak trunks, she raised the lid of the closest one and took stock of the contents. Some stockings, undergarments, and an old worn rosary with ornate wooden beads. The next trunk held some tunics in various colors, mainly whites and peaches. A compartment within the trunk contained a large green piece of cloth, folded very carefully and which took up most of the space inside. She removed this and unfurled it.

It was a cloak. An earthy green of a very fine material.

"What do you think of this, Sir Padric?"

Sir Padric studied the cloak. He gathered a handful of the soft cloth and rubbed it for quality. "It is indeed fine—but not too fine. It is light enough. I seem to recall John wearing this in the early spring, when he remarked 'the wind is most chill.' Since summer approaches, I doubt he will be needing this any time soon. Besides, I believe blue is all the rage now in town." He raised a knowing brow, making Brynwen snicker.

Once again, Talfryn rushed to the door of the wardrobe, a look of triumph on his face. "I found it!"

Brynwen shook a finger at him. "Now, brother, are you sure this is actually helpful?"

"Absolutely!" He lifted the item in question and waved it in the air. A long, cream colored tunic swayed in his hand.

"You know," she said, "I think that will actually work." The length was perfect and would almost go down to Sir Padric's knees. Both hands rose to rest on her hips, a smile parting her lips. "See, you *can* be useful!"

"I found this belt to go with it." With his other hand, Talfryn raised up a long brown leather belt. It was at least six inches wide with several tiny holes making a dainty floral pattern.

Sir Padric gaped as Brynwen sighed and buried her head in her hands. "I retract my last remark."

CHAPTER 24

The next morning, the sun finally showed itself through the sky, sweeping the swirling ribbons of clouds away to the west. Brynwen, per her normal morning routine, inspected the herb garden for any brown intruders eating at her precious leaves. She blinked away the sleep that longed to seal her eyes shut.

Eduard and her brothers were working the fields. She had left Sir Padric alone inside, out of sight, grinding and cutting herbs for her ointments and salves. When not doing that, he poured over his tutor's texts, trying to find clues about the sorceress and his predicament.

Her friends would swoon if only they knew that one of the most handsome, eligible young men in Chaddesden slept under her roof. And yet, she could tell no one.

Try as she might, she could not stop thinking about her conversation with Sir Padric from the other night. Digging into her work, her thoughts turned darker. Reason and argument rebounded off each other.

Cursed, he called himself. Would he be cursed forever? What if...what if anyone who got too close to him became cursed as well? What if it was too late and she was already cursed? She shook her head. *The sooner he has gone and dealt with Circe, the better.*

He is taking Talfryn with him...away from me.

Talfryn was a grown man.

But he is still my brother. Why should I stay while he goes off to get himself killed?

A shadow stretched over the chrysanthemums.

"Brynwen, how fare you?"

She gave a start. Peering up, a young man with brown hair smiled down at her.

"Jasper!" she cried. "What are you doing here?" Her heart raced. She hadn't expected to see her cousin today.

Sir Padric! She glanced back at the house. The door was partly open. No sign of the lieutenant. *Please stay inside,* she begged. She wasn't sure if she could explain the presence of the half-man-half-goat if he decided to hobble out the door at that moment. Brynwen prayed that Jasper merely wished to give greetings and move along.

She hastily took the hand Jasper preferred and with quick swipes brushed the leaves and dirt from her skirt and apron as she stood up.

Jasper gave a strained smile. Sweat ran down from his brow. "Pray, may I have a word?" He glanced about nervously, then met her eyes again. "Alone?"

Brynwen tried to hide her apprehension and gave what she hoped seemed a sincere smile. "Certainly."

The two walked to the side of the house and stopped just beyond in the shadows, away from the crops where her family members were working. She wanted to move farther from the cottage, but the young man's feet were rooted to the spot. She wrung her fingers in her skirts.

Jasper stood there, awkwardly gaping down at his feet, brown hair dangling over his eyes, then finally brought his gaze up and took a deep breath.

"Well?" she said, placing nervous hands on her hips. She had too much to do before the midday meal and this was not helping.

"Bryn, we've known each other a long time, yes?" he said with a serious face.

"Yes," she replied. "Since childhood."

"And I wondered if...if you would—" He hesitated, scratching the back of his neck. "If you would consider my proposal of…" He took a deep breath and let the next words out in a rush, "Would you consider—honor—me by marrying me?"

Marriage?

Brynwen's heart raced. She was thrilled, and at the same time terrified. Jasper was the one she'd always thought to marry. Giddiness built up within her as she pictured herself as his wife, making a home together with him. But was she ready? Would she make a good wife?

Taking a deep breath, she opened her mouth to answer—

A crash burst from within the cottage.

They both spun toward the noise. "What was that?" Jasper asked.

In alarm, Brynwen grabbed Jasper's arm, pulling his attention away from the farmhouse. "Oh, a…goat…Talfryn's goats keep barging into the house and upending things. You know goats…"

She thought of the mossy green eyes behind that crash…and she blushed. *No! Marriage to Sir Padric is out of the question.* Why would she even think that? He was completely off limits. Better to tamp that thought down. He'd be gone to save the world soon enough, and would never think about her again, anyway. Jasper led a conventional life and would make a good husband.

"Should we check on it, do you think? It might've broke something."

"Nay! Uh…no. I'm sure it's fine now. It is probably lying down for a little nap." She quickly moved her hand down his arm to grab his hand.

His face flushed at the contact. "What was I saying? Oh yes." He reached for her other hand. "Would you marry me, Brynwen? My stepfather suggested it's time for me to find a wife, and your grandfather has given his approval. It would be hard work—but you are used to that with your farm. We'll live with my family for a while."

Brynwen's elation cut short. Could she marry him right now, when her brother was about to leave home? She knew she would be too preoccupied to think about anything else until he returned home. Then there was her training as a midwife…

She didn't know what to do. Hurting Jasper was the last thing she wanted. And she couldn't tell him why Talfryn was leaving, either.

"I...well, I'm not so sure if now is the best time. I am still in training with the midwife," she explained. "And—"

"Oh, you won't need to train with her anymore. You'll be busy enough being my wife and doing household chores and cooking with my mother."

"But, Jasper, it is my calling. My—"

"There won't be any time for that when we have a family, Bryn. Besides, when we have children, you can use your healer skills with them. You won't need to leave the farm."

Bile rose in her stomach. Not leave the farm? Not be a *midwife*, or a healer? She really wanted to be sick now.

Motherhood was the most important vocation for a woman. Falling in love, marrying, and having children were all things Brynwen wanted very much. But being a healer and midwife were her passions. Could Brynwen give up her current way of life, when it was what gave her meaning and happiness?

Was Jasper really going to make her choose between being a wife and mother or a healer and midwife?

Rosa the midwife's husband had died shortly after their marriage many years ago and she never had children. She never re-married, though her family encouraged her incessantly. He had been the love of her life and no one else could ever replace him. As a midwife, Rosa was like a mother bringing numerous children into this world, and she was content with her role. Other than her patients, Rosa's life was her own; though sometimes when Rosa held a newly delivered baby in her arms, Brynwen could see the ghost of longing for what could have been flash through the older woman's eyes.

Jasper was a good man from a decent family. As children, Jasper and Leowyn had been close with her, Talfryn, and Samuel, and created so much mischief together. For the last couple of years, though, Jasper had looked at her differently. She thought him a potential suitor for someday. It seemed someday came sooner than expected. Her stomach twisted for what that could mean for her future. Many of her friends were married by now, so why did she hesitate?

Jasper's smile faded fast when he saw her troubled expression.

"Oh, if you think me too forward…"

"N-nay, not at all. I'm flattered. Only I…"

His face paled. "What?"

"What about Leowyn? Your brother is still missing. Is now a good time?"

Jasper sighed and released his hand to comb it through his hair, making the strands stand on end. "It isn't, not really. But it makes me realize that time is so short. We need to live *now*. Before…"

Brynwen did not say anything but glanced down at her hands. She nibbled her lower lip, then said, "I cannot make a decision. Not until things calm down." She raised her eyes to his, afraid of hurting him.

But his eyes showed the hurt all the same. "I understand you need time and that I threw this at you unexpectedly. I don't expect a straight answer now. Take all the time you need. I only ask that you consider it." He squeezed her hands and leaned in to kiss her cheek. "I promise, Brynwen, we'll make a grand pair." Then he turned to leave.

Warmth spread across her face, and she absently lifted up her hand to feel the kiss left on her cheek.

A proposal!

And a sentence.

And her grandfather was privy to it. He hadn't taken the time to mention it to her even once.

Her heart pounded in her chest. She was sure the whole county could hear it. She needed to be alone. To *think*.

Brynwen moved toward the house and then spotted a shadow through the open door. Sir Padric. Had he heard? She stopped in her tracks, picked up the half-filled basket of flowers and herbs, then dashed away in the opposite direction. Down the hill, to see Rosa—see if she needed help.

Brynwen only made it about a quarter of the way when she pulled up short. She let out the breath she had been holding since she started running, then clenched her arms and leaned against an oak tree.

She cared for Jasper. She really did. For years, Brynwen knew he was the one she would marry, and she thought she understood him pretty well. Alas, it turned out his understanding of her was not reciprocated.

Did he not realize that to never be able to use her skills in helping the midwife anymore would stifle her? Brynwen knew being a mother was one of the most important jobs a woman could ever have. The joy and determination she could see in the eyes of each woman whom she'd aided in the past year only raised her anticipation for the day when she could call herself a mother. She did not want to miss out on that experience, but Jasper's words were so final, it made her question everything.

Brynwen bristled. Couldn't she do both? Jasper certainly didn't seem to think so.

If I can't not do both, could I choose one over the other? Her heart ached at the thought.

How long could Jasper wait for an answer? And if his parents and her grandfather came to an agreement, it would happen almost immediately, she was sure. Her insides twisted so much, she didn't think they would ever unravel.

A vision of sandy blond curls and green eyes popped into her mind.

"Gah," she said, frustrated. "Not helping." How could she think of Padric de Clifton at a time like this? She barely knew him. He was embroiled in this wild sorcerous business. And he would soon be off to save the world, then back to his own life. Separate in all ways from hers.

She threw down the basket, which hit the ground with a force that showered the petals and herbs all over the ground. Letting out another cry of frustration, she snatched up the disarrayed plants. She ungraciously threw them in the basket, taking no care that the tender petals of the comfrey had crumpled.

Task completed, she stood up, taking one last sweep of her surroundings for any stray plants. Daring any of the other plants to bail out of her basket.

"Men," she said aloud to no one in particular. "Why are they so much trouble?"

Not receiving an answer, she set out once again to Rosa's home. The midwife would likely give her a lecture about taking better care of her plants.

Better than a lecture on men, she conceded.

Wait...Sir Padric de Clifton and Talfryn were leaving soon to find

Circe. Alice would be wherever Circe was. If Brynwen came along, she could hold to her promise of being Alice's midwife and also give herself time to think about what to do with Jasper's proposal. She could keep Talfryn safe from dying of hunger or wounds on the journey. Yes, it was her best option. Now she just had to convince Sir Padric.

But how?

THAT NIGHT, as she lay on her pallet, as far from asleep as could be, she hated herself for what she was doing. But she couldn't see another way. Resigned, she nudged Talfryn. He snorted with a start, then blinked a couple of times.

"It's too early yet, sis."

"I know, but I need you to do something."

Talfryn rubbed his eyes groggily with both hands. "Is it to do with Jasper? Do I need to give him a stern talking to? You've been jumpy all day since his visit."

"Nay...nay, nothing like that. I need to ask you for a favor. Please."

"Uh oh, the last time you asked for a favor in the middle of the night, I ended up doing slop duty for a week."

She grinned slyly. "Come now, brother dearest. I promise it will not get you into much trouble."

TALFRYN WATCHED Sir Padric's face turn scarlet.

"You want to do *what?*" the faun asked.

The farmer reeled backward as Sir Padric launched to his hoofs, dropping the parchment and quill on the ground. The spilled ink spread into a puddle and seeped into the grass and mud. He grabbed his side with inky fingers, wincing at the too-sudden movement. "Nay, you will not," he gasped. "I will not put you in danger."

Brynwen folded her arms together.

"I am perfectly capable of taking care of myself."

Sir Padric huffed. "Brynwen, I cannot allow this. You have your own duties here. What about midwifery and healing? They need you. And is there not *something else* you are expecting soon?"

What? Did I miss something? Talfryn wondered. He mentally ran through all the possible things Brynwen could be expecting. The midday meal? A new goat?

At that, Brynwen's eyes widened. Her face flushed. "I—n—nay," she stammered. "...nay." She stepped up to Sir Padric and jabbed his chest with her index finger. Seething through clenched teeth, she said under her breath, "How *dare* you! You will not mention this to Grandfather. Also, it is none of your business."

"Mayhap not, but I am not about to be the escape route from your responsibilities."

"I'm not running away."

The two glowered at each other for several heartbeats.

Talfryn looked from one to the other and back again, tapping his fingertips together nervously. *All right, something happened between them. Maybe I should—*

"Why?" Sir Padric gritted his teeth. "Tell me why you must go, Brynwen. Give me one very good reason."

"The same reasons as Talfryn. We both have as much at stake as you do. Our cousins and friends were taken by that sorceress. My cousin Alice is with child and will need a midwife when her time comes next month. I promised to be there for her. I *will be there* for her. If Talfryn goes, then so do I."

Talfryn nodded, but no one paid attention.

"Will the midwife not miss you?"

"I will tell Rosa that I need to visit a cousin who is heavy with child. Which is true."

"What about your family? The crops."

"The seeds have already been sown. It's only a matter of watching them grow and praying for rain. We can pray while we journey. As for leaving the farm with less hands, the miller has many sons he can lend us as payment for aiding in his latest child's birth. Besides, you would both starve if Talfryn were to cook the meals." She made a face.

Talfryn shrugged in agreement.

At a loss, Sir Padric gaped at Brynwen. Finally, he shook his head, stopping to study Talfryn. "You have been quiet. What have you to say about this? Being a member of this party, you should speak your mind."

Talfryn shuffled his feet and rubbed the back of his neck. Brynwen was his sister and he wanted to protect her. She would stay if their grandfather demanded it. She would listen to him. But could they protect her if the sorceress came back? If he could keep an eye on her along the journey, he would feel better about it. On the other hand, Brynwen had her own mind and was strong-willed. He dared a glance at his sister. Back straight, eyes bright and staring right into his own, imploring his answer. *You will back me up.*

The night before, whilst Brynwen regaled her grand plan, Talfryn couldn't stop himself from asking, "Are you sure this isn't about Jasper?"

She huffed and said, "My reasons are my own."

"So...it has to do with Sir Padric, then." She couldn't see the grin spreading along his face. "He is quite handsome, and has a title and everything..."

Talfryn could practically feel the steam emitting off the skin of her face. "I tell you for the last time, I want to help save Leowyn and Alice as much as you do. Please do not ask me any more." The last she said with so much determination, he deemed it unwise to argue again.

"Fine, so you don't like or love men with furry goat legs. Noted."

To which he could feel her eyes roll in her head.

Bringing his thoughts back to the present, he regarded his sister thoughtfully. Never had he been away from her for long. His sister, his twin. Could he bear being separated from her for several weeks or months? Would he forget her face, her hair? Her cooking? Oh no, he could not live without her cooking. He and Sir Padric would die a slow, painful death from starvation if Talfryn was in charge of cooking the meals.

Flaring his nostrils, he turned to the waiting Sir Padric. "She comes, too. I don't intend to leave her behind. She can be of great help. And like she said, Alice is counting on her to be there."

The faun sighed. He looked so tired. "There really is no way to sway you away from going?"

"Nay," the twins responded in unison.

The lieutenant clenched his jaw and crossed his arms. He would strike quite the imposing figure of authority were it not for the large baggy tunic trying to cover his furry gray goat legs. "Fine."

Talfryn stared at him in shock. He'd been prepared to defend Brynwen's coming along until he grew hoarse.

"If you are so adamant on coming, suit yourself," Sir Padric said. "You will only sneak away to catch up with us, anyway. But do not slow us down. We are leaving tomorrow, so you had better be ready to go then. Pending your grandfather's approval, of course."

"Of course," Brynwen replied.

That settled, Sir Padric stiffly stooped down to pick up the items he'd dropped. Straightening, he moved toward the cottage, crossing paths with the twins. As he passed, Talfryn saw the knight's shoulders lower a bit before disappearing around the corner.

It was the first and probably last time they would best a knight. Convincing Grandfather would be another obstacle, though. If convincing Sir Padric was a battle, convincing Grandfather would be a war. Something Talfryn didn't look forward to.

Beaming, Brynwen gave Talfryn a big hug. "My thanks, Tal. I couldn't have done it without you. We will save Leowyn and Alice. Together."

The reality of the situation hit him, and he gulped. They were leaving tomorrow to fight an evil sorceress and rescue their cousins and other villagers. Three against one was usually pretty good odds, but he wasn't so sure about betting on this fight. *I really hope we don't regret it.*

"What's wrong?" Brynwen asked.

His stomach chose that moment to growl. "Is that mince pie I smell?" All thoughts of evil sorceresses flitted away.

Brynwen laughed. "It's warming in the pot for you."

"Well then, lead the way, dear sister."

CHAPTER 25

The following morning, Padric was elated as the two riding horses and a pack horse arrived at the farm. Sir John Wilmot sent them along with a sack of grain and two weeks' worth of provisions. A note from John was buried within the sack of food. In his scrawling handwriting, Padric's friend wished him good luck, imparted some fruitless fashion advice, and informed the lieutenant that he was docking the provisions from his pay.

Padric chuckled. "The old louse."

The twins had told Eduard their plan of traveling with Padric almost immediately following his agreement. One could hear their lengthy discussion comprising heightened voices clear across the county, but Eduard finally gave in. He shot daggers at Padric from then on.

Padric looked forward to leaving the farm to search for Circe. He had lost enough time staying cooped up in bed, planning out his next course of action. His ribs still ached, especially when he moved wrong. But what were a couple of sore ribs compared to stopping an evil sorceress and the end of the world?

Despite his eagerness to be on the road, the little family and faun visited St. Mary's for Mass, prayers, and guidance. Padric made sure to wear his long cloak and pulled the hood low over his head. Afterward,

Brynwen took a little time filling a jar of holy water from the baptismal font.

Back at the farm, Eduard choked back his tears as he hugged his youngest grandchildren. He cupped Brynwen's face in his hands and kissed her forehead. "Promise me you will be safe and watch out for your brother." Padric had heard him say the same thing to Talfryn a moment before. "And bring back your cousins safely." The older man reached into his pocket and shakily held forth the contents at eye level: a dainty beaded bracelet handcrafted of smooth, fired yellow and orange rose petals. "I was saving this for your wedding day. But since I fear it will be a long journey, I want you to have it now."

Brynwen's eyes widened. She raised her hands to take the bracelet, but then hesitated. "But Grandfather, isn't this Grandmother's bracelet?"

Eduard nodded. "It is. But she would want you to have it. I hope it will be a reminder that Samuel and I are always thinking of you and love you, and we eagerly await your return."

Brynwen blinked, a single tear rushing down her cheek. She nodded, her face twisting with emotion, reverently taking the proffered jewelry. "Thank you, Grandfather," she said breathlessly. She opened her palm and caressed the perfectly round beads for a moment. Then she straightened her shoulders. "I shan't forget." She smiled and embraced him again, promising a second time that she would return.

Her brother Samuel smiled as she came to hug him. "My little sister, all grown up and going out on her own. It will do little good for me to advise you to be careful, 'cause I know you will. It's Talfryn who I worry about." He winked.

Brynwen chuckled. "I think he will be just fine. He's quite excited about this journey."

Watching them, Padric recalled his farewell to his family a few weeks ago. It pained him to avoid visiting them while he was here, to let them know he was safe. He also did not wish his mother, father, and sister to see him so. Would they be frightened of him, or turn him away? It was too much to bear.

After Edward said a final prayer for their safe journey, the three travelers turned toward the horses. Talfryn looked pensively at his mount, hands gripping the reins for dear life as he tried to figure out how to get into the saddle of the calm horse Dusty. His brow sweated profusely.

"Can you manage?" Padric asked.

"I'm fine," Talfryn squeaked.

Padric turned to Brynwen, holding the reins of Darren, with the same expression as her brother.

"Oh no. You are going to ride pillion," he said, holding out his hand to her.

Brynwen screwed up her face. "Pillion?"

"Aye. There are only two horses, thus you will ride pillion or not at all."

Brynwen looked around and raised her hands. "Who am I going to ride pillion with?"

"As your brother has never ridden a horse and is likely to get you both thrown over its head, you shall ride with me."

"With you? How am I going to ride with *you*?"

"Oh. Ah..." Padric's face flamed. He had forgotten about his new set of legs. Goat legs were not meant to ride horseback. "Disregard, you can ride as you like. I shall walk." He quickly lifted Brynwen up and into the saddle so she would not see the heat spreading across his cheeks like wildfire.

He turned around, only to find everyone else snickering.

Wonderful. His cheeks flamed a deeper crimson.

"I think I could use some help with my horse," Talfryn chided, trying in vain to hide a smirk.

"I think you have stirrups, miladdo," Padric countered, not daring a glance at his friend for fear of a sudden urge to punch something.

"Oh, so *that's* what these are! How helpful," he said, proceeding to put the wrong foot into the stirrup and ending up sitting backwards in the saddle.

PADRIC and the twins travelled westward most of the day along the Derby Road. Talfryn and Brynwen shifted often in their saddles, trying to find comfortable positions, but mainly gaining only extra pain for their efforts. The light cloak Padric wore would have been perfect for the constant windy chills of early spring. As it was now mid-May, however, the fine cloth was a bit warm for the weather, however necessary to hide his goat legs. He soon discovered that hoofs were actually quite adept at walking long distances and did not in fact miss his boots much at all. He could almost get used to this.

Unfortunately, the walk also gave Padric ample time to think. He still worried. The words of Roana the Oracle constantly ran through his head. Amulets, weapons, and devastating destruction were ever present on his thoughts. He felt like the unlucky hero in Perseus's myth. So why not add an oracle to the mix of an ancient goddess abducting innocent mortals and turning them into animals for her own pleasure? His life honestly could not get any stranger.

He also had to admit that despite his initial reluctance at allowing Talfryn and Brynwen to come along with him, he was indeed glad of their presence. Yes, he was afraid for them, and he would never stop worrying until the end. Who knew what Circe had in store for them all when they reached her lair? *If* they made it so far. As an officer, he kept on constant guard, since these two knew nothing of soldiering. Talfryn learned fast, but would it be enough? But the other tidbit an officer learns is how to trust those in his command to do their jobs adequately. Both were willing to do what was needed.

They were all headed for trouble, he knew, and would require training. But how? And when? They were on a tight schedule.

At midday, they stopped for the afternoon meal and to feed and water the horses. A nice clearing surrounded by trees meant that Padric could remove the cloak for a while. It felt refreshing to let the slight breeze rush through his tunic.

"Sir Padric," Brynwen began as she broke off a hunk of cheese, "who exactly is this tutor we are searching for? What is so remarkable about him that we travel nearly half the country in search of him? How can he help us find Circe?"

Padric finished chewing his bite of cheese and swallowed. What could he say that fully encompassed the man who taught him so much? "My tutor, Gregorio Fiori, is a well-rounded educator and has extensive knowledge of the ancients and geography. He may be able to give us a clue as to where Circe might be holding her captives. He also may know of a way to defeat her, mayhap a weapon such as an ancient magical sword or an amulet or some such.

"My father and Baron Wilmot are friends. The baron allowed me to study with his sons John and Martin." Padric explained about how he had first met Gregorio and his engrossing Latin and Greek lessons, including mythology.

"Of course," Padric continued, "old Father Dobbin would arrest of for heresy if he knew, but the baron allowed us to get away with these small concessions. I learned about Circe in a book entitled *The Odyssey*, which relates ones of Circe's better-known stories."

"Would you tell us her story?" Brynwen asked. "If only to educate us —and mayhap help in defeating Circe, of course."

"Story time means nap time," Talfryn interjected. Brynwen eyed him. "What?"

Padric wrinkled his brow. "Gregorio would be a more appropriate storyteller than I. Besides, I have not the books."

"Mayhap," Brynwen said. "But he is not here. And I imagine you don't need the books," she said, leaning on her hand, ready to listen.

"If you wish it," he said, trying and failing to hide a sappy grin. "Circe was a goddess of sorcery, skilled in the magic of transmutation, illusion, and necromancy. The daughter of Helius and the Oceanid Perse. She had a brother, Aeetes; a sister Pasiphae and niece Medea, also witches like herself, though with different specialties. Fair haired and blessed with a beautiful singing voice, Circe lived on the mythical island of Aeaea with her nymph comrades.

"In the story, the mortal adventurer Ulysses and his men landed ashore on Aeaea in a boat, and he sent twenty-two of his men with his first mate Eurylochus to investigate. Lions and mountain wolves guarded the palace, though they were bewitched by potions and were friendly and longed to play and be petted. Except for Eurylochus, who refused to enter the palace, she turned all the crew into wild beasts. Upon hearing from Eurylochus what had happened to the men, Ulysses alone went to see the sorceress. On the way, Mercurius, god of traveling and diplomacy, among other things, gave him a charm which Ulysses could use to deceive Circe.

"When he made it to Circe's home, he donned the charm, drew his sword, and threatened to kill her if she did not restore his comrades to their former selves."

Padric paused, an idea forming in his head. Could Mercurius' charm be the amulet of darkest night from the prophecy, and could it be the way to defeat her?

"Circe then knew this was the will of the gods. She promised not to transform him into an animal and would return the others to their original forms. If Ulysses agreed to stay with her for a year, she would let all the crew go free. He agreed, and soon after, she and Ulysses had two sons, Nausithous and Telegonus. After a year, when Ulysses was ready to leave, she prevailed upon him the dangers he would face and how to overcome them. He had many more adventures."

"That's not too bad of an ending," Talfryn said.

"Oh, the story is not over yet," Padric said. "Several years after Ulysses left Aeaea to return to his wife, the son he bore with Circe, Telegonus, wished to go out to meet his father. Circe gave him a spear laced with a poisoned tip as protection. In his travels, Telegonus eventually fought and killed a foe, unwittingly killing his own father."

"Oh," Talfryn said with a frown. "Never mind."

"Bereft, Circe invited Ulysses's wife Penelope and their mortal son, Telemachus, to live on her island and granted them the gift of immortality along with her and Telegonus."

By the time Padric finished, his face was flushed from the telling—not of exhaustion, but of exhilaration in sharing an epic story to a riveted audience. Brynwen sat on the edge of the log, entranced by the story. Talfryn gave the same wondrous expression.

"If Gregorio taught you all of that," Brynwen mused, "he must indeed be a great orator and teacher."

Padric's skin tingled at the complement, even if it was meant for the tutor.

"What is trans-mu-ta-tion? And necro—ne-cro…?" Talfryn asked, eyes crossing.

Padric stifled a chuckle. "Transmutation and necromancy. Transmutation is the changing of one form into another. In this case, Circe changed the men into pigs." *Or my friends and I into other creatures.*

"Ah. Lovely. Glad we had rabbit and not pork for dinner."

"And necromancy is communicating with the dead. Mainly for predicting the future. A ghastly business, as Gregorio would say." He made the sign of the cross. The twins did as well.

The twins became thoughtful, soaking up this new and wondrous information.

"How many gods are there?" Brynwen asked.

Padric shook his head, trying to recall the gods. "Hundreds, I would say. I am certain some have gotten lost through time, since much of the earlier stories were shared orally before they were written down. Also, Roman and Greek mythology are not the only pagan religions. There is also Indian, Norse, Egyptian, and more, throughout the world. Even England had some pagan religions. Gregorio is the utmost authority on the subject in the country. He could teach anywhere. I always wondered why he chose to stay in Derbyshire all this time."

And why did he leave so abruptly now?

"A fascinating tale," Brynwen said. "'Tis a pity your tutor had to leave Derbyshire."

"I still puzzle over it." Finding Gregorio was essential to the discovery of the amulet of darkest night. Once again, he looked back on his studies with the old tutor, trying to remember all he had learned from his years of tutelage. From the ancient mythological texts, he had read about all sorts of enchanted objects, many of which might have been amulets. And yet, he remembered nothing definitive about items made of any kind of black stone such as obsidian, or *lapis obsidianus*. The cheese in his stomach fluttered about. *What if the prophecy indeed referred to that stone? Of a certainty, it fits the description.*

Talfryn asked, "And you think he's near Nottingham?"

"I hope so," Padric replied. "In his previous travels, he made many trips to Nottingham. Mayhap we can learn something there." Now that he thought about it, Gregorio usually gave vague accounts of his travels, even when begged by his pupils. Nottingham being among his favorite subjects.

"Isn't that a big place?" Talfryn asked.

"It is. But we can start at the Laughing Goose. It is all he ever speaks about when referring to Nottingham."

Shaking her head, Brynwen stood up to clean up the remains of their the midday meal, which was not much. "'Tis strange...no matter how much you speak of it, I still find myself in awe that myths and magic are real. Heroes, gods, goddesses—even the creatures." Here she looked directly at Padric. "That this is all real and is happening to *us*. We are part of this."

"Aye," added Talfryn, "and in this little bit of England. Who would have thought Derbyshire, of all places, could be of interest to an ancient goddess who loves animals? If she loves animals so much, why not take them instead of men and women?"

"That is something I had not considered before," Padric said, scratching his chin. "Yet she must need humans for some specific purpose, otherwise, why take them?"

"Why indeed?" asked the twins together.

"That is one of the mysteries we must solve," reiterated Padric. "One of the many. And Gregorio is the key to unlocking those answers."

We just need to find him.

LATER, as they walked through Nottingham, Padric observed stark differences between this city and Derby. Nottingham was much bigger and dirtier. Buildings sat on top of one other, some as much as three stories tell. The people lived in cramped quarters. The streets and alleys smelled dreadful, and Padric had to hold his breath when they passed a particularly dark alley with sewage running out of it. There were more taverns, and the men from the garrison seemed to arrive earlier than would ever be permitted in Derby or Chaddesden. Padric thought the latter odd, considering the Sheriff of Nottingham and Derbyshire resided in these parts.

Following the directions of a raggedy beet seller, the three made their way toward the east end of Nottingham. They only made one wrong turn thanks to Talfryn, but eventually found the Laughing Goose. The stew they ordered at the bar had over-salty broth and overcooked rabbit, but it beat eating mushrooms for the fifth day in a row.

"The barman gave me an odd look when I asked about an Italian," Talfryn said with a mouth full of stew, gnawing a particularly tough piece of rabbit. Padric noticed that Talfryn's appetite did not seem affected in the least. He inhaled his stew and was sopping up the last bits with a chunk of fresh loaf bread.

A tray of drinks pounded on the table, sloshing grog all over the uneven wood. Some of it splashed into Padric's stew, which honestly might very well have improved the taste.

"Well, and it's about time you arrived."

CHAPTER 26

The twins' spoons stopped in mid-air, aghast at the stranger's display. Brynwen's eyes raised from the sloshing ale to the serving woman's flushed face. Wisps of dark, curly hair protruded from her cream-colored cap, and ale stained her light peach apron. A couple inches shorter than herself, the woman was young, but there was something about her that seemed ageless. Her most striking features were her purple irises. The darkest purple pupils Brynwen had ever seen. When they caught her own eyes, the orbs seemed to bore into her very soul. A shiver ran up Brynwen's spine, and for a moment she felt minuscule. Like a small child.

Padric choked on his stew. After taking a long draught of ale, he said, "Roana."

Who is she? Brynwen wondered. *And how does Padric know her?*

"Nice to see you, too, Sir Padric de Clifton." Roana stood over Padric, one hand on her hip. "I see you heeded at least one of my warnings."

"Which one?" Padric asked with nonchalance. But Brynwen saw his eyes shift.

"The shiny bauble, for starters."

Padric's lip twitched. "Yes, thanks to you, my ear is still mostly intact.

And it was hardly a bauble. Now, if that is all, we would like to finish our meal in peace."

Brynwen's eyebrows furrowed as she tried to follow their discussion. What were they talking about with baubles and ears being intact?

"You shan't find him here," she said.

Padric's eyes rounded. "What—who do you mean?"

"Your tutor. He came on a high wind and left just as quick. He even dropped off a gift for you as he departed."

"He left the tavern, or left Nottingham?"

"Both, I dare say."

"Of course, you knew we would come here," Padric said, and ground his teeth. "But how did he know we were looking for him? And where did he go?"

A grin raised her lip, meeting her purple eyes. "You of all people should be surprised by very little at this juncture. But to answer your unasked question, this is my husband's tavern."

Padric opened his mouth—

"Sir Padric," Brynwen said, interrupting him before he could say something regrettable. It was clear something about Roana rankled Padric beyond mere annoyance. That, and waiting to be let in on their coded conversation, became tiring. "Will you introduce us to your friend? Please?"

Padric's eyes sparked, his lips drawing into a thin line. "Forgive my poor manners. Brynwen and Talfryn Masson of Chaddesden, this is Roana of...The Laughing Goose."

"Pleased to meet you," the twins said.

"Likewise," Roana replied.

"Won't you join us?" Talfryn offered.

"We were just leaving," Padric stated, while at the same time Roana said, "With pleasure," and sat down on the bench next to the faun with a grace Brynwen had not expected.

"Drink up, friends. This round is on the house," Roana said, beaming, while Padric seethed. "Please, Sir Padric, don't be cross. It was inevitable that we would meet again. I must say I am pleased that you heeded my warnings."

"What warnings?" Brynwen asked. Talfryn leaned forward. "And how do you know we are looking for Signore Fiori?" She turned to the faun. "Sir Padric?"

Padric glared daggers, while Roana grinned from ear to ear, purple irises sparkling. Brynwen felt left out of a great joke.

"Please, Sir Padric," Brynwen urged.

The tension in Padric's eyes all but faded when he beheld her imploring gaze. He worked his jaw.

"We should retreat to somewhere more private," he said.

"This is private," Roana replied. "Away from prying eyes and ears."

Brynwen gazed quickly around the busy room—bursting with men and women laughing and drinking, gambling, and so on. No one seemed to be paying the slightest bit of attention to them. "But it's full of prying eyes and ears."

"These people...these *mortals*...are harmless. They are mostly concerned with their next meal and drink. And women. Nay, we are dealing with the gods and magic so ancient as to rival the druids. Gods with exceptional hearing, some more so than others."

"Old magic?" Brynwen and Talfryn said at the same time while crossing themselves. They glanced at each other.

"Sir Padric already told you some about the sorceress you seek, yes?" Roana asked.

"We've heard plenty about that wily woman," Talfryn said, nodding vigorously.

"Not all of it."

"Enough of it," Padric said.

"Yes, Sir de Clifton. Now you should tell your friends the rest."

"There is no more to tell."

"Please stop being boorish," Roana said, rolling her eyes heavenward. "You are merely wasting your own time. And mine. My husband is getting antsy at my lack of service for the evening."

Padric's cheeks flushed. "I thought it mine alone to bear." He scooted the bench back, ready to stand. Sweat beaded on his brow.

Something was very wrong, and it made Brynwen more nervous.

She knew Padric hid something. Whatever it was, if it frightened him, did she really want to know?

Yes.

Brynwen caught his wrist. "Please, Sir Padric, what is it? It can't really be anything that bad, can it?"

His eyes were anguished. Again, he glared at Roana. "You vile woman, you cannot force me to do this. It will only alarm them," he uttered. His fingers fidgeted with his half-empty mug. "Each word—each *letter*—is branded in my mind. Will it happen to them as well?"

"What?" Brynwen asked.

"We were parted too soon before." A wry smile rose up Roana's lips and her eyes gleamed. "Sometimes, young man, you cannot do everything alone. In this, at least, you will bear most of the burden. But you have friends to share in this hardship. Do not forsake them. You shall find friends in unexpected places, yet be wary of others along the way."

"Why must you always be so cryptic? A rare honest answer would be most appreciated."

The woman patted his hand. "Now, now, Lieutenant. Where would be the enjoyment in that? Enough chit-chat. Sir de Clifton, please tell them the prophecy. And no, they will not suffer the same effects as you."

The faun rolled his eyes heavenward.

"Prophecy?" the twins interjected.

"As in dire warnings, bitter omens, and all that?" Talfryn asked.

Roana nodded. "Indeed, and this one is incredibly dire."

Brynwen recalled Padric's story about his curse and the occurrences, but didn't remember anything about a prophecy. Why would he fail to mention that? Is that what he hid from her and Talfryn?

"It is your prophecy," Padric bit back. "You tell them."

"I only prophesy by the grace of Apollo. The words are not mine, but from the Olympic gods and our God."

They all stared at her as if she had lost her mind.

"I cannot remember every detail of every prophecy I speak. I recite it once, and the text transfers to the recipient. So go ahead, Sir Padric." Roana elbowed the faun in his ribs.

"Padric combed his hands through his hair, his expression seeming to say, "No use putting it off any longer." He leaned forward and recited the prophecy in Latin, then translated it into English.

> *As the heir to the charioteer of old*
> *Thou wilt bear a curse of gold.*
> *Reclaim the amulet of darkest night*
> *To destroy the weapon of untold might,*
> *And rescue those of whom you seek*
> *Ere the sun attains its highest peak.*

Stunned, Brynwen leaned back, trying to take it all in.

"That is not all of it," Padric said. His shoulders hunched, looking anything but knightly. "Roana saw the weapon's destruction of the world in a vision." Talfryn was thoughtful. "You have to do all of that before the solstice?"

"Yes. All of it."

The curse she knew about, with Padric's legs and all. But what about this amulet, and the mighty weapon that needed to be destroyed? One more devastating than the plague? The plague killed so many people, now this would wipe out the rest of the world. Her chest tightened. How could he keep that from them?

"This weapon," said Brynwen. "How bad of a weapon, and why are we only hearing of this now?" Her cheeks were scarlet as she glowered at Padric.

Sweat poured down Padric's forehead. He opened his mouth to protest.

Brynwen did not relent. "Did you not think this an important piece of information before we started out?" She was heartbroken to discover he had been hiding this from them. How could he leave something this immense out?

Head down, Padric roughly combed his hands through his hair. "I did not wish to burden you. At first, I was going alone, and I did not care to spread panic. Then you were both included on the journey. And your grandfather would have been utterly distressed—"

"How bad is this weapon?" she asked.

Roana said, "If my vision is correct, it will annihilate all of these islands and much of Europe."

Now Brynwen's cheeks lost their color entirely. She spared a glance at an equally pale Talfryn.

Talfryn said, "When were you going to tell us?"

The faun's eyes lowered to the table, then up to his. "I had every intention of telling you, but I neither knew how, nor the best time. How do you tell someone with calm and dignity the world is likely to end in a few short weeks?"

His statement did make sense, Brynwen thought with a frown. Refusing to look at the knight, she shifted her gaze to Roana. "How do you know for certain that this will happen, or is even meant for Sir Padric?"

The seer bristled. "The visions come to me and pull me toward their intended target—until I find the intended and reveal the prophecy, or vision. If I try to resist, it becomes increasingly more painful and wearisome. Of late, I let it take me as it wills. It is like a leash, and I am the dog that is being pulled one way or another. This latest prophecy came so swiftly, I had no time to warn my poor husband. He chased me down to Derbyshire. I walked much of the way, hopping on a wagon here and there. The tug was very strong, most urgent. The vision—" She cringed at the memory. "The destruction, it was most terrifying. So real." She voiced the last so softly, those at the table could barely make out the words over the crowd.

"How long have you been having these visions?" Talfryn wondered.

"Since....since the end of the plague in England, during the eclipse. I saw that within two weeks there would be no more known plague cases. And it was so. By the end of December 1349, the deaths just....stopped. 'Twas a sign from God."

Brynwen gaped. "Over six years? You must have been so young."

Eight years ago, the plague had killed more than its fair share of people in England, forever changing the lives of so many. It took Brynwen's and Talfryn's parents, but gave Roana a gift.

Another nod from Roana. "I have had premonitions all my life. Small matters. Feelings, mostly. But since the end of the plague and the immediate eclipse, these feelings have intensified, become more vivid and urgent. My husband, Hamon, has been tolerant. But this latest one has left him terrified. He is afraid to leave me alone at all, in case I run off again."

Talfryn scrunched his nose. "And how does one become a...a...whatever you are?"

"An oracle," Padric said. "For that is what you are. If not Delphi, then Sibylline, mayhap?"

"I knew you would figure it out," said Roana with a grin.

The corner of Padric's mouth raised a fraction. To Talfryn, he said, "According to ancient lore, the gift of foresight is passed from one generation to the next. Each descendent of the Sibylline Oracle has the potential gift of foresight. It is said that over time the Sibylline Oracles presented prophecies for Christians and Hebrews alike."

"Indeed," Roana said. "My family converted to Christianity many generations ago. But enough about me. All of England and Olympus, if not half the world, is at stake. If you wish to save England and everyone you love, you must make sense of the prophecy. And soon. Time is running out."

"The solstice—"

She held up a hand. "Visions given from the Oracle are rarely so clear. Some are more vivid than others, some merely bits and pieces. Almost never crystal clear. *I* do not know what exactly it all means, only that you must fulfill each part. That is why you came to see the Italian, even if you did not exactly know the reason."

"And how do you know Signore Fiore?" Brynwen asked. She avoided Padric's stares at all costs.

"Signore Fiori and I have become well acquainted in recent years, since a close friend of his was the recipient of one of my visions. He spouts non-stop about Italian culture and ancient gods. The Sibylline Oracle thinks he is charming. However, my husband dislikes his growing debt."

"That *does* sound like Gregorio," Padric mused, chuckling. "I overheard the tavern owner in Chaddesden disclose that he had not paid his tab before he left the city."

Roana smiled. "He hoped you would follow, and left a present for you, Sir Padric. It is in the next room. Now," she said, "I will bid you all Godspeed, for I must return to serving. Hamon is becoming impatient with me chatting away the hour." She grinned sheepishly in the surly barkeeper's direction. "One final thing—the amulet is the key. I am sure of it. It was in my vision."

"Thank you...for saving my life," Padric said. "Even if it was only to prove a point."

"Of course. I couldn't have you die before you'd yet begun, now could I?" She shrugged and smiled.

He chuckled, the first one since arriving in the pub, rubbing his neck. "I suppose the nudge helped."

CHAPTER 27

Padric opened Gregorio's atlas in the center of the table. "Circe's lair," he said. "I saw her Stymphalian birds fly north after they attacked us." With his finger, he drew a line. "There is no proof that they continued in a straight northward path, but I have a theory, based on a hypothetical discussion with Gregorio years ago. Circe lived on the island Aeaea, near the earth-encircling River Oceanus, at the southwestern tip of Europe. But if she moved to England—"

"Are you saying she could move her island?" asked Talfryn. "But islands don't move."

"The goddess Calliope's island moved all the time. But what if Circe traded one island for another? Made a stronghold using one of the ancient Roman fortresses sometime after Rome removed the Centurions from England in the early centuries? There would be ample space for her to do with it as she wills."

"Sounds great," said Talfryn. "What are these ancient Roman fortresses?"

"Ah, yes, that might be an important detail for you to know. I will start from the beginning. The Roman Empire conquered much of Europe long before Christ's birth. During the late Roman Republic in

AD 43, Rome sent their great Legion, or army, to Britain, to expand their empire. They built fortresses all over the country, and from the very beginning, fought to keep the native Britains under Roman control. It was not a smooth transition in the least. The Legions built temples to their gods in the cities and fortresses, where they worshipped and offered sacrifices on a daily basis. This endured for the next 400 years until Rome crumbled and the legions disbanded or returned home around the fifth century."

Padric's mind reeled with further possibilities. If Circe came to England, who was to say Mars and Minerva, the Roman god and goddess of war, had not deigned to come visit their worshipers in person? This could have been the empire's best kept secret for centuries, until Rome became disfavored by the gods.

Still frowning, Brynwen studied the map with great intent. "That is an interesting theory, but why north?"

She spoke! The tension in Padric's shoulders lessened. The hurt in her face when he revealed the prophecy and weapon affected him deeply, and he knew not why. She was a friend, no more. They had a job to do. Then why did he feel he had failed her? Talfryn seemed to more or less take the news in stride, but even he could not always predict Brynwen's mood. They were twins, but in so many aspects, quite different from one another.

"They like the cold?" Talfryn asked.

"Fewer people," Padric said. "Per my father's instruction, I have studied many maps, and between Yorkshire and Scotland, there are not nearly as many people closer to Scotland as there are to the south, near the shore and ports. And one of her great powers of illusion was used to deter those from entering uninvited. Circe and the amulet may be in this area." He circled the area in question with his finger.

He looked at the other two books from Gregorio: an ancient work by Ovid entitled *The Metamorphōsēs*, and Gregorio's small black journal. He wondered why Gregorio would leave these behind for him—how he knew Padric would need these ancient texts about mythology. Had Roana told him?

Regarding Roana, Padric could not help but notice how her character differed at this inn compared to the day she gave him the prophecy. Then, she was serious, frightened. Here, she was more carefree. Or was she now acting her part as hostess for the sake of the patrons? When she first came to their table, he thought he detected relief behind her wide smile. As though glad he decided to come.

"So, where in all that—" Talfryn pointed at the map "—can we find an amulet made of 'darkest night'?"

Brynwen raised her eyebrows at her brother. "True, the amulet could be anywhere," she said. "North or south. Or even in the ocean, or in Rome, for all we know."

Padric rubbed his nose. "There isn't any time to travel to Rome or search the ocean. It must be relatively close—in England."

They all thought for a moment.

It came to him as fast as lightning striking.

"The answer is in this journal," Padric proclaimed. "I recall Gregorio mentioning the fact when he returned from one of his trips recently...Here:

> *"In all my years of extensive research and foraging, I believe I have finally found the answer to a riddle which has hounded me since my early years: the missing amulet of obsidian. Forged near the beginning of time...the man who wielded it would have the edge over any foe. Rumor has it that the amulet made its way to England in the first century in the possession of the Ninth Roman Legion, which granted them many victories in battles against the Picts and Scots. But it is said to have transferred hands and disappeared. Soon after, the Ninth was lost.*

"Losing the Ninth was Rome's greatest shame," Padric finished.

Brynwen said, "Of course, that could be a different amulet than the one we seek."

"Yes, but do you have any other ideas? There is not time to catch a ship to Rome and return in time for the solstice."

Talfryn waved his arms in a wide arc. "Suppose we train a bird to fly—"

Brynwen threw a hand up. "Please, ignore my brother. Continue, if you would be so kind, Sir Padric." She glared at Talfryn again, and his face fell.

Padric massaged his temples. The ache was growing. "I say we search the deserted Roman temples and fortresses. 'Tis our best option. Mamucium or Linconium are the closest along the old Roman roads. Mayhap we shall even find Gregorio along our way and get some answers."

Brynwen leaned over the map, her long auburn braid falling off her shoulder and brushing Padric's fingers and the fine text. Despite the strong smells of the tavern, honeysuckle and lavender wafted to Padric. His breath hitched.

"Hmm," she said. "But which one? Sir Padric?"

Right! The map. Hurriedly, Padric swept his eyes across the document again. "Mamucium. I know not why, but something in Gregorio's journals draws me there. We should start right away while we have some daylight. There is no time to lose."

Talfryn plopped his chin on his palm. "At least the gods gave us a date to look forward to the end of the world."

"Wonderful," Brynwen said, rather unenthusiastically.

PART II
OBSIDIAN

"A man who has been through bitter experiences and travelled far enjoys even his sufferings after a time."
— Homer, *The Odyssey*

CHAPTER 28

hree days later
May 20, AD 1356

"It's ruins, all right," Talfryn said with distaste. "I think we've found it."

"It appears so," Padric confirmed with a grim grin. "Let us pray we chose the correct place to search for the amulet."

Emerging from the forest, their first view of Mamucium was the sandstone bluffs, hills of white and reddish hues. The road curved down a hill and into the decrepit main entrance of white and red stone, covered in weaving vines and stone debris. A thick stone wall encompassed what remained of the fortress, sitting in eerie silence as a massive graveyard.

Talfryn's heart sunk at the hugeness of the place. Finding the amulet in all that wouldn't be easy.

If it's even here.

They continued forward. The forest had swallowed up a third of the ruins, as though claiming the place as its own. He got the impression that the stones being overtaken by the forest seemed resigned to their fate, while the rest nearby appeared to be be trying to escape its grasp. Not only that, but the forest here *smelled* wrong. Oldness and must and rot. The odor brought back memories of the plague. A shiver ran through Talfryn's spine. *No, I'm definitely not going in there.*

A slight wind flicked at his hair, a whisper on its last tendrils caressing his neck. A cold chill shook his body when it departed from his skin.

Talfryn.

The farmer turned around, but neither Brynwen nor Padric had spoken to him. They were both studying the ruins with furrowed eyebrows.

"That was weird," Talfryn mumbled. Maybe he was only weary after several days of travel and hearing things.

Darren bickered, his ears back and nostrils flaring, eyes darting about every which way.

"It's not just you, miladdo," Talfryn whispered, patting the horse's head with a shaky hand.

He cleared his throat and raised his voice to the others. "Darren here doesn't seem too keen on entering Mamucium. Maybe we should come back another day when it's less….like that." In fact, all the horses displayed their dislike of the city: Dusty shook her main as though trying to remove a hive of bees, and the packhorse skittered, forcing Padric to hold fast to the bridle so he wouldn't bolt. Even Padric's faun hoofs tapped restlessly on the path.

"I feel it too," Brynwen said in a whisper. "As though the life is being choked out of the fortress."

Getting the packhorse under control, Padric's eyes narrowed in on the forgotten city. "Aye, there is something ominous at work here, like a restless spirit. Nevertheless, we must go in for the amulet."

Amulet or not, if it's haunted, I'm not goin anywhere near there.

"But not tonight, I am afraid," the faun said, keeping his eyes on the trees around them. "'Tis too late to venture in now."

When Padric led the packhorse around and headed back the way they came, Talfryn breathed easier. A glance at his sister showed her expression reflecting his own. That was, until Padric spoke again.

"But at first light," Padric continued with a sour grin, "we shall sally forth into the the fortress, apparitions or not."

※

Talfryn's mood lightened the farther whey withdrew from the fortress. When Padric found a place to camp for the night, a good mile away from the creepy place, Talfryn gave no qualms.

Everyone breathed easier.

Refusing to admit how exhausted he was—Padric usually took the first and longest watch—the faun had met his match that night when the feisty healer, an entire head shorter than him, shoved his bedroll into his arms and glared at him until he spread it out on the ground and laid down.

"I will tie you to a tree if I have to," she threatened. He grumbled and obliged, but promised, with a half-grin, retribution of some kind.

She would have done it, too. Of that, Talfryn was certain, chortling to himself at the spectacle.

Hours later, sitting on an old fallen log during first watch, Talfryn stretched his arms, the muscles sore from playing squire and wielding his hatchet with a well-trained knight. Never had he thought training would be so grueling! Farm work was so much easier compared to that. He was regretting agreeing to the knight's demand for training. And yet, he continued, night after night, with some improvement as his reward.

Another yawn escaped his lips, and he stared at the flames to stay awake. The opposite occurred, however, as he soon felt his eyelids droop.

Talfryn.

He snorted himself awake, peering around. Brynwen and Padric still lay asleep under their blankets, but nothing else was amiss. Again, he stared into the fire. In vain, he tried to pull his eyes away, but the dancing flames lulled him to sleep with their warmth and comfort.

Talfryn, said the voice again.

The farmer blinked. His eyes felt bloodshot, but he wished to obey.

"Yes?" he asked groggily. "Who's there?"

It is only I, Lilith. Come, the smooth feminine voice said in a soft whisper. *I have something to show you.*

"What have you to show me, Lilith...m'lady? Where are you?"

Follow my voice.

"But...I'm watching the camp."

It shall not take long, Talfryn.

"Well, I suppose I can go for a minute..."

Rising, he followed the voice, his legs heavy as lead. As he moved away from the fire, the desire to find the owner of the voice, Lilith, became stronger. The time he spent clawing his way through the thick underbrush of the forest only made his heart beat faster. All the while, she spoke to him, encouraged him.

"Am I almost to you?" Talfryn asked, straining through the thick foliage.

Yes. This way.

At last the trees cleared, and he stopped mid-step. Before him, a large lake close to the size of the Wilmots' property extended before him, the moon casting its reflection in the still water. There was no one in sight.

"Where did this lake come from?" he asked. "I don't remember it being here before. M'lady Lilith?"

From the center of the lake, the water rippled. Then, from its epicenter, something dark emerged. At first Talfryn thought it was a fish, but then he saw hair, streaks of red in the moonlight, hanging from a beautiful head, flowing straight down her back. Her loose, wet dress dripped water as she rose and moved forward, the plunging neckline borderline indecent.

The air escaped Talfryn's lips with a gasp as he beheld the beauty emerging from the lakebed. "Am I dreaming?"

The woman smiled at him, her deep red lips puckering into an evocative grin as she approached him. But before she stepped out of the water, she half-sat on a waist-high boulder, her every curve emphasized with the full moon's aid.

It was all Talfryn could do not to gulp. "M'lady Lilith," he said with a deep bow, almost toppling over his own feet in his tired, clumsy state.

"Well, if I'm dreaming, this is by far the best one I've ever had!" he said. "I don't think I ever wish to wake up." His feet moved of their own accord until he stood less than a stride away from her. He drowned in her eyes as she took the last step to meet him. Her scent wafted to his nostrils. Instead of the odor of wet person, as he would assume, she smelled of sweet red roses, and something else he couldn't quite place. The desire to kiss her overwhelmed him.

"Good," said the young woman, roving a caressing finger from his jaw to his collarbone. A tingle ran up and down Talfryn's spine. "It will be just you and me."

Lilith seemed to read his mind and closed the gap.

Their lips locked, and Talfryn's heart burst with an elation he'd never experienced. He deepened the kiss, her scent enveloping him, drawing him in, all other thoughts ceasing. Too soon, she released his lips, and he came up for air.

Don't stop now. It was just getting good.

"Just you and me," Talfryn repeated, a sappy grin on his face. He leaned forward.

"And me," said a familiar voice next to Talfryn.

Padric? What is he doing here? The one time a maid shows the slightest interest in me, and this goat-brained knight has to come and take her away from me! Get your own goat-lady!

"M'lady," the knight said to the woman with a deep, graceful bow. "At last I have found you."

"To be sure," she said with a smile of triumph. She moved around Talfryn with a grace few women he had encountered could master. "Sir Knight." She laid her hand upon his chest, and he smiled back, his eyes intense.

"Nay," said Talfryn with hot cheeks, turning on Padric. "I was here first."

Padric looked down his nose at his competition. "See here, Talfryn. I believe I have the right. I am a knight, after all. You are a lowly farmer."

"At least I'm fully human!" he retorted. "M'lady, how would you feel about goat for dinner?" He reached for the hatchet at his belt—drat, it was still at camp. No matter, he could still give the stupid knight the walloping of his life with his own fists.

"There is no need to fight over me, really," she said with a pout which made her look even more desirous. A pout that needed another kiss. "We can all be friends."

"Oh, I don't think so, my sweeting. You will have only my love in the end." Talfryn cracked his knuckles and gave the knight one of his finest smiles.

CHAPTER 29

The rustling of someone moving through camp woke Brynwen. It did not bother her in the least as as someone was always shifting around at night in her family's cramped cottage. She stretched her weary bones and blinked at the fire. The rustling stopped, but a shadowy movement caught her eye on the other side of the camp, startling her. With a quick glance around, she found neither Talfryn nor Sir Padric in their bedrolls.

Odd, she thought. At least one of them should be on guard.

"Talfryn? Sir Padric?"

No sounds.

She rushed to her feet when she heard sticks and foliage being broken and whacking one another. It came from the same direction as the movement she saw moments ago. Sir Padric would call it folly to follow the mysterious sounds in the dark. But what choice did she have? The others were missing. No, she couldn't wait.

Without another thought, she stuffed her feet into her shoes and swung her satchel over her shoulder.

Taking one last look at the now deserted camp, she took a deep breath and plunged into the darkness.

In moments she wished she had thought to bring the lantern.

Thump! Thwack!

Luckily, all she had to do was follow the sounds, and the moon was thoughtful enough to provide sporadic light through the trees for her. When her eyes adjusted to the dark, the trek became easier, despite the odd branch thwacking her in the face or arm. A couple branches tried to stab her in the gut. But she kept going, kept following the sound.

When at last she caught up to the sound-maker, she couldn't believe her eyes. The strong shoulders and curly hair were Sir Padric's. But where was Talfryn? And why was the knight-faun thrashing at the plant life as though his life depended on it? He growled as though each branch and leaf were his enemy. "Out of my way!" he shouted more than once.

Brynwen braced herself and plowed through the undergrowth harder and faster than ever she thought possible. She caught up to the knight when he encountered an exceptionally rough tree branch blockade. He chopped frantically at the branches with his sword.

"Sir Padric," she said, grabbing his arm. He did not respond, but growled at the tree. "Sir Padric, please," she begged again. "Do you know where Talfryn is?" He didn't answer, so she tried again. "We must look for Talfryn and return to camp." She twisted her body through the brush, catching her dress on a bush, and pulled his arm till he faced her.

However, his eyes would not focus on her, only in the direction he wished to go. From what she could see in the moonlight, they looked glassy, unfocused, as though in a dream. Did he sleepwalk?

"Sir Padric, I wish to help you, but I cannot if you don't tell me what's wrong."

"I must see her," he said at last, his voice choking with longing.

"Who?"

"She calls to me, my Lilith." Then he shoved Brynwen aside and worked again at getting past the thick branches. Before Brynwen could catch her balance, Padric had already found a way around the offensive trees and moved at a fast pace.

Who is Lilith?

She hurried to follow him once again. The terrain became harder now. Stones protruded from the ground amidst the trees, blocking her way, tripping her up. She had to climb over some large, crumbling stones to continue after Sir Padric.

His curly hair and shoulders were once again in sight when she tripped over a sharp stone and landed on the hard ground with a thud. She took a sharp intake of breath as her hand stung from scraping it on the stone. When she caught her breath and looked up, she found she had nearly smashed her head on a fallen log. Pushing herself up to her knees, she peered at it closer. No, it wasn't a log, but a pillar.

Her breath caught when she realized where she was.

Oh no. How did we end up so close to Mamucium?

Now that she had stopped, she could feel it. The very air made her uneasy, clenching knots into her stomach. She hadn't felt it before because of her confusion and trying keeping track of the knight through the dark forest.

Scrambling to her feet, she followed Sir Padric with greater fervor and care than before. Something bad was at Mamucium, and she needed to stop him before he got there. If Talfryn was anywhere nearby, he would be in danger too.

Her unease grew as she continued toward the fallen fortress.

Brynwen thought she lost Sir Padric until she heard a pair of raised voices coming from close by. A third voice joined in. Halting behind a tree to catch her breath, she spotted them through the foliage. Talfryn and Sir Padric stood several yards away in a heated debate. She couldn't see who the third speaker was. Then—there! A beautiful young woman stepped into view. Water dripped from her body and dress, even though there was no water to be seen anywhere. Only trees, stones, and vines.

Brynwen was about to follow them into the moonlight when something in the back of her mind warned her to stay where she was. As she watched, the debate between Talfryn and Sir Padric became a shouting match.

"I was here first," Talfryn said for the third time. "That means she is *mine.*"

"When was the last time you courted a woman?" Padric asked, hands on hips.

"I've courted loads of women," Talfryn shouted back.

"Women, as in hens?"

"Stop it," Brynwen said quietly from where she was.

Instead of trying to stop it, the woman smiled, her dark eyes glinting with amusement, thoroughly enjoying the attention from the young men.

The next thing Brynwen knew, her brother threw a punch at the faun. Padric hit him back. Then they were immersed in a deadly battle of fists, punching, swiping, and rolling on the ground like two rabid dogs.

What had happened? They had all gone to bed as friends, hadn't they? How could one woman cause them to fight with each other? Padric had called her Lilith. Did he know her? A flash of resentment swept through Brynwen's veins at the thought. What did he see in Lilith? She was obviously trying too hard to get his attention with that awful dress. Not that she cared about his tastes in maidens. Not at all.

And Talfryn had never acted so brash in his life. Where was this behavior coming from?

Brynwen tore her eyes away from the spectacle to glance at the woman again. Lilith had her hands on her hips and a wide grin on her lips. She laughed and encouraged one man every time the fighter had the upper hand. Then she switched sides just as quick when the other was winning.

But Brynwen could not pick a side. They were going to kill each other. What could she do?

Wait—what was that? Brynwen saw it for a moment, then it vanished. She thought she glimpsed red flash in Lilith's eyes for an instant.

As the fight intensified, their shouting over each other tore at Brynwen's nerves.

There it was again! Never had she seen red eyes like that. A demon? Could it be Circe, or someone who worked for her? No doubt, Lilith had some sort of control over her lads. The forest too? Each time Lilith's eyes became red, the air grew thick as though after a heavy rain for a moment, then back to normal again. But there was nothing normal about this situation. Either way, the woman needed to be stopped.

Brynwen looked for a weapon, her eyes landing on the stone around her. They were too large to lift to throw or hit Lilith with, so it forced Brynwen to be creative:

She darted out of the trees, straight for the dripping maiden.

"Leave them be!" she cried.

Lilith glared crimson eyes at Brynwen in surprise, growling loudly. "Nay, they are mine!"

She lunged a long, wet hand at Brynwen's neck, her nails growing long and curved as they neared her. Brynwen ducked out of the way of all but the last nail, which snagged on her sleeve and sliced into her arm. She landed on the ground, hard.

When she peered up, Lilith had already turned around and growled again. What Lilith had not counted on was that her two potential lovers should stop fighting. Hands around each other's throat, Sir Padric and Talfryn stared up at Brynwen and Lilith in bewilderment.

"Where's the lake?" Talfryn asked, twisting his neck around.

"Lilith is evil!" Brynwen yelled. She rolled away as Lilith tried to stomp on her with her dainty, sharp-nailed toes.

Lilith roared again. "You fool, you have ruined everything. They love *me*, not you."

This released the farmer and faun from their stupor. They jumped up and sped to Brynwen's aid. Padric pounced on the woman as Talfryn pulled Brynwen away from the raving creature. Enraged, Lilith's skin turned green as the leaves above them. Her sharp nails grew longer on both sets of fingers and toes, yet her face remained as gorgeous as ever. She stomped the faun's feet but found nothing but his hoofs. Livid, she screamed and swiped at Padric, scoring deep scratches on his collarbone and side.

"Padric!"

He grimaced but held on.

"I cannot hold her back for much longer!" Padric shouted. It was all he could do to avoid most of Lilith's swiping hands.

Brynwen tried to think how they could defeat the demon. Her claws were deadly weapons, and Sir Padric's sword was lost in the stones somewhere. Then she remembered the one item in her arsenal that might work…

"If she is a demon," Brynwen whispered to Talfryn, "I might have something for her."

"Bryn, I don't think she wants anything but my love. I mean—" his eyes crossed in uncertainty "—to kill us…I think."

"Lilith, I only wish to talk," Brynwen said louder, stepping around her brother and trying to sound calm, though her heart pounded in her ears.

"The only thing I care to talk about is in what manner you wish die."

"See?" Talfryn said.

Lilith twisted herself free from Padric's grip and rushed at Brynwen again. Talfryn moved to interfere, but the claws nearly took out his eye.

Simultaneously reaching into her satchel and dodging the next blow, Brynwen received another cut to the same arm. It stung worse than the first. She cried out, "Take this," as she unstoppered the cork of the little bottle and flung the contents at the woman.

Lilith laughed as the holy water hit her face and chest. "Did you really think that a little water could harm me? I am invincible. I am…" Her eyes bulged as every place the water touched bloomed into dark red and white bubbles. She shrieked, waking the entire forest with her cry of agony. The rash of bubbles spread all over her skin and smoldered, acrid with the scent of burning flesh.

Brynwen stumbled away with a wave of nausea.

While Lilith wriggled on the ground, Padric darted to his fallen sword in the rubble.

Brynwen tugged on Talfryn's arm as the woman writhed on the forest floor, clawing her way toward the two young men, whimpering. "Come back to me," she wailed.

Brynwen scrunched her nose in distaste. She might have felt sorry for the monster, had it had not tried to kill them just now.

Lilith's eyes locked on Talfryn. "You love me, Talfryn. I am the greatest beauty you will ever know."

"Lilith," Talfryn said. His eyes glossed over gain, and he took a step forward.

Brynwen clamped a hand on his wrist. "It's just her spell, Tal. Snap out of it."

Before Talfryn took another step, Padric returned with his sword. He didn't hesitate to strike down on the writhing monster's neck, slicing her head off.

Talfryn's body jerked at the action. "Why did you do that?"

In moments, Lilith's moldering body crumbled until all that remained of Lilith was a pile of green dust.

Talfryn's expression changed from indignation to misery. He moaned, as if he lost his dearest love.

It troubled Brynwen how Lilith had affected him.

All around them, a soft glow emanated from the bases of the tree trunks. With an eerie groan, the trees shuddered all around them, causing the ground to quake. Their shaking branches shed leaves like a winter snowfall. Brynwen's skin tingled with the energy the trees created. Humming filled her ears. She cringed, ready for another onslaught of attackers. But none came.

Wait, what is that?

The humming became louder. No, not humming—it had a pattern, like chanting. And it came from the ground.

Kneeling down, she placed her palms on the earth and closed her eyes. Three earthy "voices" reached out to her mind:

Thank you.

She has terrorized us for too long.

Far too long.

A warmth filled the pit of Brynwen's stomach. Before today, if someone were to tell her trees could communicate, she would call them dreamers. Her mind reeled at how much she hadn't known about the world before a wounded, cursed knight made his way into her life.

Whatever hold Lilith had over the forest became severed by her death.

She opened her eyes. Talfryn and Padric knelt on the ground with their eyes closed. Talfryn had a rare frown on his face, filled with hurt and confusion.

"Are you all right," she asked them.

"Fine," Talfryn and Padric said.

Brynwen raised her eyebrow but made no comment.

The three made their way back to camp in silence. The night's events still shook Brynwen. They had nearly died by a monster. Her mind replayed Lilith's claws, ripping at her skin.

Talfryn's silence was most worrying, his hands shaking by his sides, eyes darting everywhere. Padric stayed close to the twins and kept his sword ready for another attack, his stoic demeanor only betrayed by the weariness in his eyes.

By the time they reached camp, the fire was nearly out.

At last, Brynwen could take it no longer. "What happened? Who was she?"

It was several moments before anyone spoke. Brynwen thought they would never tell her.

"It was so real, but also like a dream," Talfryn said finally, slumping down upon his log.

Padric crossed his arms, peering intently at his hoofs. "She was so compelling. I...never have I been so spellbound. I simply could not refuse her." He would not look Brynwen in the eye.

In shaky terms, Talfryn and Sir Padric related their experience with the monster. Brynwen shook her head in amazement. She felt lucky Lilith hadn't tried calling her. She might have been in trouble, too.

"She called herself Lilith," Padric explained afterward. "In Roman, Greek, and other cultures, a Lilith, or a lamia, was a succubus who seduced men for pure pleasure, and then killed them." After a pause, he continued. "That was quick thinking with the holy water, Brynwen," he said, at last looking her in the eye, a hesitant smile on his lips.

Brynwen was glad it was too dark to see the blush creeping up her cheeks. "Yes, well, I suppose demons and monsters are not so different after all." She held up a roll of bandages and her miracle mix. "Now come here, let me patch you two crazed lovers up."

CHAPTER 30

The next morning, the little group traveled through the forest to Mamucium with greater caution than their two previous encounters with it.

As Mamucium came into sight, Talfryn tensed. He'd begun to wonder if the aroma of roses, blood, and decay in his nostrils would ever go away. A few times during the night he'd awoken in a cold sweat, gagging on Lilith's coppery odor. He feared it would stick with him the rest of his days.

With hesitation, Talfryn sniffed the air. He blinked. Not believing his nostrils, he sniffed again. It smelled...*clean*. Clear of malice. The heavy scents of woodland animals, tree trunks, and foliage wafted toward him, washing over him with a familiarity he missed. The forest near *home*.

Even the stones surrounded by the forest sat in some semblance of harmony. They no longer fought against each other for ground. Maybe Lilith's demise had destroyed the threat of evil here. *Maybe*.

However, his confidence waned as they drew closer. Mamucium's fallen stones and crushing ivy were just as desolate and quiet as yesterday. A lingering doubt still nagged at him. *Is Lilith's influence on this place truly gone? Or just asleep?*

Once they reached the edge of the fortress, the twins dismounted their horses. It was as desolate as could be, not a soul in sight. When was the last time anyone had ventured here? Talfryn bit down his anxiety. They hadn't encountered anyone since leaving Lilith, but he found himself glancing around at every sound.

After their nearly-fatal encounter with Lilith—which still gave him chills—Talfryn preferred staying together. He still couldn't believe he'd *kissed* her. The very idea left a metallic taste in his mouth. Even so, he found himself remembering the event, goosebumps breaking out across his skin as he relived her touch, her kiss, her...

Snap out of it!

The sudden scampering of a rabbit right in front of him set his heart plummeting down to his feet and almost chucked his hatchet at it. Right—maybe not so desolate. He was pretty sure he'd be on edge until they dealt with Circe. Now he began to understand how Padric felt all the time, looking for Circe around every corner.

If Circe were here, she hid well. But if that were the case, where would she keep his cousins Leowyn and Alice, and the rest of her captives? There was nothing left standing that would be large enough for all the captives she took from Derbyshire.

Brynwen and Padric were just as cautious with their glances and careful steps around the rubble.

"Do you know where to start?" Brynwen wondered as she tied her horse's bridle to a skinny tree branch.

Padric surveyed the rubble for a moment before speaking. "The road is in shambles. I suggest we start at the perimeter and make our way in. Do not get separated for anything," he said, unsheathing his sword.

Talfryn gulped and drew his hatchet from his belt and Brynwen pulled forth her paring knife from her satchel. He eyed his sister's choice of weapon. "Heaven forbid we are attacked by a dangerous band of fresh vegetables."

She shrugged. "It's the sharpest thing I have at hand."

"Here, Brynwen," Padric said, drawing a polished dagger from the second sheath at his waist. "I think your brother would feel more comfortable if you use this for now."

"Thanks," Brynwen said, but Padric had already turned and started hoofing it through the rubble into Mamucium.

Brynwen looked at her brother, eyebrows raised. Talfryn shrugged.

"He's excited about finding the amulet?" she asked.

"You heard the man—er, goat-man," he said, and hurried to follow the faun, Brynwen on his heels.

Thus armed, the group moved eastward on the remains of a stone-laid road, pocked with holes and chunks of gray stone strewn haphazardly about. The forest had its weakest hold in this direction.

No one could drive a cart on this terrible road, let alone traipse along it without destroying one's footwear. The horses would likely throw their shoes off or break their ankles. Talfryn wondered what the road had looked like under the care of Rome's master builders. He'd give his right arm to possess even a thimbleful of that handicraft knowledge. Although he would need his arm to do that—so perhaps he'd give his little finger.

They rounded a corner of the old wall and came upon a partially ruined building. Compared to other structures in the vicinity, it was in better shape. A hole in the outer fortress wall allowed him to enter the small yard of the building, its front door having decayed long ago.

Talfryn was the first to glance inside the shell of the edifice.

A woman clad in white stood at the center.

Talfryn's lungs nearly collapsed as he recognized her.

He lurched back, crashing into Padric, who slammed into Brynwen. Before the faun could say anything, Talfryn shoved his friend back and grabbed his sister's arm. He didn't stop until they were ducking behind a partial wall thirty yards away, out of earshot of the temple.

"What is it?" Padric whispered once they stopped. He dared a glance back the way they came.

"It's Lilith!" Talfryn hissed.

Brynwen's eyes widened. "But she's dead."

"I know, but she's in there." Talfryn thought he would go dizzy with dread. They had nearly died yesterday, and now she was back from the acid-induced grave she came from.

"It might be another succubus," Padric surmised, his jaw clenched. He gripped his sword handle tighter.

"Do you think she saw me?" Talfryn asked, hands shaking.

Padric could only shrug his shoulders. "I will check. Stay here."

Brynwen grabbed his arm and said in a whisper, "We're supposed to stick together, remember?"

"I would rather you stayed here."

"And I would rather you didn't treat me like a child," she said, her jaw set. "Besides, she might lure you a second time."

"She shall not lure me a second time," Padric said. "But just in case, keep your holy water handy."

"If I'd known we would use it on all the Lilith's in England, I would have brought a bigger bottle," she muttered, clutching the dagger and fishing in her satchel for the bottle of holy water. She found it and uncorked it, ready to go.

Talfryn fidgeted with his hatchet as he and Brynwen followed their friend back to the little temple. He tried to remember to breathe.

At the temple, the three placed their backs against the stone, Padric closest to the entrance. He peered around the corner, then turned back to his friends.

"Do not come unless I shout," he said, eyeing first Talfryn, then Brynwen. The two nodded.

Padric nodded, then disappeared through the entrance.

After a few heart wrenching moments, they heard nothing, fearing the worst.

Clenching his eyes and taking deep breaths, Talfryn readied himself to fight to the death.

"I'm going," Talfryn said, gaining courage. *I can't let him down.*

"He said to wait," Brynwen said with shaky voice.

"On the count of three." Talfryn lifted his foot from the ground. "Get your holy water ready. One…"

A shadow emerged on the ground from inside the temple. It wielded a long, jagged weapon.

Don't panic!

"Two…"

The footsteps crunched on the stone, grating at Talfryn's nerves.

Do. Not. Panic.

"Three!"

Talfryn released a yell and swung his hatchet at the would-be assailant as they emerged from the temple entrance.

CHAPTER 31

Only Padric's quick reflexes saved his life.

He parried just in time as he emerged from the temple's entrance. Talfryn's hatchet caught his sword right at the center of the blade and slid downward. The knight flicked the hatchet harmlessly away, filling the air with a metallic ring.

That was a little too close for comfort, he thought. His heart still hammered in his chest. He had only just spotted Talfryn's shadow before the blade came arcing down toward his head.

The twins stared at him with wide mouths.

"That was quite a good attack, Talfryn," Padric said, swiping the curls out of his eyes. He would feign nonchalance to his dying breath. "I think our practices have paid off."

"Stop grinning!" Talfryn shouted. "I could have killed you!"

"Yet, you did not." His grin grew wider.

"What happened?" Brynwen asked, bewildered. She replaced the cork on the little bottle. "We thought it got you."

Breathing hard, Talfryn fumed at the faun, the hatchet gripped firmly in his grasp. "Was this a test?"

A flutter of guilt stabbed at Padric's conscience. He knew he should have told them all was clear, but something stayed his voice. His intent had not been to draw Talfryn into a confrontation, yet it happened anyway. Perhaps it was the residual effects of Lilith's power over the forest and stronghold affecting his judgement. Whatever the cause, he now knew Talfryn could handle himself. Yet another reminder they would need to stay on their guard at all times.

"Not directly," Padric replied, feeling his face flush. He beckoned them inside. "Come, meet the owner of the shrine." He stepped aside for them to enter. Still dumbstruck, the twins entered with hesitation. "It is perfectly safe, I assure you...apart from the sharp stones lying everywhere."

Stepping inside once again, Padric retraced his eye along the walls and ceiling. Surprisingly, the roof still held and he thought they could camp here if the need arose.

The remains of woven baskets sat in a row at the end of the shrine, filled with decayed plant life. In front of this stood a life-size marble statue of a woman upon a dais. Despite the ruinous state of the surrounding building, the white marble was in perfect shape. The statue's details were flawless—face, hair, and body, as though she were an actual person, ready to start a conversation. Her face was the most beautiful creation he had ever seen, her hair braided and curled around her head in a crown with a laurel leaf placed neatly within the creases of each braid. Bare arms with hands clasped crossed her ample chest. Her white dress tied at the waist with an elegant cord, then flowed freely down from her hips.

"Meet your succubus," Padric said, walking up to the beautiful statue. "Fortuna, the Roman goddess of good fortune. She is the patroness of this temple." He pointed to the fading Latin inscription carved at the bottom of the statue's dais.

"She does look quite intimidating, doesn't she, Talfryn?" Brynwen asked, nudging her brother's arm.

"Well, she *could* have been dangerous," Talfryn replied, crossing his arms. He regarded the statue with a look of distaste. "If she's so fortunate, why didn't she do a better job of keeping the place up? No wonder everyone left." He kicked a medium-sized stone with his boot and winced. Hobbling over to the open window, he sat on the crumbling sill and nursed his hurt foot. Brynwen berated him for doing something so foolish.

Ignoring the twins, Padric looked upon the statue's beatific face, wondering about the life of the goddess portrayed by the statue. Did she know Circe? If she were real, would she help them with their quest?

With careful steps, he circled the statue. His eyed caught another engraving along the back of the dais. "Look here, there is an engraving with the Ninth Legion Hispana's name."

LEG * IX * HISP

"So they were here," Brynwen said.

Curiosity getting the better of him, Talfryn hobbled over to the statue, Brynwen holding his arm for support.

Talfryn nodded at the inscription as though he could read it. "Does that mean the amulet's here?"

Padric shrugged. "Not necessarily, but it is a start."

He shoved the statue, but being pure marble, it remained immobile. In a matter of minutes, the three searched every nook and cranny of the shrine for more clues, trap doors, or anything of note. In the end, they felt dejected after discovering little else of import.

A FEW HOURS LATER, Padric's mind began to fill with doubt. Had he chosen the right place? Had he misread Gregorio's meaning? He closed his eyes; the prophecy rising up in its usual fiery letters, reminding him of his impossible task. Of how much was at stake, and that there were people counting on him. Padric did not know what Miriel, Rawlins, and the others were dealing with now, or if they still lived. But he kept the determination to find them. No matter how many stones lay in his path.

Hands and feet getting sore from their labor, Padric and Talfryn brushed away a pile of rubble from a partially-intact edifice. Once revealed, they found part of a carving.

"Why is the eagle pulling the carriage?" Talfryn asked. He flipped his head from side to side to study it. "Why don't they get horses to pull it?"

"What is it?" Brynwen stopped in her tracks, her gaze resting on the carving. "What did you find?"

"A picture portraying an eagle soaring before a chariot," Padric said. "It is another remnant from the Ninth Legion."

"So, is it pulling the chariot?" Talfryn asked again.

"Yes and no. It is symbolic of the Romans expanding their empire to all areas of the world. In fact..." Padric trailed off, his mind whirling. The prophecy launched before his vision, followed by the destruction of the world.

"Padric," Brynwen said. Her hand was on Padric's arm, her eyebrows raised. "You've got that far away look in your eye. The one you get when you remember something."

A warmth filled Padric's chest, and he grinned. Was he that easy to read? These days, Brynwen seemed to know his character more than he did himself.

"You have me there," he said. "But this time, I was thinking about the first line of the prophecy, 'As the heir to the charioteer of old.' He or she might be the crux of finding Circe's lair. After all, finding the amulet will have no bearing unless we decipher who the charioteer is."

Talfryn crinkled his nose in concentration. "Hmm, I don't know much about the ancient gods, but do many of them have chariots?"

"The phrase refers to a single charioteer of old. It does not specify which god..." Padric said.

Brynwen asked, "Does it have to be a god?"

Padric's eyes brightened. He had not thought of that. "Nay...mayhap it is a mortal." From his bag, he dug out two books from Gregorio: *The Metamorphōsēs*, and Gregorio's small black journal. Again, he wondered at Gregorio's leaving them for him at the inn.

With careful movements, Padric paged through Gregorio's journal, his fingers coming away with a black chalky substance. "Gregorio lists one god in particular as riding a chariot: the Titan Helius."

Padric looked up as a memory surfaced. "This is something Gregorio, John, and I discussed shortly before my tutoring ended, when I became a knight." He carefully set down the journal and flipped through *The Metamorphosēs* until he found the page he needed. "Hold a moment...Phaethon—he was Helius's mortal son." The twins looked at him with blank expressions. "Phaethon drove Helius's sun chariot and hauled the sun around the world for a day. In fact," he skimmed some more, "it was less than a day. The boy could not control the flying horses pulling the chariot, and the sun nearly destroyed the world. This forced the hand of Jupiter, the king of the gods, also known as the god of the sky and thunder, to put a stop to Phaethon in order to prevent the world from burning to ash. Phaethon died as a teenager, and therefore, had no descendants."

"Mayhap he did not," Brynwen said. "But what about Helius?"

Talfryn slapped his leg. "His daughter is Circe! You mentioned that before."

"Precisely," Padric said. "It would only make sense that Circe has dragged Helius into this mess. Or vice versa."

Brynwen said, "But what is her end game? Or Helius's?"

The faun shook his head. "Something massive, with all of the people they have taken. But other than that..." He shrugged.

Brynwen nodded. "'As heir to the charioteer of old.' I wonder...if this Helius is the charioteer, why are you are his heir? Are you related to him somehow?"

Padric's blood froze.

"If that is so, then am also related to Circe."

Everyone sat still, stunned.

"What? How does—how does that even work?" Talfryn asked.

"But this is mere guesswork, isn't it?" Brynwen asked. "Padric? What's wrong?"

Padric's head swam. It could not be possible. Or could it? Circe's first spell had a minimal hold on him. He had broken his invisible bonds within minutes, while the others remained frozen until she released them. He still had no idea how he knew the way to break those bonds. Then the spasms of power running through his arm when touching Circe's staff. Byron touched it next and seemed to experience nothing.

Was there something inside Padric that made him unique? Something between him and Circe?

Could she be my mother? No, he and his mother Tabitha had the same eye and curly hair. Circe and Helius must be deeper down the line somewhere.

To be honest, these were questions he had shoved deep, deep down; because thinking about them made the impossible real. Substantial. It made his skin crawl.

"I..." All eyes were on him. He cleared his throat and wished he could take a long swig of ale. "Considering everything, it might not be too far-fetched an idea after all." He explained his reasonings with them. Padric took in their expressions of wonder as they connected the pieces together. If he was Helius's heir, he might have some powers. Assuming he had powers, how much was his own, and how much did Circe bestow on him?

"Do you think she knows?" Brynwen asked.

"She never mentioned it to me," Padric said. But he wondered, with the special attention she gave him at their two encounters. Not because he was in charge, but because she knew he was her descendent.

"What about your legs?" Talfryn asked.

Padric wondered about that as well. He could not understand how he broke Circe's first curse, but not his legs. With the invisible bonds, he had unlocked them by forming a key in his mind. His legs were another issue altogether. One could not use a key, at least not in the same way.

He was left with more questions and only one person who could answer them.

Padric rubbed his eyes, fatigue washing over him. "This will take more thought." Sighing, he moved on to the next pile of rubble, wondering if more clues would crop up relating his heritage to an evil sorceress.

THE NEXT DAY they covered more ground, finding additional signs of the Ninth Legion: stone markers, pillars, gold and silver coins. Statues of other Roman gods and legionaries.

Never had Brynwen's feet and back hurt so much as the task of searching through rubble and pushing over stone. She wondered if it was akin to a mother carrying a child to term.

Padric moved around the fortress tirelessly, his focus never wandering from his mission. Almost like he was obsessed. In the weeks she had known him, she had never seen him this way. He was always determined, pushing them onward, but never like this. Brynwen prayed they found the amulet of obsidian soon, before it became his downfall. She had seen the obsession happen to others, and it never ended well. Besides, the sooner they found it, the sooner they could rescue Alice and Leowyn.

"I found something," Talfryn announced late that afternoon. "A camp. And recently occupied, too."

"How many people were in it?" Padric asked as he followed Talfryn back to the campsite.

Brynwen had returned the dagger to Padric and had resumed carrying her small paring knife. They picked their way over the usual stones, but then they entered what appeared to be a graveyard. Who would camp in a graveyard?

"It looked like just one," Talfryn replied, "but I didn't take a long look around. It's a bit of a mess."

A 'bit of a mess' was an understatement. Brynwen scanned the area surrounding the campsite, finding the place completely picked through: blankets, clothes, and gear were strewn all over the place.

"It looks like some animals tried to make a nest out of his belongings," Talfryn said, poking his finger through a hole in a light gray blanket.

"There is only one set of gear here," Padric said, leaning down and examining every aspect of the camp. "But I see...three other sets of boot marks. Here is where the occupant—I assume it was him—was forced onto the ground." He pointed to an impression in the earth. "And then all four departed this way, to the northeast." The faun followed the boot marks but they ended abruptly at a pile of rubble about four yards away. The knight looked around the area for more tracks, but none could be found. He returned empty-handed and agitated.

"There is no blood, so he must not have been hurt, or at least not much. Whoever camped here had not been present very long," Padric said.

Talfryn poked at the pile of sticks near the center of the camp. He said, "Nor did he make a proper fire. The makings are here, but none of the sticks are burnt."

"Did you see that?" Padric asked, peering at the ground. Leaping over the unlit fire, the faun landed on his hoofs in front of a white stone about the size of his forearm.

Brynwen spied what caught his eye—something shiny was partially buried beneath the stone. In no time Padric dug it out with his hands.

Brynwen and Talfryn moved closer to peer at the item in his hand. It was the broken half of a silver pendant. She recognized it as something Padric had pulled out of his belongings on a number of occasions.

"'Tis the other half of Gregorio's pendant," Padric said, tracing his thumb along the dusty edges. Quickly, he dug out the original broken pendant from the pouch at his side and fitted the two broken edges together. They fit perfectly, forming a Latin inscription in the center. Padric inhaled sharply and looked at the twins, his face ashen. "This is Gregorio's camp."

Brynwen's eyes grew large. "Gregorio?"

"Yes, and someone took him."

"But why?" Brynwen asked.

"He's just a tutor, isn't he?" Talfryn asked.

"Yes, just a tutor," Padric said. "But also my friend. I failed him." He ran a hand roughly through his hair. "He was right here, and I could have saved him from these villains had I but known and reached him in time. I felt something was off from the way he hurried from Chaddesden and Nottingham. And now I am too late again. They must be long gone from here by now."

"But how could you know?" Brynwen asked softly, touching his arm.

"He never directly said he was coming this way. Didn't you say he was going to see his family?"

Padric nodded.

"Then maybe he took a roundabout route?" she asked.

"If he knew you would go looking for him in Nottingham," Talfryn said, "maybe he'd have figured you'd followed him here, too?"

Padric thought another moment, then replied, "Perhaps. He did leave me the notebook with his account about the amulet of obsidian. He must have been trying to find it when he was captured, although I have no idea why. Why would he be looking for it, and why would these people take him?"

"Should we try to rescue him?"

The faun's green eyes cast downward. "No matter how much I wish to save him, the amulet is our greater priority. Besides, they left hours ago and could have fled in any direction. We might never find any trace of their whereabouts."

Brynwen sympathized with Padric, but didn't know how to help him with the loss of his tutor. She tried to imagine what had happened here. From what little she had seen of Gregorio Fiori in Chaddesden, he was elderly and thin, so she could not envision him being much of a match against three men.

Wishing to help in any way she could, Brynwen focused on finding more clues, though she had no idea what to look for. She took a step on a loose stone and pitched sideways toward the jagged remnants of a broken column.

Padric was there in a moment, gripping her arms before she landed on the uneven ground. Her heart tripped over itself as he held her, and her feet almost gave out from under her. Once her feet were firmly planted on the ground, however, the knight kept hold of her. Glancing up, she found him looking at her, his eyes almost soft. Worry? Her cheeks heated from the gaze.

Her heart was still pummeling from the near fall. It had absolutely nothing to do with the knight, she told herself.

"I...I am quite all right now, thank you," she said, glancing away.

"Oh, of course," he said, releasing her with apparent reluctance. He took a step back "I—"

"What is that?" Brynwen asked, spying something on the ground.

She knelt down beside the rock where the half pendant had been buried. It was near the bottom, and hadn't been in view before Padric dug out the dirt beneath it. "There are letters scratched into this rock: M, T, and V." She and her brothers had learned their letters from their mother, even though most people in their station never learned theirs. It was generally something she kept to herself, but she was in the company of friends.

"M, T, V," Padric repeated, kneeling down beside her. He traced the letters on the stone with his fingers. "It must be a hint as to where the amulet is." His frown deepened. "Gregorio would risk leaving me a clue instead of hurrying to the safety of his family? Why was it so important for him to find? I am beginning to wonder who my old tutor and his family is. He never spoke much of his past, nor about his family with anything more than a vague utterance."

Straightening his back, Padric's stature transformed to the knight he was. "Well, then, if we cannot find Gregorio, he would at least wish us to find the amulet for him."

"Well said, Sir Padric. Let's go find the amulet," she suggested, squeezing Padric's hand. He nodded, his green eyes boring into hers for a moment.

Talfryn patted them both on the back. "In the meantime, I'll fetch some snacks from our packs."

CHAPTER 32

"This must be it," Padric said, nearly an hour later. They had to construct a torch to continue searching for the amulet of obsidian in the dark. After another hour of finding nothing, Padric almost gave up. Until he saw it.

"You said that at the last three similar stone markers," Talfryn said, rolling his eyes.

"But this time, I am certain of it," Padric said. He could feel something here. A sensation of energy coursing through the air surrounding the tomb drew him to it. Gregorio's clue of M, T, V was not just letters. They were initials.

They had stopped in front of a white stone mausoleum in the middle of the graveyard. The mausoleum stood in nearly perfect condition. Neither vandals nor time had desecrated it. Not even vines climbed the sides. They grew everywhere but here.

An epitaph with elegant engraving stood out on the stone door:

MARIUS TIBERIUS
VEXIL RAETOR ET NORICOR
ET LIBENTER VOLENS MÉRITO DOMINO MEO OMNIA QUÆ
VOVERIS

Padric translated, "'Marius Tiberius. First Cohort of Frisiavones. Of the Detachment of Raetians and Noricans, gladly and willingly deservedly fulfills his vow.' This is the tomb, but how do we enter? I do not see a keyhole."

Padric moved back to inspect the whole door and structure. A gate of vertical iron bars trapped the stone door behind it. At the top of the iron door, a row of eyelets was held in place by a double-edged spear. A fine craftsman had made this many centuries before, ensuring the monument withstood the tests of time.

Talfryn moved forward to inspect the gate and ran his hands along the sides, peering intently at every niche. "There doesn't appear to be any latch or knob. No release." Again, he felt along each edge.

Padric stepped forward and felt the bars. They were cold to the touch yet seemed to hum. *Alive*. Familiar. Too familiar. Cold blue eyes shot into his thoughts. With a sharp intake of breath, Padric quickly removed his hand in disgust and retreated several steps.

"Magic," he said. "Magic holds these bars closed."

At last, Talfryn let go of the bars and gave his assessment. "The double-edged spear at the top is holding the gate and door closed, but one cannot just slide it out. If we can pry it loose, the gate should open easy enough. I think."

Brynwen stepped over to her brother's side. "But how do we get that out? It's a solid piece of iron."

"Held fast by magic," Padric reminded them.

Slowly, Brynwen bent down and peered at the smooth stone near the ground. Finding nothing, she rose to her toes and looked up toward the double-headed spear. "Wait, I think there is an inscription." She pointed at the spot just below the spear. "Padric, can you make it out?"

Padric squinted at where she pointed. Indeed, another phrase had been chiseled into the stone. "I need to get higher to read it." A quick glance around gave him what he needed—a running start.

Handing off the torch to Talfryn, Padric walked away from the tomb several paces. "Clear the way." The others stared at him but moved away from the tomb. He squatted, then shot up and sprinted toward the door, launched off a large broken column, and soared into the air. Those below let out a gasp. Padric caught hold of the spear and grounded his hoofs into the hard stone between the iron gate posts with a loud crunch, jarring his mostly-healed ribs. Bits of stone crumbled to the ground.

"Hold the torch higher." He leaned in to read the second epitaph, also in Latin. This text was smaller than the text below it, though clear and made by a steady hand. Time and wind had not eroded the letters.

> *Omnes vires potest non flectere Herculis hoc vectes et possum puer.*

"'All the strength of Hercules cannot bend this bar, but a child can.'" He studied the area around the bar and epitaph. "Underneath it is a hole carved into the stone with designs around it. But they mean nothing to me. They are neither Latin nor Greek."

"What does either of that mean?" asked Talfryn.

Padric took one last look at the sentence and then dropped to the ground, landing lightly on his hoofs.

"It is a riddle. And mayhap a keyhole of some sort." Already his mind began working on solving the riddle. Never had he seen one on a grave marker. These ancient Romans seemed to enjoy keeping things interesting for the later generations."

"Then we must find the key," Brynwen said, and walked around the mausoleum, inspecting every bit of stone. Talfryn followed suit. Padric sighed and leapt down, starting on the other side. Might as well cover all the bases.

"What child could possibly be stronger than Hercules?" asked Padric. He thought a moment. "It could be figurative."

The three creased their brows in thought. Then Padric snapped his fingers together. "Hercules was very strong. A child is not as physically strong—as a rule. But they can be strong on the inside. Here." He indicated his heart. "They are resilient. With an inner strength. An innerlight."

Brynwen's eyes shone. "A child's light. A candle?"

"Or moonlight," said Padric.

The others followed Padric's gaze toward the moon. Already the clouds were trying to converge on it. The wind had shifted, he noted. "We mustn't tarry."

Talfryn scratched his head. "But how does the moon shine into the hole? It's behind the tomb."

Confound it, he had been so intent on solving the riddle, he had not thought of this problem. Absently, his hands ran through his hair, fingers grazing against the horns.

"The moon is shining on this side of the tomb," Brynwen mentioned. "But not directly into the hole. There is a shadow from the bars."

Padric let out an impatient huff. The moonlight would fade soon, and they would lose their chance until tomorrow.

"Mayhap if we had something to reflect it." Talfryn patted his pockets. Checked the ground. "A piece of glass, or even some water."

Together, they all studied the ground. Talfryn was about to fetch water from the stream on the other side of the fortress.

"Ah," Brynwen cried. "My grandmother's bracelet...it might reflect off the moon." In her hand rested the bracelet of glass and clay beads.

"That might do, after all," said Padric.

Brynwen tied the bracelet around Padric's wrist. Then he backed up and leapt onto the wall again, catching the bar easily. His hoofs slid on the old slick stone. Raising the beads into the air, the bracelet caught the moon's rays, then he pointed the reflection down at an angle into the hole.

A faint click came from inside the wall. Then iron grated against stone. The next thing Padric knew, he was lying sprawled on the ground, the wind knocked out of him. The ancient spear landed on top of his chest with a painful thwack.

Not my finest hour, he thought after his vision cleared from seeing stars.

Talfryn helped him up, the pain forgotten as he listened in fascination as a great mechanism behind the door made clicking noises. Then the stone door itself opened inward.

CHAPTER 33

The stench of must and decay wafted from the room within. Talfryn's arm covered his nose and he tried not to gag, very nearly losing his last meal. After waiting a few minutes to recover from the initial stench, Padric resolved to enter first with the torch.

"I hope the door doesn't decide to close on us..." Directly behind the faun, Talfryn lay a hand on the thick door. "I really don't want to get stuck in here for all of eternity."

"Well, go on," Brynwen encouraged, following last. "Fear not, silly, I will be right behind you."

"Thanks terribly, sis," he said wryly. Talfryn's eyes swept over the dimly lit interior. Large spider webs resided in every corner and crevice. At least an inch of dust powdered the floor and the stone sarcophagus. Only Padric's fresh hoof prints disturbed the piles of dust.

Talfryn tried to suppress a sneeze, but it came anyway. "Ach," he cried, as hundreds of years of dust assailed him, causing a second loud sneeze.

Brynwen followed after the sneezing Talfryn, then they stopped and studied Marius's stone coffin with Padric. The faun lit the old torch sitting in a sconce on the wall, further illuminating the room's carvings and frescoes. The adornments on the coffin were very intricate. Talfryn wasn't an artist by any means, but it was evident someone had taken great care making these designs for Marius.

"The great warriors and those from wealthy families were able to construct these grand tombs," Padric explained. "The details on his tomb show he had both wealth and skill. These inscriptions are full of praise." He looked up at Talfryn and Brynwen. "I almost hate to disturb him."

"But we must, I suppose," Talfryn admitted with a dry mouth. He took a deep breath. "Let's get this over with, shall we?"

Padric nodded. Bracing his hands on one side of the stone slab covering the top of the sarcophagus, Talfryn did the same on the other end. "On three." They pushed. At first the stone failed to budge, but then as if changing its mind, it gave way and slid against the top with a jarring screech that could wake the dead.

Talfryn was glad they had eaten long ago.

All that remained of Marius was his off-white skeleton and bits of his uniform that hadn't been eaten away with time. His sword was gripped in his hands, ready for when the next battle commenced in the afterlife. His hands lay in a natural position upon his chest. Talfryn half expected the skeleton's chest to rise and fall in a sleep rhythm. A chill ran down his spine just thinking about it.

"Well, that is a very fine skeleton." Talfryn tried not to sound nervous and failed. It reminded him of things he would rather not think about. Like death. The plague. His parents. "But there's no amulet. And I am *not* going through his clothing."

With a grimace, Padric examined the sarcophagus, searching for some clue. Talfryn and Brynwen scanned the room.

"There might be a hidden door somewhere in here," Padric said. "Like a priest hole."

Talfryn knew what Padric meant, but he pictured a small hole for a priest to crawl through to keep his stockpile of honey safe from his congregation. Stifling a chortle, he crouched to search down low along the walls for a hidden door.

Brynwen stopped in front of a part of the stone wall with a Roman arch partially raised out of the wall. "What is this?"

Finding nothing, Talfryn came over to investigate. Carved into the stone were three little stone blocks in relief, each with a different picture etched above a block: A man in fighting gear with a spear, a laurel, and a lamb. It's mirror image stood directly across from this arch.

The twins puzzled over the three carvings, trying to decipher any hidden meaning lying within. Brynwen tapped on each one. She sighed in disappointment when they all sounded thoroughly solid.

Talfryn moved to the other arch. This time there was a clay jar, a laurel, and a small warped-looking child. "Wait, could this mean anything? There is a laurel on both sides."

Padric looked up from the coffin. "Let me see." He moved the two steps toward Talfryn, then Brynwen joined. "Ah, the *Laurus nobilis*, or the bay laurel. It was a symbol of victory and honor. Many Roman and Greek warriors and athletes were awarded these for their great deeds. Art of the time portrayed Roman emperors adorning laurel wreaths about their heads like a crown."

Talfryn stared at the faun for a moment. "So, you are saying that these warriors or athletes were awarded a fern to wear on top of their heads? Seems kind of cheap, it being a great honor and all. It would die soon enough. Nowadays, most people bet money." Not that Talfryn had much money to bet on anything.

Padric grinned and folded his arms in front of him. "Do not get me wrong, money could be a great and frequent motivator. Betting on oneself was common, even back then."

"Well, even so..." Brynwen squinted at the stone laurel. "It *is* the exact same picture. But what does it mean?" She touched the stone laurel and it shifted. Her eyes lit up. "Of course." Then she scooted around the stone coffin again to the first arch and blocks. She pushed against the laurel block. "Try pressing that one," she instructed.

Padric got the idea and pushed against the laurel on his side. It shifted, grating against the stone wall. "I think something is happening."

Brynwen struggled with her stone. "Tal, come help me."

Talfryn helped her push the laurel until it was flush with the wall.

Nothing happened.

Talfryn ticked away the seconds. "Well, that was—"

The ground trembled beneath their feet. Stone dust rained down from the ceiling, stinging his eyes. A loud mechanism made a *click, click, click* sound.

Talfryn balked as the ground beneath their feet began to sink. He grabbed Brynwen's hand and jumped out of the way. Landing awkwardly, he caught her before bashing his hip against the stone coffin. He rubbed his aching hip, then followed the collective gazes of his two companions to the floor.

A square of four tiles shifted down together, the stones grating against each other. Once the tiles cleared the hole, they slid inward underneath the floor until they were out of site. A final *click* sounded, and the shaking ceased.

Talfryn leaned over the newly made hole. The torch light revealed a staircase leading downward into darkness.

"Ooh, a secret staircase," he said. "How exciting!" *I might have to add one of these to our cottage when we get home.*

"Care to go first?" Padric asked with a smirk.

Talfryn glanced down at the stairs again. The gloominess of the darkness at the bottom, he realized, gave him the shakes.

"Umm, on second thought, after you. You've got the torch, after all." He gave a nervous laugh.

"Watch our backs, then," Padric replied.

Great!

He disliked taking the rear. What if someone attacked from behind? Or locked them in? He raised his hatchet high, just in case.

The narrow stone staircase descended into a dark, stuffy little room. A cloud of dust rose up with each footfall, tickling Talfryn's nose. He sneezed three times in a row. *Well, it anything is down here, it knows we're coming,* he thought, wiping his nose with his forearm.

Then the torch lit up an underground room. It was filled to the brim with stone and wooden casks and boxes. Several gilt boxes and statues stood in various positions. Many of the boxes had decayed, spilling piles of gold and Roman coins all over the other boxes and the ground. A rack overflowing with rusting, dangerous-looking weapons stood at one end near the door. Scattered throughout the room lay other personal artifacts, all covered in dust. A hip-high statue of Fortuna stood on one end of the doorway, and another god of equal size, which Padric labeled as Jupiter, stood in an imposing stance at the opposite side, overlooking the treasure.

"What is this place?" Brynwen asked.

Brandishing the torch, Padric scanned the room. "It is a crypt. The items Marius and his family believed to be important in the afterlife were kept here. It appears they thought he would need quite a bit."

"I guess he didn't really need them all after all," Talfryn said with a smirk. He reached a hand out toward the rusting weapons. The leather wrapped around the sword handles had rotted away long ago.

"Don't touch that," Brynwen warned.

"She is right, Tal," Padric said, his back to Talfryn's. "Be careful what you touch. Some of these old rooms have traps."

"I was thinking more like hungry rats, but that works, too," Brynwen said.

Padric chuckled. "Just be wary of what you touch."

"Noted," Talfryn replied. "What are we looking for again?"

"An amulet of obsidian. Or 'darkest night,' if you will."

"Ah, right. Thanks. Simple task, that. An *amulet*." As though he knew *exactly* what that was. A rock? An old jar of ashes? Maybe something like Gregorio's pendant?

While searching through the heaps of ancient furniture and boxes, his stomach growled, remembering it had skipped dinner.

A chirp sounded.

Talfryn swiveled his eyes around. "What was that?"

"What?" Brynwen asked. Another trill sounded, and its echo.

"It is over here," Padric said, climbing over a pile of silver goblets, the metal chinking under his hoofs. The twins followed, helping each other mount the piles of treasure.

Then Talfryn saw it. A bird cage. About a foot tall, the silver cage hung from the center of the ceiling. How had they missed that?

An excited warble emanated from the cage, followed by a flutter of movement. A white ball of fluff.

"A bird?" Brynwen wondered, moving closer to peer inside. "What is it doing here, in an old crypt?"

"I would like to know *how* it came to be down here, and how it is still alive." Padric wondered.

"It could be a guard-canary," Talfryn said. "An alarm for when an intruder enters the crypt."

The bird twitted with contentment.

"A truly horrifying sound," Padric said, deadpan.

"I am quaking in my boots," Brynwen replied.

How *did* it get down here and then get trapped in the cage? A pang of compassion came over Talfryn. "We have to help it." He peered around for a way to reach the cage.

"Talfryn, now is not the time," Padric said.

Talfryn glared at him. "What's an extra couple of minutes? The poor bird might be starving."

"You can save it after we find the amulet."

"But it needs help now." He knew he should let the issue go, but his heart ached to see the bird in the cage.

"She does not appear in dire straits at the moment."

"You don't know that for sure." Talfryn's chest swelled with pride. He could go on all night if need be—he just wanted to help the little bird.

Brynwen touched his arm, her eyebrows furrowed. "Tal, please listen to Padric."

The kick of betrayal struck Talfryn in the chest. She was taking his side?

The faun's eyes became slits. "Talfryn. I feel for the bird, I do. But she is in no immediate danger. Help us find the amulet a little longer, then we will get her down. My word of honor."

Talfryn simmered, but he supposed Padric had a point. He just hated seeing animals suffer. "All right. But I'm helping her at the first sign she's in trouble."

"I do not doubt that."

Half-heartedly, Talfryn checked behind and around boxes and piles of treasure. Urns decorated in pictures of men fighting other men or monsters. He knew the amulet's importance, but the bird remained on his mind. Every few minutes, Talfryn's eyes drifted to the cage to make sure the bird was still alive.

"We should call it a night," Brynwen said at last. "I don't know about you, but I'm exhausted. Besides, the torch is almost out."

Padric rubbed his eyes. "You are right, Brynwen, we can resume anew tomorrow. Talfryn, how can we help?"

Elated, Talfryn started gathering an assortment of semi-sturdy-looking chests and crates. Padric rolled his eyes, but he set the torch down, and together with Brynwen, helped Talfryn stack items into a haphazard staircase. When it was finished, Talfryn carefully climbed up the rickety, makeshift stairs. Padric and Brynwen remained on the ground to keep the staircase steady.

When Talfryn lifted his fingers up to the cage door, the bird cooed again. "Hello, little maiden," he cooed back. "What is a lovely little thing like you doing in a dingy old place like this, eh?" He tried lifting the little latch to the barred door, but it was stuck fast. "Well, my friend, I am afraid we will have to take the cage, too."

The cage ring released from around the hook. "There you are! Let's go."

A *click, click, click* sound came from the ceiling. Then, just as abruptly, it stopped.

Talfryn's eyes widened, and he peered around in the dark. "Ummm, what was that?"

The grating of stones scraping against each other started and grew louder than the clicking.

"That cannot be good," said Padric. He gave Talfryn an I-told-you-so look.

Stones shifted directly above them, shaking pebbles and dust from the ceiling down onto the little group. The bird flitted around and around in the cage, twittering in terror while Talfryn's nose tickled agin most dreadfully. *Not a good time, nose!* He let out a series of sneezes.

"We should leave," Padric said. "The door is closing!"

He seized Brynwen's hand and launched over the treasure debris. Pushing her up the stairs, the faun immediately turned to Talfryn.

Talfryn froze to the spot, another sneeze building to crescendo. *Why now, sneezes? WHY?*

Without another glance, Padric snatched a handful of Talfryn's shirt and shoved him up the stairs after his sister. The birdcage clanged against the statue of Jupiter, knocking it to the ground.

"Achoo! Sorry!" Talfryn cried to both the bird and statue as he bolted up the stairs. Padric was directly on his tail. About halfway up, Brynwen's feet disappeared through the stone trap door. As he got closer, Talfryn's heart pounded as the trap door seemed to slide closed faster. *It will seal us in forever!*

By the time he was five steps away, it was more than halfway closed.

"Faster!" Padric yelled. Talfryn tossed the cage through the hole, then leaped up the last three steps, pulling his feet out as Padric crawled his way up on hands and knees. No room left to jump. The sliding stone pressed against the faun's thighs, and he gave a shout as it pinched his fur.

Talfryn and Brynwen lunged for his arms and dragged him up and out as stone slammed into stone. Padric's hoofs barely cleared the exit in time.

With Padric's weight, all three crashed to the floor of the mausoleum in a heap of cloth and limbs. A great cloud of tomb dust burst from the floor shaft, covering them head to toe.

Taking a couple shaky breaths, Talfryn sat up, the excitement of the last few minutes slowly withdrawing from his system. He patted his limbs to make sure they were all there. Brynwen and Padric seemed to be in one piece, too. A big dent marred the cage, but the bird inside was otherwise no worse for the wear.

He ran a hand through his hair, staring at the stone floor that nearly trapped them in a dark crypt forever.

I can't believe we made it!

"This is one of those instances where thin ankles came in handy," said Talfryn.

From the light of the torch, all three adventurers' clothes and faces were smeared with dust, dirt, and perspiration. The bird fluttered around in its cage, flinging dust everywhere, its little voice trilling and trilling.

"The amulet!" Padric cried, staring at the closed crypt door. He flung himself at the sealed stone floor. The stones were so close together, it was difficult to tell where the floor had parted. A long cut on his forearm dripped blood onto the stone. "What will we do now?"

Brynwen knelt next to him and studied the floor. "We will find another way." She glared unappreciatively at her brother.

"What?" Talfryn asked. "How was I supposed to know the cage was a trap?"

Padric studied the floor. "Do we have a chisel?"

"Not that I am aware of," Brynwen replied.

Meanwhile, ignored and left to ruminate about his ill-judged actions in the crypt. *Well, it looks like I did it again. Somehow*, he mused, *I will make it up to them. But how?*

The little bird flitted about, eager to be free of her cage. "Calm down, little one. I'll have you out in no time. Can I call you Nessie?" Now that they had better light upstairs, Talfryn could see the bird wasn't yellow at all. "But you're no canary. You're white as snow, like a dove."

Jiggling the lock for a couple minutes, the rusty latch finally released, and the door snapped open. The white bird zipped out of the cage and made circles around the interior of the mausoleum, singing sweet songs of freedom.

Talfryn felt his heart lighten at her cheerfulness.

"Well," he said with a sigh, "at least one of us is happy."

A gleam of torchlight caught the reflection of something at the bottom of the cage. He shook the cage a little.

He cleared his throat. "Beg pardon..."

The faun and healer continued to scrape at the stone, ignoring him utterly.

"What color is obsidian again?"

"Black," both Brynwen and Padric said.

"Like this?"

Brynwen and Padric turned back to Talfryn.

At the bottom of the cage lay a round object—a gold ring with an ebony gemstone.

Obsidian.

Everyone stared at the little ring.

"That must be it!" Padric exclaimed. He procured the ring from the cage, his eyes sparking with excitement. It seemed to shine more brilliantly in his hand.

Leaning in, Brynwen gasped. "It is beautiful. And to think it was in the cage the whole time. Who would think to look there?"

Well, maybe just me, Talfryn thought, puffing his chest out a little bit.

"So much trouble for a little trinket," Padric said. His cheeks flushed, and he set a hand on Talfryn's shoulder. "Tal, I am..."

"Thoroughly contrite?" Talfryn said, putting as much dignity in his speech as he could. "Well...apology accepted."

Brynwen flung her arms around her brother's neck, then kissed him on the cheek. "I will never doubt you again, brother."

"I should say not," Talfryn said, setting the bird cage down.

The little dove circled above the three, then alighted on Talfryn's shoulder.

"Nessie is appreciative, too."

CHAPTER 34

Brynwen startled awake. Her eyes wrenched open as a blinding light made her squeeze them shut again. Another peal of thunder crashed down. The storms this time of year were just awful. She tried to fall asleep again, concentrating on the rain pattering on the roof and the ground outside.

After the night they'd had, nearly getting trapped in the crypt, they trudged back to camp just in time for huge drops of rain to alight on their heads. A godsend, the temple of Fortuna's allowed them shelter. They barely got everything under cover before the sky opened up.

Brynwen rolled onto her side and glanced about the fire-lit camp. The smoke rose to the ceiling, fogging up the air before eventually creeping out the windows. Her brother slept peacefully, his chest rising and falling evenly. Next to him, the bird Nessie slept soundlessly in its cage, the door open wide.

Another bolt of lightning illuminated the faun's features. He stood at a window looking out. His broad shoulders and athletic muscles, the slim waist leading down to furry, bent legs in short trousers, and the short fuzzy tail sticking out the back. Little horns protruded from his curls made silver in the lightning. His face set in a frown, worry creasing his forehead. When the lightning dissipated, the fire barely showed his silhouette.

Figuring she wouldn't fall asleep for a while, she got up to wander over to the faun. Her foot struck a pebble, and he turned to her.

A slight grin crept up his lips. "You could not sleep, either?"

Brynwen sighed and stopped next to him to follow his gaze out the window. "It was a close call in the crypt."

"I still cannot believe Nessie was the amulet's guardian," said Padric.

"And the smug look on Talfryn's face when he discovered the amulet. We will never live that down."

"Aye," he replied, and they chuckled.

They stood in silence for a few minutes, listening to the rain.

"Now that the first part of the prophecy is accomplished, you still have to destroy a weapon, right?" Brynwen asked.

"Aye, and find all the missing people, in just under a month."

"What is it like, the prophecy? You mentioned it a little at Roana's inn."

Padric squeezed his eyes shut and shook his head. "I feel the prophecy tug at me, day and night. If I try to turn my attention to something else, this prophecy barrages me. It is quite literally burned into my brain. I do not begin to understand what sort of power the Oracle holds, but I cannot forget, no matter how hard I try. It feels…violating."

She was angry for him, and thought of many ways to end Circe, but none of them were satisfying enough to avenge Padric's turmoil. Had Circe sent the oracle to him to be a distraction? The sorceress might be devious that way. The prophecy would have a two-fold effect: to warn Padric, but at the same time tear him apart, leaving him to know his own destiny. Set him up for failure.

"Could—could you change the prophecy somehow?"

"I wish I knew how, if it were possible."

The faun's silver curls swished with a gust of wind and rain spatter, making him and Brynwen wince. A silver curl strayed on his forehead. An impulse overtook her to move it back to its rightful place, but she resisted.

As he turned to look down at her, dark shadows covered his eyes. A dry, humorless laugh escaped his lips. "At the beginning of the year, I felt all had finally fallen into place. Rising to lieutenant, attaining my first real assignment. But it has all been torn asunder since then. I begin to wonder if I was somehow cursed before that. As if the gods and the Fates conspiring against me. They hold the string of my existence in their hands. And to top it off, now I have dragged you and Talfryn into this mess." He shivered despite the warm evening. He leaned against the window ledge, allowing the rain splatter to wet his clothes and face.

Brynwen shifted. "See here, I don't know about these *Fates*, and what they have in store for you, Talfryn, and me. Nor do I know if the prophecy is set in stone. I sincerely hope not. I certainly would like some leeway on how I live my life. But if there is a way to change things for the better, we must do it, mustn't we? God will see us through."

Padric's eyes sparked for a moment before dimming again.

"Indeed, we must. For everyone's sake." He hung his head forlornly. As he said it, the silver reflected in his hair and the deep shadows made him appear twenty years older than his eighteen. He took a deep breath. "It is not for my own sake that I worry. If I must forfeit my life for the sake of others, then I shall do so willingly. Such is the life of a knight, bred to take the brunt of the world's problems to protect those who cannot. And those I care about most, I will protect with my life."

He would. She had always known that. The prophecy did not specify if he would live or die in the end. The talk had taken a scary turn, she realized, and she wanted to shift away from that. Padric needed hope, not more to worry about. As though with a stubborn woman in labor pains, she spoke to him with all the authority she could muster. "We will beat this. We will find a way, together. You have to believe that. We will save everyone and return to Chaddesden. All of us." That statement made her feel brave, and before she realized what she was doing, her hand shot up and finally brushed away the stray curl from his forehead.

Padric reached up and gently took her sweeping hand in his. Held it. Then his free hand came up and caressed her cheek and his lips gently kissed where the hand had been. Her heart rose in her throat. The remnants of the kiss lingered on her skin, warm to her bones.

"I thank you for your kind words. He is lucky to have you," he said, carefully placing her hands down on the stone window ledge.

She smirked. "Oh, Talfryn can take care of himself, given the need."

"I was not referring to Talfryn."

"Oh, well..." Brynwen had almost forgotten about Jasper. She twirled her braid between her fingers, guilt filling her belly. In fact, she had not thought much about him in days. "Oh, your arm."

"What about it?"

"It is wet from the rain. Let me put a new bandage on it," she said.

"I think I can live with a damp arm."

"Do you wish it should fester?"

Padric set his mouth in a thin line. "Nay."

"That's what I thought."

"You healers always seem to have the upper hand," the faun said with a smirk, and followed her to the fire where Talfryn still slept soundly.

Thoughts still on the kiss, Brynwen rummaged through her pack for her bandages and salve, removing a few of its contents while searching through the innards of the dark bag.

"What is that?" Padric asked.

He plucked a little stoppered vial from among the contents from her satchel.

Heat brushed Brynwen's cheeks. No one was supposed to see that. *He will probably think it is a foolish hobby.* "'Tis but a little project I am working on. May I have it back, please?" She held out her hand for it.

"But what is it? Powders of some sort?"

The flush deepened. Why couldn't he just give it back? "This is my first attempt at a new herbal mixture."

She lunged for it, but his reflexes were too quick.

"Not your miracle mix?" He brought it closer to the fire for a closer inspection, a grin widening on his face.

"It's for a different set of ailments. The powders are layered by color and are meant to be pleasing to the eye. Now stop stalling and give me your arm."

Padric reluctantly handed the vial over. "Whatever it is for, I have no doubt it will be most beneficial."

"Like I said, it is only my first attempt, I tell you. Stop moving, or...What's wrong?"

Padric's head had jerked up, as Talfryn's dog Finn's would when he heard a noise.

After listening for a couple more heartbeats, Padric said, "Forgive me, I think the stew must have disagreed with me."

Unsure what to say to this, Brynwen nodded slowly. *Odd, I don't remember him having a troubled stomach over my cooking before.*

Once Brynwen finished tying off Padric's bandage, he yawned. "Best get to bed then, my eyes refuse to stay open another moment." He reached behind him, then slid a dagger in a leather sheath on the ground toward her. "Wake Talfryn," he breathed.

He slunk into the darkness before she could respond. The rain covered the clap of his hoofs upon the stones as he moved from shadow to shadow, until he was all but shadow himself.

Brynwen's heart pounded as her fingers trembled on the satchel's clasp. Whatever he was about, it couldn't be good. He had heard something. But what? Where?

Laying down with her head in the shadows and the dagger gripped in her hand, she pinched her brother's shoulder. After three pinches he stirred. In a few short, whispered sentences she relayed the situation. It didn't take much for Talfryn's eyes to widen into wakefulness.

When Padric did not come back after a few minutes, they began to worry. Every few seconds Brynwen felt for the dagger, ensuring it was there, ready.

"Should I go after him, do you think?" Talfryn asked.

Before Brynwen could answer, a handful of drips appeared on the floor near the fire.

Then a mess of silvery-blond hair touched the edges of the firelight.

"Well?" the twins asked simultaneously.

"No one is directly outside," Padric whispered. "But I did hear something out there. Could have been a couple of stones shifting or an animal finding shelter. The darkness and rain hid anything tangible. I will check again at first light."

"Do you think someone has followed us here?" Talfryn asked.

"I have been followed before," Padric replied. "Roman gods are not known for playing by conventional rules."

"You will be wanting this back, then," Brynwen said. Now she noticed for the first time it was the dagger Padric always wore at his side. The de Clifton family crest, an embossed gold shield with a seahorse and rose in opposite corners, reflected on the sheath in the dying fire's rays.

"Keep it," Padric said. "I would feel much better if you had a weapon upon your person. Something other than your small paring knife."

She wanted to argue that her paring knife was a perfectly good weapon, but thought better of it.

With that, he popped his head back into the shadows to keep watch.

On her pallet, as Brynwen closed her eyes once again, her brain wouldn't tune out the scenes which had played out a few minutes ago. The kiss on her cheek. The way Padric tensed when he heard a sound. Clutching his dagger. If anyone hid outside. Her chest constricted, not knowing what to do, receiving no answers or sleep.

CHAPTER 35

*L*ack of sleep did nothing to ease Padric's apprehension.

He had stayed up most of the night keeping vigil. Something lurked out in the rain the evening before. It did not feel like Lilith or the forest, and the stag had all but disappeared. It would pop up here and there to remind him of its presence. But in the last few days, it was either very well-hidden or had fled to wherever it hailed from. Whatever it was seemed different. More menacing.

After several hours of leaning against the stony temple wall, he finally dozed and Talfryn took over. The feeling of being watched was a constant worry, grating at Padric's every nerve. Circe likely had many means by which to watch them and could and would attack at any time of her choosing. He reckoned that pretty much nothing he did was a secret to her, but he had to take his chances as long as possible. If she did attack, would he be able to use the amulet against her?

Meanwhile, Talfryn attempted to free the bird Nessie, but she refused to leave him—or the cage, for that matter. She clung to him like glue, sweeping around his head, frequently landing on his shoulder. She pecked menacingly at Brynwen for a while, until the healer gave Nessie some seeds. Then she was content. Nessie believed Padric's head of hair was a nest and tried at every opportunity to either sit on it or steal some for her cage.

As they had gathered up Gregorio's belongings to take with them that morning, Padric worried about his old tutor, the guilt weaving through his chest at not going after him. He still failed to understand what Gregorio's involvement was in all of this, or who had taken him.

Roana's prophecy and vision of world destruction barged its way through his thoughts. *This amulet better be worth it.* Otherwise, Gregorio's disappearance, along with everyone else's was for naught.

Before they left Mamucium, Padric and Talfryn gave Brynwen quick instruction on how to use the dagger in self-defense. The lesson ended in Talfryn very nearly losing an eye and everyone involved receiving a few abrasions. But all-in-all, Padric had commented with a bright smile she had done "quite well" regardless of the short lesson.

They traveled much of the day beneath the unending canopy of trees, traveling northeast along the decidedly better-kept Roman roads. Per Gregorio's map, they took the Roman road north called Wattling Street II, then at *Bremetannacum* would head east to pass two cities called *Olenacum* and *Verbeia* to reach *Eboracum*, or York.

"If we were not so pressed for time," Padric said, studying the map, "I might wish to visit longer at Bremetannacum. Gregorio has a theory that King Arthur and Merlin may have come from this area."

"Truly?" asked Brynwen.

Padric gave an involuntary wince as something sharp nipped at his hair. "Talfryn, is it really necessary for your bird to treat me so ill?"

"Come on, Nessie likes you."

"By attacking his head?" Brynwen asked with raised brow.

"Sitting on my shoulder I could handle," Padric said, dodging another downward swoop of the little bird. "It is the leaping about and tugging at my hairs that is most meddlesome."

"She is just thrilled to be free," Talfryn replied with indignation.

"Then she can be free atop *your* head."

Talfryn scoffed. "Alas, Padric, your golden locks are more desirous than my own plain dark tresses, my friend." He brushed a hand against his short hair.

Stifling a snicker, Brynwen leaned forward in the saddle. "What if Nessie lays an egg on his head? Is Padric to be her nest until the egg hatches?"

Talfryn drummed a finger to his lips. "I daresay, that would be a sight."

"Could we make another nest for her?" Brynwen suggested. "I've got some cloth, and she can add twigs to it."

"I think Nessie has other ideas," Talfryn said.

Padric sighed. He had to agree with Talfryn on that.

Nessie tried on no less than four more occasions to sit in and yank on Padric's hair. Not only sit in it—but also hobble and chirp atop his head till his cranium pounded. Finally, he bade Talfryn to either close her in the cage or leave her behind on the road.

Talfryn closed the cage door.

That accomplished to his satisfaction, Padric and his aching head withdrew from the twins and scouted ahead for a small clearing to spend the night. There were no signs of travelers, yet he remained anxious. After a relatively short time, he found a delightful clearing with a nearby stream north of the forest road.

As they made ready the camp, Padric took stock of the supplies as Brynwen removed them from the bags and laid each item out on a bit of cloth: two crumbled journey cakes, a gnarled wedge of white goat cheese, and several small squirrel bones with which Brynwen said could be used to flavor a broth.

"We are running low," Padric surmised.

"Would you go hunting?" Brynwen asked. "If you find a boar, it would last us a while."

"I think it unwise. We should stay together. Whoever lurked outside the temple could be nearby. For all we know, they were the ones who took Signore Gregorio."

Brynwen placed a hand on her hip. "Have you seen any other trace of them since we left?"

He shook his head.

"Then they're likely not here. Mayhap they are lost travelers too embarrassed to ask for shelter. If you see anyone suspicious, you can return to us immediately. Talfryn and I will be fine until your return."

"We've got our guard canary, too," Talfryn said, indicating said bird.

"If you are so worried, just be quick about it," Brynwen said.

"As you wish," Padric replied finally. Yet he could not drop the increasing notion that something or someone out there followed them. "Keep the dagger with you at all times. Please, if only to humor me."

Brynwen acquiesced, eyes shining. "If you see any berries, will you please pick some? I desire to make a compote."

"I will keep my eyes open," he said as he adjusted the quiver across his back, hiding his worry behind a quick smile. "Will you hold onto this for me until I return? I fear to lose it in the forest."

He removed the chain holding the amulet ring and his St. Christopher medal from around his neck and placed them in her open palm with care, brushing her fingers as he let go. A slight tremor rent through his stomach.

"Of course. I shall keep it safe." Her brow furrowed. Then her hazel eyes brightened as she said conspiratorially, "You best be quick, for I am going to make something delicious for our evening meal—I am unsure as yet what it will be, but it will fill you up to be sure."

"Of that, I have no doubt." Unable to stop smiling, but to hide his blush, he gave her a little bow, and wheeled around toward the road.

Talfryn turned from brushing down Dusty. "If you make it back before it gets dark, would you feel up to sparring for a bit? I don't wish to get rusty."

"Certainly, if the woodland animals do not put up too much of a fight."

Padric wandered south and crossed the road into the forest. His eyes danced around looking for wild game. Within a few minutes he found a rabbit trail and followed it. It was a marvel how, as time had passed since meeting the twins, he had become defter at walking silently with the hoofs bestowed unto him, thanks to Circe. Perhaps the one thing he could accept inheriting from her. Now he could pass through the forest almost as stealthily as when he wore soft leather boots. Rare was the animal that scampered away at his proximity.

As he traveled, numerous easy targets of squirrels and birds presented themselves, but they moved off too fast, as though in a fright of something—though there were no signs of any people. However, his unease lingered. Even the scent in the air seemed off somehow.

This overshadowing in the forest made his thoughts turn dark. If he was never restored to a fully human body, could he ever fully return to the human world? He could not hide beneath his cloak forever. If he could make Circe change him back...what then? The future was unknown and, in all parts, dangerous. The fact that he was bound to face the sorcerous and a monster did not fail to remind him that his life could be forfeit in as little as a few days or weeks at most. He thought back to his conversation with Brynwen in the temple, how he had allowed his hand to linger on her cheek then kissed her...What had he been thinking? If he dared to reveal his desire for Brynwen's heart with the threat of death looming, what would that say about him? His chest tightened as he resolved to avoid breaking her heart regardless of his actions. He did not even know if she harbored the same feelings. No, he hated to admit it, but she would be much better off with Jasper.

A burst of white stopped him short. Tiny white berries encased in a round, green bush. Similar to honeysuckle, he had never seen berries this stunningly white before, and wondered if they were only native to that part of England.

Realizing the late hour, Padric picked a handful of the precious little berries and carefully rolled them in a cloth. Securing it with a bit of twine, he placed the bundle in his pouch. *She shall have her compote.* Brynwen would be thrilled at the discovery of this bush. Should she wish for more, he would return with her in the morning.

A strange feeling came over him, like an animal sense.

Had he left Talfryn and Brynwen in danger, too?

I should not have left them. I should return to them now.

He spun around. Then shook his head and scoffed.

Perhaps my imagination is making me paranoid.

After another quarter of a mile with sightings of neither man nor beast, he became suspicious. The forest no longer greeted him with its earlier comforts. It should be alive with the twilight-active animals, not the stagnant air that crept into his lungs, filling his ears. Not even the rustle of birds settling down for the evening bothered the trees. It was nothing like Lilith's power over the forest near Mamucium, but he could not explain what this feeling was. The hairs on the back of his neck rose.

Slowly, he nocked an arrow.

Then—the faintest hint of a noise. Leaves and twigs crunched under something heavy.

He spun on his heel.

The stag stood directly in front of him. Its long, smooth antlers emerged from the majestic animal's head like long, slender fingers curving toward the sky. And the diamond mark above its heart. Once again, the faint shimmer hovered over its back, giving the impression of wings. The stag peered directly at Padric, not giving the hunter the satisfaction of showing an ounce of fear.

Padric's heart raced. *At last*, he thought, *I can kill this infuriating creature. It does not even flinch at the sight of my bow.* He raised his weapon, gazing once again into the stag's eyes, and saw something almost human about them.

A shiver ran down Padric's spine, making him pause. The deer shook its head, as though a circus of gnats were flying around its ears. When it stopped, it cocked its head to the side and gazed in the distance behind Padric.

Was it trying to communicate with him?

If he started a conversation with the creature, he wondered if it would respond in kind. It suddenly struck Padric that the stag could be from Derbyshire. Could it be trying to tell him something? The stag began to advance, when Padric did not so much as hear, but *felt* the presence of others. He could almost smell their odor. Sweat, pine, and blood. Could being part animal contribute, he wondered, or had his senses toned since he began to learn the art of knighthood? His ears opened to the sounds of the forest. An instinct told him to lean to the right.

The *whoosh* of an arrow whistled past his ear, nipping his hair in the process.

His heart quickened. He pivoted around and fired the arrow originally intended for the stag.

A human grunt came from the direction of his spent arrow, followed by the thud of a body hitting the ground. Chest heaving, a twinge gripped his stomach. *How many more are there?*

The answer came quickly as a volley of arrows descended upon him.

CHAPTER 36

Without skipping a beat, Padric launched himself at the nearest tree. He made himself as thin as possible while waiting for the volley of arrows to pass around the tree. Heaving deep breaths, he took stock of the situation. Quick peeks around the trunk revealed each visible enemy's movement. He spied caps of various sizes and colors of forest greens and browns, and near them, the glints of weapons. In all, he counted six men. *But there could be more hidden*, he reminded himself. He pulled forth all of his military training. Made calculations. Who the easiest target was from here. Where each man might move to next. Who seemed to be the leader. He sincerely wished Rawlins had his back in this. His kidnapped friend was perfect for stealth missions. Pushing down the regret, he formulated a plan of attack.

He had little time to care who they were. It was clear they wanted him dead—the barrage of arrows was evidence enough. If they were after the amulet, it was safe with Brynwen—and she along with it—he hoped.

The lieutenant unclasped his green cloak and let it fall to the forest floor. Next, he pulled out an arrow from the quiver and licked the red contrast feather. Detected the wind's strength and direction. North by northeast.

Another arrow shot from the far side of the distant tree, barely missing his nose.

He took a deep breath and lifted the bow. His left arm ached up near the shoulder. A warmth trickled down his tricep. It must have been hit during the volley of arrows. *No time to think about it.* He inhaled, stepped out into the open, aimed at the first target he had spied earlier, and let fly. Not waiting to see if it struck true, he kept moving.

As much as Padric hated to admit it, the faun legs gave him more speed and agility than human legs with boots. A rush of euphoria, a type of freedom thrilled through his chest. Whether these legs were an inheritance or a curse, they were undoubtedly useful.

Out of the corner of his eye, he spotted the glint of an arrowhead. The bowman came out into the open for a quick shot. Padric bounded two steps up the nearest tree trunk and then pushed off into the air, arrow loosed directly at the man's heart. A half twist in the air and Padric landed on his haunches gracefully, one hand on the ground for balance. The bowman's startled face contorted as he beheld the arrow sticking out of his chest. Then he keeled over.

How many more?

Just as Padric bounced back up, a large man emerged from the trees. Hat askew on his large head, he had broadsword in hand and shouted vulgar obscenities in the Padric's direction. Padric thought of a return retort, but decided against it. Instead, he deftly drew the sword from his back scabbard and met the berserker head on. Their steel clashed. Padric wondered if the loud report could have been heard at the campsite.

"Who are you?" Padric asked. His sore arm would become a burden soon if he did not give it some rest before entering another skirmish. "Why are you doing this?"

The man merely grunted and shoved against Padric's sword.

Their swords separated, and they parted a few steps. The assailant swung again, and Padric brought his sword up with both hands to deflect the blow. His left arm burned where the arrow remained lodged. He swung the sword around with his right hand and pushed off. Retreating a step, he then lunged forward before his adversary could recover. The other man's sword rose and deflected his thrust. Steel clashed again. The enormous man pushed with a great grunt, and Padric found himself briefly in the air. Crashing to the earthen floor, he rolled over and over like a rag doll as his sword skittered across the ground. The arrow in his arm snapped off upon impact with the ground, wedging the arrowhead deeper into his flesh, leaving an agonizing throbbing. Spots danced across his vision. Helplessly, he panted for breath.

Cracking open his eyes, he spied his sword lying on the grassless forest floor two arm lengths away. In desperation, he stretched his good arm toward the weapon. A shadow covered the ground between his fingertips and the sword.

"Well, confound it," he groaned.

THE GLINT of metal caught Padric's eye just in time. The faun rolled out of the way as the sword tip smashed into the ground directly where his chest had been.

Taking two gulps of air, Padric shoved his hurt arm under his body. Leaving the bow on the ground, he lurched toward the sword and scooped it up. He launched back to his hoofs as the assailant stepped in for another attack.

Again, their swords met.

Padric's shoulder throbbed. He could feel it weakening as the man shoved against him. They each released the hold and Padric stepped back. The assailant immediately returned, this time nearly cleaving a hole through Padric's stomach. Too close.

The more he moved, the greater the blood loss affected his actions as well as his concentration. This skirmish needed to end soon, or else he was finished.

The two circled each other to catch their breaths. Padric knew he had to find a weakness in this fellow, otherwise, he was done for. He cleared his mind. *Think about sword training with the captain. With Rawlins.* A crafty fellow, his friend was a formidable adversary on any given training field.

He stepped up again and they continued.

Thrust.

Parry.

Clash.

His breath grew ragged as he lunged again. As he moved, he discovered the weak spot he was searching for. He drew up his sword again and they moved as before. This time, he raised his elbow and sliced at the man's armpit. A blood stain immediately sprung from the place where Padric's sword pierced. The man shimmied away several feet, then dropped his sword. He fell to his knees but moved no further. A curious pose for a wounded man.

Padric had no time to take more than a couple of breaths before the sixth assailant came out of the woods. Holding his sword with shaking hands, the lad scowled at Padric.

"You do not have to do this," Padric said.

"But I do. These men you beat are my friends," the lad said, and charged.

Padric took a breath and stepped in to meet the youth's weapon. Not as versed with the sword as the previous assailant, Padric defeated him easily. The poor youth was younger than Padric, perhaps only sixteen. He left the lad with a wound that would encourage him to seek a different profession.

The boy lifted watery eyes to Padric. "Just finish me."

Padric knelt and looked over his wound. "Not today. I am afraid you will live."

"Please finish me off, for they surely will have no further use for me when I return."

The faun's eyes softened. "I am afraid I must decline. You would do well to diverge from this dangerous occupation when you recover." The lad shook his head and moaned. Padric turned the conversation. "Who are you, and why did your group attack me?"

The lad swallowed. "I... we are trappers. We were trapping along the river when this man came along and offered to pay us handsomely for taking care of a few travelers who stole something from him. Two men and a woman. He promised extra if we found a gold ring."

Padric's insides twisted. So they *were* followed. He had not imagined the noises of the night before. And they knew about the amulet. "What were you to do with these travelers once you relieved them of their possessions?"

The boy's face flushed. "We were to do with them as we liked. Extra for their heads in a sack. We figured you must have done something terrible to him to want vengeance like that."

"And you would gladly participate?"

He shrugged and coughed. "It was all or nothing, Drogo said. I didn't have much say in it."

Padric glanced around, but none of the fallen men had acted like the leader. "And where is Drogo now?"

"He went after the other two."

Padric's heart froze. Brynwen and Talfryn were in danger, and he left them alone. He gripped the boy's tunic. "What did this man look like, the one who hired you?"

"I never got a good look at his face. He stayed in the shadows, but he was of average size, and sounded youngish—but extra gruff, like he was trying to disguise his voice."

Unfortunately, the youth was in terrible pain and fainted straight away before he could answer any more questions.

Frustrated at his waste of a perfectly good opportunity, Padric rocked to his hoofs, taking far more effort than it ought. The undertaking made his head swim and the landscape danced in front of him as he found a tree to lean on.

Brynwen and Talfryn...

Despite the excruciating pain and swooning head, Padric ran. His friends were in trouble. It could already be too late.

I must go faster. To save them, he needed the swiftness of a horse. The centaur. But how could he do that again? Desperate, he pulled the memory up. Lived it. Experienced it—chasing the stag...the wind rushing through his hair, his limbs, the landscape dashing past him.

Something snapped inside him. As though his limbs twisted as he ran. About halfway to the camp he stopped at a tree to catch his breath, then a hideous pain racked his stomach and legs, bringing him to his knees, tearing him in two.

CHAPTER 37

Talfryn led the horses to the fresh spring. Dusty took long sips of water. Beside the mare, Darrin picked at the long grass, which grew in the pocket where the sun managed to reach between the foliage. It was peaceful here, with no sister to argue with him, nor his friend constantly making plans—the ever-vigilant knight.

He looked forward to the training sessions of their mornings and evenings. Being a knight, Padric needed the constant exercise, and Talfryn was appreciative that his friend took the time to include him, though he had not quite the same skill to which his friend was accustomed. Yet he was learning, and Padric was patient when Talfryn made mistakes—and there were many, many mistakes. "Knights err time and again," Padric confided. "Per the captain, we must work toward achieving perfection and ingenuity through constant application."

To which Talfryn responded, "And not accidentally cutting someone's head or arm off."

"That would be preferable, yes." A companionable laugh. Then another lunge and parry.

Talfryn was glad to get out of the sessions with merely scratches and bruises. It was fortuitous that Padric was an experienced fighter, or else it could all have gone completely awry.

A twig snapped and broke his reverie.

The hatchet was in Talfryn's hand in an instant. He whirled and lifted the axe level with his ear.

"Tal!" Brynwen exclaimed, almost tripping over her skirts as she stepped back.

Heart a-flutter, Talfryn took a deep breath. "Bryn! Don't sneak up like that! I could have given you a scalping."

"I just came to get more sticks for the fire. How was I to know you would be right *here*?" She pumped her hands on her hips.

"Still," he said, and lowered the hatchet. "Just be careful, all right?"

"Yes, brother dearest. Now come, help me gather some wood for the fire, if you will." She then proceeded to look for useful pieces of wood. Her satchel, which housed her prized herbs, was slung over her shoulder. She had not put it down since they left Mamucium.

Talfryn hitched his weapon to his belt and bent over to pick up a few fallen pieces of wood lying at his feet, a couple as thick as his forearm.

Their thirst quenched, he gathered Dusty's and Darrin's reins in his free hand and turned to go. "When we return to camp..." he began but trailed off at Brynwen's expression.

She stood stock still, a load of sticks gathered in her arms, ogling at something in the trees on the other side of the stream. After a moment Talfryn's eyes focused on a man, dressed like the trees. He wore a green and brown tunic and matching leggings. His full beard, a russet brown, made it impossible to tell his age.

Talfryn espied at least two to three others standing in the trees as silent as this first man. He could not make accurate count, however, for they all dressed the same and blended in with the surroundings so well.

Talfryn opened his mouth to speak, but at first nothing came out. He cleared his throat, then spoke to the bearded man with a wide smile. "Ho there."

"Ho there yourself," the man replied. He came out of the shade of the tree and stopped not three yards from the brother and sister, only the stream between them.

"How can we be of service?" Talfryn asked.

"I am Drogo. Jeffrey over here's brother was out hunting, and a boar managed to wound him. We have cleaned him up as best we can, but I fear of infection in this dreary wood. We hoped you would be able to help."

The twins' eyes met, and Talfryn pursed his lips. He quickly peered back at the man, but not before catching the warning in Bryn's eyes. "Where is he?" he asked. "We would be happy to assist in any way we can." He could sense her unease. In fact, he felt the same. There was something about these men that disturbed him. "Sister, would you not agree?"

Without skipping a beat, she replied, "I agree, brother. Pray, sir, what sort of wound did he receive?"

The bearded man answered, "To the arm. A large, deep gash." He drew his finger from his wrist, up across the forearm, and ending at the elbow. "Come with us, and we will bring you to him. We can return you to your camp in no time."

Brynwen retreated a step. "First I will need to fetch supplies from our camp. I'll return directly and then we can go." A deliberate fib, Talfryn thought as she carried her supplies wherever she went in the satchel hanging from her shoulder.

Brynwen rearranged the satchel in question ever so slightly so it was hidden behind her. *Ah, the amulet is inside.* Padric had given her the amulet before he left to hunt. Where was he now?

Talfryn harbored deep reservations about these men. Could they be trusted, or were they bandits...or worse, Circe's henchmen? Regardless, there were no doubts that he and Brynwen were being lured into a trap, with little chance of escape. All of this went through his head in the time it took to blink twice.

"There is no time," the woodsman grumbled. "He needs help now."

"We will return directly. We promise, it isn't far." Talfryn picked up the horses' reins again and spun around. But not before he caught the glint of the man's long pike.

"Do not take one more step toward those trees," Drogo warned and drew his pike forward.

Talfryn stilled, his chest tightening. He guessed their farce of a conversation was over now. Really, a 'wounded brother back at camp' story? His goats could come up with a better excuse. He needed to stall. "Surely it is not so dire that his arm will be lost with the loss of a few extra minutes?"

"It might," came the sharp retort. The others behind him also drew their arms, spears and gnarled clubs.

"Sister, what do you say to cooperating with these fine gentlemen?"

His sister gave him a puzzled glare. "I don't think—"

Talfryn grinned, a terrible idea forming in his mind. It probably wouldn't work, but he could see few better choices. "Me too, I have changed my mind, I think." He stepped forward. His foot slid on the wet bank, and he teetered, waving his arms for balance. The strangers stared at him intently as he launched the wood he carried at Drogo. The woodsman's mouth opened in an "O" as the wood hurtled toward him. Talfryn might have laughed until Drogo batted at them away with his spear, knocking most of them aside. Only a few sticks struck his large body and fell harmlessly into the spring.

With haste, Talfryn retreated and slapped Dusty's rump hard. The quiet horse startled. With an angry snort, it dashed off toward the intruders, empty reins flapping around her head. Talfryn slapped Darrin next, and the horse followed his fellow into the woods, scattering the woodsmen as they passed. Two men dove into the brush and foliage. Darrin's frantic foreleg kicked a fair-haired man who then went tumbling.

"Run, Bryn!"

Brynwen pulled her dagger from its scabbard.

"*Go!*" he shouted again. He lunged toward his sister and grabbed her arm, propelling her away from the dangerous men.

Scurrying one step behind, Brynwen managed to keep up with Talfryn's longer legs.

Through the trees they darted to the clearing where their disheveled camp lay.

An arrow whistled past Talfryn's ear. Another followed. A sharp pain lit his right side on fire. He cursed below his breath. *This will not work.* Simultaneously he grabbed the bird cage and again Brynwen's arm as they dashed to the other side of the clearing. An arrow struck a nearby tree trunk. The imbedded shaft swished up and down wildly, sending bark flying everywhere.

In a few steps Talfryn halted.

"Keep going and find Padric," he said, and shoved the bird cage into Brynwen's arms. Nessie was too frightened to make any sound.

"I'm not leaving you." Her hazel eyes gleamed with the defiance she wore so well as she clenched his forearm.

He shook off her grasp. "Will you listen to me for once and go? I'll keep them at bay." He reached for the hatchet at his hip. Next to this, his hunting knife hung snug in its holster. A backup weapon, just in case.

"Did you hear me?" Brynwen argued. "I'm not going anywhere. And Padric will probably be back any moment."

"Bryn—"

"I'm staying."

Talfryn huffed. "Fine. Just keep out of sight."

His sister nodded, then he motioned for her to duck behind the closest tree.

"Be careful, Tal."

He nodded in return. "Now for some sparring practice," he said with a false confidence. Heading back to the clearing, he hid himself behind a tree and peered at the camp. The forest stood still, but his heart beat as though trying to escape his chest. The insufferable silence unnerved him—even the animals knew trouble was brewing. He gulped back a lungful of air.

Where did they go? What would Padric do in this situation? Talfryn wished he'd had more training. Maybe even spent a few weeks in the barracks learning different fighting strategies. Instead, he had only learned some sword play, staff-fighting, and hatchet-throwing.

But he would die before he let anything happen to Bryn.

He glanced down at his burning side. A red gash ran alongside his rib, staining the brown tunic with dark red blood. It wasn't a deep wound by any means, but Brynwen would be irritated that he had ruined yet another tunic. In his defense, it wasn't as if he had *asked* to be shot at.

After a few more heartbeats, he decided to move around to seek better vantage at a different location. Another fine specimen of a tree stood about a quarter of the way around the clearing.

He only took three steps when the faintest sound caught his ear. Leaves rustling on the ground—a foot dragging in the foliage. An uneducated woodsman or a wounded squirrel? Talfryn inched closer, hatchet lifted at eye level for a strike, if one came, and peeked an eye into the clearing.

A gnat picked this time to land and climb up his nose. *Shoo!* he told the gnat mentally. He wiggled his nose. A sneeze came on. *Bad timing, fly!* He drew the hatched up to shoo away the annoying winged insect when—

Dink!

The point of an arrow glanced off the metal head of the hatchet and shifted its way into the side of a tree. But the force pushed the blunt hatchet edge into his cheek. He pitched into the tree behind him, scratching his ear and shoulder on the rough bark. Bright colors filled his vision, followed by angry bursts of stinging on his whole face. The blasted weapon struck his cheek but managed to miss his nose. It might have been sliced right off...

"He's there," a call came from a short way off.

Might as well get it over with.

Talfryn said a quick prayer, braced himself, and sauntered into the clearing.

BRYNWEN OPENED her ears to the sounds of the forest. It was made difficult, however, with the pounding of her heart against her rib cage.

Dusty and Darrin's stampede had only slowed the huntsmen down for a few moments, but they would catch up soon. Where was Padric? She knew she shouldn't have sent him away, but they needed food, and Padric seemed to need a little time to himself for a little while. She never expected someone to find them so fast, if at all.

She heard Talfryn's muffled voice in the clearing. He had met with someone. *Please be careful*, she begged silently and sent up a prayer for his protection.

Stretching her concentration for any signs of the men following her, she clutched at the ring atop the bird cage. Were all the huntsmen with Talfryn? She dared take a glance at her brother's fight. If only to see if she could help in some way.

Within the cage, Nessie cooed softly, though Brynwen could detect its distress. "Keep quiet, little one," she whispered, though she experienced the same anxiousness.

With slow steps toward the clearing, she paused every so often to listen again.

A sharp rustle in the brush sounded to her right.

Brynwen jumped and launched herself behind the nearest tree, drawing Padric's dagger in her shaking hand. Breaths coming in short rasps, she took a gander around the tree. A brown rabbit, thin as a bare spool, emerged from the brush.

She let out a sigh of relief.

"A might sore sight for a rabbit, you might say," a raspy voice said from behind.

Brynwen's breath caught.

Slowly, she turned her head toward the speaker. She recognized him instantly as one of the men by the stream. He was a tall, spindly man, the skin of his face bearing the signs of a hard life outside in the sun. Brown and worn as a piece of old leather. His beaklike nose had been broken at least twice, and never set properly. A knowing smile revealed a wide gap between his front teeth.

"T'wouldn't be right proper to fix 'im up in a stew. All skin and bone." He shook his head. "It'd barely flavor the broth a'tall."

"Why," Brynwen swallowed, while trying to hide her rising fear, "you could add a number of spices and herbs to season the stew. And a few vegetables. Like carrots."

"Nah, carrots'd ruin the pot. I'm a game man, meself." He winked at her. "Now, if you'd be so kind as to hand over your knife there, we can get a move on." She shrunk away from him. "Be a good lass and don't give us trouble."

"I—I think I will keep it. Thanks all the same."

"Oh, but Drogo won't be pleased one bit if I brought you back hurt, like. Not pleased a'tall."

This would not end well. She needed to keep him talking until she could formulate a plan to get back to Talfryn and Padric. "He doesn't have to know. I can just be on my way, and you can say that I got away." She took a small step back.

"Come on, love." He moved closer, raising his hand in supplication. "Give it to old Teddy."

"What is that?" Brynwen asked, peering around his shoulder in the distance.

"What?" Teddy turned around in a lazy half-circle.

"In that clump of birches. I saw something move."

"I don't see nothin'."

She bolted—in the opposite direction from where Teddy stood stupidly gazing at some boring birch trees.

Anyone following her could find her easily, she knew, as she must be throwing all flora and fauna into a tizzy with her loud thrashing. But how long did she have to run before she was safe?

She dove behind a thick tree trunk. A long, thick branch lay on the ground. Hefting it up, she swung just in time to smash it against Teddy's chest. He cried out and fell backward head over heels, feet flying into the air.

Without waiting, Brynwen continued the mad dash.

A sound picked up behind her—feet crashing through leaves. They clomped heavier than Teddy's thin frame could muster.

Brynwen's stomach lurched. *He's gaining!* The trees swept past. The road was only a few steps away—

Her body jerked back, an explosion of color filling her vision. Then darkness.

THE POUNDING in her head roused Brynwen, and a groan escaped her dry lips. Then a short bout of coughing took her. She blinked. Then blinked again, her vision clearing somewhat. She lay on the hard ground, still in the forest. A man stood over, his face twisted in a scowl. The man with the beard from the spring. *Drogo.*

Oh no.

He had caught and yanked on her braid, hard, when she was just steps from the road. Hard enough to pull her feet out from under har and tumble to the ground.

She glanced from left to right, trying to find an escape. There had to be something she could do. But Drogo would not be easy to fool like Teddy.

"You run like a jackrabbit, young lady. I almost didn't catch you." Drogo's full beard encroached upon her spotty vision. Gray eyes peered into her own. "Now come along, my friends are waiting. And we'll see if they're done playing with your brother." She could almost see the cruel smile under his ugly beard.

She glowered at him, but deep inside her stomach twisted. *Is he speaking the truth about Talfryn?*

Brynwen flinched as he yanked her up by the arm. She tugged back, but his grip only tightened. Alarm bells rang in her head as the woodsman reached for her satchel.

"Nay!" she cried and swatted at his hand. She turned to run.

He restrained her hands, bruising her knuckles. Deftly he plucked the dagger Padric had given her out of the bag. "This is nice. You won't be needing this."

"I will if you don't let me go." Fury boiled behind her eyes, but she paid attention as he flipped the blade in the air, caught it by the hilt, and tucked it in his belt.

Drogo laughed. He shrugged as he said, "If you can get it, go ahead and try."

Before she could brush off her skirt, Drogo grabbed her wrists again and tied them together. Then he shoved her forward. Biting her bottom lip, she held back a smart remark.

Keeping his viselike grip on her arm, he led her back the way they had come. He held the cage in his free hand. Brynwen worried for the bird. Taking a quick peek around the woodsman's wide stomach, she spotted Nessie sitting on the floor of the cage. Quiet, but unhurt—that she could see.

"He shan't be pleased that you'll not cooperate," Drogo said. "But he wouldn't be surprised if you did cause trouble."

"Who is 'he'?"

"You'll see. Come along."

Puzzled, Brynwen trudged alongside him. She wondered if Drogo and his men also took Signore Gregorio.

The skin was sore where her hair met her scalp. She imagined angry red welts there. It irked her that he would use her own hair against her. In good news, the satchel still resided around her shoulders, and the man had not moved to take it. Only the dagger. Why?

Teddy caught up to them, rubbing his chest. He glared daggers at Brynwen.

As they plodded onward, she hoped Padric or Talfryn would come leaping out of the trees and fight Drogo. Where were they? Were they alive? Did Talfryn escape, and did Padric get attacked, too? She prayed for their safety. *If they escaped, surely they would come looking for me. But how will they find me?* If she had gotten completely off track, they could be in a separate part of the forest. No, Talfryn was a decent tracker, and Padric even more so. Their combined skills would successfully find her if they came searching.

But as each step progressively led them to the campsite, back to where she had last seen her brother, a cold fear ripped at her heart that something had gone terribly wrong for both of them.

CHAPTER 38

Talfryn stood at the edge of the clearing. "You found me," he said to anyone within earshot. "How clever of you. I suppose it's my turn to be the seeker now. Shall I close my eyes and count to ten, or do we start over? I can't ever quite remember the rules."

From the trees, a man emerged. He was smaller than the bearded Drogo, maybe a few years older than Talfryn, but otherwise had no interesting facial characteristics. The one outstanding feature on this man was the tight muscles which fought against the woolen fabric of his tan shirt, indicating he was no stranger to hard work. Probably fighting, too. His right hand clutched a spear with a wooden shaft. A perfect weapon for launching at a wild boar. Talfryn just hoped he himself wouldn't be considered a wild boar. Could this be the "Jeffrey" the bearded man had spoken of?

"I think," said Talfryn, "the rule states that you are supposed to hide until I find you. But, instead, I see you are surrendering. I accept."

Without a word, Jeffrey launched the spear at Talfryn. It traveled straight for his heart.

The spear whistled past as Talfryn dove out of the way. Before hitting the ground, he cast his hatchet. The blade lodged itself into the nearest tree with a loud *thunk*. Eyes wide, Jeffrey only just narrowly missed receiving the hatchet in his temple.

"Surrender now?" Talfryn asked.

His adversary smirked. "It'll take more than a puny farmer as yourself to make me surrender."

How did Jeffrey know Talfryn was a farmer?

Cracking his knuckles, Jeffrey continued. "You're no match for me, lad."

"With your tiny stick and my hatchet? I think it wouldn't exactly be a standstill."

"What do you say to hand-to-hand combat?"

"Suits me just fine." Roughhousing had been common enough for Talfryn growing up. He fought often with his brother Samuel, cousins, and friends. All for the sake of boredom, arguments, or pretty maids. Most fights ended with a laugh and a slap on the back, sometimes a call for a rematch.

Talfryn threw the dagger from his second holster into the ground two yards away as Jeffrey tossed a long knife from his boot toward a sapling.

Then they began. They each took a few steps in a circle. Jeffrey made the first move, lunging with a meaty fist. Talfryn sidestepped away and tapped Jeffrey's shoulder. Talfryn rallied as the woodsman grunted.

Now they grappled in earnest, neither giving an inch.

This close, Talfryn could smell the sweat reeking off his opponent. Stale ale wafted from his seething mouth into Talfryn's awaiting nose.

"When this is over, mate, you should take a bath. There's a nice stream over there..."

That got Jeffrey's ire up. He loosened his grip to swing at Talfryn.

His hand hit air, though, as Talfryn nudged him in the ribs.

Jeffrey howled in pain and released his grip. He had barely retreated a step before Talfryn pounced on him. They rolled on the ground, punches flying and grunts blaring. The wildlife seemed to come alive during their fight. They were likely disrupting the whole forest. Jeffrey's friends would probably descend on them at any moment.

Before long, Talfryn was partially blinded when a cut on his brow bled into his eye. He tried blinking it away, but it only got worse. He didn't even realize it when he elbowed Jeffrey straight in the forehead. The woodsman's head fell to the forest floor like a rock.

Talfryn remained on the ground next to the unconscious Jeffrey, catching his breath and trying to sop up the blood on his face with the sleeve of his ruined tunic. His elbow throbbed, but probably not as much as Jeffrey's head would when he awoke.

He was about to get up when he heard a *snap* of a branch nearby.

My hatchet!

"Tal!" a female voice shouted behind him.

Is that Brynwen? She's all right!

"Look ou—"

He whirled, but before he could move far, something hard hit his head.

It took a couple heartbeats to get his bearings. He lay on his face with a pounding headache.

People spoke directly above him. It sounded muffled at first, but then cleared up.

Something touched his arm.

"I said don't touch him!" Brynwen shouted.

Despite his headache, Talfryn jerked around. She wasn't alone, and by the tone her companion likely wasn't Padric.

"Stop struggling, lass. It will all be over soon," came a man's gruff reply. Drogo.

Drogo shoved Brynwen forward. With a cry, she took two stumbling steps toward Talfryn, her mouth distorted in a scowl. Her hands were tied together in front of her.

Talfryn's chest burned. "Leave her be," he warned, getting to his feet as fast as he could—which wasn't very fast at all. Brynwen's eyes lit up. But they soon darkened again as she winced from Drogo's vise-like grip. The scrawny fellow from the stream stood next to them, in stark contrast to Drogo's bulk.

Talfryn wondered at his chances of taking on two men at one time. Maybe if he could take the scrawny one down first...

The bearded Drogo set down Nessie's cage and turned to the thin man. "I will take care of this. Teddy, watch her." The thin mad stepped forward and grabbed Brynwen's arm from Drogo.

Slowly, Drogo approached Talfryn, no weapon in hand. Talfryn's unease grew as the bearded man drew closer. Even though Talfryn had bested brawny Jeffrey, Drogo's sheer strength and size nearly doubled Talfryn's own. The man was as large as a bear. In fact, Talfryn wouldn't be surprised if Drogo had actually fought a bear single-handedly, without a weapon, and won. He probably lifted whole tree trunks before breakfast as a light exercise.

This was life or death. *If I fail, I'll probably be dead. But if I'm dead, I can't protect Bryn. She has the amulet, and they could steal it from her. Then Padric won't be able to save the world.*

No, he couldn't lose.

Bracing himself, Talfryn prepared for the slaughter. "I don't suppose you'd care to surrender? I mean, poor Jeffrey didn't. And look at him." He dared take his eyes off Drogo for half a heartbeat to steal a glance at his sister. Her face had turned white as a sheet. Wonderful, even *she* had no faith in his abilities.

"A lucky blow's more'n likely," Drogo said. "You should've stayed down, lad."

Behind him, Teddy nodded sagely.

Drogo was upon him in half a stride, swinging a bear fist at Talfryn's face. Talfryn backed up and got a cuff to the chin. Drogo swiped again and again. Talfryn punched the man's chest, but his knuckles came back bruised and nearly broken, having no effect on his target. *What is this guy made of? Bricks?*

Intending to bowl the man over, Talfryn plunged forward. But Drogo punched him in the face instead. Again, the farmer found himself groaning on the ground.

Breathing hard, Talfryn turned his aching head toward his sister. Struggling to get free of Teddy's grip on her forearms, it was all he could do to keep her at bay. Tears streamed down her cheeks. She kicked at her captor, begging for release. "He'll kill him!"

Drogo leaned over and picked Talfryn up by the arms without any effort and set him on unsteady feet.

Through the haze, Talfryn heard Teddy clear his throat. "Just finish 'im off, boss. It's getting dark."

The bearded woodsman grumbled. "A woodsman who is afraid of the dark. Unbelievable." He lifted his arm and slapped Talfryn across the cheek. Talfryn's head snapped around, and he stumbled.

In the waning light, out of the corner of his eye, he spotted a cloak of green hidden just within the shadows. Padric! Talfryn's heart leapt at the sight of his friend.

The hood was pulled down low over his face, so Padric's expression was completely hidden. Why didn't he jump in to help? Maybe he waited for his chance to help when he could have the advantage.

Instead of rushing out into the melee, Padric gestured toward Brynwen, beckoning her to come to him.

Brynwen spied him as well and looked to Talfryn for guidance.

Talfryn's priority was to get her out, to safety. He nodded. *Go.*

To keep the woodsman distracted, he swung his arm up for a cut to the chin, but it was deflected with ease. Again, he tried, and lost his balance. Drogo caught his shoulder with an elbow, making the farmer lose his footing. Talfryn tried pivoting out of the way, but the larger man took a long stride behind him. Twisting Talfryn's left arm painfully behind his back, the larger man wrapped his other arm around the farmer's throat.

Before Talfryn could raise a finger to fight back, the arm tightened around his throat, squeezing the air from his lungs. His fingers pawed and clawed at Drogo's face and arms. The breaths were squashed out of him. He was sure his face resembled a ghastly shade of blue.

The cry from his sister was loud enough to wake the dead. "Leave him alone!"

Brynwen tore out of Teddy's grip and ran forward to save her brother. But before she could reach him, Teddy yanked a chunk of her dress and hauled her back.

"Keep her quiet," Drogo growled.

Talfryn continued to struggle, though the effort quickly took its toll. It would not be long now. He couldn't hold back forever. She had to get free.

Drogo pivoted just enough so Talfryn could see Brynwen elbow Teddy in the face. He gave a cry and let go of her arms. Her shoe smashed his foot, and in the same step dashed over to pound on Drogo's back in a fury.

Incensed, Drogo elbowed Brynwen in the chest, and she bowled over to the ground. Padric leaped out and grabbed her, hauling her back into the shelter of the trees. She'd barely had time to catch the ring on Nessie's cage as they passed.

Black spots danced in front of Talfryn's eyes as his breathing became more labored.

His knees buckled.

A faint sound of muffled voices caught the edge of his attention. But he was too far gone to make out the words.

Bryn is safe.

Peace spread in his chest, even as the last bit of his breaths petered out.

CHAPTER 39

Do not black out.

Padric panted against the harsh bark of a birch tree near the clearing where he had left the twins earlier. It took everything to keep his wounded left arm steady as he aimed the bow, even as warm blood soaked the back of his tunic. The broken arrow shaft remained in his arm. *One more time*, he willed encouragement to his shaking limb.

After the change back into a centaur, it took a minute for his body to adjust before being able to rush back to his friends. For their sakes, he prayed it was not a minute too long.

Stepping out into the clearing on four hoofs, bow ready to shoot at anything, his breath caught at the sight before him.

A bear of a man stood choking the life out of Talfryn. His face as white as a Christmas goose, Talfryn clawed limply at the strong man. Another man—dangerously thin—sat nearby, rubbing at his bloody nose and unshod foot. His worn boot lay on the ground. A fourth man struggled to sit up, a large knot growing above his eyebrow.

But where was Brynwen?

Talfryn's knees buckled.

Panic constricted Padric's chest.

"Let him go," he shouted.

The thin man turned around and gave a startled cry when he saw Padric. "Ahh, Drogo..."

"I'm a little busy here, Teddy."

"Halt," Padric called. His arm thrummed in protest, but he ignored it. He let loose a warning arrow. It shot forward and embedded itself into the ground less than an inch from the woodsman's large foot. This time Drogo glanced up, and his eyes bulged.

"Wh-what..." he stammered, nearly dropping the limp Talfryn. He stared with wide eyes at Padric. "What are you?"

"Release him." Padric had already nocked another arrow. "Now, or you will have a hole large enough in your forehead for a third eye. Your friends shall call you Triclops."

Drogo regained his composure and grinned. "I'd like to see you try."

Padric tightened his grip on the bow string. "Do not tempt me. I have had a tiring day and am in no mood to argue."

Teddy glanced nervously between the two men, sweat covering his forehead. "Drogo, give him up, mate. It's not worth it."

Scowling, Drogo threw Talfryn's lifeless body on the ground like a sack of flour. Padric restrained himself from shooting the man in the face anyway.

The bear of a man's eyes betrayed a small twinkle of surprise, then clamped down with gruff annoyance. "You'd better watch your back, son."

"Where is the maid?" Padric asked. If anything happened to her...

The large man eyed Teddy, still holding his bleeding nose. "Teddy, where did she go?"

"She went that-a-way," Teddy said, waving his arm to the right. "Someone came and scooped 'er up. Then poof, they was gone."

"And why didn't you follow her?" Drogo asked.

"I'm crippled, Drogo! Can' ye no' see me foot's crushed?"

"Never mind," Padric snapped. "Some of your other men are lying wounded south of the road. I suggest you go tend to them."

Drogo took a dangerous step forward.

The bow string twitched between Padric's impatient fingers. "Go before I change my mind."

Drogo stared intently at Padric for a moment, then his expression turned grim. "Good luck with everything, mate. You're going to need it where you're going." Drogo said "mate" with as much charm as a venomous snake. Padric wanted to scream when Drogo kicked Talfryn hard with his boot as he walked past, his friend's head bobbing to the side.

Teddy helped the wounded, muscled man to his feet. He took one last nervous glance at Padric before limping off after Drogo.

As soon as they had gone, Padric staggered over to Talfryn. Dropping the bow and arrow to the ground, he carefully knelt over his friend. The large red and purple welts covering his face and throat made Padric swoon with nausea. He shook his friend's arm. "Talfryn. Wake up. Tal..." A wave of relief swept over him as Talfryn's chest rose and fall.

The farmer's head lolled, and gave a weak cough, eyes fluttering.

Padric patted his cheeks with the back of his hand. "*Talfryn.*"

With effort, Talfryn opened his eyes. "Pad—Padric." The farmer's voice rasped, and he let out another bout of coughing. "You came back. Where's Bryn?" The farmer attempted to sit up, clutching at Padric's bloody shirt.

Padric grabbed his arm for support. "Someone took her. We must help her."

Talfryn's eyes surveyed Padric, blinking back his confusion. "Your cloak...where is it?"

"My cloak?" Puzzled, Padric looked around him. "I must have left it back where I was attacked. Come, we must go after her. Can you run?" He stood up.

That was when Talfryn let out a startled cry.

"What? What is it?" Padric circled around and reached for his sword. "How did you—when did you—"

Padric did not like the way his friend stared at him. "What?"

Without a word he pointed at Padric. More to the point, at his legs.

Padric glanced down. Four chestnut legs. His cheeks flushed. He had forgotten that the twins never saw his centaur form. "I—I will explain later. Come, there is no time to waste."

Talfryn caught Padric's bloody sleeve. "Go after her. I'll catch up."

"Nay, I will carry you. Get on."

"Fine, just...hurry," Talfryn begged, voice ragged.

THE LIGHT GREW dimmer as Padric, with Talfryn on his back and holding on for dear life, broke through the trees at breakneck speed. Twigs and leaves scratched at their faces and arms. Padric leapt over fallen logs while dodging tree trunks and limbs. Roots attempted to trip him up every few feet.

None of that mattered if they failed to save Brynwen in time.

Breathless, as they reached the clearing, much of Padric's stamina reached its limits. Panting heavily, he leaned over to catch his breath. Power—that was the only way he could describe it—seeped out of him, and in moments he shrunk to his knees onto the ground, every extremity writhing in pain. Talfryn rolled off his back and shrunk away in horror as he witnessed the transformation. When at last Padric opened his eyes, the draining and twisting of his gut had mostly stopped, and he took great gulps of air.

With the help of the nearest tree, he rose to his hoofs. Back to faun form.

Not too far away, a feminine shout caught his ears.

Brynwen.

"Go," Talfryn said, still on the ground.

Hastening toward the edge of the trees, Padric pulled forth his bow and spied two figures in hot debate on the other side of a rocky clearing with tall grass at the edge of a hill or cliff. One was Brynwen. The other, their back facing the faun, wore a hooded cloak—Padric's cloak. They argued over something she held at bay. She backed up a few steps, but the other followed, not letting her escape. The bird cage rested at her feet, and Nessie twittered frantically within.

So it was true, someone took his cloak while he fought Drogo's men. Why would they do that?

Taking a deep breath, Padric slung the bow across his shoulder and unsheathed his sword.

Despite his hoofs, he was able to sneak up unheard. As he crept closer, Brynwen peered in the faun's direction for a fleeting moment.

Whatever she was doing, it had the cloaked person's attention. Now if she could only keep it until he caught up to them.

He sprang forward, picking up speed on the last steps over uneven ground. Tall grass swished at his heels.

But just before he could take Brynwen's captor by surprise, the figure wheeled around and sprang into attack, flashing steel. Padric pulled his sword up just in time. The cloaked man and Padric fought tooth and nail. Foot and hoof. Despite his earlier exertion, the fight gave Padric a burst of energy. For every one of Padric's thrusts, the other parried easily, and vice versa. Padric sidestepped, and the other followed. Almost as though each knew every move the other would make. There was something quite familiar about his movements, but Padric could not put a finger on it. One thing was sure—he had military training.

Dusk fell quickly, and the shadows darkened, barring any hope of seeing his antagonist's facial features above the stubbly chin. Cloak, as Padric called him, never uttered a word, and barely even a grunt.

Cloak stumbled on a loose rock, opening his defenses wide. Advantage granted, Padric lunged at Cloak's chest. As he drew near enough to draw blood, a glint of steel reflected off the setting sun. With reflexes like a cat, Padric grabbed at Cloak's wrist. Together, they struggled with the dagger.

"Brynwen, run!" Padric shouted.

Padric struck Cloak's wrist and the knife flew from his fingertips landing at Brynwen's feet.

With her hands still tied, Brynwen picked it up and retreated a ways. The remains of the sun glinted off the other item she held: gold on a silver chain.

The amulet.

Cloak lunged at her, hand outstretched toward the chain.

Brynwen cried out and raised her dagger. The glint of steel arced and sliced Cloak's forearm. In shock, he retracted his arm.

Good lass, Padric thought as he moved toward the pair.

Again, Brynwen retreated a step. Her foot connected with the birdcage, and she tottered. She took another faulty step to compensate, but too late. Rocks cracked and the cage slid on the ground. Brynwen's eyes grew wide as her body swayed over the edge. The cloaked man made one last lunge for the amulet.

"Bryn!"

A step behind the maiden's kidnapper, Padric stretched out his free hand toward hers.

"Padric!"

"Take my hand—"

Their fingers grazed as he reached toward her wrist.

Eyes wide, she struggled to grip his arm.

A great force struck him in the side and knocked him off balance. Their fingers untangled. Still groping for Brynwen's hand, he caught a glimpse of her expression, terror filling her eyes and a scream forming on her lips and then ringing out as she fell.

He hit the ground hard with a grunt, the cloaked figure landing on top of him in a tangle of green cloth. He shoved Cloak off but was too late.

Brynwen was gone.

Over the edge and into oblivion.

CHAPTER 40

"*B*ryyyyn!"

Padric stared at the place where Brynwen had stood only a moment before. It was as though daggers were piercing his heart. Padric felt his guts twisting and wrenching. Taking a deep, painful breath, he desperately shoved the assailant off of him. The hooded man grunted and almost tore the green material.

"Brynwen!"

Padric rose to an elbow, but before he could jump to his hoofs, a black boot connected with his cheek. Lightning flashed through his eyes with a sharp throb.

Shaking his head, his sight cleared in time to see the flash of metal. At the last moment Padric rolled to the side—the dagger lodged itself harmlessly into the ground.

He turned his head to find Talfryn at the edge of the wood, peering down at the river. Then without a word, the farmer took off into the trees. Cloak dislodged his dagger from the ground and disappeared into the woods in the same direction as Talfryn.

Please let there be a ledge, Padric hoped in desperation. *A branch...anything.* He scrambled to his knees and peered over the edge. His hope plummeted with the sheer drop of no less than forty feet. Directly below jutted rocks that could smash a body to pieces, and beneath those, a rushing river. There was no sign of Brynwen, but her body could have been swallowed up by the rapids and swept away with the current.

Gone.

And the amulet went with her.

Crimson filled Padric's vision. Heat expanded in his lungs. It radiated off his body.

Brynwen was gone.

Gone.

And Cloak was responsible.

An animal rage launched Padric to his hoofs. Chest heaving, he sprinted after the murderer.

❧

As Talfryn dashed through the forest, he cursed himself for coming too late to Brynwen's rescue. He had only caught the last trace of his sister falling over the cliff's edge, Padric and the green-cloaked man locked arm in arm as she fell.

He charged to the edge of the cliff just in time to see her satchel surface and then get carried away down the river. But his sister did not arise from the water with it.

A crazed desperation drove him to find the satchel now. She had to be with it. She would never leave her precious bag of herbs and medicines behind.

The woods descended down a hill at a steep incline, making Talfryn very nearly collide with at least three large tree trunks in the growing darkness. But as he emerged from the forest, he was relieved to find that the satchel floated close to the shore, the current less swift as it neared land. As Talfryn splashed in waist-deep and reached for it, the waves he created pushed it away again.

No, no, no, no, no.

"Bryn!"

He followed it before it ventured farther out to where he could not follow. For he had never learned to swim and didn't care to learn just now. Splashing to chest height, he stretched out to reach the long arm strap but came up empty.

He got it on the next try.

Into the water he waved his free arm frantically. "Bryn!" He called her name, the distress rising in his breathing, mind, and heart. He lost track of how many times he called her name.

Perhaps she was farther downstream.

Not giving up, he pulled the soggy satchel to his chest, then carefully turned around on the slippery river bottom.

The cloaked man stood on the shore, breathing heavily, a dagger glinting in his hand.

Wordlessly, the assailant gestured for Talfryn to approach.

"Are you serious?" he said to the dark one, bracing his feet on the river bottom. "You killed my sister, you—" He slipped on a slick stone and flung backward, his head going under and inhaling a mouthful of water. Spluttering back to the surface, he found a foothold and coughed miserably.

The hooded man stepped into the river and waded toward him, his dagger raised at eye level. Talfryn was trapped.

Without a weapon, he was virtually defenseless against the sharp steel. He hadn't had time to retrieve his hatchet before chasing after Brynwen. Talfryn stood his ground, though. He wouldn't lose the last thing in the world he had left of his sister.

"You're not taking it."

The cloaked man neither agreed nor argued as he continued to approach. Then he launched at Talfryn. The farmer sidestepped to dodge the blow, almost losing his balance again. With his free hand, Cloak grabbed Talfryn around his already sore neck and yanked hard. Talfryn cried out, spun, and crashed his elbow into the man, then tried to wriggle free of his grip.

Another loud splashing joined their cacophony.

Please, not more woodsmen.

Talfryn craned his neck and saw Padric approach. Grabbing the cloaked man by the arm, Padric sent a punch into his covered face. The man grunted and released his grip on Talfryn.

The water now reached almost to his chin, and he couldn't steady his feet on the slippery bottom.

Panic flooded his brain as he waved his free arm about helplessly. This did absolutely nothing to help his predicament, as Padric and the cloaked man were too busy fighting one another to notice Talfryn being pulled away by the rapids. His head pitched under, and he swallowed another lungful of water.

A wild thought struck him as he was carried away: he might find Brynwen at the end...

&

From the trees, Padric had seen Talfryn struggling with the cloaked man. When at last he splashed into the water, they were more than chest deep. Wishing he still had his dagger, Padric grabbed a chunk of the stranger's cloak and yanked, sending swift punches to the man's covered face, back, and shoulder.

Alarm filled Padric when he lost sight of Talfryn. *Where did he go?* He never made it to shore.

Ten yards downriver, Talfryn's head popped up. He gasped for air, splashing.

Talfryn!

First Brynwen, now Talfryn. He could not lose both twins.

He pushed off the loose riverbed to go after him.

Cloak's arm blocked him, sending Padric's head below the surface. Padric emerged and gasped a breath. A long hunting knife greeted him.

Padric dodged whirled, shoving Cloak back. They scuffled in the water, every movement slow.

His knuckles connected with Cloak's jaw when an explosion of red and white and black filled his vision. Something slid against his skin. Padric's eyes grew wide with the shock as a radiating warmth spilled endlessly from his abdomen. Cloak raised his bloody, dripping dagger from the water. Padric sensed a smile form beneath Cloak's hood.

Fury raced through Padric's veins. He thought of Brynwen as she fell to her death. Talfryn, as he raced away down the river. Padric's rage only grew.

"No, I refuse to die at your hands," he said.

Padric lunged at him. Cloak fumbled the knife, losing it to the water. Exerting all his energy, he pummeled Cloak. His left arm burned with each exertion, but he agonized through the pain.

Before they knew it, they moved deeper into the water. Thrashing at each other. Rolling over and over, each spluttering in turn as their heads resurfaced to spit out the vile river water.

Then Cloak released his grip on Padric's arm. With a weary shove, he leaned back and separated himself from Padric, kicking toward the other side of the river. They stared at each other for an eternal heartbeat, then Cloak swam clumsily toward shore.

Every ounce of strength Padric had dwindled to almost nothing. Too weak to do much other than trying to keep afloat, Padric continued down the river. Everything hurt. How far had Talfryn gone? He hoped to heaven that he had not drowned.

Then—there he was, on the south side.

With the last burst of his strength, he made long strokes to where his friend clasped desperately to the very end of a heavy, leafless branch of a fallen tree lying in the water. Talfryn's brown head dunked for a heartbeat, and Padric feared he was lost, when he came up with a splash and a gasp.

At last, Padric reached the tree branch and clenched onto the thicker part of the limb. Tugging a fistful of Talfryn's tunic, he pulled against the current. Padric let out a huff of exertion as Talfryn reached for the larger, sturdier part of the branch and took firm hold. His face paled in the ascending moonlight. He looked ill and had likely swallowed much of the river.

Weakening from loss of blood, dark and lighter spots intermingled with each other in Padric's eyesight as he vied for a firmer hold. But his fingers were clumsy, fumbling for a better grip on the tree.

In the back of his mind, he knew he should be panicking. But his brain and body were too numb.

Talfryn shouted something, but Padric heard little over the loud water rushing by his ears. Too exhausted to hear.

"Are you all right?" Padric asked, his tongue heavy.

"I...think so," came the response. At least, he thought that was the reply.

"Good enough." And his fingers let go of the branches, letting the river carry him away.

Talfryn's eyes grew wide. He lurched toward the faun, but just missed his hand. Padric thought he heard his name from afar.

A cold darkness swallowed him up as his consciousness faded in and out.

Then his head dipped under the water.

CHAPTER 41

anic.

Giant chicken.

Panic.

Darkness.

Kisses.

Long, slobbery, smelly kisses.

"Get lost, Finn," Talfryn said, groggily swatting at the dog. A thorough licking commenced on his face again. Dog breath. *Argh.* As he shifted away, a roiling began in his stomach, and he thought he would be sick.

Scratch that, he was most definitely going to be sick.

After what appeared to be a quarter of the river completely evacuating his stomach, he rolled again onto his back.

A snout nuzzled him. "Finn. Can't you see I'm trying to sleep here?" But the nuzzling continued. At least the barking had stopped.

Talfryn groaned and groggily cracked open an eye.

Large, dark orbits met his. Blinked. But they did not belong to Finn.

Startled into a sitting position, Talfryn scrambled back a pace. In the darkness, the creature's eyes appeared to crinkle—as though in amusement.

Talfryn wiped at his tired eyes. "This is not funny," he said to the universe.

The universe did not answer back.

The stag continued to stare at him, the dark river rushing about two yards behind it.

But where was his dog Finn? Oh, right, he stayed at home.

What was strange about the stag, besides the fact that it willingly stood a couple feet away from him, was the giant bird wings hanging from its back. And the long sweeping tail full of feathers. A...chicken-stag? He recalled how, his eyes blurry from river water, he could have sworn that a giant chicken was coming in to land on top of him. "I must still be dreaming. Or Dead. Unhappily dead."

The chicken-stag shook its head, *No*.

He scratched his head. This stag...chicken....thing....had saved him. "Umm, thanks, for saving me, Sir Stag. Where are my friend and sister?"

Talfryn followed the gaze of the chicken-stag to a long, dark lump next to him. There was only one lump. *Padric?*

"Padric." The faun didn't move. Heart racing, he turned Padric over onto his back. It took quick work to glance over his body, and he found two deep, dark splotches. One on his arm, the other at his side.

No, no no.

Talfryn placed his head to Padric's chest and heard a heartbeat. Sighing gratefully, Talfryn pulled at a large tear in Padric's tunic to get a better look at the wound. He gasped at the deep gash cut into the faun's left side. Ripping off his own sopping, ruined shirt, Talfryn squeezed as much water out of it as he could, wadded it up, and shoved it into the knife wound.

His heart sank. How could he help him? Brynwen was the one with the medical knowledge. Where was she?

At that moment, the stag appeared next to Talfryn. Clenched in its teeth, Brynwen's satchel hung from the strap, large droplets of water dripping all over the grass.

"Please tell me you found my sister, too."

No answer.

The stag nudged the bag at him. Talfryn peered at the bag, then at the stag, then back at the bag. A knot tightened in his stomach.

"Don't look at me like that, Bryn can fix Padric up when she gets here. Should be any time now, I expect. Better yet, I should go search for her."

In the dark?

He glanced at the unconscious Padric. He needed help *now*.

"Fine," Talfryn said, yanking the bag out of the stag's teeth. "I'll—I'll start and then Bryn can finish up when she gets here."

The memory of her falling from the cliff brought a lump to his throat. *She will be here. She* will.

Then he remembered that he was talking to an animal, and the only other human in the group was unconscious.

He didn't have the time or resources to make a fire, so he worked in the moonlight. With a sigh, he dumped out Brynwen's stores and sniffed the contents of each jar and soggy pouch to find Brynwen's miracle mix. The stag nudged a substance at Talfryn. He had no idea if the stag knew what it was doing, but at this time he didn't care. He needed to save Padric.

"Where's the needle and thread?" he asked. This was his least favorite part. He took several deep breaths in an attempt to steady his shaking hands. "Dear Lord," he prayed, "please don't let me botch this up. In the dark."

At long last, the Shadow received the knight's signal.

He has obtained it!

The Shadow squeaked with glee as it faded from its hovel and emerged in the brightly lit cave. The fire crackled and spit sparks, the tongues of yellow and orange flame licking the roof. The low ceiling made the fire seem larger than it actually was.

The knight huddled in the corner cooking a rabbit on a stick and pensively staring at the object dangling from his hand—a small gold object on a silver chain.

In its excitement, the Shadow distorted and convulsed against the dark stone and dirt of the cave's walls in the firelight.

Let me see it!

The blaze intensified twofold as the Shadow jumped out from behind the fire, taking the knight off guard. Wide-eyed, the dark-haired, drenched youth kicked out, both the gold object and the stick with the skinned rabbit almost flying out of his hand.

"A little warning would be nice," the young man said with angry eyes.

Show it to me, quick!

The knight pulled the object closer to himself, then thought better of it. "Here." He held it closer to the fire, another drop of water falling from the ancient gold. Blood dripped simultaneously from his forearm. Greedy shadowed fingers flexed eagerly for the piece of gold. Then the hands froze and shrunk away.

But what is this? Where is the ring?

The knight huffed. He knew he was in trouble. "She tricked me. The little tart tricked me." He held up his wounded arm. "In my defense, it was dark."

You useless—

"Come now, don't be too hasty. There is still time. I'll scour the riverbed for their bodies. Hopefully they shan't have washed out to sea before morning. Mayhap the woodsmen will finally do their jobs right. I paid them enough." The knight made a sour face.

Leave no pebble unturned in your search. You do not wish to displease the master.

The knight screwed up his lips. "Mayhap we don't need the amulet. It's just a precaution, right? And now that de Clifton's gone, and the farmers are out of the picture..." He shrugged. *Good riddance.*

For your own sake, it better be so.

"First thing in the morning."

First thing.

CHAPTER 42

A frantic nudge jostled Talfryn awake. "Staggy, we need to talk about boundaries." He pushed the deer's head away as it chewed the grass nearest Talfryn's knee. Sleep still encumbering his eyes, he rubbed them, trying to wake up. He was too groggy to think very hard, but he felt a nagging that he was supposed to do something.

Now that he was awake...Awake—that was it! He was supposed to stay awake! He cursed at his own ineptitude at doing one simple task. Scripture came to mind: Even the apostles Peter, James, and John were unable to stay awake with Jesus for one hour as he prayed at Gethsemane...

Once again, he pushed away the emotions that threatened to leave him flailing as a newborn, as he removed Padric's bandages and examined the wounds. The wound in Padric's side looked particularly gruesome in the morning light, especially with the uneven stitches. He willed himself not to think of the perfect stitches with which his sister would have sewn the wound closed. The arm was healing better, though it was still a rough sight.

Upon glancing at the unconscious faun's face, his complexion ashen and covered in sticky sweat, Talfryn could sense an unwelcome sign of illness had crept up overnight. The slightest touch of his forehead burned against Talfryn's fingertips. Yes, Padric had lasted the night. But would he last another? Despite the June morning heat, Talfryn shivered.

With each hour that passed without a sign from Brynwen, Talfryn began to lose hope—for both his sister and his friend. Staggy refused to leave their sides all night, despite Talfryn's urging to seek her out. It was as though it knew something...

He bid the stag to stay with the wounded knight while he went to gather water. As he took a quick splash in the stream to drench his face, Dusty, Darren, and the packhorse sauntered up to graze in his area. Talfryn was overjoyed at their return. He even found his hatchet and knife in the clearing where the fight with Jeffrey and Drogo occurred.

Upon his return, with horses, water, and weapons in hand, he found a surprising sight: the stag stood protectively over the prone Padric as a sentry to a castle, hovering over his charge in the morning light, strips of drying linen hanging from his majestic antlers. Indeed, a force to be reckoned with.

While he worked to redress Padric's wounds, it occurred to Talfryn that something was missing. Something obviously other than his sister's missing person. Once again, he checked the contents of the medical satchel, and came up short one item. He remembered when they were avoiding the woodsmen, Brynwen held the bag protectively to herself—it had contained the amulet. And now it was gone.

The gorge tearing its way through his chest widened.

How could I have missed this before?

Because there were more pressing issues, Stupid.

But still...we need that wretched piece of metal! Brynwen died over it. The least it could've done was stay in its place inside the satchel.

A tear slid down his cheek as he glanced at the sleeping knight, each breath labored and uneven.

"Stay strong, Padric. I need you—you're all I have left here. Prophecy or no, I need to know this wasn't all for naught." He was tired. So tired. "Mayhap once we have our revenge on Circe and do what we came to do, we can be at peace."

More than anything, he wished he could believe his own words.

Hours later, when the sun was near to sinking below the tree line, Talfryn lit a prayer candle from his belongings. Bowing his head, he prayed for the repose of his sister's soul, that she may rest peacefully, wherever her corporal body may lie. It was perhaps the hardest thing he'd had to do in years.

The plague had taken his parents, a sorceress's lackey had taken his sister, and now he was about to lose Padric as well.

His thoughts spiraled in all directions. But mostly about Brynwen and their childhood. And Nessie the Bird, who had fallen with her. Her cage must have sunk right to the bottom of the river with the silt.

What would he do if Padric died? He didn't even want to think about continuing alone. But he would have to, somehow.

The ache in his heart was unrelenting.

Another slash of the sword thrust through his heart. *Guilt.* He should have run after her right away, despite his ailments. If Padric could run with a giant arrow in his arm, and get stabbed, Talfryn could just as well run with half the life choked and beaten out of him.

"Oh Bryn," he said into the empty space in front of him. Tears beaded down his cheeks. "Why did you leave me? Whatever shall I do now?"

A distant memory caught at his mind, of a conversation he and his sister had one evening, late into the night when they were quite young. Just after their parents had died. They were scared and felt alone, even though Samuel slept next to them, his arms around them for protection, and Grandfather downstairs in his bed. They decided that if something ever tore them from each other, by thousands of miles or death, the other would know it immediately.

As he sat here, now, he did indeed feel a gaping hole, her phantom presence constantly right beside him. Yet he didn't feel completely severed from her. Almost as if—as if she still lived and breathed somewhere. He couldn't explain it. And he didn't know if the feeling was true, or just some desperate desire.

Whatever his feelings, he would not tell Padric. How could he explain the things that only a twin would understand?

How desperate the child who holds on to these precious little wisps of hope.

And yet, he grasped with all his might.

In this life or the next, he would see her again.

"I promise."

PART III
LOST

"My name is Nobody."
—Homer, *The Odyssey*

CHAPTER 43

Padric sat along the river, water lapping over his hoofs. Clouds covered the sun's rays and the river water rushed by merrily, as though no one had died in it, that a small battle never occurred in it, or that blood ever ran through it.

He stood up, his emotions sour and body sore.

I should continue the search. But his heart was not really in it. Not anymore. After a week of coming up empty, what good would searching one more day do? Brynwen was gone and the amulet with her. What hope did he have of succeeding against Circe and rescuing her captives now? The prophecy was useless.

The knight released a breath. He limped along, his hoofs leaving prints upon the shoreline, listening to the birds and watching the water for signs of Brynwen and the amulet of obsidian.

Padric felt eyes upon his back. He turned to find his father, Garrick de Clifton, in full uniform, standing at the tree line with a grave expression. The captain of Derby and thirty knights had arrived four days ago while Padric was still convalescing, taking charge of the situation immediately upon their arrival.

Fearful for their safety, Talfryn's grandfather, Eduard Masson, had informed the captain about their plans to head north and fight an evil sorceress. It had not taken long for the regiment to follow their route.

Padric limped to the older man, wary of each jarring step. Despite his best efforts, his left hoof dragged along the ground. When he approached, he squared his shoulders and asked, though he knew the answer, "Captain, have you found anything?"

"Lieutenant," Garrick said with a shake of his head, eyes up, pointedly away from his son's cursed legs. "Nothing more than the night before. I doubt those brigands will return, though." They had searched up and down the river multiple times each day and came up empty. No Brynwen or amulet.

"Are you sure you looked far enough? She could have landed down river, or—"

"At this point, there is little to hope for, Padric. Sometimes you must know when your battles are lost."

"But—"

"Enough."

All of Padric's hope shattered to pieces by his father's abruptness.

Garrick pinched the bridge of his nose and took a breath. "My sincerest condolences to you and your friend for your loss, but sometimes these things happen. We cannot save everyone."

"Nay, sir, we cannot give up, not after all we have been through. Talfryn and I will continue the search ourselves, if need be." *If he would but speak to me.*

Garrick shook his head. "If we are going to beat this Circe woman, we had better head out first thing tomorrow, amulet or not. Nay, do not look at me that way. 'Tis for the best."

When they had arrived, Garrick had a hard enough time coming to terms with his son's goat legs. However, it aided Padric in convincing his father that a sorceress was responsible for kidnapping the villagers.

"Sir..."

Roana's prophecy and vision of destruction flashed through Padric's mind with such force his knees buckled.

As the heir to the charioteer of old

Thou wilt bear a curse of gold.
Reclaim the amulet of darkest night
To destroy the weapon of untold might,
And rescue those of whom you seek
Ere the sun attains its highest peak.

"Mayhap you should sit down, Padric," Garrick said. "Your complexion worries me."

Padric shook his head. This was not working. His father did not understand all that was at stake. "Sir, you must reconsider. Circe will rend you and our legion to shreds. She—"

"I think you underestimate my knights' abilities. We have trained our entire lives for this. We have a plan and will not back down. Our numbers will outmatch her."

His knights' abilities? And what plan? Padric had been privy to no plans concerning Circe. "Father, you do not comprehend her power. You have not seen it. She rendered four trained knights helpless with but a word. Think what she could do to a whole battalion. What can I do to make you understand?"

Garrick sighed. "Son," he said, grasping Padric by both arms, sorrow filling his eyes. Padric held in his grimace at the contact. "This is my fault. I...I set too much responsibility on your shoulders. I thought, 'My son can do anything he puts his mind to. He is bright, strong, and capable.' Now I see I have set the standards too high, put too much pressure on you. Like that inventor fellow's son..."

"Icarus."

"Err, yes, him. There is nothing you have to prove to me, lad. You have done your best, and 'tis all you can do. In fact..." he said, staring into his son's eyes, then finally glancing down at the furry goat legs and hoofs, his eyebrows forming a deep frown. "You are still recovering, mayhap you should stay here and concentrate on getting well." He gave Padric a half smile that did not quite reach his eyes.

Padric's own grew wide with shock. "What? You cannot do that! I would see this through." *It is* my *prophecy, after all.* "Only say the word, and I will be ready to march within the hour."

Shadows darkened the captain's eyes. "Padric, as much as I wish it, this is no longer your affair. My word is final."

Padric's heart plummeted to his hoofs. Without another word, Garrick patted his son's shoulder and stalked off to see to his regiment.

Not caring where his hoofs took him, Padric stumbled down the shale of the river, numb. His own father had shut him down. Shut him *out*. And now Garrick and all the knights of Derbyshire were to march to their dooms, and he had no way to stop them. What he had feared from the beginning was now all coming to pass.

Perhaps he could speak to Talfryn about it and convince him to help the captain see what they were up against. His friend still refused to speak to him because of what happened to his sister, but Padric had to try.

He encountered three knights scanning the trees and rocks along the riverbed. Aeron Drefan, Will, and George. Padric paused to hail them, but none of them noticed him. As Padric approached, he stopped and greeted Aeron. The knight did not pause in his search, as though he had not heard Padric at all.

"Sir Aeron, ho," said Padric.

The knight spun, darting his eyes at Padric. "Oh, ho there, Master de Clifton." The other knights hesitated for a moment, then continued as before.

Padric refrained from wincing at the slight of station. Since when had he been demoted to a civilian? "Sir Aeron, have you searched the shallows and the woods all along the other shore?"

"Aye, Master de Clifton, we've already checked those places. It's a waste of time if you ask me. Now, I think George, Will, and I have got it under control here."

Padric opened his mouth to protest, but closed it, clenching his jaw. So, this was how it was to be. "I will leave you to it, then," he said, and continued in his slow way past the knights.

That night, Padric could not sleep. All night, he wondered what he could have done better. How could he have let his father, his friends, the whole world down? How did he think he could ever stop Circe in the first place? His pride had led him to this place. And Brynwen paid the ultimate price for it.

After hours of tossing and turning, he emerged from his bedroll, eyes bloodshot and side burning. Resting against a thick tree in the forest at the edge of the fire's light, he glanced up at the moon. The constellations were bright, the sky full of heroes who, if they could talk, would give him no peace. He could imagine their frowns and glares upon him.

He awoke at dawn with his back chafing from the tree bark and a crick in his neck. Stretching, he was about to rise when he heard a rustle in the forest.

Has the cloaked man returned?

His fingers gripped the new dagger at his side, ready to pounce.

"Here is a good place," came a familiar voice.

Talfryn. Padric released his grip upon the dagger. This was his chance to speak with him. The farmer had not spoken a word to Padric in days.

"You sure this is far enough?" said another voice. "Your friend won't come looking for you?"

"He's no friend of mine," Talfryn replied in a rush. "I should've known better than to follow him. I should have listened to my sister in the first place. She never trusted him a wink."

Whilst Talfryn spoke, Padric moved in for a better view.

"Aye," said the other.

It irked Padric that he could not place the voice, though he had heard it before. What other knight besides Leowyn knew Talfryn? Padric moved one step closer and saw them, not more than five paces away.

He was taken by surprise at the young man speaking with Talfryn: nearly identical in appearance, but where Leowyn's hair was light, this man's hair was dark. It was Leowyn's younger brother, Jasper—and Talfryn's cousin. *Brynwen's betrothed.*

What was he doing here? Padric squinted at the pair, searching their apparel. Talfryn wore the same clothing as usual, but his cousin wore a black uniform. When did Jasper become a squire? Padric had never seen him in the barracks.

Jasper continued, his chest puffed. "Aye, Sir Padric has done enough, I say. He took yer sister away from you; my bride from me. He ain't nothin' but a boastful braggart who wished too heartily for his time in the sun."

"Don't I know it! He made it all sound like a grand adventure. Fame and glory! I thought he was strong, and smart, but I guess I was wrong. When we were attacked, he let that—that *murderer*—kill her, right in front of my eyes. While he did nothing! He didn't even try to stop him."

"Well, the captain's makin' sure he don't hurt anyone no more. We'll get vengeance for our Bryn and Leowyn. I'm glad your grandfather told the captain."

"Aye," Talfryn said, folding his arms across his chest. "I wish I had never met Padric de Clifton. If I see him again, I'll probably rip his face off with my hatchet."

"We'll do it together, 'cuz. You'n me," Jasper said, raising his dagger for emphasis.

Padric did not wait to hear Talfryn's reply. He spun on his hoof and crashed through the forest, not caring if they heard him or not.

This cannot be happening! Is everyone against me? First his father, then the knights, and now Talfryn. *What have I done? I have made a mess of everything.*

Without halting, Padric dashed out of the forest. It was obvious, he was not welcome in the knights' camp any longer. He trudged to the riverbed, not caring that his hoof dragged, his side ached, or his heart was about to burst.

The prophecy flashed behind his eyes again.

"I do not want this prophecy any longer! Do you hear me, Oracle of the Sibylline? I renounce my involvement in your grand schemes. Find another hero to do your dirty work. There are plenty of knights to choose from. You can have your pick from among the best."

The rustle of wind brushing against some leaves was his only answer.

Something floating just off the shoreline caught his eye, hooked in a small sand bar littered with stones and tall grass.

He hurried over to it. Through the grass, it appeared to be cloth of some sort. Brushing aside the greenery, he drew a sharp intake of breath.

It was *her*.

Her body floated in the water, face up with closed eyes, hair loose from the braid and framing her face, blouse and skirts swirling around her wherever the water moved them.

He nearly forgot to breathe.

"Brynwen." He whispered her name, reaching down and cupping her cheeks in his hands and lifting her head out of the water, her hair a heavy weight. He still lacked the strength to lift her entire body. So pale, the skin of her face and neck seemed almost translucent. "Wake, Bryn. You must awaken. Please."

As if bidden, her eyes fluttered and opened. Hazel eyes peered directly into his own. His heart leapt, and he laughed with joy. "I can hardly believe it! We searched everywhere for you. Fret not, you are safe now, Bryn."

She smiled back at him, and said, "Am I safe? Truly?"

"Aye. I was so afraid for you. We had all but given up hope, but Talfryn and I believed you were still alive."

"But I am not."

"Not what?"

"Alive."

"That is not humorous, Brynwen. Would I be talking to you now if you were not alive?"

"I might be a ghost. A ghost of her that was."

Her tone turned the blood in Padric's veins to ice. "What are you saying?"

"You did not save me."

Padric shifted, the weight of Brynwen becoming heavier and heavier. The water continued to flow from atop her body and drip into the shallows.

"Nay," she continued, "I am not alive. You let me drown. Drown in this foul-tasting water, where not even the fish care to dwell! You let the sorceress take me to the watery depths. My poor brother, how he must miss me, and curse you. For the rest of his days, he will rue you to your grave."

Then, Brynwen's eyes transitioned—brighter, from hazel to light blue, and then to sapphire. At the same time, her nose and cheekbones morphed. Her hair color changed to blonde, and the sapphire eyes radiated with intensity. Wild.

Circe.

Recoiling in revulsion, Padric dropped her head back into the water and crawled his way backwards to the shore.

Circe rose from the water. "Oh, young Padric de Clifton, former lieutenant of Chaddesden, Derbyshire, you cannot win. 'Tis a pity, watching your struggles, your hardships. Everyone you love has forsaken you, for will you not in the end forsake them? You could not save your friends before, and you certainly cannot now. Your entire regiment of knights is marching to their deaths, you see. You can do nothing to stop the course of the world's destruction. It breaks my heart to tell you that your journey will end in tragedy, and for all your pains, not a soul shall you save. A pure Roman tragedy, nearly worthy of Homer's papyrus."

A light sound escaped her throat. The sound grew louder, evolving into a low chuckle, then a cackle—a beautiful, though insane, cackle.

The laughter grew louder and soon became so intense, it drowned out everything, including the river itself. Padric cupped his hands over his ears and clamped his eyes shut to drown out the noise. His heartbeat intensified. He knew he should flee, but his furry legs remained rooted to the spot.

A loud cry escaped his lips, pleading it all to end.

CHAPTER 44

adric gasped.
No!

Colors ignited in his eyes as a barrage of pain erupted throughout Padric's entire body. Taking quick little breaths, he tried to bite back the great pangs as he writhed and reached for his sword. He collapsed back onto his pallet, weapon in hand. The blanket was strewn haphazardly to the side. Never had he felt so dreadful in his entire life.

"Bryn...*danger*..."

A shadow stood over him, blocking the sun.

"Circe!"

"Calm down, Padric, it's me!"

Strong hands clenched his arms, preventing him from swinging.

"Nay, vile witch!"

"Relax," said Talfryn's voice. "There's no one here. It's just a dream—a nightmare."

Instantly, Padric opened his eyes to find his friend leaning over him, expression of concern, begging him to calm down.

"Nay...I saw her..." Padric's eyes roamed around in a frantic search for Circe. Sunlight streamed through tree branches—tall trees and grass surrounded them on all sides. The two horses grazed in a lazy manner to the side, the packhorse a little farther off. "She will return. Get the captain."

"What captain?"

"Did they already leave?"

"Who?"

Rage filled Padric's lungs. "Captain de Clifton and his knights, you fool. They have been here for days."

"Padric, no one's here besides you, me, Staggy, and the horses."

Padric blinked and peered around again. "But...they were here."

"Here, let me give you something for the pain," Talfryn replied, gently pushing down on Padric's chest.

"Is Brynwen here?"

Talfryn's brows creased, and after a moment's hesitation, shook his head.

Images of the dream—was it really a dream?—flashed through Padric's mind with intermittent blasts of stabbing pain from his side and arm. His breath caught.

Brynwen is really gone. And it is all my fault.

Closing his eyes, he attempted to refrain from thinking of Brynwen, Circe, or anything. Just breathing was excruciating. He heard Talfryn rummaging through something and mumbling to himself.

When Padric opened his eyes again, it was dark, and his friend was lathering a sweet-smelling ointment onto the skin on his left side under the ribs.

Where he had been stabbed.

Padric recalled the fight with the cloaked man. He had worn Padric's own green cloak as he practically threw Brynwen over the cliff, her eyes pleading for him to help her...

He bared his teeth as Talfryn applied too much pressure on the wound.

"Sorry," Talfryn said, easing the application somewhat. "I'm not very versed in this."

The aroma caught Padric's nose. "What is it?"

"It should be comfrey. At least, partly comfrey and some other ingredients in Brynwen's Miracle Mix." He saw the skepticism on Padric's face. "Well, it's not poisonous, if you must know. And you haven't sprouted any leaves or buds, so that's a positive sign. Worst case scenario, I've been rubbing chamomile all over you, so you'll taste just dandily to the wild animals." Talfryn managed a smirk. "I've used up most of this on you, and you haven't died yet. So just hold still."

Talfryn finished with the ointment and rummaged around in his pack again. "I have water boiling for tea. Which I am quite certain *is* chamomile." He winked and turned back to the small fire and steaming pot.

"How long was I out?"

"Three nights and two days. You had a dreadful fever on the second day, but by nightfall you came around." He spun on his heel holding a tin cup. For the first time, Padric noticed the bags under his friend's eyes. His chest squeezed, knowing Talfryn must have slept very little in trying to keep him alive. And to look for...

Shaking his head, he tried to avoid the question. But the words slipped out, nonetheless.

"Did you find...any...anything else?" He gulped.

Talfryn's gaze fell to the ground, and his eyes twitched. Shaking his head, he leaned back on the balls of his feet, staring down at his hands. "I looked everywhere up and down the river during the last two days, but never found Bryn or the amulet."

"Could she have survived somewhere farther downriver?"

"*We* barely survived. And only by the grace of God. I searched as far and long as I dared but didn't find a thing."

Padric's heart tightened. Cracked. To see his friend grieve so about losing his sister. And about his own failings at saving her. Another person he couldn't save. He had left them. He had thought he could take care of it himself. How could he even start to apologize to his friend? His breathing grew more ragged.

"But I did manage to find one thing," Talfryn said. He tossed a folded green cloth on the ground beside Padric.

His cloak.

For several moments, Padric stared at the blasted piece of fabric. Barely above a whisper, he asked, "Where did you find it?"

"It was down by the river, discarded, after he..." Talfryn trailed off, silent tears running down his face. "He just discarded it."

Padric felt his own cheeks growing hot and looked away.

"Who was he?" Talfryn asked. "The man who stole your cloak?"

"I must admit, I have not the faintest idea. He never said a word, not once, and the hood completely covered his face. But his fighting style seemed very familiar and evenly matched with me, as though we had fought before, somewhere. 'Twas as if he knew my weaknesses."

"Mayhap he does know you. You said he never spoke, mayhap he was hiding his voice in case he failed to kill you."

"Mayhap."

"But that still begs the question, why did he want to kill us at all? He was certainly after the amulet. But why not just threaten us and take it?"

"Because he knew we could track him down to get it back. Or he has some vendetta against me. In either case, he will be sorely displeased when he finds out you and I yet live." He sat grimly for a moment. "It leads to the next question—why did he want the amulet, and how did he know we had it in the first place? Or that we were even searching for it? I told no one other than you and Brynwen."

"Could he have overheard us at the inn?"

"It is entirely possible." Padric sighed. "We will never know unless we catch up to him."

"Right. And get the amulet back. If he has it."

Padric's chest constricted.

"Padric? Are you in pain?"

"More than you know," he said under his breath. "I saw Brynwen put it in her pocket."

Talfryn's face twitched. "Then it is lost with her. What will we do now?"

They had no amulet. No direction.

"Honestly," Padric replied, "I know not."

They were lost in every way possible.

CHAPTER 45

Discomfort whittled its way into Padric's subconscious. At first it was just a small nuisance. But as time lingered on, it gradually became harder to bear, until it wedged a giant hole in his side.

Drops of water drizzled across his forehead, cool, with a scent of lavender. Breathing in deeply, his discomfort lessened a fraction. A memory played through his mind of one such time when someone with hazel eyes and gentle hands had soothed his ills.

All too soon the pain nagged at him again. The ache in his tricep and side increased, to distraction. He opened his eyes to find a set of hazel eyes staring down at him. He gasped.

Then he blinked.

Heart sinking, he realized they were not the hazel eyes from that memory.

Talfryn leaned over him. "There you are. Sorry about the rough handling. But I'm happy to report that you're on the mend. Wouldn't you agree, Staggy, that our patient looks much improved?" Talfryn turned his head toward the stag. The animal gave a nod so slight, Padric fancied he must have imagined it.

It took no time for Padric to recognize it. The intricate antlers. The red diamond mark over its heart.

"What is that thing doing here?" Padric asked. In the many weeks since their first encounter, the animal had toyed with him, leading him around the country, never coming within more than a few yards. Now it stood in their midst, an arms-length away, its white wings folded at its sides.

Padric blinked twice to make sure his vision did not deceive him. He was correct, the stag had a pair of *wings* on its back. He remembered the stormy night when he had chased the stag through the forest and glimpsed what appeared to be a shimmering set of wings along its back. But neither before nor since had it shown its wings as such. Why reveal them now?

"Staggy here has also been very helpful in keeping wolves and other nasties at bay," Talfryn explained.

"Staggy? *It has a name?*"

"Yes, Staggy. We're calling him 'Staggy.' Or Rupert. I haven't quite decided yet."

An ache grew between Padric's eyes. With slow strokes, he rubbed the sides of his nose with his index finger and thumb. "You have had entirely too much time on your hands to go around naming all the animals in the forest." Again, he glared at the stag. "Why do you not return to your mistress? Certainly, she has more people for you to spy on elsewhere and let the invalids convalesce in peace."

"He was instrumental in saving us. We owe him our lives."

The ache grew stronger. "What are you talking about?"

Talfryn pursed his lips. "Staggy plucked us out of the river. He didn't take us to Circe, or that hooded man, or let us drown. He saved us. And he hasn't left your side except to forage periodically for food."

"Or mayhap he withdrew to give Circe our exact whereabouts and general health."

"Are you not grateful that he saved us? You could have died, Padric. Death is the end."

"This prophecy will not let me die. Not until it is finished."

"Don't talk like that," Talfryn said in a quieter voice.

"Do not talk like what? Everyone I care about has been affected by her. My friends, so many people from Derbyshire, and now Brynwen.

And Circe knows every step we take. She even sent her agent to keep an eye on us."

"You aren't the only one who has lost loved ones, remember? He is our friend. He saved you—"

"So he could spy on us further! Do you not see? How are you so blind? We are at the mercy of an insane woman with a scepter. A cunning sorceress who uses seemingly harmless animals for her own ends. She probably gave *Staggy* here wings just so he could continue her dirty work. No wonder he is everywhere we are. He merely has to soar into the air and peer down at us to know our exact location."

"Mayhap he switched sides."

"Are you serious?"

"Look. He hasn't left your side since you fell ill. He has stood protectively over you whenever I've had to leave for even a short while. And no person or creature has attacked us once." Talfryn crossed his arms, which reminded Padric of the monkey he had once seen with a traveling circus.

"Mayhap he told them not to. He could be waiting for the right time to signal them to attack again." Padric glanced around, searching for his weapons. "And we should be ready for them." He made to move off the palette, and then quickly regretted it as a rush of nausea overcame him. Too fast and perhaps too soon to try to return to normal. Though what normal could possibly be after this, he dared not ruminate about. "The man in green could return."

"Not without this." Talfryn held up the green cloak. It had been washed in the stream and looked less worn for the wear.

"Of course not, it is in your hands. And I simply do not think he would return for it because it made his legs look quite fetching in such a lovely shade of green."

"If he was to come back, he already would have. He could have easily killed us in our incapacitated states."

"He could be searching for reinforcements," said Padric.

"Not likely."

Padric leaned back again on his good arm, the nausea dissipating somewhat.

Talfryn clucked his tongue like an old woman. "You shouldn't exert yourself yet. You have a grave wound, and you won't heal unless you receive proper rest. I think we should see a physician in York. It's only a day's journey east—when you are feeling strong enough, that is."

Padric lay back down. "But the deadline—we must make haste."

"Hang the deadline. I'll not lose my first human—or *half-human*—patient. Besides, we have plenty of time before the solstice—almost three weeks. And we need more supplies, most of which we should be able to find in a large city like York."

Padric lacked the strength or will to argue with the farmer. It frustrated him to no end how much time they continually lost. Between their time finding the amulet, fighting mysterious woodsmen and now his wounds, they had lost an entire week. And they were still unsure of the exact location of Circe's lair, let alone how to defeat her and her weapon without the amulet.

Padric nodded. "Mayhap you are right." Then he closed his eyes to lessen the dizzy spell that followed.

Yet despite his fatigue, Padric's mind wandered. In between the ever-present etchings of the prophecy, images from the other day flashed through his mind.

Try as he might, he could not figure out the stag. Was it really working for Circe? Everything led him to believe so: it was there the day he met Circe, and had followed him for weeks thereafter. And yet, it had saved both him and Talfryn that night. It had guarded him while he slept. There was no denying Staggy was connected to Circe in some manner—but if not as her spy, then what? There was a deep nagging that the beast hid something for its own reasons.

What irked Padric most was the fact he could only have a one-sided conversation with Staggy. Among other things, he wished to elicit information regarding Circe's prisoners and the weapon from the prophecy without receiving a blank stare as the answer.

His mind swirled to the two men he had wounded or killed in combat on the night Brynwen died. Never before had he killed a man. His father had once lectured the new recruits, relaying that a knight always remembered the first death they dealt. Padric's actions were self-defense, but they affected great remorse, regardless.

However, he would have had fewer qualms in killing the man in green. Even without the cloak, Padric was sure he could recognize the man. His bearing, the breadth of his shoulders, his fighting style, his gait. The way he loomed over Brynwen before she fell, her hazel eyes terrified, pleading with Padric to save her. Their fingers brushing for the briefest moment before—

Over and over, that scene played in his mind, haunting his every dream. Every waking moment filled with scenarios of how he could have done it differently—how he could have saved Brynwen and defeated the cloaked man. Guilt piled on top of guilt.

Then something ticked in Padric's mind. What kind of person was he turning into? Vengeance had no place in a knight's heart, yet he could not deny the evil feeling creeping up his chest, poisoning his soul. Would God consider forgiving him for that?

Would God, in fact, forgive him for leading Brynwen to her death? He had already failed so many in Derbyshire. Rawlins and the knights, Miriel and Isemay and their servants, the villagers—they were all collateral damage of his own perilous choices. Roana's prophecy was always right there in his mind, yet he did nothing until it was too late. Everyone would pay the ultimate price for his actions. Brynwen was but the latest casualty to add to his growing tally. Chances were high Talfryn would soon follow in her wake.

"I see now I set the standards too high, put too much pressure on you."

Even though he knew it to be a dream, the words his father had spoken still haunted him. What would he say if he were here?

He would say they must move forward. After all, they only had three weeks left to prepare for the end of all things.

A SHORT TIME LATER, Talfryn poured the sad excuse for chamomile tea into two wooden cups and handed one to Padric. His culinary skills were lacking but might have improved had the honey jar retained a never-ending supply of the golden nectar. His honeybees were probably suffering for want of his attention. He sincerely hoped his brother didn't neglect them. Maybe he should have left more proper instructions before departing.

Sighing inwardly, Talfryn turned his attention to his friend. Downcast did not remotely account for Padric's forlorn countenance. He sat there, utterly taciturn, his arm and sides bandaged tightly. He looked like something out of a tale from *Lais of Marie de France* he had once heard from the Derby bard. Brynwen never let Talfryn forget how he cried like a baby the first time he had heard the bard's rendition of "Nightingale."

Honestly, Talfryn didn't know how to start a conversation anymore. But the quiet between them was almost too much to bear. At last, he broached a subject that Padric might approve. "If you are well enough, we should head out for York tomorrow."

Padric shrugged his shoulders and winced. Both hands fumbled the cup, absently sloshing the contents about. Some spilled onto the grass in front of him.

"Here, mate, that's perfectly good tea." Talfryn didn't know why he was defending the tea. It was rubbish and he knew it.

"You call this tea?" Padric spat back.

"Yes, it took much care to make that tea."

"You boiled water and threw in some tea leaves. That's all you did."

"But it takes a certain amount of finesse."

"That is the problem. Finesse is something you lack altogether."

Talfryn could not believe those words came out of Padric's mouth. The usually thoughtful Padric, always with the right thing to say. He was depressed, and why shouldn't he be? Talfryn's heart was broken too, didn't he see that? He thought of a sharp retort but stifled it down.

"She wouldn't want this," he murmured.

"Would not want what?"

"Us quarreling."

"We are not quarreling." Despite his words, Padric's expression was unconvincing.

Talfryn took a long breath. "Padric," he said softly. "I know you're miserable in soul and body, but so am I. We have to keep it together."

"What is left to keep together? We have already lost so much, and there are only the two of us left. My incompetency is so acute, I know not why I even continue on with this charade. I thought I would be good at it—born to it, even. But I could not save my men, my friends, and now Brynwen is gone, too."

"She—"

"And the amulet!" Padric cried. "Lost to that man or the river, we will never know which. We cannot even find Gregorio. How are we to free anyone? Am I so inept that I cannot keep even that promise? Despite my best efforts, we have been thwarted at every turn. Our mission is cursed. *I* am cursed. Even the Lord has forsaken us. What is the point of going on? We shall fail, as we have failed before. How do you not hate me, or even deign to forgive me for what happened to your sister?" He placed his head in his hands.

Again, Talfryn did not know how to respond.

After a moment, Padric shook his head. "It was Circe who has shown me for what I truly am: a failure, and I clearly lack the skills to be anyone's savior. I knew someone was following us, but I acted too late. And to taunt us further, Circe's agent openly watches us. He stands mere yards away, listening to our very drivel. Do not look at me in that way. You know it is true. How else did he know to come at that particular time to save you and me, but not Brynwen? She should have lived, and I should have died in her stead." His face grew taught, hard as a stone.

Talfryn sat quietly, his face a distortion of emotions. He knew Padric made several correct points. At last, he replied, "It is true. I probably should hate you for not saving my sister and withholding vital information. But what about me? I have just as much claim to the blame as anyone. *I* let her talk you into having her coming along. *I* sent Bryn into the arms of a trickster—a murderer. I thought her safe. If I had known of his deadly intentions, I would have run after her in an instant. We are both at fault. But Circe—the instigator—most of the blame falls on her. I shall curse her to my dying breath." He clenched and unclenched his fists. "And it is true: we were tricked. We were blind to the things directly in front of our faces. But...is that not how we learn? We are only human—well, mostly human." He smirked, but Padric did not return the gesture.

"That is my point," replied Padric in a soft voice. "Our mistakes are too costly."

"And *my point*, miladdo, is that we cannot give up. Brynwen would want us to move forward. She believes in you. We have a mission to fulfill—to rescue our friends and family from the evil sorceress who took them. You have a prophecy, which states very clearly what will happen if we do not face her. Countless lives are at stake. The oracle gave *you* the prophecy."

"What if she chose wrong?"

"She traveled a long way to find *you*. And if she did choose wrong—not that I have any experience with prophecies, but mayhap you can change the prophecy like you can your own form. And you have escaped her grasp twice. How many people have done that? With these attributes and your fighting ability, there's a chance we can do this."

Padric's expression betrayed skepticism. "Without the amulet?"

Talfryn shrugged. "Mayhap a very slim chance."

Nevertheless, Padric nodded, whether in agreement or out of exhaustion, he did not specify. He regarded Talfryn carefully, deciding something. "Sometimes you are too much, you know that?" He cast his gaze down at the grass and with his good hand plucked some tiny pieces of the green shoots, twirling them between his forefinger and thumb. "And sometimes, you make excellent points."

Talfryn beamed.

"But I suppose you are right." Padric lifted his gaze. "We have come all this way and should see it through to the end, no matter the outcome. Brynwen was not one to give up. We should do our best to not disappoint her. I will not lose anyone else to this venture, this I vow." His expression turned thoughtful. He became silent and focused on the cup with great interest. At last, he looked up and lifted his cup in the air to make a toast. "To Brynwen."

"To Brynwen."

Both men took a long sip.

Padric wiped his mouth. "Your speech was admirable, Talfryn. But there is one thing which requires critical aid."

"And what is that, pray tell?"

Padric downed the last drops of his cup and scrunched his nose in displeasure. "Your attempt at making proper tea."

At that, Talfryn scoffed and threw his empty cup at his friend. "I fear, my friend, that is utterly hopeless."

CHAPTER 46

Still unsure how he let Talfryn talk him into this ridiculous idea, Padric, garbed from head to hoof in his traitorous green cloak, followed his friend inside the monolithic Minster of York that bright Sunday morning.

The day before, a York barber who claimed to be versed in medicine had seen to their wounds outside the city walls. When Talfryn came up with the excuse that bandits had assaulted them on the road, the barber eyed the healing bruise on Talfryn's neck. He said in a wry tone, "I see, clearly someone in this bandit group wasn't happy with either of your living conditions."

After the barber left his charges in clean bandages and a minute bottle of unappealing, aromatic elixir, Talfryn turned to his friend with a spark in his eyes. "You should come to Mass at the Minster with me tomorrow. It is the most magnificent church you have ever seen!"

And here they were. Padric did not feel like going to Mass at all, yet Talfryn dutifully nag-nag-nagged at him until he finally gave in. Despite his apprehension, its greatness drew him in.

In truth, Padric used to love attending Mass. He had been very devout, and never missed a one. When Saint Mary's was built seven years ago, he truly enjoyed the beautiful new church and Father Philip.

But soon after the good Father departed for the abbey. His replacement, Father Bernard, was more difficult to understand, and his theology seemed lacking. Padric still dutifully attended, but his training in knighthood had taken precedence over the last three or four years.

Talfryn made them stand in line for another hour waiting for the confessional. Padric found himself sweating as he awaited his turn. When Talfryn went in to face the priest, Padric contemplated walking away. In the end he stayed, unsure if it was the influence of Talfryn or the Holy Spirit keeping him in the queue.

As he stood there, discerning his sins, he discovered something about himself. The realization was like a punch to the stomach. It was not the act of confession and the fact that he had killed men—which was terrible, and he truly felt horrible about that—that bothered him most. No, it was the magic.

Could he be forgiven for having—and using—pagan magic? Was magic inherently evil, or was it the wielder? This was what tore him up on the inside. This, and failing those he has sworn to protect. Miriel, Isemay, Brynwen, his knights, and the missing people of Derbyshire.

A sob formed in his chest and a tear tore down his cheek as he found himself clumsily walking in his green cloak toward the confessional curtain, his hoofs clacking on the smooth cool tile.

A few minutes later, he emerged from the confessional much lighter than when he had entered. The priest had listened attentively and gave more than the normal penance of saying a dozen prayers which was usually prescribed at St. Mary's. Hearing the priest's penance, Padric hung onto every word. He prayed his atonement with a full heart, gave alms, and then found a place to stand near Talfryn with a column to lean against during Mass.

The Mass was surprisingly quite pleasant, and the priest—the same one from the confessional—was as good a celebrant as a confessor. A good portion of the city's population attended the Mass, which made it crowded, but not overly so.

Afterward, Talfryn took a self-guided tour of the inside and came back to relate to Padric the details. The nave was only completed in 1340, which took over sixty years to build. The current construction and scaffolding which blocked the east end piqued Talfryn's interest to no end. Padric suffered through Talfryn's in-depth descriptions with a surprisingly light mood—although he did deem it necessary to sit down during this portion of the verbal tour.

Two hundred and seventy-five steps to the top of the Minster. Padric walked up the steep, winding staircase with Talfryn, which seemed like an extra penance in itself. There was no railing, and it was quite claustrophobic, tiring the faun after only thirty steps. Worse, the cloak dragged him down. But he continued climbing.

After two hundred, Talfryn had the nerve to be barely winded. "I could do this all day!" he said. Seeing Padric's ashen face, he was contrite and asked if Padric needed to sit down or return to the bottom.

Panting, Padric shoved his friend up the next step. "We are almost there, you jester. Only seventy-five more."

The view from the top was striking; it would have taken his breath away if he had any left after the climb. Five counties could be seen from here.

"I wish I could show this to Brynwen," Talfryn said.

"Aye," replied Padric.

Talfryn and the other fit spectators walked the entire perimeter over five times, while fatigue settled itself on Padric's shoulders after only one turn. In spite of the fact that he thoroughly enjoyed the sights and wished to see more, his body retaliated with each step. At last, he slumped to the ground and watched his friend peer over the edge in excited bursts. Sometimes he shouted to Padric, "You have to see this!" Padric waved at him and smiled. He would look at it after a breather.

Sitting by himself, Padric clasped his hands and bent his head. He had been putting it off for weeks, but now it was time. The trip to the confessional had opened the door he had wedged shut for far too long. He needed strength for what was to come. And he needed guidance. Most of all, he needed a miracle.

Taking a deep breath, Padric cleared his mind and began: *Dear Lord, if ever you deemed it worthy to aid this poor sinner...*

Minutes later, Padric rummaged around in the pouch at his belt until he found what he was looking for and wrapped his fingers around it—

the little stoppered vial filled with colorful powders. Each layer placed with the utmost care. He knew he should not have taken it the morning before when it spilled from Brynwen's satchel, but some deviant imp inside him refused to return it.

His heart still harbored guilt for what had happened. Not only the guilt of Brynwen's death, but also something more: As though a vast hole emerged without her company. He could speak freely around her and always looked forward to their conversations. She had so much potential, such a talent for healing and midwifery. Her smile, her bright eyes, her heart—lost forever.

He thought his heart would burst with the ache.

Talfryn plopped down beside him, prattling on about all he saw around every corner.

Shoving his thoughts deep, deep down, Padric let out a grunt and pushed his hands on the limestone to heave himself to his hoofs. Further surveillance over the ramparts revealed a wide view, and he checked the sun's location. Nearly mealtime.

"Come on. I've got to check the rabbit snares," said Talfryn, nudging Padric's good arm. Talfryn's face was flush from the excitement and exercise of the day. In fact, his mood seemed much lighter since he emerged from confession, as well.

"Wait," said Padric. "There is something out there, to the northwest." He pointed outside the city walls near the horizon. "Do you see it?"

"What is it?" Talfryn shaded his eyes with a hand. "I only see farmland. Looks pretty rich." He shrugged his shoulders.

"Beyond that. A shimmer or something. I cannot tell from here. Like sunlight reflecting on a lake, but in the sky." Padric checked his pockets. "Blast, I do not have Gregorio's map on me. Cataractonium is to the northwest, is it not?"

"Yes, I recall that on the map."

"Aye. I could be wrong, but I think it is in the same distance as that bit of shimmer."

"The shimmer that I don't see."

"Precisely."

Talfryn's eyebrows gathered in a frown. "Mayhap you need to rest. Come, let's go down and eat rabbit stew."

"Talfryn. I need you to think about something other than your stomach for once. I know Cataractonium is a fort to the northwest."

"But why there? Why not go to Scotland?"

"Scotland is a long distance to travel to obtain people from Derbyshire. Though with all of Circe's magic, I am sure it could be done. But that shimmer. It is similar to the one that coats Staggy's—oh, you have me saying it now—the stag's wings."

"I haven't seen the shimmer of Staggy's wings."

"That is because you aren't filled with magic."

Talfryn lifted a finger to argue, then promptly lowered it. "Oh. Right. Continue."

"So, if that is the same source of magic cloaking Cataractonium from mortal eyes, then we can deduce that it is Circe's lair, hidden in that very spot." A feeling grew in his gut. *This must be right*, he thought with determination. Not just any feeling: hope.

"Brilliant." Talfryn clapped Padric on the arm. The injured arm this time. He looked contritely at Padric. "Apologies."

Padric rubbed his arm, biting his lip to stifle the pain. "I am not some fragile kitten, Talfryn."

"I know, but I just got you all better. I don't want to re-break you."

"You shan't." Turning toward the stairwell, he flashed a grin at Talfryn, a second wind filling his lungs. He sent up a little prayer of gratitude. "The last man to camp gets to skin the rabbit."

"You're on."

CHAPTER 47

Oh yes, we're going to die.

Together, a shape-shifting hero and a half-trained farmer without amulet would be up against a woman wielding magic.

"What could go wrong?" Talfryn muttered.

He sighed again as he clenched Dusty's reins for the third time that morning on the road to Cataractonium.

On the other hand, since leaving York, it seemed something changed within Padric. His stamina had increased. He ate and drank what Talfryn gave him. He even laughed at Talfryn's jokes! Now that he had a physical target, what once seemed a hopeless mission was at last coming to fulfillment. And, Talfryn suspected, confession at the Minster had done wonders as well.

Though the subject generally upset Padric, Talfryn had been dying to ask the faun a certain question for days. "Pray tell, O Scholar, what kind of mythological creature is Staggy?"

As predicted, Padric eyed him steadily for what seemed a full minute before he shrugged and spoke.

"To be honest, I am not at all sure what, exactly, he is. He reminds me of a gryphon, but in somewhat reverse. You have heard of a gryphon? Nay? Well, a gryphon is a mythical creature—a combination of two animals in one: it has the head and wings of an eagle, but the body of a lion."

"So what's Staggy, then?" Talfryn asked again.

"As you have well noticed, our *friend* is the combination of two animals: the head, body, and forelegs of a stag, but the hind legs, wings, and tail of a bird. 'Tis nothing I have encountered in Gregorio's books, though."

With a pang, Talfryn missed the proud stag who had helped them. Just like that, Staggy up and left them before arriving in York, but why? He refused to believe Padric's accusation that it had a hidden agenda. "I suppose I can't call him a chicken-stag anymore."

Padric chuckled dryly. "Until we know what he is for sure, you can call him whatever you like."

Talfryn had just taken a bite of his tough venison strip when a chirp caught his attention. "Did you hear that?"

"Birds," said Padric, chewing on his own meal. "It is called nature."

Talfryn rolled his eyes. "Thanks."

Before he could look up, a small streak of white dashed directly in front of him. "What the—" Throwing up his hands in defense, a brown streak zipped past his face, something soft brushing his arm. Feathers.

Ready to fight, Padric drew his bow and arrow.

Talfryn turned his eyes upward as the shadows passed overhead. Two birds. A brown hawk chasing a smaller white bird—a dove.

They flew and circled each other. The hawk gained on the little dove, extending and retracting its claws mid-flight. It nipped the dove's tail. A squeak escaped from the dove, and a chunk of white feathers were dispatched into the air. The bird gained some speed, but then it began to tire. It limped in the air, if that was even possible.

Talfryn watched the spectacle in horrified amazement.

"Is that..." began Padric.

"It's Nessie!" Talfryn shouted. "We have to help her. Padric, what can we *do*?"

Another squeak came from the dove, followed by an exhilarated hungry call from the hawk.

"It will *kill* her!" Talfryn shouted.

Padric's eyes grew wide. "What do you expect me to do? I cannot leap that high."

"I don't care, just do something. Please."

In one smooth movement and with careful aim, Padric let fly two arrows in quick succession. Neither hit the great bird, but they whizzed directly in front and to the side of its beak. It was enough to frighten it. The hawk dropped the hunt, squawking its annoyance down at the humans.

After an interminable time, the dove descended on shaky wings—more like fell, into Talfryn's outstretched hands.

"Nessie!" Talfryn cried as he cradled her in his arms. "However did you find us?"

"And where did you come from?" Padric wondered, peering in the direction they were heading. "She flew in from the north. From Cataractonium."

Talfryn jerked his head up. "What?"

The faun's eyes sparkled and he combed a hand through his hair. The sun glinted off a curved horn. "I think...I have a hunch. I cannot explain it now, not until I am certain. But we must make haste to Cataractonium."

༺ ༻

Padric and Talfryn caught rare glimpses of the sun peeking through the clouds for much of the day. Light rain dropped on their heads, soaking them to the bone, and they had all but forgotten what it felt like to be dry. After some time, it finally gave evidence of dissipating, but not enough to make a difference.

To Padric, Nessie appeared glad to be back in their company. She made a quick, full recovery thanks to Talfryn's ministrations. In celebration, she frequently flung her little body from his lap to Padric's shoulder or hair, then back again. Sometimes she would soar in circles directly above their heads. Even in the rain. Just watching her flit about gave Padric some comfort.

For the last several miles, Padric could distinguish the sheen that emanated over the hills through the sheet of rain. It was as if the rain intensified the shimmer. He was still all amazement that Talfryn could not see this obvious phenomenon. But he supposed that the latter had not been touched by magic the way he had. The hill in question rose to the northwest of the road. As his eyes drifted up the rocky terrain, the hairs on the back of his neck rose with them. This was it, he was sure of it.

The hasty cold breakfast he had consumed did not sit well in his stomach.

Family or not, the imminent discussion he would have with Circe was at last a reality. He both shuddered and thrilled at the prospect of confronting her. The truth about everything—why souls had been taken, why Brynwen had been killed. To rescue the kidnapped villagers. It would all come to an end.

Just over that hill.

Yet...

Questions flooded his mind. Would he find his friends alive and well? Would Circe allow him a chance to fight, or merely kill him and Talfryn outright? How would he fulfill the prophecy if he was dead?

He peered over at the farmer, staring with equal intent upon the crest of hill. The bird on his shoulder followed his gaze.

Talfryn squinted. "So, this is it."

"Aye."

"The shimmer is just over that hill."

"It is."

"And there is no turning back after that," Talfryn said in a husky voice.

"None whatsoever. This is your last chance to turn around. I will not hold it against you. You have come farther with me than anyone else probably would. No matter your decision, I am proud to have you as my friend."

Talfryn stared at Padric for a few moments, considering.

Worry snaked through Padric. After everything they had been through, he had not considered Talfryn abandoning him now, even with the offer. Not like his dream father or Staggy. Not when he needed his friend the most.

"Oh no, I've come this far, I am not turning back. I brought you back to health and lost a most cherished sister. We have an evil sorceress to defeat. Friends to save." Talfryn smirked. "*You* can turn back if you want to. I won't hold it against you either. Prophecy or no, I'm wiping that witch's smile off her face for no other reason than my own satisfaction."

The tightness in Padric's chest lessened.

"And you would do this singlehandedly?"

"With one hand behind my back. And my eyes closed." He considered for a moment. "Mayhap I should have brought my bees."

Padric could not help but laugh at that. "So they could sting her into submission?"

"And why not?" Talfryn said indignantly. "Those bees can be quite wicked when incensed."

"'Tis quite brilliant."

"Really?" Talfryn looked hopeful.

"Nay. It's terrible. But my thanks for making me laugh."

"Anytime."

With difficulty, they coaxed the three stubborn horses up the rocky hill, careful to avoid rocks and holes. At the top, the terrain flattened out to a plateau, but it was just as craggy as the ascent. Padric scanned the large barricade of stone interspersed with vines and lush, thorny green bushes covering the ground in front of the magical curtain.

Padric nocked an arrow and gripped his bow tight as Talfryn drew his hatchet. Who knew what lay behind that veil?

A slight tingling touched Padric's skin as he passed through the shimmery curtain. Gloomy rain had been traded with sunshine.

Despite the pleasant weather, Padric's blood ran cold. Because atop that stone wall sat Circe.

Talfryn stopped dead in his tracks. "Is that her?" he whispered.

Padric could only nod.

Blonde hair swept into an elegant bun atop Circe's head, adorned with a gold circlet, and ending in a perfect braid that spilled gracefully off one shoulder. Her sapphire dress—different from their last encounter—perfectly matched her eyes and appeared to be spun from the finest silk. The material flowed around her body, accentuating her delicate frame. Her staff lay horizontal in her lap.

On either side of the sorceress stood two maidens, equal in height and build, each bearing a polearm crafted of ash wood and bronze tips on one end. Long, braided brown hair surrounded nearly identical, green-skinned faces. Muscles on their bare arms, though delicate in appearance, indicated warriors. They wore exotic sky-blue blouses with translucent, flowing skirts similar to Circe's Romanesque style. In short, these green-skinned maids reeked of danger in balance as well as stance.

Instead of attacking, however, they remained still, eyeing the newcomers.

"My sweet Padric," Circe said innocently. Then as an afterthought, she said, "And friend. Welcome to my humble home."

CHAPTER 48

*P*adric's arrow tip pointed directly at Circe's heart. He could not miss at this distance.

His recovering shoulder protested greatly at the groaning strain of the bow string. He could let loose the arrow, and it would all be over. A simple thing. Forget the prophecy. Yet his friends might suffer the consequences of such a decision.

To his surprise, the warrior maidens remained still. Why? He expected them to at least change to defensive stances. Could he shoot both before they moved to attack?

A sweet smile lit Circe's lips. She clenched the staff as though daring Padric to take it again. The orb gleamed reflections of the enchanted curtain behind him. He wished he had snapped the wretched thing in half weeks ago when given the chance. Yet he refused to take the bait. If he stepped forward, her guards would be on him in an instant.

"Your home is doomed, Circe," he told her. "Hand over your prisoners. You can do this the easy way or the hard way. It is your choice." He tugged the bow string a fraction more for emphasis.

Circe laughed. Crystal clear and as beautiful as the siren song she had sung for him in May. The faun was taken aback and nearly fumbled his weapon. He quickly cleared his mind and thought of Brynwen instead. Of his missing friends. How he needed to help them.

"You are quite determined, I must say, Padric de Clifton." A playful pout puckered her lips. "Once you crossed the hill, you entered my territory. Besides, my spies saw you from miles away."

With a frown, Padric wondered if Staggy warned her of their approach.

Circe swept her hand in the air with a graceful stroke, drawing Padric's attention to the sky. Three large Stymphalian birds circled overhead.

Perfect. Even if he managed to release a shot, the Stymphalian birds would tear him and Talfryn limb from limb. He could possibly pick off one or two before their enormous wingspans delivered their deadly claws from directly overhead. An encounter he did not wish to repeat, as he remembered the talon slicing into his arm mere weeks ago. The warrior maidens were no less threatening.

A warning clicked in the back of Padric's brain to run, but he pushed it down.

Without taking her eyes off the intruders, Circe acknowledged the two green maids. "These are my trusted friends, Nalini and Eliva."

The maids gave a slight nod.

Not letting up on the bow, Padric bore his gaze at Circe and her friends. "You have taken our friends, our families, and sent underlings to hunt and kill us. We demand your prisoners be released this instant. Otherwise, do not think we will show mercy. We will do anything to return what was lost."

Amusement played on the sorceress's lips. "Anything?"

Padric inwardly scowled at his own poor choice of words.

"You had my sister murdered," Talfryn shouted, his leggings ensnaring themselves in a bramble bush behind him. Nessie chirped loudly, as if berating him for being so clumsy. But little did that faze him at the moment as he ripped his leg free. His voice was thick with emotion. "She died fighting your minions. You couldn't even be bothered to come yourself to finish her—or us—off."

"It was not I who sent them," she said.

"Lies!" shouted Talfryn.

Circe cocked an eyebrow. "I knew you would not believe me." She studied them for a long heartbeat. "Then come, my children. Release your vengeance if you think it will serve you and your brethren. Show me your mettle, if you have any."

Padric's chest constricted with anticipation. This was it! His mind raced. Was this truly the end of the prophecy? He need only defeat Circe, and her prisoners would be free. And yet...something was missing. He was without the amulet. And what of the great weapon—could it be her staff, perhaps? Doubt entered his mind, but there was nothing for it.

Talfryn's face set in determination. Bending to a fighting stance, he twisted the hatchet in his fingers, his eyes sparking with danger. Gone was the laidback, witty farmer Padric had known. Everything he had suffered in the past weeks—nearly dying at the hands of their assailants, Brynwen's death—came to the forefront. He looked to Padric.

"I made a vow to never beat a woman," Padric declared. "But I retract my oath for this one instance."

Talfryn nodded. "Aye. Just this once."

Both Nalini and Eliva took defensive stances, identical to one another, their polearms at the ready. Padric could now see physical differences between the two—the one on the left had a Roman, or aquiline, nose. He decided she would be Nalini.

He had only sparred with someone wielding a spear or staff a handful of times, only once coming close to victory. Combat with a sword against a staff was another matter, but not impossible.

Sparing Talfryn a glance, he gave the signal. Padric released the arrow at Nalini.

She deflected it without losing a step.

Dropping the bow, Padric sprung forward, freeing his sword from its scabbard on his back as Nalini and Eliva spun their polearms above their heads. Talfryn dashed in a half step behind.

Nalini blocked Padric's blow, and the next.

"I do not wish to hurt you," Nalini said.

Padric grinned. "Why? So I may become your slave, too?"

She gave him a coy smile. "Would it be so dreadful?"

When their weapons unlocked, she spun in a graceful circle, her dress flowing out like the petals of a flower. It was as though she and the polearm were one entity.

She swung and Padric parried and slid the polearm away with a swipe, shoving her away to gain a better stance. Warm blood spilled down his cheek from where the bronze tip had nicked him. First blood spilled. Another frustrating thing about spears and staffs: they kept their enemies at a distance. Padric would have a time getting past the bronze tip without grave injury.

With a swift pivot, Nalini moved to Padric's right. Only just did he catch the flick of her eyes and he blocked her high feint. Then she grinned. With a quick jab of her arms upward, the polearm sped down over the sword's edge and jabbed him in the thigh.

Padric parried and riposted. The movement cost him. It was all he could do not to stumble, the agony in his side, leg, and arm were that great. He heaved deep, burning breaths. The stitches would tear by the end of the battle, he knew—whether he lived or not. Leg and side throbbing, in a tick he weighed his options, at the same time allowing for a short breather, never taking his eyes off Nalini. Having not been well enough to train much over the last several days, every one of his muscles were taut.

His movement was not wasted, as he spied a trickle of blood slither down Nalini's arm.

To his right, Eliva battered Talfryn's hatchet. They fell into a short rhythm for a time, Talfryn taking a beating, never retreating, yet rarely leaving any marks on her. A frown creased the maid's brow when the hatchet scored a mark on the fine wood of her polearm.

"So," Circe said with a wicked grin from beyond the warrior maids. "The great warrior has not quite healed, has he? In both body *and* mind." She clucked her tongue in mock sympathy.

"I know not to what you refer. I could fight all day," replied Padric with a confident smile—a confidence which he sorely lacked, as dark clouds threatened the edges of his vision. He could not afford to lose—his friends and the world were counting on him. Apart from that, the prophecy was not yet complete. "I did not come this far to be beaten now."

"Good. Then this courtesy respite is now over."

Nalini twirled the polearm above her head, then leaped at Padric. He parried the blows with all his strength, and lunged, managing a few hits past her defenses. Deflecting the polearm away, he spun and thrust his sword at her midsection. Shooting a worried glance his way, the maid pivoted. Before she could set her foot on the ground, Padric caught her polearm in his hand and shouldered her in the ribs. She sprawled to the ground with a thud, the polearm rolling and bumping into his hoof.

Lungs a'flame, Padric tossed the polearm to Talfryn and made to approach Circe. In all honesty, he knew not how much more he could take. He was near to exhaustion.

Talfryn's fight with Eliva waned in her favor. Taking a misstep to avoid a polearm in his gut, Talfryn stumbled into the bramble bush, landing on his back, and shouting out in surprise.

Padric bounded over Talfryn as Eliva's polearm arced down toward his chest. As he moved, the stitches holding Padric's wounds stretched painfully. Sliding the sword down the shaft, he knocked Eliva in the head with his hilt.

She sunk to the ground without a word.

Without taking a moment to catch a breath, he turned to the sorceress. "Now, sorceress, 'tis your turn. Are these your best champions?" He and Nalini were fair to evenly matched, as the wounds she had dealt reminded him. Yet she did not need to know that.

Circe stepped forward, gripping her staff ever tighter. "Mayhap," she replied.

Nalini got to her feet with little effort, a scowl on her face. Before she could take a step toward Padric, Circe halted her. "Nay, you have fought well, Nalini. I shall finish this, now."

Raising and twisting the staff in the air with expertise, Circe approached, her gaze set with determination. Padric could not help but wonder how the orb on the staff would affect her balance, and at the same time knew being struck by it could incapacitate him if he was not careful. If not being thrashed and cut by the glass, then by its silver holder. His aching muscles and side already dragged down his own movements, his lungs burning with the exertion used. Could he last another round? If he failed, would Talfryn be able to defeat her? Unlikely.

To defeat Circe, he must somehow catch her off guard. But how does one outmatch a centuries-old deity who has likely seen her share of battles? Though there were no existing records depicting Circe as a warrior, that did not mean she never learned. Of course, it was plausible she picked up skill with the staff after the stories were written. He counted himself fortunate it was not Minerva or Mars he faced.

He took the time to adjust his grip on his sword and study the goddess. Why did she not use her magic to defeat him?

"I do not need magic to fight you," Circe said, as though reading his thoughts. "You can surrender now, though I know you will not."

"I would rather die."

"Then so be it."

Circe lunged with a similar attack as Nalini. Padric maneuvered and the staff narrowly missed his chest within an inch. He brought the sword up and her staff naturally deflected it with an arc. They grappled, Padric holding his own, sweeping Circe closer to the wall overlooking Cataractonium.

After a feint on Circe's part, Padric saw his chance. He rolled to the left as she swiped over his head.

Then—

Eyes sparking, she slammed the staff into the ground. The translucent orb caught the sun's rays and its reflection frolicked around the hill and into the eyes of her foe. Blinded, Padric lurched back to cover his face.

Without slowing, as though in a dance, the goddess twirled her staff low and swept the impaired Padric off his hoofs. He landed on his back, directly into the bramble bush next to Talfryn. The sword slipped from his sweaty fingers.

Long, sharp thorns stabbed his neck, arms, and torso. But it did not just stab at him. It grabbed at him, jabbing the thorns deeper into his flesh, clenching onto his clothes. Talfryn writhed beside him, desperate to get free, his back and arms covered in bloody scratches.

"Even...even Circe's plants are weapons," Talfryn said through gritted teeth.

A shadow loomed over them. It were as though watching water flow. Circe followed through, twirling the staff again and again, all in one fluid motion.

Padric caught the spark in her sapphire eyes. He knew that look—

With a devious grin, Circe careened the orb down toward his head, and all Padric could do was watch.

CHAPTER 49

The staff arced down at Padric's head.

Then rough hands shoved him, the thorns rent from his flesh and tunic with all the ceremony of ripping a bandage from a bloody wound.

He landed hard on his hands and knees. His arms were numb, and everything burned and ached. With great effort, he at last peered up. Talfryn lay sprawled in the bramble bush, arms outstretched over where Padric had been a moment before. A long crimson gash crossed his forehead. He remained still.

"Talfryn?" he called.

But his friend did not answer.

No!

First Brynwen, now Talfryn. Padric's chest threatened to explode in agony. Leaping to his hoofs with a newfound energy, his eyes saw only red. The glare he gave Circe would frighten even a score of vipers. The goddess's eyes flicked a note of concern. For her safety? Most likely.

Sword lost to the bramble bush, he charged at the sorceress. He avoided her urgent swipe at his head and then stomach. As she followed through after the second swipe, he tackled her to the ground onto her back.

He caught the staff in his hand—this time the staff sent no jolt of lightning through his arm, to his surprise. Lowering the staff to her neck, he pressed it against her windpipe.

She gasped, clutching at the staff with desperate fingers.

Nalini and Eliva raced forward but Padric only pressed the staff harder against their mistress's throat.

"One more step," Padric warned, "and she dies." At least, he hoped that was true. If nothing else, he might scar her.

They halted, grimacing.

Perhaps there is merit in my threat after all.

"You cannot kill her," Nalini said.

"Dare to argue, lest you are wrong? I have broken her curses before." Well, one.

"Release the prisoners," said Padric between heaving breaths.

"Nay...I..." Circe croaked.

"Release them! You have killed another one of my friends. I should kill you now, but I shall give you this one chance to redeem even an ounce of your cold heart."

Circe shook her head, despite the limitation. She rasped a reply: "I...cannot."

"What do you mean, you cannot? You are in no position to negotiate. Likewise, your nymphs seem a tad hesitant to move against me at present." He lifted the staff a fraction so she could better answer.

Closing her eyes, the deity inhaled a deep breath. Opening her eyes once again, a hint of weariness crept in behind the shield of mirth lacing her sapphire eyes. And....*fear?*

Heavy silence filled the hillside.

"No games this time," Padric said. "No trickery."

Quick as lightning, the mirth all but fled Circe's eyes. They still sparked, but with a different determination. "They are not mine to free."

"But it was you who took them."

"I shall not deny it. Regardless, my actions were not upon my whim. Have you asked yourselves who, besides me, could be behind your friends' disappearances?"

For some reason the first line of Roana's prophecy came to Padric's mind: *As the heir to the charioteer of old...* But that would mean—

"And your young female mortal friend," she continued, "did not die at my hands."

The faun glared at the sorceress, assessing her declaration. There were numerous ways to read into what she stated. She gave the air of sincerity, but he had been lured by her before. Others had fallen prey to her words, to their doom.

Padric leaned forward, his voice laced with venom. "Then by whom?" *The charioteer?*

"You misunderstand. She did not die—neither by my hand nor anyone else's. She is alive, and she is here."

CHAPTER 50

"Truly?" The barest whisper came from behind Padric. "Bryn lives?"

Padric whipped his head around to find Talfryn still ensnared in the bramble bush, awake. *Alive.* Nessie sat very still on his shoulder as if attentive to Circe's answer. A flood of relief filled Padric's chest.

And Brynwen...

Dare it be true?

"Where is she?" Padric asked Circe, his voice husky to his own ears. His heart tried to overtake his brain at the news, ready to rush to her rescue. When he and Talfryn reunited with Nessie outside Cataractonium, a glimmer of hope had filled his chest that perhaps Brynwen had survived, too. It took great effort to put aside his feelings now, if only for a moment.

"You would not lie to us to get your way?" he asked, not wavering from his hold on the staff. He could not let down his guard, no matter what.

Circe rolled her eyes. "Please, do you really think I would harm her?"

The men stared at her, unwavering.

She bristled under their scrutiny, perspiration forming on her brow. "Well, I suppose you would see it that way, given our past history...But I assure you she is safe." Receiving no response, she reiterated, "She *is* safe in my city, and you need not concern yourself with her at the moment. There are larger issues at hand, and we have little time."

Shaking his head, Padric said, "You are wrong, we have every intention of concerning ourselves with Brynwen. We do not abandon one of our own on the word of a sorceress."

Padric pushed the staff a millimeter further into her throat. "You will release Brynwen and the prisoners, now."

"I am afraid I cannot do that," she replied, her face turning scarlet.

"Care to change you answer? I have you in a bind," Padric said.

Despite her circumstances, Circe snorted. "Hardly."

Padric scowled, a readied retort on his tongue.

"Please, m'lady," Talfryn pleaded from the bush, his voice barely above a whisper. His eyes were filled with unshod tears. "Brynwen is my sister. I just wish to see her."

Circe spared a look at Talfryn, her sapphire eyes sparking a sorrow Padric had not expected. What was this? Conflicting thoughts wracked Padric at her show of an emotion. Was it genuine, or a ruse? He mentally shook his head. This was getting them nowhere.

"Enough," Padric said to the trapped goddess. He glared at the nymphs before returning his gaze to the sorceress. "The prisoners' release, or a swift death. These are your choices. Decide—*now*."

Circe shook her head. Not one golden curl came loose in the act. "Foolish mortals," she said, and before Padric could stop her, she glided her hand over the translucent orb on the end of the staff. Padric felt a tingle run up his spine. "I have decided. Long ago was it decided. It is you," she pointed one polished finger at Padric's chest, "who has something to decide. Not I."

Padric remained stone-faced, though his thoughts whirled, heart racing. Whatever did she mean? What could he possibly have to decide?

Then it occurred to him the Stymphalian birds hovering overhead had stopped making noise. In fact, they stopped *moving*. They were frozen in the sky!

"What the..." said Talfryn with awe and rubbed his wounded forehead.

Even Nalini and Eliva stood motionless.

Circe grinned at their surprise. "I have created a magical barrier to freeze time, so we may speak plainly."

Padric glared at her, unconvinced. "And your friends Nalini and Eliva?"

A sadness filled the sorceress's eyes. "Alas, my nymph friends must be kept in the dark. The more they know, the more danger they will find themselves in. I cannot risk it."

"But you would risk us."

She nodded and let out a sigh. "There is little time to explain, but *I* am in great need of *your* aid."

"How could *we* possibly aid you? And what on earth could make us fancy to help you?" Padric asked.

"For one, it is not I whom you need fear, but my *pater*—my father, Helius."

"Your father is the charioteer." Padric grimaced. Sometimes he loathed being right. "What is his stake in this?"

"Everything." The exasperation on her face was completely genuine. "He is the one behind it all. And I am powerless to stop him."

Padric stared at her in disbelief. He knew the magic her staff had wielded. "How are *you* powerless against him?"

"I—" She glared at Padric. "For Olympus's sake, will you remove this staff from my throat? It is altogether distracting."

Padric flinched. "Why should I believe you? What is to stop me from ending you right now?"

"You can kill me, but it shall not return your friends and family to you. My father shall remain in charge, and you shall fail. Besides, I could deflect your weapons. Mayhap I allowed you to beat me," she said with a cocky grin. Yet her heaving chest told otherwise. "Or mayhap...I tire of fighting." A bluff?

Padric grimaced at the turn of the conversation. "If you wanted our help all along, then why have us go through all the trouble of fighting you and your nymphs?"

"Were I to invite you into my home with open arms, would you have deemed it prudent to accept my offer without reproach or hostility?

Would you stay your weapons and harken to me as I pled my case to you? Nay? Besides, your actions on this hill shall only serve to increase his approval of you. As well, he wishes to determine how your strength has returned. Most excited is he to meet you, yet it must be on his terms."

Padric's eyebrows furrowed. "Will your father not suspect your ruse?"

"Not if I send him an illusion of my defeat at your hands."

"If you can produce an illusion to appear before him, why not illusion the fight?"

"And allow you to keep all that rage pent up inside your chests?" She chuckled. "It had to be real for my father to believe it. Besides, I need you level-headed when you meet him."

Hesitating, Padric removed the staff from her throat. But still he held the weapon ready in case of the treachery he more than half expected.

"If you would allow me..." She snatched the staff from Padric's hands and used it to haul herself to her feet. Then she tapped the ground with it, as though ensuring it were in one piece. Brushing the grass off her blue robes, she continued, "My father has been...*unwell* the past two thousand years. Unbalanced, I should say. It started with the death of my mortal half-brother Phaethon."

Still keeping an eye on the sorceress, Padric helped Talfryn out of the deadly bush.

Padric remembered the tale from Gregorio's books. "He rode Helius's chariot and lost control, forcing Jupiter to kill him."

"Yes. My father always blamed himself for the death of Phaethon. He could have stopped Jupiter from killing him, but he did not, and has lived with the shame of his own failure. He retired from the skies with his horses to my island of Aeaea. Father meant to return to the skies someday, to regain his former glory—but not whilst Jupiter yet reigns in Olympus. After a thousand years we moved here with the Roman Empire, then when they crumbled we stayed in Cataractonium.

"However, being the god of the sun, his very essence is influenced by its phenomena, and vice versa. The last two hundred years has been the worst. He has lost his grip on his solar powers, and what used to give him strength now makes him ill and out of sorts. Blinding solar flairs and total eclipses wind him up, afflicting him with severe mood swings, up one moment, down the next. I watched as the total eclipse in December finally sent him over the edge."

"December, you say?" Padric asked. The wheels in his mind turned. "That was when the first people started disappearing from Chaddesden."

"Indeed," Circe said with a grave nod. "It was then he came up with the idea to build a vast temple in his own honor. But he needed workers to accomplish such a feat. There were not enough nymphs in all of England to build such a structure."

"Let me guess, that is where you came in?" Talfryn asked.

"Yes," she replied with a grimace. "He made me swear on the River Styx to help him with his endeavor. One does not swear lightly upon the River Styx. It is as signing a binding contract. To which, if you fail to fulfill your obligation or willingly break your oath, dire consequences occur. It would hinder not only me, but also those around me.

"I was charged with finding workers to build the temple. At first, I borrowed a few from sporadic villages. Then he needed more and more. I blindly believed the sooner he finished his project, the sooner he would become himself once again. But there was one problem."

A tear formed at the corner of her eye.

"He lied to me."

That admission caught Padric's attention. "How did he lie to you?"

The single tear traveled down her face as she replied, "Only recently did I find out he has had a hidden agenda all this time. The temple is only the first part of his grand scheme. His ultimate venture is to kill Apollo."

CHAPTER 51

"What?" Padric asked, shocked. "How does he plan to do that? And why?"

"With a great weapon," she replied. "An eye for an eye for the god who killed his son."

To destroy the weapon of untold might.

The oracle's vision of destruction came to Padric's mind. "The weapon will not stop there, will it? Helius Would destroy Apollo and the world with it. None will be spared."

Circe nodded grimly.

Padric clenched his fists. "How could you let him build it? Why did you not destroy it when you had the chance?"

"Do you not see? My hands are tied. I swore to my father upon the River Styx to help him." The humans stared at her blankly. "Helius is very powerful. One wrong move or word, and all I have worked to achieve could come down on our heads. Including all of the people that reside in the valley below. It is near folly in confiding this to you, but it is a risk I must take."

Padric crossed his arms. "But surely there is something you could do."

"I did do something," she said, her eyes narrowing. "I found *you*."

"Because of the prophecy," Padric said lamely.

Circe pursed her lips, thoughtful for a moment. "It is unclear exactly how prophecies come about, but Apollo might have that answer. It is also possible my staff awakened the prophecy. I have had this staff for thousands of years and yet at times it still manages to surprise me."

Padric was still skeptical. "Yet...why me? Why did the prophecy choose me? I am no one. A mere knight. Why should I have sudden powers, where others do not?"

"There is more magic in the world than you know, sweeting." Circe placed a hand on her hip, a wry smile upon her lips. "From the moment I saw you, I knew you were special, that you were of my blood. You look exactly like my...Ulysses. I will tell you more later, but know now you are my great-grandson, over sixty generations."

As the heir to the charioteer of old
thou wilt bear a curse of gold.

Padric grimaced inwardly. It was difficult to show no emotion as he spoke. "Then it is true. The charioteer in the prophecy is Helius, and I am his many-great-grandson—his heir." His ability to overcome Circe's staff suggested it, and now she confirmed it. They were relations of his whether he liked it or not. But what about changing into a mythical creature? Was he Ulysses' relation as well? There were too many questions to ask, and so little time.

Talfryn's eyes widened as he took in all this information. "Uh, as a family member, does Padric get a staff, too?"

Circe chuckled. "Nay. That is not a condition of our little family circle." She turned back to Padric. "Yes, my little demigod, we are related. Is that not delicious?" A wicked smile spread across her face, reminding him of the first time they had met weeks earlier. It felt like a lifetime ago.

"We may be family," Padric said, "but it does not make kidnapping right."

Circe's countenance changed with a drastic swiftness. The air around them chilled. "Mark me well, *grandson*. As I already explained to your tiny mortal brain, I cannot openly defy my father. That is why I have tested you from a distance. In doing so, I performed my father's will in spying on you, but at the same time aiding you. As his heir, you are the only one who may be able to sort this predicament out."

She looked at the sun and banged her staff on the ground. "Quickly now. Whilst we waste time chatting, my power grows weak. I can only hide our little discussion from my father for so long. You know his power."

Padric had heard what Helius's great power was. Per the texts, besides pulling the sun around the world behind his golden chariot, the god could hear conversations down on the Earth. Back in ancient times, anyone could call upon him and he would bear witness, be it a wedding, a death, or a war.

Padric's stomach pitched as he realize what that meant. "Then he can hear everything we have said. Our plans—"

"Are not private, no. He has known for some time of your trials and impending arrival. He must have sent those swine after you to apprehend the amulet you found."

In a low voice so only Padric could hear, Talfryn asked, "Does everyone know about the amulet? And is she looking less shiny to you?"

Furrowing his brows, Padric gave the goddess another glance. Indeed, her sunny cheeks had sunk, paling despite the sunlight. Her perfect golden ringlets began to droop. Even her shimmery dress lost some of its sheen. Trembling white knuckles clenched the wooden staff.

Padric wondered at her story. If she spoke the truth, then her family had born much hardship in the last couple thousand years. He had met people who had lost everything and turned to a life of crime or drowned themselves in drink. Why not a god, too? The myths of the gods he had grown up learning about were fraught with tension and emotion, so Helius's reaction to his son's death was not completely unexpected. It made him seem almost human.

"This spell, my grandson, is holding Helius back, but I cannot maintain it much longer. You must listen to me, for my servants are on their way now, under his orders. But I must prepare you. Your first test was to get past me. Know when you are beaten. When you are taken to him, you must demand that he release those he has taken. Make him swear to it. He will demand a payment in return, and you must cede to his demands. 'Twill be a heavy price, but in order to save those you care about before the solstice, it must be so."

This is it. The rest of the prophecy will take place here.

A war raged within his chest. Elation at fulfilling the prophecy, as well as defeat, because he must surrender to Helius. It was no little thing, giving himself to the god. *Would he make me swear on the River Styx as well?* It could mean losing his soul. To save everyone, he would.

"The solstice," Padric said, "is his greatest day of the year."

"Yes, he is strongest on that day. He will use his weapon when the sun is at its zenith."

"Then I concede." Everything sore, Padric bent over with care for his bow and arrow, still expecting large adversaries to attack at any moment. "And the amulet? The rest of the prophecy?"

"All will make itself known to you in due time. You will find your amulet when the time is right." She walked up to her many-great-grandson, her eyes returning to their previous mirth. But for a moment, he detected kindness in them. "I am afraid your trials have only just begun, Sir Knight. You are strong and smart as your forefathers, and I see many great things in your future, young Padric, should you survive. I have put my faith in you. Do not prove me wrong."

"What about me?" Talfryn asked, back straight as an arrow, but bloody and disheveled as ever.

"You." Again, Circe's lips curled. Feigning boredom, she said, "Will be of some use, I gather." She cast her gaze to Nessie, who had again taken roost on Talfryn's shoulder. "Take care of that caladrius."

Padric wanted to ask what a caladrius was, but knew there was no time. "Can we count on your aid to stop Helius?"

A small smile raised the corners of Circe's lips. "I will do whatever is in my power to aid you. But our alliance cannot reach my father, or all is lost. Once I release the spell around us, we will have little by way of communication with one another. Should my father suspect we have formed an alliance, I will claim ignorance. Is that clear? Good. I will leave you to it, then. And Padric?"

"Yes?"

"Helius has many spies in Cataractonium, so choose your friends wisely. May the gods be with you."

Then she tapped the staff on the ground and the freezing spell lifted with another tickle up Padric's spine.

CHAPTER 52

In less than five heartbeats, they were surrounded.

The servants Circe had spoken of were neither nymphs nor mere woodland animals. No, they were of a wild variety Padric had only ever heard of in nursery tales, each creature more ferocious than the last. Large animals from the most dangerous parts of the world. A wolf, a tiger, a lion, and a great brown bear.

Eliva and Nalini moved once again to Circe's sides, their eyes set, ready for a second round. Circe resumed her haughty stance, looking for all the world as though she had not frozen time to have a clandestine conversation with Padric and Talfryn. The goddess's wide grin took Padric off guard, giving him doubts as to the goddess's earnestness. However hard she tried to hide it, he could detect the slight shift in her bearing. He prayed she really was on their side. For if not, they would all be dead by the solstice.

"They seem friendly," Talfryn observed of the animals, his voice nearly cracking.

The lion's jaws opened wide, showing razor-sharp teeth, and released an impressive roar that pricked the nerves of the animal part of Padric.

"What did he say?" whispered Talfryn.

"They are inviting us to tea," Padric explained.

"Really?"

Padric snorted. "Of course not. Do you honestly think I speak lion?"

Talfryn stared ahead at the creatures, his hand shaking, white knuckles clutching his hatchet. Trying his very utmost to put on a brave face. "There are only four of them. We can take them."

"Be my guest," Padric said.

The claws and teeth alone on each animal could tear him and Talfryn to shreds in no time. Let alone the fact that Padric was bone-tired and sore. His many wounds burned and ached with a frenzy. Talfryn fared little better.

His years of training had taught Padric three things: A knight should weigh each and every available option, fight for what he believes in, and know when beaten.

The latter option appeared to be the wisest course in this situation. Even after weeks of training, Talfryn might take on one, but not all of them. And even with his own faun and centaur abilities, Padric could only outdistance them for a time.

"Do you surrender?" Circe asked, her grin wide yet again, as though they had never held a private conversation but moments before.

Rage filled the knight's chest—he was helpless once again. He nudged Talfryn as the farmer opened his mouth to voice his confusion. Looking at his friend in consternation, it was all Padric could do to convey his thoughts via eye contact. At last, Talfryn relented, though with a grunt in response. With a clenched heart, Padric hoped to high heaven Circe was as trustworthy as she had claimed.

"We surrender," Padric said to the sorceress and the lion.

Talfryn raised his hatchet and—froze. "Wait, what? Just like that—we're giving up?"

Under his breath, Padric muttered, "We have to stay alive to save the others. I seriously doubt our ability to do so should we perish before we even arrive in Circe's compound."

"Oh." Talfryn let the hatchet drop to his side. "When you put it that way..."

Both sets of weapons clattered to the ground, along with any hope of escape.

"Excellent choice," Circe said with authority. "Now, be good lads and obey the guards. My father is most eager to meet you." She nodded at the animals.

The large cats and wolf comprehended her directions without hesitation. As one, the four animals unhinged themselves from their fighting stances and parted, stepping aside for another creature to approach.

A winged stag.

Talfryn gawked. "Staggy?"

The other animals bowed their heads toward the regal stag.

The stag's appearance bristled against Padric's nerves. It's abandonment hurt Talfryn the most, and for this Padric had difficulty forgiving it. For days Talfryn looked up to the skies awaiting its return.

Padric regarded Staggy with a look that could pierce armor, but the stag peered right back at him, not giving an inch. Why did that look remind Padric of his father?

"So," Padric said, his blood seething. "I see you have returned to your mistress. What a pleasure to alight in your company once again after such a long absence." If Staggy truly was a spy for Padric's newfound family, he wanted no part of it. The quicker they completed the prophecy and left Cataractonium, the better.

"Ulysses," Circe said, waving her staff toward the hill. "Please guide our guests into the fortress."

Padric whipped his head around to peer at the sorceress, his anger squashed for the moment. "Ulysses? As in the hero?" Why would she name a stag after the Greek hero?

"Something like that," she replied with a sly grin.

The stag named Ulysses gazed at the two captives with dark brown eyes filled with something akin to remorse.

From the wall, two green snakes with black spots slithered toward the prisoners.

"Staggy?" Talfryn asked with a gulp. "What's going on?"

"Do not move," Padric said to Talfryn, sweat covering his brow as he watched the creatures slink toward him.

"Are they poisonous?" asked Talfryn.

"I would not provoke them to find out."

Talfryn and Padric stood stock still, waiting to see what the snakes would do. To both young men's chagrins, the snakes slithered directly up to them, curled over their feet and hoofs, and started ascending their legs.

"Pa-Padric...What are they doing?"

The knight was too petrified to even think about what the snakes would do. His hair stood on end, waiting for venomous fangs to protrude and end it all. Slowly, Padric's snake slithered up past his hip, and found his wrist. The green and black creature curled around the wrist twice, then launched itself to twist around the other arm. Then, with a quick tug, it pulled his arms together like a rope. The snake then gazed up directly into Padric's eyes and stuck out its forked tongue, as if asking Padric to inspect its handiwork.

"This is a bit of overkill, don't you think?" Bound in the same manner, Talfryn scrunched his face, lifting the snake a couple of inches, who in turn hissed. "They must think we are very dangerous, with such an escort and bindings."

Once satisfied with their helplessness, Circe, followed by the nymphs, Ulysses, and the other animals, escorted the captives down the hill toward Cataractonium, and to Helius.

Talfryn looked to Padric and said in a low voice, "Right. Now that the plan is underway, what's our next move?" He indicated the snakes around their wrists.

"Not yet," Padric replied in kind, a plan of action sprouting in his mind. "First, we must gain our bearings in Cataractonium. I shall need you to keep your eyes and ears open for anything of import. And should you locate any of our friends..." Again, his heart leaped at the hope of finding Brynwen alive and well. Rawlins, Miriel, and the others he too looked forward to seeing.

The lion grumbled beside them, making Padric's heart rate quicken all the more.

Talfryn was nodding with minimal movements. "What will you be doing?"

A sly grin slid up Padric's lips. "Why, keeping them from noticing you, of course. Whilst they are wary of my every move, you will have the advantage of blending in."

"Why does that sound like a highly more demanding job than yours?"

"Because, my friend, it will be."

To be continued in *Treacherous*

WANT to find if Padric survives his quest? Start reading book 2 instantly here:

https://books2read.com/SusanLaspe-treacherous

A WORD FROM THE AUTHOR

Thank you for taking the time to pick up *Sorcerous*!

If you have a moment, I would really appreciate it if you would take a couple of minutes to leave a review on your favorite booksellers and social media sites. Reviews help authors find new readers and receive feedback about their works.

If you enjoyed this book, would you consider leaving a review on:

- Amazon
- GoodReads
- Barnes & Noble

To receive alerts about Rise of the Charioteer series, sign up for my newsletter at: susanlaspe.com

HISTORICAL NOTE

There were a number of plagues during Europe's rich history, each one darker than the next. The Bubonic Plague, also known as The Black Death, spread across Europe from AD 1346-1353 via infected fleas on rats. Possibly coming from the Middle East or Far East, it arrived first to the ports of Italy and then spread in quick succession around Europe. It only reached England in the spring of 1348, but was gone by December 1349. Even though the plague lasted only a year and a half in England, the effects were astounding—nearly forty to sixty percent of the population was lost. Like most bacterium, the spread of disease runs rampant in warm weather, but lies dormant in winter. The harsher winters of the British Isles likely helped to assuage the fleas and bacterium from continuing to disease the populace for a longer period of time.

Ancient Romans were not very creative where their mythology comes into play. When they became the dominant force in Southern Europe, they took much of the Greeks' stories, adapting and renaming most to suit their religious and language needs ([G]Helios/[L]Helius, [G]Kirce/[L]Circe, [G]Heracles/[L]Hercules). Few names such as Apollo retained their Greek names, though the pronunciation may change with the language. You may also notice that there are a few different versions

HISTORICAL NOTE

of many of the mythologies, making it hard to keep track of what information came from where. Homer's *The Odyssey* and *The Iliad* were each only one version of their heroes', gods, and monsters' stories. I also took the liberty of using other European mythological creatures within the story, such as the *peryton* (part stag and part bird). Be on the lookout for more mythical creatures in future stories!

The Ninth Roman Legion spent most of their time in York (*Eboracum*), but I took liberties in having them spend some time in Mamucium for story purposes. The Ninth Legion disappeared in England in the first couple of centuries AD, and little has been discovered regarding their fate. For further historical fantasy reading about this legion, I recommend reading Rosemary Sutcliff's *The Eagle of the Ninth* (also a major motion picture: The Eagle).

ACKNOWLEDGMENTS

This book would not be possible without the invaluable help of these amazing people:

To my readers, thank you for giving my book a chance. I sincerely hope you enjoyed it.

Kelsey Gietl for helping me brainstorm whether in the parking lot or library, and giving tips on the writing and publishing process. Thanks for always being there to answer my silly or repetitive questions! You are awesome!

Anne Poelker for our brainstorming sessions during lunch breaks. The story wouldn't be where it is today without your creative brain! (When in doubt: "because magic.")

Mark Laspe for reading the story and giving valuable suggestions, as well as for your patience as I spent hours "locked" in the office working on my book.

Patrick Tebeau for the wonderful Latin translations used by the Oracle and Circe.

My great beta readers: Kelsey Gietl, Kirstin Wright, Rachael Johnston, Kimberly Camp, Brittany, Jennifer Reinsch, Srivalli Palaparthi.

My advance readers.

Jennifer Reese for her marvelous editing skills and developmental insight.

And last but not least, my Lord and Savior, who is present in everything I am and do.

ABOUT THE AUTHOR

Susan has loved watching television and movies, reading, writing, and art since her earliest memories. Her push to create her own stories was influenced by Greek mythology, Grimm's Fairy Tales, and the Percy Jackson book series, as well as a love of history (her favorite subject in school). When not working or writing, she can be found doing one of too many craft projects, scrounging the cupboard for chocolate, or playing board games with her husband in St. Louis, Missouri.

facebook.com/Susanlaspeauthor
twitter.com/SusanLaspe
instagram.com/susanlaspe_author

Made in the USA
Monee, IL
06 April 2024

55945292R00204